For my Mom

Thank you to my fabulous beta readers, (J., R., & D.). You guys catch all my little mistakes. I owe you so much!

CONTENTS

CHAPTER ONE

Late Thursday Evening
Barrington, Illinois

Shards of pain reverberated against Chase Humphry's skull. He strug-gled to open his eyes. "What the hell...?" he groaned. His breathing came in short hot pants as his heartbeat sped up. He attempted to lift his hand and remove whatever covered his eyes. "What the hell! What's happening?" He licked his lips, cringing as his sandpaper tongue scratched their surface.

"Shit." He wrestled against the restraints. "C'mon. This can't be happen-ing." The itchy fabric tied around his head, pinched his eyelids closed. "Hello? Where am I?" His voice quivered. Every breath he took became more labored. The more he yanked against the leather straps around his wrists and ankles, the tighter they became.

His chest constricted. Each breath harder to take than the last. He curled his fingers into a fist as he concentrated on remembering what happened. His mind flooded with fragmented visions. He'd left his office around five p.m. and stood at his car, finishing a conversation with his girlfriend. "Jacey," Chase whispered. "Jacey," he said again as he focused on the phone call, on her sultry voice. He couldn't recall anything after that moment, past the conversation, or even the conversation.

His lips and chin trembled. "I don't know what kind of game this is, but it isn't funny. Doug? Chris? If this is a joke, haha...now fucking untie me!" He shifted in the chair. "Fuck," he said, yanking against the straps. "This isn't funny anymore."

Chase's throat burned. He swallowed what little saliva he had trying to stop the searing pain. He sweated profusely causing his linen shirt to stick to him. "Hello? Hey, what the fuck is going on?" He screamed out, twisting his head from side to side. "Anyone here?" Yanking against the restraints, he hoped the chair would move around and loosen the straps. The chair didn't budge.

"What the hell is going on? Someone fucking answer me?" he screamed as he wrenched on his restraints. Starbursts erupted behind his eyes. A wave of nausea crested over him. He breathed in through his nose and hissed it out through his mouth, wanting to keep the vomit at bay. A heater kicked on. *Goosebumps erupted on his arms when the warm air clashed with the sticky coating of sweat on his skin.*

Chase dropped his chin to his chest. *The vomit hovered at the back of his throat. The caustic bile eating away the already raw tissue. As his pulse slowed the thumping in his head subsided. He swallowed gagging on the thick mucus.*

"Please. Someone, please help me." His posture straightened when he heard a faint motorized hum. *Within moments, a familiar smell wafted around him. He lifted his chin, sniffing the air. He cocked his head to the side, inhaling deeply through his nose. "I know that smell."*

Keeping his excitement in check, he waited for the chimes. With no sense of time, he had no idea when or if the old grandfather clock would fill the room with his favorite sound. When the first chime echoed, he blew out the breath he didn't realize he held. "I'm in my home." A slight giggle escaped as relief washed over him.

"That you are my friend. That you are."

Chase's body stiffened as the sound of heavy booted footsteps walked towards him. *He angled his head in the direction of the intruder's voice. "Who are you? What are you doing in my house? I demand you let me go."*

Kerry threw his head back and laughed as he stood in front of his captive. *"You really are an ass, aren't you? I don't think you're in any position to demand anything."* Kerry walked around the chair, pulling on the restraints making sure they hadn't loosened. *He placed a second pair of latex gloves over his hands, giving him another barrier of protection.*

"Why are you doing this? Is it money? I can give you money. Tell me what you want."

"Chase, you always thought money was the answer to any problem. Even when we were kids. I have my own money; I don't need yours. I have quite a bit actually." He leaned down next to the man's ear. *"I made a killing in the tech market."*

Chase fixated on the man's voice. *"What do you mean when we were kids? How do you know me?"*

"I can't believe you don't recognize my voice. You and your delinquent friends heard my screams enough." Kerry dragged a chair from the other side of Chase's living room, placing it in front of the pathetic man. *"Hmm, sorry. I think I scratched your wood floors. It's too bad, they're exquisite."* He glanced around at the flooring. *"Brazilian Walnut. I bet you dropped a*

pretty penny on these."

Chase squirmed. "*I don't think you're here to discuss my wood floors. What is it you want?*"

Kerry ignored the man's question as he moved to the table positioned against the wall for easy access. He lingered in front of it, analyzing his choice of tools. "*I think this will start us off nicely,*" he said as he picked up the ice pick.

"*Who are you?*" Chase lowered his voice, trying to hide the quiver. He angled his head towards the sound of the intruder's footsteps.

Kerry sighed, sitting in the chair. He placed the ice pick in his lap as he crossed his legs. "*I'm sure it will all come back to you shortly. However, before we take a trip down memory lane, let's discuss what you've accomplished in your life up to this point. You definitely capitalized on the whole misfortunate kid thing.*"

"*I didn't capitalize on anything. I worked hard to get to where I am. No one handed me anything. I earned it.*" Chase lifted his chin as he puffed out his chest.

"*I guess we all tell ourselves a few good rationalizations to help us get through the day.*"

"*What are you referring to? I don't have to rationalize anything.*" Chase clenched his hands into fists.

"*I understand your company recently went public. That had to boost your bottom line tremendously. Seems to have given you a lot of options.*"

Chase tilted his head to the side. "*I still don't understand what my company has to do with this. Why are you here?*" He jutted out his chin.

Kerry raised an eyebrow. "*Do you think if your past ever came out your company would have had such success? I think if the public knew who you really are and what you did, I bet your company would tank in a heartbeat.*" Kerry stood pushing his chair back a few inches. He stuck the ice pick in his back pocket.

"*There is nothing in my past I have to worry about.*" Chase sucked in air, holding his breath. He began coughing. The more he coughed, the more his throat burned. Swallowing, the metallic taste of blood made him gag.

"*I think there is.*" Kerry reached down next to the leg of his chair and picked up a two-liter bottle. "*Where are my manners,*" he said. "*I bet you're thirsty. The drug I injected you with has a nasty side effect of making your throat feel as if you are gargling hot coals.*" Unscrewing the top, Kerry grabbed Chase by his hair and yanked his head back. "*Here you go. Have a drink."*

"What—what are you doing?" Chase asked before his assailant pinched the sides of his jaw forcing it open. He writhed under the man's firm grip. "Stop, please. What are you doing?" Chase screamed before a rush of liquid ran down his throat. He struggled to swallow the onslaught of the caustic fluid. He shook his head from side to side, but his assailant's grip was too firm. His gag reflex kicked in as he coughed vomiting some back up.

Pain erupted along the entire length of his esophagus. Chase sucked in air, coughing it out. Saliva drooled from his mouth, dripping off his chin. His coughs turned into hacks as droplets of blood spewed from his mouth. Tears streamed from his eyes, dampening the fabric covering them. The opening of his throat felt as if it had constricted down to the size of a straw. Chase wheezed, his lungs felt as if they were filling with fluid.

The corners of Kerry's mouth tugged upwards at the edges as he watched the man's discomfort. "As unpleasant as that was, it won't kill you. At least not immediately. I still need answers from you." Replacing the cap, he set the bottle on the floor. "I remember when I begged you and your asshole friends for something to drink, you guys thought it would be fun to piss on me. Do you remember that?"

Chase panted, dry heaving. Thick strands of mucus ran from his nose, dripping down his lips. Every breath in through his mouth felt like the flame of a blow torch. "I don't know what you're talking about." The slight swelling of his tongue distorted his speech.

"Come on. You don't expect me to believe that, do you?" Kerry pulled the ice pick from his back pocket, pricking his finger on the tip. He smiled at the sharpness of the point.

"I don't care what you believe. I would never do something so disgusting." Chase coughed. He tasted blood. He spewed out the nasty, thick bloody mucus, gagging.

"You're such a liar." Kerry stood moving towards the blindfolded man. He rechecked the straps. Chase jumped at the contact. "My, my, my, a little touchy aren't we?"

"Please tell me what you want from me. I'll do whatever you want," Chase whimpered as full body tremors engulfed him. He squeezed his eyes shut behind the blindfold.

"When I begged you and your band of assholes to stop your near-daily torture of me, you never did," Kerry said.

Chase twisted against the man's grip of his wrist. The pressure from the hold forced his palm flat against the arm of the chair.

"Do you know how long I smelled like piss? No matter how many showers I took, I could never quite get rid of the smell."

Chase shook his head in denial. "That wasn't my idea."

"Oh, so now you remember?"

"Patrick was the one who thought it would be funny." His voice high pitched as his breathing came in quick pants.

"You were the one who pissed on my face. When I threw up, you laughed at me."

Chase's nostrils flared. The sound of his heartbeat thrashed in his ears. "We were kids, teens. I would never do those things now. I would never condone that now."

Kerry chuckled. "You knew what you were doing."

"Please, please, let me go," Chase begged.

"I want you to suffer as I did." Kerry dragged the tip of the ice pick across the top of Chase's hand. "I want you to suffer as Sierra did."

"I—I didn't have anything to do with her." Chase jerked back pressing himself against the chair. He shook his head. "I swear. We did what he told us to do."

"You gave Pops a big donation a few weeks back. You knew what kind of man he was. You know what he did to the girls in his care. How could you give him money?" Kerry applied more pressure to Chase's wrist.

Chase flinched back. "I didn't have anything to do with what Pops did. We were all scared of him."

"Only recently, as a grown man, you gave him money, why?"

"I can't..." Chase stuttered. "I...I...."

"C'mon Chase. You're going to have to do better than that."

"I'm sorry. I was a kid. We were stuck in that place. I wanted to survive and get out. I didn't know any better." His chin and lips trembled.

Kerry raised the ice pick. "You're a liar. And it's time for you to reap what you sowed all those years ago." He jammed the pick through the back of Chase's hand. The tip of the weapon stuck in the wood of the chair. He had to yank with force to get it out.

Chase's scream echoed throughout the house.

Kerry raised the ice pick and stabbed the hand again. And again.

Chase screamed, throwing his head back. "Please, please, stop. I'll do whatever you want. I'll tell you whatever you want." He gulped in air through *his sobs.*

Kerry smiled as he jabbed the pick into the mutilated hand. He used such force the hilt of the pick, broke several bones in Chase's hand. The man's screams sounded like a mortally wounded cat. He left the eight-inch pick stuck there as he reached around the man's head and grabbed the blindfold. Yanking it off, he stepped back waiting for Chase's eyes to adjust.

Chase blinked, squeezing his eyes tight. The tears stung, and the brightness from the glaring overhead lights made it hard for his vision to focus. He sobbed at the blood oozing from the holes in the back of his hand. The sharp pain from the broken bones brought back the nausea. "Why? Why are you doing this?" His gaze focused on the man in front of him. "I don't remember what happened. Why do you care so much about her? I didn't have anything to do with what happened to Sierra."

"You'll say anything to cover your ass. You did whatever Pops wanted. And he let you and your friends have extra privileges. You didn't have to do anything to survive." Kerry walked over to the table. He picked up a pair of pruning shears and the ball-peen hammer.

Chase turned his head; his gaze following his attacker. "I promise. I don't know what happened to Sierra. I wasn't there."

"You helped Pops cover it up. I want to know where she is. I want to find her."

"Patrick. He was older. He did whatever Pops told him. He made me and Maggie help him."

"You both benefitted, though."

"Pops was a mean man. He had his favorites, and if you weren't on his list, you suffered. We did what we had to."

Kerry walked back to his captive. "I need something from you, Chase. I need some answers from you. And 'I don't know,' isn't going to work."

Chase's eyes bulged at the pruning shears. "I'll answer anything you want me to." He wriggled in his chair. "Please, stop, let me go. Please don't hurt me anymore."

A malicious smile spread across Kerry's face. "Chase, I'm going to do more than hurt you." He lifted Chase's right forefinger and opened the hand-held pruning shears placing the finger between the blades. "First, you're going to tell me what I want to know," he said winking at him as he squeezed the shears together, cutting off the finger. Chase's shrill cries of agony made his smile broaden. "Then, I'm going to kill you."

CHAPTER TWO

Early Thursday evening

After the three-hour drive from Chicago to Davenport, Iowa, the sun was beginning its descent. Damien turned on the road leading to Dillon's grandparent's farm. His breath hitched as the edge of the farm's property came into view. The glow from the early February amber sky cast a golden hue on the dusting of snow blanketing the property. The entire farm had a 3D look as if it popped off a movie screen.

The farm had remained closed to the public. The townspeople showed their support by placing flowers and stuffed animals along the entire length of the fence line. Various cards hung by nails and twine affixed to the cedar posts.

Damien glanced in the rearview and saw Joe and his girlfriend, Taylor, staring in Dillon's direction, waiting for her reaction. Damien reached over and lifted Dillon's hand from her lap, kissing the back. "Hey baby, how are you holding up?"

He waited for her to respond. She stared out the passenger window. Her long honey blond hair hung forward, blocking her face from his view. He watched her struggle to find the words. Dillon shrugged before turning towards him. Damien's heart stopped for a split second at the sight of her tear-streaked face. "Honey, we shouldn't have come so soon."

She wiped her face with her sleeve. "No. I had to come and talk to the lawyer. I have to make decisions impacting the farmhands. I wasn't ready at the funeral. It can't wait any longer."

"Dillon, we could've done this by phone." Damien slowed the vehicle.

She squeezed his hand. "I'll be okay." She peeked over her shoulder at the two love birds snuggled in the back seat. "Having all of you with me will make this easier." Looking in Taylor's direction, she continued. "Although I think you two should've taken a vacation while Joe and Damien are suspended from work for three weeks."

Taylor reached over the top of the seat and touched her shoulder. "We would never let you do this alone. And we can take a trip any time.

This is way more important."

Gunner, the big chocolate Mastiff, who had been quiet for the last twenty minutes, let out a howl as if he agreed with Taylor.

"See, even Gunner wouldn't let you do this alone," Joe said as light laughter filled the SUV. "They gave us the suspensions to save face with the higher-ups at Division Central. I actually only got a two-week suspension, and it was with pay. Your boy here took the hit for me."

"You shouldn't have been suspended in the first place. I was in command, and I was solely responsible. At least they listened to me when I said to take my pay and leave yours intact," Damien said.

"I'm your partner and your best friend. I would never have let you handle that op without me," Joe said squeezing Damien's shoulder.

"Who the hell said you were my best friend?" Damien asked winking at Dillon.

"Man, I'm the only friend you don't have to pay—to be your friend. Which qualifies me as the best friend." Joe smirked at him in the mirror.

"Look at all the flowers," Dillon said as they pulled up to the gate. The entry of the driveway was filled with potted plants, flowering plants, and bouquets of flowers. Lumps swelled at the back of her throat. She swallowed, trying to shake off her emotions. "The key code is 5954."

Damien rolled down his window and punched in the security code. The new electronic gate opened up. His father installed it after Dillon's grandparents were murdered. The Martins, the couple who were caretakers to her grandparent's farm, had been so grateful for the security system, they sent a fresh fruit basket to Damien's father's company, Kainetorri Securities.

Entering the gates, Gunner sat up in the very back of the SUV gazing out the window and whimpered softly.

Damien looked in the rearview mirror and saw a glimpse of sadness in the dog's expression. His droopy jowls seemed to sag a little bit more than usual. Gunner had barely survived the attack the night of the murders. Had it not been for the fast-acting paramedics, Dillon would've had to bury the dog as well as her grandparents. Damien's weighted chest made it hard for him to take a deep breath. Not sure how either the dog or Dillon would react to seeing the inside of the house for the first time since their death.

Damien tightened his grip on Dillon's hand. "The crew I hired to clean, sent me photos. Everything from the dining room has been re-moved. The Martins put in a dining table they had. It's not the same one your grandparents used."

Dillon remained silent. She barely managed a nod. Blowing out the breath she held, she glanced over at Damien. Looking away before she caught his deep blue eyes. They always bore through her as if they could read her thoughts.

Dillon loved him, his family, and the Shermans. They were all she had left now. Her heart sank at the thought. She wondered if Damien had done anything different, would the outcome still have been the same. She pushed those feelings aside telling herself none of this was his fault.

Damien drove down the long drive. Following the curve, he stopped in front of the porch steps. Damien patted her leg. "Let's get the dog and cat inside, then we can get our luggage. Okay?"

"That's a good idea," Dillon said.

Damien went to the rear of the SUV and lifted the back. He watched as Gunner jumped out and ran to Dillon's side, who stood frozen at the passenger door of the vehicle.

Taylor grabbed Coach's portable cell.

The cat bellowed out a long meow.

"I bet you'll be glad to get out, huh?" Taylor asked as she looked at him through the crate door. She walked over and stood next to Dillon.

Damien leaned into Joe, who lifted the bags from the SUV. "I still think this is a bad idea."

"She needs to do this. You're going to have to let her, Damien." Joe peered around the edge of the vehicle, then turned back. "She's the strongest woman I know. She'll be okay." His Irish accent taking on a reassuring tone.

Damien wasn't as sure. It had only been two weeks. Her physical wounds hadn't even begun to heal. Her psychological wounds would take far longer. And he worried this trip would set her back. He left Joe and took Dillon by the hand. "The Martin's have stocked the fridge. The bedrooms are made up and ready to go. Are you ready?"

Dillon nodded. Her eyes never left the front door. She wrapped her fingers tightly around his. They walked together up the stairs. Her heart-beat thrashed in her ears. She blew her breaths out through taut lips. Her body trembled, making her legs feel like rubbery noodles. She leaned into Damien, glancing over her shoulder, she noticed Taylor and Joe had lingered behind at the truck. She hated the feelings of vulnerability. She hated herself more for allowing it to drape over her.

At the front door, Damien stopped and took both of her hands in his. "It's going to get easier as we stay here. If it is too much for you to be here, we can leave."

She shook her head. "No. I want to stay here. Promise me you won't make me leave. Do you promise?"

He angled his head down before looking her in the eye. The beautiful whiskey color always made his stomach flutter. The golden ring surrounding the iris gave them a fiery glow. "Dillon, as long as you can handle this, I will not make you leave."

Gunner nudged her leg with his head.

She smiled as she reached down and scratched his ears. "You ready boy?"

He barked at the door.

"Let's do this." Damien pulled open the storm door and used the key. He stepped in first and switched on the lights. As they entered, they were hit with the smell of a clean and sanitized house. Rounding the corner as they walked towards the dining room where both of her grandparents had been murdered, he reached out and pulled Dillon into his side. "You okay?"

She blew out a shaky breath. "Yeah." The video David had made her watch of him killing her grandmother and grandfather, flashed in her mind. Her body stiffened, as she squeezed her eyes shut, blocking out the horrible images and cries of her grandfather. The opening of the front door brought her out of her trance. She shook it off, turning towards the sound.

Joe and Taylor entered, carrying Coach and the luggage.

"Which room gets what?" Joe asked, carrying all the bags.

Dillon smiled. "Put our stuff in the room on the right. You and Taylor will have the room at the other end of the hallway. Before you get to the room at the end."

Taylor put the pet carrier on the floor and opened the door. "There you go handsome," she said as Coach sauntered out meowing. Taylor swooped him up and nuzzled him. "Oh, you sweet boy. This is your new home for a few days. Are you hungry?" She glanced over at Joe as he walked back into the living room. "Will you text Jenkins and make sure Muffin is doing okay?"

Joe smiled. "Yes, I will. You realize it's been like four hours, right? That old cat probably doesn't even know you're gone yet."

She squinted at him. "I know how long it's been, and I want to make sure she is okay. Jenkins said he would check on her during his lunch." She stood with Coach purring in her arms.

Joe pulled out his phone and texted Jenkins, one of the detectives in the Vicious Crimes Unit where he and Damien worked. When they weren't suspended. "You know he will be there until we get back. I told him to sleep at our house." Joe looked up with a scowl. "Which means he will probably fuck someone in our bed. You know we will have to buy a new bed."

Taylor giggled. "I doubt we have to buy a new bed. We can throw away the sheets." She stepped over to him and wrapped one arm around him while still holding Coach. "That's why I put our oldest set of sheets on the bed."

"I like your thinking, woman." His phone pinged. "I think Muffin is fine." He held his phone out. The hundred-year-old cat was snuggled up next to a cute pink teddy bear, her front paw draped over the belly of the small bear.

"Awe!" Taylor clutched Coach tighter to her chest. "She looks so happy."

Joe rolled his eyes. "Yes. He says he sprayed the bear with some of your perfume. He didn't want the cat to be anxious."

"I love Jenkins. We need to buy him something." Taylor beamed a big smile at him.

Joe frowned, shaking his head. "We don't need to buy him anything."

Taylor waved him off as she went back to her previous task of feeding Coach. The cat meowed nudging and kissing her. She carried him and the bag holding his cat food, small litter box, and supplies into the kitchen. Setting him on the floor, he danced around in circles as she put a can of stinky wet cat food in his dish. When she placed the bowl on the floor, the cat growled as he ate. Taylor giggled at the creature. "Do you have to prove how tough you are by growling at your food, Coach?"

Damien looked on in feigned disgust. "He likes to think he killed it."

Taylor placed some dry dog food in a bowl and set it on the floor opposite of Coach.

They all turned at the sound of Gunner whining. He had laid down on the spot where Dillon's grandfather had died a few weeks earlier.

Dillon knelt next to him, rubbing his head. Tears rolled down her cheek. "I know this is hard Gunner. I promise, you and me, we'll get through this."

Gunner raised his head, licking her face and nuzzled her.

She kissed him, then rose. She turned to find everyone staring at her. "Stop looking at me. I'm okay. I promise." She wiped her cheeks with the palms of her hands.

"Okay, then." Joe glanced at his watch. "It's almost time for dinner. You guys want to see what is in the fridge and we can make something?"

Taylor clapped her hands and squealed. "Ooh, sounds perfect. I can cook something." She spun around, heading towards the fridge.

Joe glanced at the fireplace. "I'm going to get the chill out of the air." Loading up the last of the fresh logs onto the fire rack, he used some of the kindling from a basket set to the side of the hearth, and got a fire going. Stepping back, he admired his work.

Damien sniggered at him. "What a boy scout."

"You're jealous of my skills," he said, flicking his shoulder.

Gunner ran from the room and slid into the door at the end of the hallway. He barked at the closed door.

"What's up with him?" Damien asked, turning towards Dillon.

She smiled. "His room is down the hall. It's not big enough to be a bedroom, so my grandparents made it his room. He's probably looking for one of his old chew toys." Dillon walked down the hall and opened the door, returning to the living room.

Gunner ran in, grabbed his big bed, and dragged it out to the living room.

Everyone stopped what they were doing and watched as he growled, dragging the bed alongside him. Even Coach watched as the dog weaved his way around the furniture.

"What is he doing?" asked Taylor.

Dillon couldn't hold back the giggles. "I guess he wants his bed out here."

Gunner ran back to the room.

Damien watched as the cat meandered towards the big oversized pillow. Spinning around several times until he got the right spot. He snuggled into Gunner's bed, in front of the fire. Damien laughed. "This isn't going to end well."

Joe laughed at the expression on the dog's face as he bounded around the corner and stopped dead in his tracks, carrying one of his chew toys. "Umm, poor guy. All that work and a fat cat took your spot."

Gunner whined as he slinked over to his bed. He dropped his toy and walked around it, stopping and staring at Coach. He nudged Coach towards the edge. When the cat didn't move, he growled at him.

Damien looked over at Dillon. "What do you think he will do?"

She shrugged. "I don't think he will hurt him. They haven't had any trouble at the house."

Taylor moved next to Joe and wrapped her arms around him. "Coach, can't you share the pillow?"

Coach looked up and huffed, snuggling in deeper, ignoring her question.

Gunner barked and then stepped onto the pillow, spinning around several times as Coach had done earlier.

Coach didn't budge. He cracked open one eye and went back to sleep.

"See. I told you there was nothing to worry about." Dillon smiled at Damien.

They all followed Taylor back into the kitchen.

"I took a quick inventory of the fridge and the cabinets. The Martins did a good job stocking this place. How about if I make some chili and cornbread?"

Joe opened the fridge. "Sounds fantastic. Is there any beer to go with the chili?"

"Yes. Out in the mudroom is another refrigerator. It is usually stocked with beer, wine, and soda pop," Dillon said.

"Woohoo!" Joe bounded into the mudroom connected to the back of the kitchen. "You want a beer, Damien?" He called back over his shoulder.

"Sure. Grab several for the fridge in here, and a bottle of wine."

The phone on the wall rang. Dillon walked to it. "Hello?"

"Dillon? Is that you honey?"

Dillon smiled into the phone. "Yes, Agatha, it's me."

"I wanted to make sure it was you guys I saw over there. How was the trip?"

"It was good. Thank you for buying all the groceries."

Agatha sighed on the other end. "I hope I got what you guys wanted. I remembered many conversations with your grandfather about Joe and Damien and how much they can eat. Especially Joe. I made sure to get lots of stuff. Ralph made sure I got plenty of beer and wine too. He said there was some whiskey in one of the kitchen cabinets."

Dillon giggled. "You did a great job. The lawyer is supposed to be here tomorrow at ten a.m. He has requested you guys be present."

"Yes. He contacted us. We will be there." There was an awkward silence before Agatha spoke again. "Are you okay, honey?"

Dillon leaned against the wall. "I'm okay."

"You know we love you, Dillon. We're here for you."

"I know. Thank you, Agatha. We will see you tomorrow at ten."

"Okay. You call me if you need anything."

"I will." Dillon hung up the phone. She paused as her hand rested on the receiver. *Block out the memories.* She took a deep breath before turning around. "What can I do to help, Taylor?"

Taylor tossed her an onion. "You can chop."

"I can do that," Dillon said.

Damien took the beers from Joes arms and placed them in the refrigerator before he grabbed the keys to the shed off the wall. "Joe, come help me get some extra wood for the fire," he said walking through the mudroom to get to the backyard.

Joe took a quick sip of his freshly opened beer, setting it on the counter. "You got it, boss." He kissed Taylor on the cheek.

Gunner ran out with them the minute they opened the door.

CHAPTER THREE

The light covering of snow crunched under their feet. The last of the sun had disappeared below the horizon filling the night sky with stars and blackness. The shed was located at the back of the grounds. Not too far from the mudroom. A motion sensor light kicked on flooding the back yard with a bright white light.

Joe looked up. "Is that one of yours?"

Damien nodded. "My dad set them on all the buildings, even the Martins' house." He pointed to the house located about a half-mile to the right from where they stood. The dim lights of the house were noticeable in the dark of the night. "He made sure this whole place was loaded with a new system. Everything can be tracked from the main farm building," he pointed to a large structure off to the left, "and from this house and the Martins' home."

"That's good. I know it makes the Martins feel safer." Joe noticed the tightness in his friend's face. "Don't do that to yourself. That asshole would have still found a way to get to them. Your security systems aren't foolproof. They aren't a guarantee they would still be alive today."

"I know. I still think she blames me. On a deep level, I think she blames me."

Joe grabbed Damien's shoulder as he reached out to unlock the shed. "No, she doesn't. I'm not saying she might not go through a stage where she lashes out at you. It's part of the grieving process. But no way she blames you. And you need to stop blaming yourself."

Damien's head hung. He dragged a hand through his black wavy hair. "I'm trying, Joe. I really am."

"Well, try harder."

Gunner ran through the yard, sniffing every inch.

"I bet he's glad to be back here," Damien said.

"I wonder if it's hard for pets. You know coming back to where something awful happened."

Damien watched the dog scamper through the snow. "I don't know. I do know the paramedics found him barely alive laying with his head on Dillon's grandfather. You know, I think if he hadn't caused the damage to David he did, I think he would've killed Dillon before we got to her. I owe Gunner a hell of a lot."

Damien unlocked the shed and pulled the string for the hanging lightbulb. The soft glow of light cast swaying shadows across the interior.

Joe rummaged through the shelves. "This has got to be the cleanest woodshed ever."

Damien chuckled. "Between the Martins and Dillon's grandparents, this farm is well run. I bet the Martins came through and cleaned this place after the murders." He followed Joe's lead and inspected the shelves. "You and Taylor should've taken a nice vacation."

"No way. We can go on a trip at any time." Joe picked up a jar from the back of one of the shelves. "Holy shit, I can't believe anyone would eat this." He lifted the jar.

Damien's brow wrinkled. "They don't waste anything on a farm. I personally wouldn't eat pig's feet or snout." He picked up another jar. Holding it up to the light, he glanced over at Joe. "What the hell is this?"

Joe leaned in, peering at the unidentified object in the jar. "I don't have a damn clue. Who were these people?"

Damien laughed. "I have no idea what this is. I don't want to know either." He replaced the jar. "How are you and Taylor?"

Joe leaned against the shelving unit. "We are fine. Why do you ask?"

Damien smirked as he inspected another jar. "I keep waiting for you to get cold feet. This has been one of your longest relationships."

Joe shrugged. "True. But my heart and head are thinking this time. Not my *gooter*."

Damien laughed. "Jesus man, where do you come up with these words?" He chuckled some more. "I remember when your girlfriends had a shelf life of three months."

Joe shook his head. "Those were the good ole' days."

Damien glanced around the shed once more. "I don't see much of anything of value. Most of the tools are kept in different buildings. It looks like can goods and stock for the main house are kept here." He reached down and grabbed a few logs. "Quit stalling and grab the wood. I don't want to have to come back out for a few days."

"You are such a slave driver." Joe picked up several logs, pulling the light's string as he and Damien exited the building.

Damien fumbled with the wood in his arms as he locked the shed.

Gunner stood next to the back fence. His ferocious barking echoing through the blackness past the yard.

"What's got him riled up?" Joe asked.

"I have no idea. Gunner! C'mon boy."

The dog turned and bounded towards them. Running around in circles, occasionally stopping to glance back at the woods.

Before entering the mudroom, Joe looked back over his shoulder, staring at the dark area behind the farm. "Maybe a monster is out there waiting to pounce."

Damien opened the back door of the house, entering the mudroom. "I hope he gets you first." Damien placed his logs on the floor next to the door leading into the kitchen.

"Some friend you are," Joe said as he put his logs down next to Damien's stack.

As Damien opened the door, they were greeted to the sound of soul music and the delicious smell of chili. Damien and Joe glanced at each other then back at the two women who danced around the kitchen. Coach sat on the counter, waiting patiently for scraps.

"Do you have our dinner ready, or have you been dancing all this time?" Joe asked as he lifted the lid from the pot on the stove. He grabbed the beer he had left on the counter a few moments ago and chugged it down, letting out a loud burp.

Taylor swatted him before he could taste the chili. "Yes, we did. We're waiting on the cornbread."

Dillon picked up Coach and snuggled him. She cradled him like a baby, stroking his belly, still swaying to the music.

"Quit that. It's disgusting," Damien said as he took a beer from the fridge. "Plus, look how jealous Gunner is." He pointed to the dog who watched her, staring at the cat in her arms.

Dillon smiled. She kissed Coach and placed him on the floor. She knelt next to Gunner. Grabbing his cheeks, she kissed him on the nose. "You know I love you." She smooched him again. "You're my baby, too. You're just too big to hold."

Gunner nudged her chest with his big head, wiggling his butt bumping into her. His massive bodyweight knocked her from her perch. He straddled her, showering her with kisses.

"Okay, okay," she said, laughing as she pushed him away. Damien reached down and grabbed her hands, hauling her up to her feet. She wrapped her arms around his waist. "I love you most of all." She stood on her tippy toes and gave his lips a whisper-soft kiss.

"Sometimes, I'm not so sure," Damien responded as he tightened his arm around her waist.

"Can we stop the smooching and eat already?" Joe asked as he grabbed another beer.

Taylor removed the cornbread from the oven. "Everything is ready." She turned towards everyone. "Get some bowls and plates and dig in." She lifted the lids off the chili and pot of white rice. On the counter sat a bowl of shredded cheese, a bowl of sour cream, a jar of salsa, and a bowl of chopped onions, along with a bag of Fritos. "We will do this buffet style. Help yourselves."

Dillon removed a bottle of wine from the refrigerator and grabbed a corkscrew from the utility drawer. Once the bottle was opened, she poured Taylor and herself a glass. She set them on the table and then filled her bowl with chili loaded up with all the fixings.

Once they were all sitting at the table, a comfortable silence filled the room as they devoured their food. After a few moments, Gunner broke the solitude with a loud bark. Dillon jumped startled by the booming noise. She clutched her chest. "Dang, Gunner."

Damien looked at the dog. "What's his problem?" he asked as he looked in the dog's direction. He stood in the kitchen facing the door leading into the mudroom. "He was barking at something out past the back fence when Joe and I were getting wood."

"I'm telling you, it's a monster." Joe grabbed another piece of cornbread.

"It isn't a monster. At the most he sees some of the wildlife living around here," Dillon said as she took a sip of her wine.

"You're wrong, lassy. It's a monster or maybe Jason or Michael Myers. You watch." Joe wiggled his finger at them.

"You watch way too much TV," Damien said.

Taylor took a sip of her wine. "He had a *Friday The 13th* movie binge night the other evening. He then checked the apartment three times before bed."

"Jason lives. I'm telling you."

CHAPTER FOUR

Dillon glanced at the clean kitchen. Joe and Taylor were snuggled on the sofa, while Damien was looking at some of the books on the shelves. She stared at the spot on the floor in the dining room where her grandfather had laid dying. An intense desire to run flooded over her. Her legs trembled as she stood her ground. Battling the urge to scream out.

She glanced over at Taylor, who giggled as Joe whispered in her ear. If it hadn't been for her bravery at the shack where David held Dillon captive, she and Damien would be dead. Probably Joe as well. Dillon glanced back down at the spot. The blood had been cleaned, leaving behind a slight discoloration where her grandfather had bled out. Bloodstains never entirely disappear. No matter how much sanitizing may be done.

Dillon quietly slipped out of the room and into her grandparent's bedroom. She opened up the closet and stared at all their clothes. One of the shelves had her grandfather's cologne and watch. She picked up the bottle and smelled the spray nozzle. Closing her eyes, she pictured the last time she was with them. The tears stung. No matter how tight she squeezed, they crested over.

She picked up the watch and smiled as she gently rubbed the face of it with her thumb. "I miss you guys." She jumped, spinning around at the sound of someone behind her. "Hey."

"Hey yourself. Are you okay?" Damien asked, leaning against the doorframe. "I was wondering where you had gotten off to."

She placed the watch back on the shelf. "I wanted to be close to them." She walked over to her grandmother's side of the closet. She pulled down one of her sweaters and held it to her nose. "I don't know how to move past this." She looked at Damien, tears running down her face.

"Baby," he said, taking her in his arms. "I'll be with you every step of the way. Whatever you need from me." He held her as she clung to the sweater.

"I miss them so much. Several times these last two weeks, I started to call them, then realized they weren't there to answer." She buried her face against the sweater and cried.

Damien's grip on her tightened as she let it out. "I know being here is hard. We can leave right after the lawyer in the morning."

She stepped back, shaking her head. "No. I want to be here. I need to be here. I know I'm a blubbering mess," she hung up the sweater as she spoke. "This is where I need to be right now. I have some decisions to make soon, and being here will help me with those." Dillon wiped her face gathering her emotions and stuffing them back down.

"Whatever you want, Dillon. I'll do whatever you want." Damien followed her out of the closet and back into the living room.

Looking at her watch, it was barely eight p.m. and Dillon wasn't' ready to settle in. "Anyone want to go walk around? I can show you the grounds. We can go look at the horses." She grabbed her jacket from the coat rack next to the front door. Opening the control panel on the wall behind the coat rack, Dillon flipped a few switches.

Taylor popped up. "That sounds great."

"I'd love to," Joe said, disappearing down the hall, returning with his holster and weapon.

"What the fuck is wrong with you?" Damien asked as he put on his jacket and gloves.

"I'm not about to go out there and let Jason pop up and kill me. And ten bullets to the head will stop him once and for all." He glanced over at Taylor. "I love you, but on the off chance they don't kill him, you better run fast, because I'm not helping you. I'll be running, leaving all you fuckers behind."

Damien shook his head. "You're a shitty friend."

"Friendship has nothing to do with it. I'm not going to be a victim and get hacked up by Jason Vorhees." He put on his jacket and followed them and Gunner out the front door.

Damien was about to shut the door, when he turned to Dillon. "Do I need to grab a few flashlights?"

She shook her head. "No, I turned on a few of the floodlights. Not all of them, but enough for us to walk around."

Following the gravel pathway from the side of the house, they walked between two smaller pastures. "This area is where some of the livestock are held for certain things. Like maybe if they need to be quarantined from the rest of the herd." Dillon pointed towards a large barn off to the left. "There is a larger pasture out past the barn where they usually stay. The milking barn is past the main barn."

"How large is the herd?" Taylor asked.

"I think at last count 150 milking cows, and fifty for breeding. My Grandfather had recently started breeding for beef sales. He wasn't sure he wanted to get into it or not."

They came up to the main barn. Several horses were out in the pasture. "There are ten horses here. Most are used for herding the cattle. A few are used for trail rides. You can pay to ride out with the ranch hands and get a feel for rounding up the cattle."

Entering the main barn, several horses peeked out from their stalls. The smell of leather, hay, and oats filled the massive structure. An older man with a shotgun stepped out from a spacious tac room located off to the right.

"You aren't...Oh, my Lord. Look what the cat done dragged in," said a tall, lanky man, with smooth buttery skin.

Gunner ran up to the gray-haired man, howling and barking.

"Well, I'll be damned." Jethro Parks leaned his weapon up against a nearby hay bail and knelt next to the big bullmastiff. "I didn't think I would see you, big fella."

"Hey, Jethro. I should've called out. I thought everyone was gone for the night." Dillon stood ogling him. She stepped forward towards his outstretched arms. She fell into them, burying her face against his chest. He smelled like her grandfather, and she had to fight back tears.

Jethro rested his head on the top of hers. He could feel her trembling against him. He held her in his arms for several moments before moving her to arm's length. He blinked as the tears welled up in his own eyes. "I'm sorry about your grandparents." He lifted her chin when she looked down. "You know we love you and this place will keep running. Whatever you want to do. We support you."

She wiped her moist cheeks. "Thank you. I know you do. I'm not going to change anything. I know between you, the other workers, and the Martins, this place can keep going. I know my grandparents made provisions for all of you. I hope you know that."

He brought her in close to him for another hug. "I know, baby girl. I'm more worried about you. We will all be fine, and so will this place."

Dillon inhaled one last time before letting him go. "Jethro, I want to introduce you to my friends. This is Joe and Taylor. You remember Damien, of course."

"I sure do," he said, bringing Damien in for a hug.

"It's good to see you again, Jethro." Damien stepped back. "This is my partner, Joe."

Jethro held out his hand. "Nice to meet you," he said, shaking both Joe's and Taylor's hands. "You guys going a little stir crazy at the house?"

Dillon smiled. "Sort of. I thought I would show them around. Introduce them to Missy and Gertrude."

"I know they will be happy to see you and Gunner." He led them to a set of stalls at the far end of the barn.

"Who are Missy and Gertrude?" Joe asked as he followed Jethro and the others.

"Two of the best mares ever born." Jethro stepped up to one of the stalls and unlatched the door.

Missy turned at the sound of the squeaking hinge, lifting her head and neighing.

"Hey there pretty girl," Dillon said, walking into the stall. The horse recognized her former mistress and rushed to her. The Paint nudged her, snorting and sniffing. Dillon scratched her ears and broad cheek. Kissing the tip of her nose.

Her hide, pinto spotted coloring of dark brown and white, was silky smooth and shiny. The smell of the horse brought on a rush of memories. For a moment, she could hear her grandfather's laughter as she pushed Missy to her limit. Racing her grandfather and some of the other ranch hands across the pastures as the sweet aroma of the fields filled her nostrils.

"She's beautiful," Taylor said, entering the stall. She reached out and rubbed the flank of the horse. Gently sliding her hand along the mare's hide.

"She is, aren't you, girl?" Dillon glanced over at Joe, who stayed at the entrance. "You're not afraid, are you Joe?"

Joe laughed. "Not at all, lass. Used to ride my fair share of horses back in Dublin. She is fabulous." He moved next to Taylor and patted the horse on the side of her neck.

Dillon turned towards Jethro. "Where is Gertrude?"

A big smile spread across his face. "She's down at the end. She's been separated for a bit. You want to see why?"

Dillon's brow furrowed. "Is there something wrong with her?"

Jethro laughed, waving the clan to follow him. "Not at all, baby girl. C'mon, let me show you."

As the group made their way down to the other end of the barn, Dillon's heart began to race. Her mind ran through scenarios causing Gertrude to be separated from the other horses. Of all the mares on the farm, Gertrude needed to be around the others the most. One of the most social horses she had ever met, she couldn't fathom what would have the old girl sequestered.

As they neared the stall at the end, Gunner ran ahead and sat at the entrance. Enthralled by whatever had captured his attention beyond the gate.

Damien glanced at Dillon. "I'm sure it isn't anything to worry about." She nodded, keeping her silence.

Jethro stopped at the entrance. "One at a time, inside."

Dillon's heart thumped in her chest. As the stall came into view, her eyes widened. Her mouth hung open. "Oh my gosh!" She turned to Jethro. "When, how?"

"She and Oliver have been hanging out a little too much. We never expected this."

As Taylor stepped up next to Dillon, a squeal of delight erupted. "A baby!"

Gertrude turned at the sound of late evening visitors. When she saw Dillon, she too neighed and raised and lowered her head. She moved towards the gate, getting as close as the barrier would allow.

Dillon unlatched the hinge, pushing the mare back, she entered. "Hey, mama. Look at you." The horse nudged and nibbled on Dillon's jacket, always mindful of where her colt was. The young horse hugged his mother's side. He ventured closer to Dillon, allowing her to gently stroke his nose, before retreating to the hind end of his mother, and the safety of distance. "He's so handsome," she said, looking over at Jethro.

Damien stood with Joe and Taylor on the other side of the gate. Enamored at sight of the young colt, and the happiness on Dillon's face. "When was he born?" he asked.

Jethro leaned against the railing. "About a week now."

The impact of Jethro's statement hit Dillon hard. As if Gertrude knew what she was thinking, the docile mare nudged her chest, pushing up against Dillon. "Just after..."

Jethro nodded solemnly. "Yeah, sweetie."

"What's his name?"

Jethro smiled. "We haven't named him yet. Been waiting to see his personality."

"Can I do it?" she asked.

"I think that would be great. Got anything in mind?" Jethro asked.

"No. Over the next several days, I'll spend some time with him, and something will come to me."

"I think that's a great idea. Anything will be better than what Rodney came up with."

Dillon snorted. "I can't imagine. What was it?"

Everyone turned towards Jethro. He sheepishly glanced at the clan. "Pickle McPickleFace."

Dillon raised an eyebrow at him. "Huh?"

Joe snickered, then laughed. "What the hell kind of name is that?"

"He was eating a pickle at the time," Jethro said.

Dillon doubled over laughing. "That is the dumbest thing I have ever heard."

The sheer stupidity of the name made everyone laugh, lifting the dark cloud threatening to descend on the moment of joy.

Dillon looked at Gertrude. "Gurty, girl, I won't let them name your baby boy. I will come up with the right name." The horse nodded in agreement at the same time the young colt bucked and spun around in the stall. Dillon took her cue to leave and let the pair rest.

Jethro looked at his watch. "Well, I was due home a bit ago. Martha will want to come see you. How long are you going to be here?"

"Several days. Have her come over whenever she wants to. I'd love to see her." She hugged the man again. Inhaling the familiar smell of her grandfather.

He kissed the top of her head. "I love you, Dillon. We all do."

She nodded as she stepped back. "Maybe we can take a few horses out for a ride tomorrow?"

"Tell me when, I'll get them saddled up for you." He placed the shotgun in the tac room, back on the rack. Grabbed his jacket and headed out of the barn waving as he left. "Lock all the doors before you leave for me."

"Will do." She called out to him. "You guys want to ride tomorrow?"

Taylor nodded excitedly. "Horseback riding sounds like fun."

"Joe, I think you will need to ride, Juniper." Dillon's lip quivered as she tried not to smile.

"What the hell kind of horse is Juniper?" he asked as he followed Dillon back down the long corridor of the barn to the opposite end.

"Dillon, you can't put him on Juniper," Damien said smirking.

Dillon giggled. "Juniper will know how to handle Joe."

"That's not what I'm worried about," Damien said.

"Okay, what the hell? What's up with this Juniper horse?" Joe asked.

Nearing the end of the barn, hoof stomps and snorting could be heard coming from the last stall on the left. Taylor and Dillon reached the stall gate first, followed by Damien and Joe.

Taylor's eyes bulged. "Holy cow!" she gasped.

Standing before them was a massive creature. The Percheron turned his head, a wild gleam in his hazel colored eyes greeted them. His all-black coat had a glistening sheen, and his tail hung almost to the floor. His mane hung wild and covered his head almost to his eyes. He reared back and on his hind legs and snorted. Rushing the gate at the sight of visitors.

"Are you trying to kill me?" Joe asked, stepping back from the gate.

Dillon and Damien died laughing. Dillon could barely contain the tears. She clutched her sides, doubling over with laughter. "Oh man, the look on your face was so worth it."

Damien tried to stifle the laugh, making a snorting sound instead. He had never seen fear in Joe's eyes until that moment. Pure terror. "I wish I had snapped a photo."

Dillon patted Joe's arm. "No. I wouldn't let you ride him. I'll have you and Taylor ride one of the other more docile horses. One of the trail riders. I'll ride Juniper."

At the sound of his name, he came over to Dillon. He nibbled on her clothes then nuzzled her chest. Raising his head until she patted his cheeks and scratched his ears. "He looks like a force to be reckoned with, but he has an easy-going personality. Loves to run the open fields."

All of a sudden, the floodlights outside the open barn doors flashed on. Gunner ran to the edge barking, darting off towards the fence line. His bark laced with an edge telling the onlookers he wasn't playing.

"What is this dog's problem?" Dillon asked.

Both Joe and Damien stepped out of the barn. Damien went to the right, while Joe went to the left, drawing his weapon.

Dillon and Taylor scanned the back fence and the dark woods beyond.

"Off to the left is the main pasture. A fence line runs along the area. My grandfather's land includes the woods. If the cows get back up in there, it's too hard to round them up. Grandpa left those woods untouched. He liked the backdrop to the farm."

Damien and Joe walked back up to the pair. "Well, I didn't see anything. The lights don't filter far enough towards the fence," Damien said as he glanced at Joe. "See anything on that side?"

"No. Nothing. Gunner!" Joe yelled, followed by a whistle. He held his weapon at his side. The dog raced up, wiggling his butt. Carrying something in his mouth. "What you got there, buddy?" Joe bent down and removed a shop towel from the dog's mouth. "Is there a mechanic shop around here?"

Dillon nodded. "Up behind the barn. If you follow the drive up past where we are, that's where all the work on the equipment is done." She took the towel from his hand. "I have no idea how this got all the way over here. Randy doesn't let these things leave the shop. He's kind of anal about that kind of shit." She pocketed it. "I'll ask them about it tomorrow. After we speak with the lawyers."

Joe looked at her. "Taylor and I can speak with them, while you guys are talking to the lawyer. I need to get some answers anyway. Something doesn't feel right here. Joe re-holstered his weapon, keeping his hand on it. "I'm telling you, something is going on out in those woods."

CHAPTER FIVE

Friday Morning

Joe sat at the table, finishing his full Irish breakfast. "When is the lawyer coming?" He asked as Dillon handed him the shop rag from the night before.

Dillon swallowed her bite of food. "At ten." She glanced at her watch. "In about thirty. Dang, we all slept late."

"That's what a forced vacation will do for you. Make you all kinds of lazy." Damien winked at her as he stood and took his plate to the sink.

The rest followed suit and began to clean up the late morning breakfast.

"Do you have any idea what he wants to tell you and the Martins?" Taylor asked as she loaded the dishwasher.

Dillon shook her head. "None whatsoever." At the moment, a knock at the door echoed through the house. Her eyes lit up. "That must be Agatha and Ralph. I want you to meet them." She ran to the door, squealing as she flung it open.

Agatha's long silver hair hung loose around her shoulders. Her plump figure wrapped up in a puffy warm jacket. Ralph's tall skinny figure towered behind his wife. His pale blue eyes were filled with warmth and joy. He wore his favorite red flannel jacket with a hole in one of the chest pockets. Dillon threw her arms around the woman she considered a second grandmother. Overwhelmed by the full force of emotions, she buried her face in Agatha's neck.

"There-there, child." Agatha stroked the back of her head. She nodded to Ralph to go on by.

He entered the living room, embracing Damien. "How have you been, son?"

"Pretty good. Ralph let me introduce you to Joe and Taylor. Joe is my partner at the VCU, and Taylor is his girlfriend."

Ralph shook both their hands. "Nice to meet both of you." He removed his jacket and hung it on the back of a dining room chair.

Dillon raised her head, wiping her wet face. "I'm sorry, Agatha."

"Sweetie, there is no reason to be sorry. Sometimes things need to come out." She placed her hands on Dillon's cheeks. "I'm always here for you. All you have to do is call me."

Dillon nodded.

Gunner, who had sat patiently waiting for his turn whined at the feet of Agatha.

"Well, now. Look at you." She bent down and kissed the top of the dog's head. "We have surely missed you."

Gunner ran to Ralph's side, waiting for more attention.

"How is he getting along with you guys?" Agatha asked as she stepped further into the living room, removing her coat.

"He seems to be doing well. If for any reason I see he is missing this place, he can always come back here," Dillon said.

Agatha took Dillon's hand in hers. "No, sweetheart. He belongs with you. You and he need to heal together. You need him, and he needs you. The two of you can come and stay here any time." She winked at her before turning to the new people in the living room. "Now who is this incredibly handsome man?" she asked eyeballing Joe.

Damien chuckled at the blush on Joe's cheeks. "This is my partner Joe and his girlfriend, Taylor." He took Agatha's coat and hung it by the front door.

"Well, now aren't you a gorgeous girl. Do you have a bat handy to keep all the girls away from him?"

Taylor laughed. "Yes, except I will use the bat on him. Not the other girls."

Agatha roared back with a hearty laugh. "You are my kind of woman."

Ralph shook his head. "Don't encourage my wife."

They continued the conversation until another knock filled the room. Gunner ran to the door barking and growling.

"It's okay Gunner." Dillon made her way to the door, pushing the dog to the side with her leg. On the other side of the glass, stood Andrew Wright, her grandparent's longtime lawyer. "Hi, Andrew, come in."

Andrew Wright was a short stocky man. His lack of height overshadowed by his boyish good looks. At fifty-five years old, his youthful vitality pegged him for a forty-year-old.

He stepped into the crowded living room. Nodding at everyone as he removed his hat. "Hey, Agatha, Ralph." He stepped up to Dillon, who towered over him, he placed his briefcase on the floor. And rested his hat on top of it. "Let me look at you."

He studied the young woman before him. Her eyes were filled with a sadness he knew wouldn't leave for quite some time. "Your grandparents were proud of who you are and what you do. They bragged about you to everyone. You need to remember that." He took her in his arms and hugged her tight. "My wife and I are here for you, too. All you need to do is call us."

"Thank you, Andrew. I am grateful to have such wonderful people in my life." She moved to the side, staunching her desire to run from the house screaming. "Andrew, this is Joe and Taylor. You remember Damien."

"I do. It's nice to see you again, Damien." He quickly shook Joe's and Taylor's hands. "Pleased to meet you both. I think we should get this meeting started. I have a lot to tell you," Andrew said, smiling at Dillon and the Martins.

Joe nodded to Taylor. "We're going to head to the mechanic shop. We'll be back in a bit. Give you all a chance to talk."

"Okay. Let Jethro know we will ride as soon as we are done here," Dillon said.

"Will do." Joe and Taylor left the house, taking Gunner with them.

CHAPTER SIX

Joe took Taylor's hand as they walked down the pathway leading to the mechanic shop. "Farm life isn't for me. Although, I wouldn't mind coming back here for a visit."

Taylor laughed leaning into him. "I think I would love to have a bed and breakfast on a working ranch or farm like this."

"Nope. Don't even go down that road."

"Well, I like the city too much to do it now. Later, in our old age, it could be a thought."

"No. In my older age, I'm going to own a proper Irish bar." Joe wiggled his eyebrows at her. "With the sexiest waitresses around."

She smacked him on the shoulder. "Not a chance. I know your proclivity for waitresses. They will be old hags." A crooked smile filled her face. "We will have the sexiest bartenders around."

"I don't think so. If I have to have old women as waitresses, you get old farts for bartenders."

As they entered the shop, they heard two men arguing.

"Where the hell did they go, Stan?"

"How the fuck should I know. Now you're accusing me of stealing shop rags?" Stan crossed his arms as he leaned against the wall of the office, mainly to keep from punching Randy.

Randy plopped down in the office chair. "Ah, hell. I'm not accusing you, but something is going on around here."

"Well, it isn't me. Fuck. I got my own tools and shop rags; I don't need the farm's."

"Umm, hello?" Joe said as he rapped on the open doorway.

Randy stood. "The farm isn't open to visitors. How did you get in here?"

Joe held out his hand. "I'm Joe, I'm here with Dillon."

Randy's expression and stance softened. "Oh, hell. I forgot she was here." He reached out, shaking the big man's hand. "I'm Randy, this is Stan."

"This is Taylor. I couldn't help overhearing you're having some thefts?"

Randy sat back in his chair. "Yeah. Small tools, shop rags, and other weird stuff have been disappearing."

Joe pulled the shop rag from his pocket. "These?"

Randy reached out and took the rag. "Where did you find it?"

"Last night, we were up at the barn looking at the horses. Gunner brought it back after chasing something or someone along the fence line. He acted strangely back at the main house too."

Stan's eyes lit up. "Where is Gunner now?"

Joe glanced around. "Hell, he was right behind us a minute ago." Joe stepped out of the office and let out an ear-piercing whistle. Both the men covered their ears, as he did it again.

"Holy shit," Stan said. "How do you do that?"

Taylor laughed. "It's a talent. Just don't encourage him."

A moment later Gunner ran full force into the shop. He slid past the door as his weight was too much on the smooth flooring. His legs slid out from under him as he lost his balance slamming into the wall.

"Gunner, you big dork. Are you okay?" Joe started towards him when he jumped up, wiggling his butt at the sight of the two familiar men in the office.

Gunner ran to Randy whining and howling with glee at his old friend. He turned to Stan bumping into him, almost knocking him over.

"Hey buddy," Stan said as he knelt next to the massive dog. "We miss you. How you been?"

Too excited to stand still, Gunner ran to Randy, who didn't hesitate to lavish attention on the dog.

"He looks like he is healing nicely." Randy ran his finger over the scars showing through thin patches of fur.

Taylor nodded. "He is. He's been doing well."

Randy peeked over at Stan. "How's Dillon?"

Joe leaned against a table located on one of the walls. He stuck his hands in the front pockets of his jeans. "She's doing as well as expected for what she's been through. She needs more time." He cast a sidelong glance at Taylor. Removing his hands from his pockets, he rubbed his palms on his thighs, then crossed his arms. "When did stuff start going missing?"

Randy shrugged. "Maybe three weeks ago. Before the murders. Nothing to do with those. They seem to have picked up a bit in frequency, after them."

"Have you had any unwanted visitors or Lookie Lous on the property? Trying to get a glimpse of the murder scene?"

"Nothing like that. Everyone has been super respectful." Stan scratched Gunner's ears.

"Have things gone missing from everywhere, or a more concentrated area?"

Randy sighed. "As best we can tell, it's everywhere."

"You think anyone has been squatting in the woods, and they're looking for items to use or sell?" Joe asked.

"The items taken are small, nothing of major value, except a few small tools. Sometimes some of our food goes missing." Randy glanced over at Stan. "I guess it could be someone in the woods. The food items have been taken from the fridges and pantries. Sometimes the trash."

The walkie talkie went off. "Randy, this is Jethro. In fifteen minutes, meet us at the main farmhouse. Round up everyone else over that way. Dillon and the Martins need to speak with us."

Randy stood. "I have no idea what that's about. You think it's bad?" he asked Joe.

Joe shrugged. "I don't think so. I know they had a meeting with the lawyer." The men started to leave the shop. "Hey, do you mind if I investigate this and see if we can get you some answers while we're here?"

Stan spoke up first. "I would welcome it. Forget what this bastard says. I'm tired of being blamed."

Randy smacked the man on the upper back. "Fuck you, hosehead," he said, laughing. "Listen, any help you want to give, we would readily take."

"Great, we will have some answers for you soon." Joe watched them leave. Gunner moved next to Taylor. "I think we have a case to solve Watson."

She frowned at him as they started to leave the building heading towards the barn. "Why do I have to be Watson?"

"Duh, I'm the detective. I'm Sherlock."

"Pfft. I'm smarter than you, I should be Sherlock," Taylor said, stepping into the barn.

Joe spun around, pushing her up against a stack of hay bales. He peeked out the open bay door and saw all the employees gathering at the start of the driveway getting ready to head towards the main farm-house. He turned his attention back to Taylor.

Her stomach fluttered at the look of desire raging behind Joe's emerald green eyes. She sucked in a breath as his hand unzipped her jacket and shimmied up her shirt. He pinched her nipple through her bra, squeezing her breast.

"What did you say about you being smarter than me?"

"Hmm, am I in trouble?"

"That depends on the answer you give."

She felt the rush of wetness dampen her panties as she licked her lips. "I said, I am way smarter than you." She leaned into him and bit his bottom lip.

He spun her around, bending her over the hay bales and unzipped her pants, as he did the same to his with his other hand. He sprang from the constraints of his jeans, rock hard. One quick look out the bay door again showed everyone walking towards the house. He reached between her legs and placed his lips next to her ear. "I think you like making me angry." He eased a finger into her and was rewarded with the warmth and gush of fluid.

Taylor moaned at his fingers inside her. Her legs trembled, waiting for the moment when he would fill her with more. "Please, don't make me wait."

"Greedy too." He removed his hand and entered her from behind. Her walls cinched around him. Her warmth coated him, allowing him to move in and out with ease. He quickened his pace; he wasn't going to last long. He leaned close to her ear. "Come for me, baby."

Taylor shivered as Joe's warm breath brushed over her neck. Unable to speak with the onslaught of pleasure, she moaned as her orgasm inched closer to climax. Her entire body began to tremble. "Joe. Don't stop. Harder, please harder," she whispered the command.

Joe slammed into her. Her round ass sticking up as he pushed her upper body down against the hay. "Taylor, I'm so close." His muscles tensed before he exploded inside her. He grunted, holding back a scream of ecstasy. He panted, leaning forward he lifted her torso up. "You okay?"

She pressed her back into his as he extracted himself from her. She pulled her panties and jeans back into position. "Are you sure you wouldn't want to live on a farm?"

He laughed zipping up his jeans. "I guess when you look at it like that, it wouldn't be too bad." A noise caught his attention. He turned to his left to see Gunner staring at him. "Uh, oh."

Taylor spun around. "What? What happened?"

"I think we were watched the whole time."

She gasped, covering her mouth with her hand. "No. Please tell me no one saw us."

He looked over to his left.

She followed his stare. Her eyes widened. "Gunner. Did you watch us?"

He twisted his head to the side as if he was trying to think of an answer.

"As long as you don't tell anyone. Promise?" Taylor asked.

He barked and ran out the bay door.

Joe took her hand. "I think we're safe. No one would believe him anyway."

CHAPTER SEVEN

Friday Afternoon
Chase's house

Kerry twisted his head to the side, listening. Every breath Chase took was followed by soft gurgling. "Still alive. Impressive, Chase, very impressive."

Chase's shirt was covered in blood and vomit.

Kerry walked to the table and picked up the straight edge razor. Standing next to Chase, he sighed. "Chase? Hey Chase?" he smacked his cheeks.

The man barely moved his head.

The air still had the stench of burnt flesh from the cauterization of his ankles and wrists. Kerry was pretty sure Chase had crapped his pants sometime during the night. "Man, you stink Chase." He smacked Chase's cheeks again, this time the man blinked his eyes open. "Wake up Chase. I wouldn't want you to miss this last part."

Chase whimpered; tears streamed down his face. "I'm sorry."

"What exactly are you sorry for, Chase?"

"I'm sorry about Sierra. I should've stood up to Pops. I should have stopped him. All of them." Chase's head hung limply against his chest.

"Yes, you should've. No worries, they will all pay a steep price for what they did to her." Kerry grabbed Chase by the hair, yanking his head back. "I think this is going to hurt." He stuck the edge of the razor into the corner of the eye, slicing upward following the curve of the eye socket along the edge of the brow bone.

Chase's blood-curdling screams echoed throughout the living room.

"Stop struggling." Kerry held onto his hair tighter, holding his head in place. He sliced through the muscles and optic nerve, allowing him to pop the eyeball out.

At some point, Chase passed out. Just as well, Kerry thought to himself. "Almost done now, Chase. You've given me what I needed." He patted Chase's head. "Almost done now."

CHAPTER EIGHT

The Farm

Dillon squirmed in her chair at the dining room table as Andrew removed a folder from his briefcase. She reached under the table and took Damien's hand in hers, squeezing his fingers.

Andrew stared at Dillon. "Your grandfather has some specific things lined out in his will. First, in the event you want to sell the farm, there are specific provisions Jonas made."

Dillon lifted her hand. "I have no intention of selling this property or this farm. There is no issue there. Agatha and Ralph have been with my grandparents for a long time. I may not want to run it, and that's why they will."

Andrew smiled. "Your grandfather knew you would say that, but, and I quote, 'You make sure to tell Dillon, she can do whatever she wants.'" He opened the file. "With that said, let me spell out a few things. Agatha and Ralph's house and the surrounding acreage around their house is theirs.

"Should the property ever be sold, Jonas had a survey done, and their property will not be for sale in the final deal. The will also gives them two hundred and fifty thousand dollars." He glanced at Ralph and Agatha. "Your property is worth over two million dollars."

Agatha gasped at the amount of money. "We can't accept that."

Ralph sat back in his chair, too stunned to speak.

Andrew held up his hand. "That's not all. Whatever amount is owed on their home shall be paid. I will have the estate pay that for you."

Ralph's eyes glassed over. "I can't believe this."

Dillon wiped her face. "Grandfather thought of you as family. I'm not surprised."

Andrew turned towards Dillon. "The ranch hands will receive one hundred thousand dollars each, and their mortgages are to be paid as well. Everything else as far as the eye can see goes to Dillon. Along with all cash and retirement funds. Those can be withdrawn as needed. Or you can continue to let them accrue interest the way they currently are.

"Jonas set up everything in a trust fund, and when you need any of the monies, we can discern which will carry tax penalties and which won't. I have some bank cards and papers for you to sign, which will give you access to monies with no fees attached. You can add to that account or transfer to another as you see fit."

Dillon's eyes widened as she looked over at Damien. She turned back to Andrew. "I don't understand. The amount of monies set aside for the ranch hands, and Agatha and Ralph are quite substantial, I can't imagine the money leftover warrants a trust fund."

Andrew searched through the file. He had to make sure he got the number right. He knew that no one knew of the wealth that Jonas and Kitty had acquired. "I know Jonas kept the finances from you. He never wanted you to be burdened with anything after the death of your family when you were younger. He made sure to set up this farm and all his investments so that one day, you would have everything you needed."

Dillon's grip on Damien's hand tightened. Her right knee bounced up and down at a furious pace. "I still don't understand."

Andrew's mouth twitched. He hoped the news of her new-found wealth would ease her loss. No money could erase her pain, he did hope it would remind her what her grandfather did to protect her.

"Please. Tell me." She stared at Andrew, waiting.

"Dillon, the entire property, even after the payouts, which to be honest, I have already pulled everyone's mortgage amounts. You're going to inherit over ten million dollars. That sum doesn't include the value of the property, the herd, or the working farm."

Everyone gasped at the table.

Damien who had been stoic coughed trying to catch his breath. "Holy shit!"

Dillon's hand covered her mouth. "I don't believe this." She turned towards Damien. "I don't believe this."

Damien reached over and put his right arm around her. "Your grandfather was a brilliant man. I am not surprised he set it up like this."

"As long as you don't withdraw money from three of the main accounts in large chunks, they will continue to grow and accrue interest. You will stay a wealthy woman. And as this farm continues its operation, it will only add to the bottom line of your wealth," Andrew said.

Dillon blinked rapidly, glancing from Damien to Andrew.

Damien leaned into the table. "I'm assuming Jonas made a provision for the Martins to continue with the daily operations, and if there are any major things they need or want, they have to run that by Dillon."

"Yes, he did. He hoped you would let the Martins continue running the farm. They know what Jonas and Kitty wanted. They will move the farm forward under your tutelage."

Agatha reached across the table, taking Dillon's hand in hers. "We would never change anything about this farm. This is your farm. We will do whatever you want."

Dillon smiled as she took Ralph's hand in hers. "I know you will. I will leave all that for Andrew to go over with you." She looked at Andrew. "I would like for you to continue to act on my behalf and on my grandfather's wishes for the farm. I'm guessing he has laid out specific provisions on how to advance their wishes for the property."

"He has. Everything will come to me and be forwarded on to you. If you don't agree with something, it won't happen."

"Well, I trust Agatha and Ralph. I'm pleased about the ranch hands. I can't wait to tell them. I need whatever information you want me to pass on to them so they can get their properties paid for." Dillon blew out a shaky breath.

Andrew handed her several business cards. "All they need to do is call me, and I will take it from there."

Dillon looked at Ralph. "When we are done here, can you call them all to come here and we will tell them the news together?"

"As soon as you want me too." He pulled the walkie talkie from his hip. "One click away."

CHAPTER NINE

It was after lunch by the time the ranch hands and the Martins left the house. Damien sat across from Dillon at the table. "They all seemed pretty damned stunned at the news."

She raised an eyebrow at him. "No, shit. I was more than stunned." She took a sip of the whiskey he had poured for her. "I can't believe this."

"Get used to it. You're a very wealthy woman." He shook his head when she frowned at him. "I'm not making light of the circumstances that brought you to this point. Jonas made sure to set you up when he and Kitty died. I know this isn't the way he wanted it to happen."

Her posture relaxed. "I realize you didn't mean anything like that."

Damien drank his whiskey and refilled his glass with the bottle on the table. "The ranch hands were thrilled. Did you see the looks on their faces? They were stunned, happy, and then instantly guilty about their joy."

"I got that impression as well. Agatha did a good job easing their discomfort." She took a long sip of her drink.

"What do you think of the plan she came up with?" Damien asked.

Before she could answer Joe, Taylor, and Gunner entered the house.

Gunner stopped at his bed nudging Coach who slept on one of the corners. The cat rolled over, baring his belly for him as if Gunner was going to rub it. The dog sniffed Coach then snuggled up next to him. Soaking up the warmth of the fire.

"Hey guys," Joe smiled as they sat at the table.

Damien smirked at Dillon who grinned at Taylor. "What have you two been up to?"

Taylor's eyes widened as she watched Joe point to his hair. She couldn't figure out what he was trying to tell her. Her gaze shifted between Joe, Dillon, and Damien. She could feel the warmth spreading across her cheeks.

Dillon raised an eyebrow at her. "I think Joe was trying to tell you, you have hay stuck in your hair."

Taylor reached up and felt around, pulling several strands of hay from it. "Oh my. I have no idea how that got in my hair."

Damien laughed, unable to catch his breath. "Yeah, right."

Joe looked up at Taylor and shrugged. "Cat is out of the bag now."

Damien shook his head. "You two can't help yourselves, can you?"

"Hey, it was her fault," Joe said.

Taylor's jaw hung open. "I can't believe you."

Dillon sighed. "You two have to be the horniest people I know. Next to Damien."

"You aren't bringing me into this debauchery," Damien said.

Joe grabbed a beer from the fridge and a glass of wine for Taylor. He handed it to her before he sat back down. "Why did all the employees come over here? Did something happen at the reading of the will?"

Damien stared at Dillon, nodding. "You could say that."

Taylor glanced between them. "Can you share it with us? The suspense is killing me."

"Dillon, you want to explain it or would you like me to?" Damien asked.

"My grandfather made provisions for all the workers." She went on to explain to them how each of the men was taken care of, and the Martins as well.

Joe ogled her. "That's a lot of money. Is there much leftover for you?"

"Joe!" Taylor exclaimed.

"What? It's a legit question."

Damien grabbed an empty glass and poured some whiskey in it, sliding it over to Joe. "Go ahead and tell them the rest."

Joe looked at the glass of whiskey, turning towards Dillon. "Well, I'm waiting."

"It seems my grandfather was a damn good businessman. Even after the payouts for the employees, the cash alone amounts to over ten million dollars. When you add in the value of the property and farm, the total goes upward of twenty million."

Joe downed the glass of whiskey. "Holy shit. Will you marry me?"

"Joe!" Taylor said, laughing. "Marry me instead, Dillon."

They all laughed.

Dillon glared at Damien. "I'm still after your money, I want it all."

Damien raised his eyebrows. "Together, we can rule the world."

Joe's look turned somber. "Dillon, I didn't mean any disrespect. I know you could care less about the money. I know you would rather have them back here with you."

"I know you didn't mean anything." She glanced around. "I don't want anyone outside this house to know. I don't want people treating me differently."

Each of them nodded.

"You don't have to worry. No one will hear about it from us." Damien downed the last of his drink.

An evil sneer pulled the corners of Joe's mouth slightly upward. He leaned into Dillon. "Well, as for me, my silence is going to cost you."

She rolled her eyes at him. "I expected nothing less."

Taylor sat back and smiled. "I'm thrilled for you Dillon. What's going on with the farm?"

"Damien and I were about to discuss the plan." She refilled her glass with more whiskey. "Before their deaths, my grandparents and the Martins had talked about building a cottage and making this a bed and breakfast, where people could be immersed in as much of the 'working farm experience' as they wanted. We decided to go ahead and use this house. We're going to make it a little more luxurious. Fix up the bedrooms and bathrooms and fill the house with new furniture. Make Gunner's room a craft room for families when they stay here." She stared down at the hardwood floors. "I think I might suggest they change out the floors."

Damien agreed. "I think that may be a good idea."

Taylor's eyes lit up. "That's a fantastic idea. Not the floors, I mean the bed and breakfast thing." Her stomach growled. She looked at her watch. "Holy cow, it's almost two. Who else is hungry?" She giggled at all the hands being raised. "I will find something for us. Keep telling us about the B&B."

"Well, the Martins are going to get everything started. Ralph has a friend who does construction. When we leave, they will get some of the updates done, then she will furnish the bedrooms. I told the lawyer to use his best judgment on expenses, unless it's a major expense. I'm not worried, though. The Martins know what my grandparents wanted to do."

Damien peered over at Joe. "She needs to go through the house and take what she wants of their personal belongings. They don't want anything of personal value left in the house."

Joe nodded. "You know, out in the shed, there were some stacked flat boxes behind one of the shelving units. We can bring those in. You pack up stuff, and we can rent a truck if need be."

Dillon frowned. "There are only a few things I want. Everything else the Martins can have. I know some of the workers asked for some stuff to remember my grandparents by. They don't have anything valuable. I know Kitty has some jewelry I want to keep. I have some important stuff from my family that Jonas kept. Everything I want should fill a few boxes, if that."

Damien chuckled. "You say that now, but I can see you going through the items and saying you want that, you want this. You might as well take everything, and when you're prepared to go through it, we can do it together at the house."

Taylor chimed in. "I think that is the best idea. You're too close to the loss of them. I don't think you're ready to make decisions of that magnitude yet."

Dillon sighed in resignment to Taylor's suggestion. She really wasn't ready to make those decisions. "I think you're right. I will box up everything and go through it later. I can set aside some of the specific items for some of the workers."

"After we eat, Damien and I can go out to the shed and get those boxes," Joe said as Taylor set a plate of sandwiches on the table. Footlong hoagies stuffed with meat, cheese, lettuce, and tomatoes. She also set a bowl of chips and cut up fruit on the table. Joe's mouth watered. "Babe, this looks great. Thank you." Joe grabbed a sandwich and a handful of chips, placing them on one of the plates she had set on the table.

"Yes, thank you," both Dillon and Damien said as they filled their own plates.

"You're welcome." She placed half a sandwich on her plate, along with fruit and chips. "Dillon, how do you feel about this house being used as the B&B?"

Dillon's brow wrinkled as she shrugged. "I don't know. On some levels, I'm fine with it. On others, I don't want strangers in here. Agatha showed me what she and Kitty had been working on regarding the B&B and Jonas was all for it. I can't let my personal feelings block something they were going to do," she paused, "if they were still alive. I don't think I can do that."

"I think it's a great way to honor your grandparent's wishes. I think it's also a great business choice. This house will get used. You will bring in an income that will cover expenses without touching revenue from the farm. And it will only build community relations keeping the farm and ranch at the forefront of the industry." Damien swallowed.

Joe nodded. "I agree. It's a great way to honor Jonas and Kitty. I know having people in here may seem intrusive." He reached across the table and took her hand in his. "I wouldn't take all their personal stuff out. Leave a few things behind, so visitors get a sense of who they were. That's what makes this place so great. Honor them with letting everyone know what kind of people they were. How they took care of their family and the ranchers. What your grandparents have done for their employees shows their love of others. That's what should be celebrated. Don't try to erase them, embrace who they were, and share them."

Everyone sat gaping at Joe.

He glanced around. "What? Did I say something wrong?"

Dillon looked at Taylor. "Who is this man?"

Taylor shrugged. "I have no idea. I guess our roll in the hay must have done something to him."

Damien's eyes narrowed in on his friend. "Who are you, and what have you done with Joe?"

Joe rolled his eyes and waved them off. "*Stai zitto.*"

Damien gasped. "Using my own language against me."

Dillon stood and moved behind Joe. She wrapped her arms around his neck and kissed his cheek. "Joe, you are absolutely right. I have an idea I think will work for just that." She squeezed his neck and kissed him again. "I love you, Joe." She glanced up at Taylor, with tears in her eyes. "I love both of you. I'm grateful I have you two in my life."

She picked up her plate, and as she walked past Taylor, she gave her a one-arm hug and a kiss on the cheek. "When you're done getting the boxes we will go horseback riding."

"Ooh I can't wait," Taylor said.

"You almost finished?" Damien asked, standing.

"Almost." Joe finished his sandwich and gulped down his beer. "Hey Dillon, you know your grandparents canned some weird shit out there in the shed."

She turned towards him. "What are you talking about?"

"There are some weird jars of stuff out in the shed," Damien said as he put his plate in the dishwasher.

Joe leaned against the counter as he handed Damien his plate. "I can understand the pig's feet, snout, and ears, but there are a few jars with things that make me wonder if Jonas and Kitty weren't trying to recreate *Motel Hell*."

Dillon crossed her arms. "I don't know what you guys are talking about."

Joe angled his head down. "Have you seen what is in some of the jars in the shed?"

Dillon tilted her head to the side. "I can't imagine...oh, wait. I know what's out there. Whenever one of the livestock dies, if possible, it is butchered to eat, if it is contaminated, then Grandpa would butcher it so students who visited the farm could see those organs."

"That explains so much." Damien patted Joe on the shoulder. "Let's get those boxes."

"You got it, boss."

"I should punch you," Damien said as he walked out the door of the mudroom, turning to face Joe as he held the door open.

Joe stopped and swung his arms in a Kung Fu karate chop. "No way, you can get past these lightning fast moves."

Damien raised an eyebrow at him. "You are seriously delusional."

CHAPTER TEN

Friday evening 9 p.m.

Joe walked in the front door carrying a large duffle bag Damien had in the back of the SUV. Gunner ran to him, sniffing the bag. "Hey buddy," he said, rubbing his ears. He moved towards one of the empty chairs across from the sofa and placed the bag between his feet, grunting as he sat down.

Damien looked up from rubbing Dillon's feet. "Did the horseback ride make you sore? And what are you doing with my tactical bag?"

Joe turned his attention to Damien. "No, the horseback ride did not make me sore. To answer your question as to why I have the tactical bag, while you guys were talking to the lawyer earlier, Taylor and I spoke with Randy and Stan over at the mechanic shop. They both said over the last few weeks, things have gone missing from different locations on the farm."

Dillon swung her legs over the edge of the sofa. "I haven't heard about things being stolen."

"Randy said it started about three weeks ago. Little things like rags, small tools..."

"And food," Taylor said, lifting a pair of night vision goggles out of the bag.

"Taylor, be careful. If you turn those on with the lights on, you'll be blinded," Joe said, shaking his head at her.

"Okay. Still doesn't explain why you need the tactical gear," Damien said.

"I thought we could do a late-night investigation." He glanced at Dillon. "You'll need to let the Martins know what we will be doing and inform them the floodlights will be turned off. They'll need to stay in their house too."

Dillon giggled. "What the hell am I going to tell them?"

"The truth. We're going to see if we can find who or what is stealing from the farm." Joe pulled out a few small infrared flashlights and four small ultra mag lights.

"They're going to think we have all lost our minds." Dillon headed towards the master bedroom to call the Martins.

Damien knelt next to the bag. "I think I have enough equipment in here for all of us." He reached into the interior side pocket, removing a small pouch.

Taylor squealed in delight. "Oooh, do I get to wear one of those again?"

"Babe, I love you and your *giblets*, but you are a serious dork," Joe said, blowing a kiss to her.

"OMG! I can't believe you said that."

"What, giblets or dork?" he asked.

"You won't get my giblets if you keep it up."

"Stop," Damien said chuckling. "I don't want to hear about Taylor's giblets."

"Do I even want to know what you three are discussing?" Dillon asked, walking back into the living room.

Damien shook his head. "No. Trust me on this."

"Alright. Agatha said no problem. However, she asked us to do it Saturday night instead of tonight. They're entertaining some friends this evening."

"That'll work," Joe said. "We can make smores tonight."

"Yes," Taylor said, jumping up. She grabbed her butt cheeks with her hands. "My ass hurts."

Dillon and Damien frowned at Joe.

Joe's brow wrinkled. "Don't give me that look. I didn't do anything."

Taylor turned around with bright red cheeks. "You two are disgusting."

Dillon's eyes widened. "I wasn't thinking that. Whose fucking mind is in the gutter now?"

Taylor laughed as she waddled to the kitchen. "I haven't ridden a horse in so long. I used muscles I didn't even know I had."

Dillon followed her. "I'm a little sore too." She helped Taylor load up a plate with chocolate bars, graham crackers, and marshmallows. "Hey, Damien?" she called out.

"Yeah, babe?" he strolled to her. His gait a little slower than normal.

She smirked at him. "Are you sore?"

Damien nodded. "A little. Nothing a long soak in a hot tub wouldn't fix."

"After smores, that's what we will do. Well, we will soak in the bath-tub. That's as close as I can get to a hot tub." Dillon gave a quick kiss on the lips. "Will you grab some wine and beer from outside?"

"Anything for you," he said, walking out to the mudroom and the outside refrigerator.

Joe looked up at them as he put the last of the tactical gear back in the bag. "There is enough equipment for all of us to use." He wiggled his eyebrows at them. "This should be really fun."

Taylor shook her head. "You would think hunting for Michael Myers or Freddy Krueger would be fun. I hope it isn't a big bear clan. Momma bears are mean."

Damien walked back in with a bottle of wine and six beers. He placed four beers in the fridge and grabbed two wine glasses and the corkscrew. Barely able to balance all of them in his arms. "Hey," he said, walking back into the living room. "Grab the wine. I can feel it slipping."

Dillon walked to him and grabbed the dangling bottle. "If you had yelled, I could've helped you."

"You are helping," Damien said as he handed a beer to Joe.

Dillon used the corkscrew and opened the bottle.

Taylor took the two wire coat hangers they had brought out earlier that day when Joe had first mentioned smores, and straightened them. "I think these will work." She handed one to Dillon. "I love smores." Taylor placed two marshmallows on the end of one. Before she stuck it in the fire, she made sure two graham crackers were ready with a piece of chocolate.

Dillon followed suit and placed two marshmallows on her hanger. "Shouldn't we do one mallow at a time?"

"No. This way, we can all eat one at the same time." Taylor stuck her marshmallows into the fireplace.

Coach and Gunner sat right next to her, eyeballing the plate with all the goodies.

Dillon glanced at the pair of furballs. "Don't even think about it, you two."

Both pets looked at each other then back to the plate.

"Don't act like you don't know what I'm talking about." Dillon rotated the marshmallows.

"Don't burn them," Damien said as he placed the tactical bag near the end of the sofa. He sat down on the floor next to the cat and scratched his ears. "She's mean, huh, Coach?"

"That cat is spoiled rotten." Dillon put a marshmallow one of the crackers and chocolate. She used the other half of graham cracker to slide the caramelized sugar cube off the hanger.

Taylor handed one to Joe.

"Now this looks like heaven." Joe took a bite. Gooey marshmallow squished out. He licked his fingers, getting off what he could before it stuck to him.

Damien took his from the plate Dillon held out. "Mhmm," his eyes closed as he savored the sweet concoction.

Coach pawed at him, meowing.

Twisting to the right, he lifted his smore up out of the cat's reach. Coach was faster and managed to get some of the treat on his paw. Damien laughed as the fat feline struggled with the sticky mess.

He shook his paw, licking the once soft goo. Now hard and stuck between his toes. Coach licked and tugged, making more of a mess.

Taylor took pity on the poor cat. "C'mon sweetie, let's go clean your paw," she said scooping the cat up in her arms.

Damien continued to giggle as he finished off his smore.

"I can't believe you didn't help him clean it off." Dillon began roasting two more marshmallows for Damien and Joe.

"I would've eventually. After I entertained myself watching him struggle for a bit." Damien took the second smore off the plate Dillon held out.

Joe moaned as he ate his second one. "These are so good."

Coach ran back into the living room and sat on the dog's bed.

Gunner didn't even notice. He was busy watching the plate holding one lone graham cracker. He kept licking his chops and shifting his eyes from the plate to Dillon.

Dillon rolled her eyes as she stood. "Here." She handed the cracker to Gunner. He wolfed it down and looked for more. "That's it. I got nothing else." She showed the dog her empty hands before taking the plate to the kitchen.

Taylor's phone pinged. She glanced around. She removed it from her back-pocket reading the text, quickly darkening the screen as Joe walked up to her.

"Who was that?" Joe asked.

"Huh?" Taylor asked, smiling. "Um, nothing. An automated text about my credit payment being due. I think I'm ready for a bath. You want to join me?" She traced her finger along Joe's chest.

"You don't have to ask me twice," he said, dragging her behind him. "See you guys in the morning."

Dillon heard giggling and squeals from Taylor as she shut the bathroom door. "I think they are going to have sex."

"When do they not have sex?" Damien asked, laughing. "Can we go have sex?" He wiggled his eyebrows at her. When she didn't acknowledge his question, he didn't push it. "You want to go sit on the porch?"

She nodded. "Gunner needs to go out anyway." Dillon followed him out the door, both grabbing their jackets on the way out.

Damien sat on the porch swing as Gunner bolted down the steps, running around the yard.

"Wait." Dillon walked back into the house.

Within a few moments, lights flooded the yard as the motion detectors kicked on and picked up Gunner's movements. Shortly after Dillon came back out with two beers in her hand. "Oh sweet," Damien said as he took the beer she held out.

She sat in the swing with him. Taking a long pull of her beer, she sighed. "I love sitting out here. Whenever I would come home from college, I would spend hours out here. On this very swing."

Damien used his legs to sway them gently. He watched as Dillon curled her legs underneath her. "I can see why. It's so quiet compared to the city." He lifted his head, sniffing the air. "I love the smell too."

"I love the way this farm smells. Something about this...I'm glad we're here. Thank you for this." Dillon reached out and took his hand.

"Dillon, I want you to be happy. Whatever it is you need. I will do it."

She smiled at him. "I do need something from you."

"What?"

She took a deep breath. "I need you to quit treating me like I'm going to break."

His brow wrinkled.

"Don't try to deny it. Ever since the cabin, and the hospital, you have treated me with kid gloves. I can't stand it."

Damien drank his beer.

"I need you to treat me like you always have. Get mad at me, tell me when I'm a pain in the ass. I need you to treat me like...I'm normal."

Damien looked at her. "I guess I was trying to make it easy on you. I didn't realize it was driving you crazy."

"I just can't deal with it...the pity, the long stares wondering if I'm going to break down."

Damien kissed the back of her hand. "I won't do it anymore. I promise."

"Okay. I understand when I get back to work, I'm going to have to deal with everyone tippy-toeing around me, I don't want to deal with it from you or Joe."

"This whole treating you normal thing, does that mean I can jump your bones?"

"Soon. I just need a little more time."

"I can wait." He took her hand in his. "I love you, Dillon."

Gunner ran up to them, wagging his butt ready to go back inside.

Dillon stood. "Let's go to sleep. I'm tired. We will take our bath tomorrow."

"That's fine with me. I'm tired too. I hope Gunner and Coach stay off the bed tonight."

"Like that will happen." Dillon closed the front door. As if on cue, Coach and Gunner both ran to the bedroom, staking out their spots.

"Make sure, Agatha puts a king-size bed in here," Damien said as he followed Dillon into the bedroom.

CHAPTER ELEVEN

Early Saturday Morning

Damien's chest was weighted down. He had a hard time breathing. *Am I drowning? I think I'm drowning.* Funny, he wasn't scared. He couldn't be drowning. He'd be scared. *I can't breathe. Why can't I breathe?*

His heart rate began to speed up. He couldn't move. Pinned. His head buzzed. No, it wasn't his head. *Bzzz, bzzz, bzzz.* Something smacked him on the chest. His eyes fluttered open as Dillon hit him a second time.

"Your phone...answer the damn phone."

"Huh?" He tried to move. He was stuck. Dillon was draped over him, Coach was laying on his left shoulder snuggled between him and Dillon, and at some point, Gunner had laid between his legs with the upper half of his body crushing his pelvis. "I can't believe this." He would've laughed if he could've breathed. Reaching for the nightstand, he fumbled with his phone. "Kaine."

"Damien, it's about time you answered your phone." Captain Mackey's voice boomed in his ear.

Damien sat up, sending Coach to Dillon's side of the bed in a huff. Gunner didn't move. Damien squinted at the clock on the stand, almost nine a.m. "I'm on vacation, you know. Why are you calling me this early?" His heart stopped for a split second as he waited for his captain's reply. Not sure of what news he was about to hear.

"You and Joe are reinstated as of now. You shouldn't have been suspended in the first place. It is what it is, though, politics."

"I don't understand. I have two weeks left, Joe has one. It must be something awful to bring us back." Damien pried Gunner off his body and swung his legs to the side.

Gunner made his way to the vacated spot right next to Dillon.

"There's been a murder. A horrific murder. The chief wants you two on the case. It's going to get nasty, too. Be ready."

"Who?"

"Chase Humphry."

"You've got to be kidding me." Damien stood and grabbed a pair of underwear from his bag. He heard Dillon stirring. He grabbed his jeans and quietly left the room.

"No, I'm not. He was found today in his home. Or what was left of him."

Damien zipped up his jeans and sat on the sofa. "I can get us there in probably two hours if I drive like a maniac."

"Do it. Put on your sirens and lights. If you get pulled over tell them to call me. I'll text you his address."

"Can the body stay there until we get there?"

"Sure, no problem. Dr. Forsythe said he's in no hurry. It's going to be hours before they can figure out how to move him."

"Crap, what happened? You got any details?"

"He left his office Thursday evening. He had travel plans for this weekend in Washington. His housekeeper showed up early this morning. She wasn't scheduled until Monday, but she had some kind of appointment, so she opted to do it this morning, get it out of the way. That poor woman is going to need counseling. All the officers on-site could get out of her was that he was supposed to be traveling. That's all we know for now."

"Alright. Joe and I will leave here in the next half hour. We will get there as quickly as we can."

"Okay. Damien?"

"Yes?"

"I'm sorry it all went down the way it did."

"I know it wasn't your fault, Captain. It was mine."

"No. You did what I would have done if my family was in trouble. Both the chief and I went to bat for you. They tied our hands. Just know, you have our support."

"I appreciate it. So, I'm reinstated, fully? Back in charge of the VCU?"

"Yes. Of course. Your men will be glad to see you. Lieutenant Stevens has done a good job of running it, but I know your men miss you. We all miss you. Text me when you get there. We will need to have a briefing early Monday."

"I will." The line went dead. Damien wasn't sure how he felt. A roaring battle waged inside. He was sure he wanted to leave the VCU, and yet, at this moment, he was happy. Happy to be going back to work. Although he didn't want leave Dillon, he knew she had to stay.

He walked down the hallway towards Joe's room. Knocking on the door, he eased it open. "Joe?" He heard light snoring. "Joe?" He called out louder.

"Yo. What's up?" Joe asked.

Damien opened the door and stuck his head in. "The captain called."

Joe bolted up. "Get the fuck out. What's going on?"

"We need to go. We've been reinstated." Damien leaned against the door frame.

"Oh shit. It must be bad." Joe swung his legs over the edge of the bed.

Damien averted his eyes. "I don't want to see your junk, man."

Joe laughed as he pulled on a pair of underwear. "Why? Because it makes yours look like a Vienna sausage?"

"You got me." Damien turned to leave, then turned back. "Taylor and Dillon can rent a truck and get home. She will stay with her, right?"

Joe looked up at the concern he heard in his friend's voice. "She will stay with her. They could use the time together. Don't worry buddy, she'll be fine."

"Okay." Damien went back to his room. As he entered, both Coach and Gunner cracked an eye at him making no other effort to move. Both had snuggled in next to Dillon. Her arm was draped over the big dog's body, and Coach had nestled himself right between the two. He wondered if she even knew he wasn't there.

He sat on the edge of the bed and brushed her hair out of her face. "Hey, baby."

Stirring, she swatted at his hand.

"Dillon, sweetie? I need you to wake up."

She sighed as she snuggled in closer to Gunner. "I don't want to get up. It's too early."

"Dillon? I need you to wake up."

Her eyes opened at the stern tone in his voice. Realizing he wasn't in bed, she twisted her head to look at him. She glanced back at the dog. "I thought...how did Gunner get here?"

He chuckled. "He took my spot when I answered a call from the captain."

"Captain Mackey?" she turned over and sat up facing him. "Why did he call you?"

"Joe and I have been reinstated."

She cocked her head at him, with wide eyes. "Something bad has happened. What?"

"It looks like Chase Humphry is dead. And from what Mackey said, it's nasty. He wants us at the scene as soon as possible."

"Wow. Humphry. That's like, big news. You guys are going right back into the fire, aren't you?"

Damien grabbed his bag and started packing. "It's going to bring out the vultures, that's for sure. The guy is worth millions. I have a feeling, whatever got him killed, is going to make our lives miserable."

"Do you need me to come with you?"

He stopped and sat next to her again. "No. I think you and Taylor should stay here. Get what you need to do done. And get the masked bandits taken care of. I think it will be good for you two to be here. Taylor can help you." He reached out and held her hand. "Let her in, you hear me?"

She smiled at him. "You know me so well, huh?"

"I know you don't like to let people in, but in this instance, let her in. She loves you, let her help you."

She kissed him. "I will. Coach and Gunner can stay with me. We will get a truck or whatever we need to get home."

"I think Taylor has a lot of time off. Stay as long as you need to. If she needs to come home before you are ready, rent her a car. I'll pay for it."

She nodded. "I don't want to stay much longer than a week. Don't worry about us."

He reached over and rubbed Coach's head and Gunner's belly. "Gunner, Coach, you guys keep her safe." He turned back to the woman who held his heart in the palm of her hand. "I love you, Dillon."

"I love you more." She kissed him and watched him walk out the door. She glanced at the clock, nine twenty. "It's too early to get up." She snuggled back under the covers. Coach purred, and Gunner snored as she drifted back to sleep.

CHAPTER TWELVE

On the road to Chicago

Damien ate his breakfast sandwich. The traffic was light on the country road. Glancing at the dash clock, he shook his head. "I bet we roll into Chicago right in the middle of Saturday shopping traffic."

"Didn't the captain say they were in no hurry to move the body?"

"He also said get there as quick as we could." Damien turned off the siren, leaving the lights flashing. "Actually, Humphry lives in Barrington."

"Shit, in the gated community," Joe snapped his fingers. "The one that looks like it stepped out of a Norman Rockwell painting?"

"Chandelier Heights, that place is impressive. It's guarded like Buckingham Palace." Damien downed his diet soda and opened the second one he had bought when they stopped for gas and food before heading out.

"Well, now you and Dillon can move out there." Joe snickered at the glare Damien shot his way.

"Don't say that to her. She will punch you." He paused. "I can't believe how much money her grandfather had. Who knew farming was so lucrative?"

"It sounds like he invested well. Why is Dillon so uncomfortable being rich?"

Damien sniggered. "I don't know. She hates it when I do nice things for her with my money. Even if it doesn't cost much. She will probably never touch that money. Unless I can talk her into buying our bar for us."

"Now, you're talking. She can put up all the funds. Damn, I came close to telling you I don't want to go back to work."

Damien shot him a cockeyed look. "You mean like quit altogether?"

Joe nodded. "Yup. I feel like sometimes we keep putting these fuckers away, and another one pops right up. Maybe we should think of leaving."

"I had this same conversation with Dillon. She said something, though. She said, you, me, her, and all the others who choose this line of work, we do it because we were meant to. And if it isn't us, then who?"

Joe sighed. "She's right." He was quiet for a few minutes. "We could always do this on our own. Start our own little detective agency."

Damien stared out the front window. The flat plains of Iowa rolled by. "I think we open a bar and run the detective agency on the down-low. Like the *Equalizer*. We help those the system can't."

Joe smacked his leg. "Yes! When?"

Damien roared back laughing. "I don't know. How about we get this case solved. We get Dillon back to work, and back to normal. Then you and I can make a decision. Sound good?"

"Okay. Sounds doable. Let's do a one to three-year plan. I think knowing we have an out, will make this job not seem so fucking bad." Joe finished his second breakfast sandwich. Balling up his trash and putting it in his bag, he looked over at Damien. "You know, I got to say, I'm glad to be going back to work. As much as I say I want to leave, Dillon has it right. We were made for this. When it's time to leave I think you and I will know."

"I think you're right. You know this case is going to be baptism by fucking fire. I have a suspicion this is going to get ugly."

CHAPTER THIRTEEN

Saturday 12:15 p.m.
Barrington, Illinois

Joe had fallen asleep shortly after their conversation. Damien had enjoyed the quiet, the calmness before the storm. As he rolled into Barrington, he smacked Joe's leg. "Hey, we're almost there."

Joe sat up, yawning. "Crap, why did you let me sleep so long?"

"Dude you must have been tired. You were out. We were talking, I asked you something, and you had fallen asleep."

Joe rubbed the sleep from his eyes. "It's the last week, not having to get up in the morning. I will miss that. I have enjoyed being lazy."

Damien snorted. "I hear you." As he followed the GPS on his phone, a knot began to form in his gut. "The captain said the scene was pretty horrific. I wonder what we're rolling into?"

No sooner were the words out of his mouth, the entrance to Chandelier Heights came into view. The guard stations were staffed by a small army, with several Chicago PD patrolmen assisting with crowd control. The news crews had gathered in force outside the gates.

"Oh, fuck me," Joe said.

Damien flipped on the siren. All eyes turned towards the SUV. As he pulled up to the entrance and rolled down his window, the news crews swelled towards them, trying to get a glimpse of who was being allowed through the hallowed gates. He handed both their ID's to the guard.

The guard clicked the radio attached to the shoulder of this uniform shirt. "I have a Lieutenant Kaine and Detective Hagan waiting for entry."

"Send them through. The ME is waiting on them."

The guard passed their ID's through the window. "Thank you, Lieutenant Kaine," the guard said. "Turn to the right. You will see the house down the lane."

"Thank you. Has anyone spoken with you about any video or entry logs?" Damien asked.

"Yes, sir." He thumbed through his notes. "It looks like Detective Davidson already requested the information. We are putting it together now."

Damien nodded. "Tell me this, are these gates manned twenty-four hours?"

"Yes." The guard winced.

"What are you not telling me?" Damien asked.

"Last Thursday night, we had some kind of alarm, and it pulled our guards out of the gatehouse. It was later found to be a false alarm. However, for about an hour, the gate was on automatic entry."

"What does automatic entry mean?" Joe asked.

"Well, every resident has a sticker on their car. When there is a guard at the gate, we scan the bar code on the sticker, it pulls up the person's picture and address. If the gate is unmanned, they have to use a special key card, and they punch a special six-digit code to get in."

Damien glanced at Joe, then turned back to the guard. "Is there a camera that takes a photo at entry when that system is engaged?"

"There is. I have included it in the requested information your detective asked for," the guard said.

"Okay. Thank you." Damien drove through the open gate. He looked in the review mirror watching the news vultures trying to snap photos as it closed behind him. "Are you ready for this?"

"Fuck no. I think we should turn around and run. Run the fuck out of this town." Joe retrieved his weapon from the glove box and clipped onto his belt. He placed his ID back in his shield case.

Damien followed the lane to a house with the ME's van parked in the drive, along with three more Chicago PD vehicles. "I'm glad Davidson in on this with us. He'll be a big help."

"I bet you lunch today he has on the brightest damn shirt in his closet."

Damien shut off the SUV. "That's a sucker bet." He clipped his badge onto the front of his jeans and his weapon on his side. Glancing around the neighborhood, he estimated the houses were on one acre plus lots, making the distance between the houses a fair amount apart. "According to Captain Mackey, Chase was tortured. The space between houses would definitely allow for privacy."

Joe frowned. "I bet the walls of this house are soundproofed as well. You're not going to fork over this kind of money and not a have a quiet house."

The brown shrubbery sat in stark contrast to the dark green lawn.

Damien assumed the dark green color on the grass came from a recent weed treatment. Three tall pillars lined the covered porch area. The brick of the house was a dark red, and all the trim was stark white.

"Let's go see what is left of our victim." Damien led the way to the front door where a few officers from Division Central were standing on the landing.

Officer Randolph turned around at the sound of approaching footsteps. "Excuse me? Hell no, they let you back, huh?" he asked with a smile and outstretched hand.

"Hey Randolph, how's it been going?" Damien asked, shaking his hand.

"It's going to be a hell of a lot better with you guys back." He looked back over his shoulder towards the front door. "It's a mess in there. Whoever did this had a good time torturing this guy. I hope you haven't eaten recently."

Joe's shoulder's slumped. "This is going to be a nightmare, isn't it?"

Officer Randolph nodded. "I have to say, I like having you two back, although I wouldn't trade places with you. After everything, you guys went through, and now this case, you'll be lucky to get out with your careers intact." His radio squawked. "Excuse me," he said, stepping away.

Joe reached out and pulled Damien towards him. "You think that's why they brought us back for this? To be the sacrificial lambs?"

Damien's brow furrowed. "I don't think the captain would knowingly support sandbagging us, nor the chief."

"I don't know, Damien."

"Let's not worry. What's the worst thing to happen to us, we'll be fired? I guess we'll start our bar and detective agency a little sooner than we thought," Damien said.

"I guess that's the bright side." Joe followed him into the home. "Wowzy! Get a load of this entryway."

A massive chandelier rose over forty feet in the air. Each of its eight rungs was adorned by large glass droplets, each one a different pastel color. A floor to ceiling window drew the eye into the ample living space.

All heads turned towards the familiar voices.

Detective Davidson, who was standing inside the hallway to the left of the entryway, stepped out. "Hot damn," he said as he walked to his lieutenant, hugging him and Joe. "Damn, I'm glad to see you guys."

"I missed you, too, Davidson. Not your damn shirt and tie, though." Damien raised his eyebrow at his detective.

Davidson looked down his chest, lifting his bright blue tie. "I thought it brought out the blue in my eyes."

Joe laughed. "What's the excuse for the shirt?"

Davidson held out his arms, looking over his choice of clothing. He lifted the tie and pointed to the pink in the rainbow arching over the unicorn. "I wanted the shirt to bring out the pink in the tie. It's called color coordination." He glanced over his shoulder at the ME who stood in front of their victim. "You know why I wear what I do?"

"You have deep-rooted issues that counseling hasn't helped?" Joe sniggered.

"Ha, no. We see so much nasty shit, I refuse to wear stuff that doesn't make me happy," he said.

"That's the best reason, Davidson. Where's Jenkins?" Damien took in a deep breath, thankful Dr. Forsythe stood in his line of sight of the body.

"I didn't see any reason for him to show up. I told him I would call if I needed him later when I got back to Division Central." Davidson peered around the room. "My in-laws are supposed to come over for the day."

"No need to say anymore." Damien smiled. "I spoke to the guard at the gate. He said you asked for all the videos of entry through the gates."

He nodded. "I was going to pick it up on the way out." Davidson led them to the victim. "What have you been told?" He asked, glancing back at his boss.

"That it was messy." Damien stepped closer to the body. "Holy shit, he wasn't exaggerating, was he? Damn, whoever did this, was pissed."

"And hated this poor guy. No one should die like this." Joe said as he made the sign of the cross. "How much of this shit was done while he was alive?"

Dr. Forsythe stood next to the body with one of his assistants. "Most of it," he said, turning towards them.

Damien smiled, realizing how much he missed seeing his friend. "Hey, Doc. It's good to see you."

Dr. Forsythe grinned at his longtime friend. He lifted his hands, palms out. "Don't touch me. As you can see, it's a mess. I'll save the hug for later when I'm not covered in this shit."

Damien gave him the once over. "Appreciate your thoughtfulness, and for not moving the body."

The doc sighed. "The captain called me first thing after your conversation. It wasn't a big deal at all. I know you like to see the victims." He turned to move away, then turned back. "How's Dillon?"

The knot in Damien's stomach tightened. "She's doing better. She's at the farm. She and Taylor stayed behind."

"You let me know if I can do anything for you guys," Dr. Forsythe said.

"Thanks. I will. I promise."

Dr. Forsythe nodded.

Joe stepped to the side and pointed to the fingers, hands, and feet. "Doc, those look like they were cut off while he was alive."

"They were. The holes in the back of his hands and thighs were made with that." He pointed to a bloody ice pick laying on the floor next to the chair holding what remained of Chase Humphry.

"Damn. How many stab wounds?" Joe asked.

"I won't know for sure until I wash him off back at the morgue. My guess, more than three dozen. From the looks of the wounds, the ice pick was the warm-up."

Damien stared at the empty eye sockets. "Have you found his eyes?"

"Yes, we did. Our guy is creative if nothing else. Let me show you." Dr. Forsythe walked to the back of the vast living area. The three men followed.

There was a baby grand piano in the right-hand corner. On the wall adjacent to the piano, hung a large mirror. The eyes had been placed on two metal skewers dangling from a fancy skewer holder. Both eyes faced the mirror.

"Hey, Taylor and I ate at a Japanese restaurant a few weeks ago, they served our hibachi shit on a skewer like that." He frowned. "I'll never look at those things the same way again."

Damien glanced at them. "Got any ideas on what the killer is trying to tell us?"

"I'll leave the head shrinking to you and Dillon," Dr. Forsythe said.

Davidson shrugged. "What about him thinking he was better than everyone else, you know what I mean?"

"What, like Chase here is a vain guy?" Joe asked.

They all walked back to the body.

Damien studied the dead man's injuries. "Doc, did he remove the eyes while he was alive?"

The doctor nodded. "Yes, at least one." He pointed to the right eye. "The eyeball is held in the eye socket by several muscles, fatty tissue, and the optic nerve. You can see the crudeness of the cut and the amount of blood in and around the injury." He pointed to the other eye. "If I had to guess, I'd say he cut the right out first, then the left eye after he was dead. You can see the left eye has a smoother cut and there is much less blood around and in the wound. He also didn't cut the eyelid like the first one. Tells me our guy was dead at that point."

Damien looked back at the eyes. "I think the eyes mean something more than being vain."

"Like he saw something he shouldn't have?" Davidson asked.

"No. The eyes mean something more profound, something personal." Chase Humphry had pissed someone off, Damien thought. Besides his fingers being cut off, and his eyes being removed, the man had been gutted, from crotch to gullet. He bent down and took a closer look at the man's sliced open belly. "What else did he remove?"

Dr. Forsythe laughed, then stopped abruptly. "Sorry. I have no idea why that made me laugh." He used the back of his gloved hand to rub his chin. "He removed his guts and his balls."

Joe squeezed his legs together. "I bet the balls were probably the last thing he did to Chase before he died."

"Good guess. I think with this level of cruelty, it's a strong possibility it happened that way." Dr. Forsythe stepped closer to the body. "Alright, let me go through the injury timeline for you. Remember, this may change when I get him on the table."

"I understand," Damien said.

"Let's assume Chase was sedated and tied here to this chair. The chair came from a pair in the library, and you can see our killer anchored it to the floor." He motioned towards the three detectives. "Once Chase was secured, he made him drink bleach. You can see the irritation around his mouth." He wafted his hand over the dead body. "You can get a whiff of it every so often. Plus, this bottle," he pointed to the floor and a two-liter bottle, "still has some in it."

"That wouldn't have killed him, though," Joe said.

"No, it wouldn't. It would be very uncomfortable, however. I'm fairly certain, this is industrial strength sodium hypochlorite. I will, of course, have it tested to confirm my theory. Once swallowed, the caustic fluid would burn the lining of his esophagus. His reflexes would cause him to gag and cough only irritating it to the point of spewing droplets of blood. This solution is much stronger than everyday bleach." The doc continued with the timeline. "I'm speculating he used the ice pick on his hands first, then his thighs. Whether the eye came first or the fingers, I'm not sure. I liken the fingers first."

Damien hissed out a breath. "I would remove the fingers first."

"Especially if you want some information from him," Joe said.

Detective Davidson pointed to two of the fingers. "Were those the first two?"

"No. Look at this finger." He lifted what was left of the right forefinger. "Smooth no hesitation or struggling." He pointed to the bloody pruning shears located on the floor near the body. "I don't think Chase was expecting his finger to be cut off, so he didn't fight it." He pointed to the next two fingers. "I believe these two were next. The jagged slanted cuts tell me Chase struggled against losing any more digits. Your killer may have decided to restrain his hands afterward, the rest of the fingers have cleaner cuts."

Joe sighed. "What about the man's hands and feet?"

"Ahh, yes. He cut those off before he killed Chase. You can see the pooling of blood. He cauterized the wounds to keep him from bleeding out." The doctor pointed to the charring around the amputated limbs. "The guy came prepared. At one point, everything sat on the table near the wall." He pointed to the right, where a long wooden table had been placed. "The killer retrieved whatever tool he needed. There are drops of blood on the table. I bet when we test it, it will be the victim's blood."

"Our killer takes Chase, sedates him, gets through the gate, brings him in here, ties him up, and goes to town on him," Joe said.

"It looks that way. After the hands and feet were removed and the wounds sealed, he could've done a few different things. He could've cut out the right eye, or he could've cut the balls off." Dr. Forsythe pointed to the gut. "Again, speculation. He could have taken the balls first, then the right eye, lastly slicing him open and removing his guts."

"Where are the balls and innards?" Joe asked.

"That's what leads me to believe the last scenario I mentioned is the correct version. In the kitchen, we found a frying pan with his balls sliced and sautéed."

Damien's jaw fell open. "That's so wrong. Do you think our killer ate them?"

Dr. Forsythe shook his head. "No. I think he fed them to Chase." He motioned towards the body. "I found some vomitus on his shirt. When I analyze it, I bet we find remnants of his genitals."

Joe exhaled a long hissing breath. "Motherfucker. This guy really pissed someone off. I'm almost afraid to ask, but did you find his guts?"

"We found them in the blender," Dr. Forsythe said.

Damien dragged a hand down his face. "Damn."

Dr. Forsythe sighed. "I can tell you the killer took his time. There is significant coagulation of blood between injuries."

"Or Chase here passed out from pain and our killer had to wait for him to wake up," Davidson said.

"Why would you go through all this trouble? Run the risk of getting caught just to torture someone? If you wanted them dead, kill them. This guy wanted something from Chase, more than information alone." Damien glanced at Davidson. "Dig up all you can on this guy. Get Detective Travis from the Electronics and Cyber Division to help track this guy's life from birth to now. Something in his past led to this point."

"Yes, Sir. Hey, you know about this guy, right?" Davidson asked.

Damien raised an eyebrow. "What do you mean?"

"This guy grew up in some home, I don't know, like an orphanage or something."

"Do you know the name?" Damien asked.

Davidson tilted his head to the side. "I think I remember, something like Sunshine Vista, or Sunshine Valley, yeah, Sunshine Valley. It's down near Indiana Dunes, what fifty-four miles outside the city. He made a big contribution to them not too long ago. There was a big to-do about him and his company and what he was doing in the community."

Damien looked over at Joe. "Did you know any of this?"

"What, do I look like Chase's best friend? How the hell would I know anything about this guy? I know he's rich and he's dead. That's all I know," Joe said.

Damien smirked at him. "How did you get to be a detective?"

"Haha, asshole. Davidson, when you start looking into this guy, see if you can get a list of names from the home when he was there." Joe turned his attention to Damien. "You got to figure, if this guy tortured him, it had to do with either his time then, or his time now. Right?"

"I'm not going to narrow the field on anything yet. I think the way you're looking at this is a good line to pursue. I don't know how much you can get, if the records are sealed, I don't even know if they are sealed."

"What about Dillon? Can she help us?" Davidson asked.

"She is still on medical leave," Damien said. "I might reach out to AD Reynolds."

"I don't know if that's the best idea. You aren't his favorite person," Joe said

"Surely he can't still be mad about the glass. I had the repairs completed within a few days." Damien frowned. "What else does he have to be mad at?"

"You can't be serious?" Joe rolled his eyes. "You remember the whole cabin and killing the bad guy thing. He was thoroughly pissed you did what you did. I don't know withholding evidence, all that shit. Ring any bells?"

Davidson laughed. "He was pretty pissed."

Both Joe and Damien glared at him.

"What are you talking about?" Damien asked.

"Sorry man. Forgot you weren't there. Okay, after you two were suspended, he came in and wanted all your files from your office. I gotta tell you, Lieutenant Stevens told him to get the fuck out of the office. He said he wasn't about to give him anything and he had no right demanding it."

Damien looked at Joe. "Did you hear about this?"

He raised his hands in a defensive pose. "Don't look at me. Shit, this is the first time I'm hearing it."

"What happened next?" Damien asked.

"AD Reynolds marched his butt up to Captain Mackey's office then to the chief's. They told him the same thing. They explained the files pertaining to the case had been rightfully turned over. The FBI had no jurisdiction asking for any other cases."

Damien's brow wrinkled. "He let it go after that?"

"Hell no. He tried to get a warrant. Shot down in a ball of flames. The state said the same thing the Chief said. The FBI doesn't have the right to any of our case files they are not directly involved in. And even then, it's only what they need for the case."

"Let me get this straight. Reynolds wanted all my case files, every case I ever worked on?" Damien squinted at Davidson.

"Yeah. Seemed a little odd AD Reynolds wanted everything." Davidson shrugged. "I don't think I would call and ask him for any favors."

"Thanks for the information," Damien said nodding.

"No worries. Hey unless you need me, I'm going to grab the stuff from the guard and get back to the VCU. Get Travis and ECD on this ASAP. He's on duty today."

"Sounds good. Thanks, Davidson."

"No problem Damien. Hey, it's terrific to have you back."

"Davidson, as soon as you get the shit from the gate, and notify Travis, go home. Enjoy your Saturday with your family," Damien said. "Hopefully nothing else will happen, and you can enjoy Sunday too."

"You and me both. I'm on call, I'm expecting the worse. You know how to find me." Davidson waved as he walked out the door.

Damien turned towards Joe. "Call the ADA. Make sure we have warrants for Chase's office, his vehicle, and all his electronics. Call ECD and have someone come out here and get all the house security files. Make sure they take any laptops or computers as well. I want everything."

"You got it." Joe walked out, making phone calls.

"Doc, how long before you get him back to the morgue?" Damien asked.

Dr. Forsythe stretched his back. "A few hours. Maybe less. I'll text you when I get him on my table."

"Thank you."

"Don't worry about AD Reynolds. He was mad about you besting him and the FBI when it came to finding and saving their agent."

"I know. I hope he doesn't take it out on Dillon."

"You listen to me. If AD Reynolds tries to take anything out on Dillon, Director Sherman will have his ass. And you make sure you tell him. He and his wife love Dillon like their own daughter. He will not go for his own agents and ADs holding a grudge against her." Dr. Forsythe stepped closer. "I'm telling you; if you don't tell him if something happens, I will."

Damien smiled at his friend. "Are you threatening me?"

"You're damn right." Dr. Forsythe laughed. "I love both of you. And if you're mother and father caught wind of AD Reynolds messing with Dillon or you, the wrath he would face from them alone would rock his world."

"I need to call my family and let them know Joe and I are back." Damien checked his watch. "It's almost noon. Are you going to do the autopsy today, or wait until in the morning?"

"Like Davidson, I'm on call. I might as well do it. Hopefully, I'll be home for dinner." Dr. Forsythe turned to his assistant. "Peter, let's get him bagged up as best we can."

"You got it Doc." The tech went to work, bagging the body parts.

Damien and Joe headed out to the SUV.

Joe glanced back over his shoulder. "Do you think our killer got what he wanted and this ends with Chase?"

Damien smirked unlocking the truck. "Not in the least. I think Chase was just the beginning."

CHAPTER FOURTEEN

Damien drove out of Chandelier Heights. "Still glad to be back on the job?"

Joe shook his head. "I'm not sure. Why couldn't we get the average run of the mill murder?"

"Run of the mill murder?" Damien asked, chuckling.

"You know wife kills her husband, husband kills his wife...maybe something simple like a scorned girlfriend."

"Do those even happen anymore?"

Joe shrugged. "Probably not. It would be nice." He glanced out the window. "Where to next?"

"Let's hit Kaufman's first, get lunch. Then we'll head to Chase's office." Damien pulled into traffic on the highway. "Where are our warrants?"

Joe pulled out his phone and checked his email. "Looks like ADA Flowers got what we need. Everything for his home and office, the warrant includes everyone's comps if we need it. Along with all files, correspondence. It covers everything."

"Good. Did you call ECD about the home?"

"I did. Travis was sending someone over to collect all the electronics."

Damien nodded. "Our killer had to know how to get through the gates. And he had to be familiar with Chase's security system."

"Where's Chase's car?" Joe asked.

Damien frowned. "Fuck." He used the Bluetooth controls on his steering wheel to call Davidson.

"Hey Lieutenant, what do you need?"

"Where is Chase's car?"

"It was in the garage."

Damien glanced at Joe. "Okay. Did you get all the files from the security gate?"

"I picked them up on the way out. What's up Damien?" Davidson asked.

"Our killer drove his car from the garage. Keeping anyone from finding it and questioning where Chase was. How did he get out? Did he drive to Chase's place and then call a cab, leaving his car there? How far do the security tapes go back?" Damien heard some papers shuffling over the speakers.

Davidson sighed. "According to the written log, I got dates going back about a week, maybe two. Not sure about video logs."

"Alright. Call the gate. Ask them if they have video and written logs going back a month. Our UNSUB had to plan this, and he would've had to do some research, maybe even recon. Let's look at odd deliveries to Chase's place or possibly to other homes, anything giving this guy a way in and out, especially on the night Chase was taken from the garage."

"I'm on it. You guys coming into the office?" Davidson asked.

"No. We are going to Humphry Enterprises. Check out everything at Chase's company." Damien paused. "Get your shit done and go home to your family."

"I will. I've given the electronic files from the gate to ECD. Travis is going through it now."

"Okay. Thanks, Davidson." Damien disconnected the call.

"What are you thinking, Damien?" Joe asked as he searched the console for some gum.

Damien sighed. "We aren't dealing with a hack. This guy knew what he was doing. Remember the guard at the gate had said there was an alarm, leaving the gate unmanned for at least an hour. I'll lay nine to one odds, our guy caused the alarm." He glanced at Joe. "How did our guy get out of Chase's place? If he left his vehicle at Chase's house, how did he get in and out, and when?"

"Okay, maybe he had a bike. He rides it to Chase's work. Puts it in the car. Voila."

"I guess."

"Listen, Damien, if this guy is as smart as you think, then he got in and out without anyone seeing him. He's a ghost."

"It's going to needle me."

"I know, buddy." Joe sighed. "What happened to the good old dumbass killers? You know the ones who leave a trail right back to them. Boom, case solved in like a day." He placed two pieces of gum in his mouth, holding out the pack to Damien.

Damien laughed, shaking his head. "I don't think I have ever had one of those." He smacked the steering wheel. "Yes, I do. Do you remember our last case at the 17th?"

Joe's brow wrinkled. "Are you referring to the one where you told me you signed my ass up for the VCU without my permission?"

"You aren't still mad, are you? Look at what being in the VCU has done for you."

Joe flinched back with wide eyes and a half chuckle. "What the fuck has it gotten me? Let's see, I've been shot and almost died. You were shot and almost died. Dillon was run off the road. Taylor had to kill someone to save both our asses." He turned in the seat to face his partner. "Have I missed anything? Oh wait, it got me suspended and on the FBI's shit list. Can't forget about that."

Damien's jaw hung open. "You can't be serious? You wouldn't even know Taylor if it weren't for the VCU."

"That's all you got, isn't it?"

"Anyway, if only our guy was like—what was his name," Damien snapped his fingers. "Mallory, George Mallory."

Joe laughed. "If only the world had more stupid guys like Mallory committing homicides. He was an idiot. You remember when he went over the balcony?"

"I remember wishing it was further than two floors." Damien turned into Kaufman's taking a spot right next to the front door. "Maybe. The other thing you got by leaving with me...is me. If I had left you behind, you'd be lonely."

Exiting the SUV, Joe draped his arm around his best friend. He pulled his head towards him and gave his temple a big fat kiss. "If I had let you go alone, you would never have lasted."

"Will you quit kissing me in public?"

"Never. You know you love it."

CHAPTER FIFTEEN

Pulling in front of the Chase Humphry's business, Damien placed the on-duty placard on his dash, visible through the windshield. He sent a quick text to Detective Travis at the VCU, asking him to send someone to the offices. The building was located in the heart of downtown Chicago. The twenty-five-story building housed other businesses. The bulk of the top floors were solely dedicated to Humphry Enterprises.

Joe whistled as he glanced up and down the street. "This had to cost some bucks."

"No doubt. I'm sure the rent he charges other businesses more than makes him a profit." Damien stood on the curb. He pointed to a driveway off to the left. "I bet the parking garage is down that ramp. Let's go in and talk to the security and find out where Chase parked. Maybe they have some surveillance."

They walked into the spacious lobby.

Damien glanced upward. The floor to ceiling atrium allowed for light to filter in from the glass roof. Filling the indoor garden with soft glowing light. Several people stuck working a Saturday stood at the glass wall surveying the space below them. Five banks of elevators lined one corridor. Damien suspected one of those elevators led directly to Chase's office.

"Can I help you, gentlemen?" asked a security guard as he approached them.

"I'm Lieutenant Kaine, this is my partner Detective Joe Hagan." They both held out their shields. "We need to get up to Chase Humphry's office."

The guard walked back to his desk. "I'm guessing you have a warrant?"

Joe held out his phone. "Give me an email or text, and I can send it to you so you can print it."

"All I need is the warrant number. Hold your phone up again, please."

Joe pulled the picture up, narrowing in on the document number.

The guard took it down, then led them to the last elevator on the right. "This will take us up to his office. His executive officer and their secretaries are also located up here. Along with the financial officer and his secretary." The guard stepped into the lift holding the door for the two detectives. He used a key card to access the upper floor. "I'm Harold. Harold Jones." He held out his hand.

"Nice to meet you, Harold," Damien said, shaking the man's hand.

"Has there been any odd deliveries, or visitors lately? Maybe someone asking questions about Mr. Humphry?" Joe asked as he shook Harold's hand.

"I'm not sure what you mean. Why are you guys even here?"

Damien leaned against the railing. "It seems Mr. Humphry was murdered sometime over the weekend."

Harold's face paled, and his eyes widened. "Are you serious?" his gaze shifted between the two detectives. "Have you notified his XO? Or his girlfriend?"

"No. We will need their names, addresses, and phone numbers. We also need any tapes from the parking garage from Thursday, all day into the evening."

Harold nodded. "I can get them for you. The garage tapes are recorded and kept for a month. I can pull them off the hard drive." The door opened to another opulent entryway. "I think the XO is still here. I didn't check the log. I know he came in a few hours ago and I didn't see him leave." Harold unlocked the door leading to the upper echelon offices. "I'll have the tapes for you when you leave."

At the sound of the door opening a man stepped out from an open office doorway. "May I help—oh Harold, it's you." He walked towards the men. "Who are you two?"

"I'm Lieutenant Kaine, this is Detective Hagan. Can we speak to you in your office?"

Harold smiled at Samuel Prichard, the executive officer. "Mr. Prichard, I'll leave you three. You can call me if you need me." He nodded at the detectives and headed towards the elevator.

"I'm Samuel Prichard. I'm the executive officer of Humphry Enterprises." He held out his hand. "I'm not sure what brings you here. On a Saturday no less." He led them into a spacious office.

"Wow. Nice view of the city," Joe said, looking past the man. The entire city could be seen from this vantage point.

Samuel let out a nervous laugh. "It can make it a little distracting when working. Have a seat. Please."

Damien pulled out a small note pad from his back pocket before taking the chair. "Mr. Prichard, it appears that Chase Humphry was murdered sometime between Thursday evening and early this morning."

Samuel's eyes bulged. His mouth gaped open. He covered it with his hand before he spoke. "You—you must have made a mistake."

"No, sir. There's been no mistake. Can you tell me when you last spoke with him?" Damien asked.

Samuel leaned back in his chair. Unable to speak. He pinched the bridge of his nose, trying to stop the tears. It didn't work. He pushed the palms of his hands into his eyes, then wiped the tears from his cheeks. "I can't believe this." He stood and looked out the window.

Damien gave a sideways glance at Joe. He allowed the man a few minutes before he spoke. "Mr. Prichard?"

A few moments passed before Samuel turned towards the detectives. "I'm sorry." He took his seat. "What do you need to know?"

"When did you last speak with Mr. Humphry?"

Samuel Prichard squeezed his eyes together, exhaling a sharp breath. "Thursday. We had meetings all day. He was going to head out early. He was traveling to Washington on an early morning Friday flight. Chase had meetings scheduled for today."

"Who knew about his travel plans? Were they common knowledge?" Damien asked as he jotted down some notes.

Samuel Prichard shrugged. "I don't know. I mean, everyone here knew. I would imagine he told Jacey." His eyebrows drew together. "Oh, no. Jacey. Has anyone told her yet?" He leaned forward, placing his elbows on the desk. "How am I going to tell her?"

"We can tell her for you. It might be better if we did it anyway."

"If you don't mind, I would like to do it. She's at her parent's house this weekend. I can call her there."

"That's fine. Tell me about the parking garage. What kind of security is there?"

Samuel closed his eyes as if he had to give his mind a few seconds to process the question. "Um, everyone who works in the building has a sticker on their windshield. They have a key card allowing them entrance through the gate. Anyone else has to take a ticket and pay as they leave."

Joe leaned forward. "Harold said he would get us the security footage for the garage. Can you tell us about the surveillance cameras in it?"

"Cameras are pointed on the entrances, exits, and the elevator entrance. There aren't any cameras around the parking spaces."

"How long have you known Mr. Humphry?" Damien asked.

Mr. Prichard dragged a hand down his face. "Shit. I've known Chase since college, at Perdue. We were in the same fraternity together."

"Are you aware of his past? When he lived at the Sunshine Valley home as a kid?" Damien asked, watching the man's reaction.

"Yes. He never shied away from his time in the home. He actually used it."

"What do you mean he used it?" Joe asked.

"Chase never kept his past a secret. He often said the time spent at Sunshine Valley made him the man he is—was." Mr. Prichard sighed. "He received several scholarships to Perdue. They paid his entire way through college. Shortly after graduation, he started this company."

"Do you know how he ended up in the home? Did his parents die, what was his story?"

Mr. Prichard nodded. "Both his parents were into drugs. His father was murdered in a drug buy, and his mother went to prison. She was supposed to be released when he was sixteen. From what I gathered, she killed someone while in prison. Got like twenty extra years. At least that's what he said happened."

Joe's brow furrowed. "Do you think he was lying?"

"I don't know. I researched him once when we were in college. I couldn't find anything on his parents. Maybe they sealed his records, I don't know. I didn't care, I guess I was curious."

Damien scribbled in his notebook. "I understand Mr. Humphry recently gave the home a substantial donation. Can you tell me anything about the donation?"

Mr. Prichard looked at his hands. "I didn't like it."

"Why?" Damien asked.

"I went with Chase a few months back to the home. I met the guy who runs it. Umm, his name is..." he trailed off with his eyes closed. "Shamus MacDougal."

Joe smiled. "Sounds like a Scot."

"He was. Had a heavy Scottish accent." Mr. Prichard glanced between the two detectives.

"What is it, Mr. Pritchard? You look like you want to say something." Damien raised an eyebrow. "You need to tell us everything. Don't hold back."

"I don't know. When we were there, at the youth home, it seemed like..."

"What?" Damien asked.

"Everyone seemed to like him, Shamus. Yet, at the same time, it seemed as if they were afraid of him. I know that doesn't make sense. It felt like something was simmering under the surface." Mr. Prichard blew out a long breath. "I was waiting in this considerable living space. The house was huge. An old, renovated mansion. I'm in the living room, and Chase and Pops were standing inside the doorway to the kitchen. I could see them, but I couldn't hear what they were saying. I swear, it was the only time I saw Chase look—I don't know—scared. They were arguing but not really."

"Pops?" Damien asked.

"That was Shamus' nickname. All the kids called him that."

"What makes you think he was scared?" Damien asked.

"He kept glancing over at me. His eyes had a look like, he wanted me to step in. I know this makes no sense. All I know is Pops kept poking Chase in the chest and finally Chase shook his head and walked away. And we left. I asked him about it; he wouldn't tell me anything. Next thing I knew, Chase was making a big donation to the home. I voiced my opinion, but he told me to drop it."

"Had he made other donations to the home?" Joe asked.

"Not from the company. Now if he did it from his personal finances, I don't know. Chase was worth millions."

"Who inherits everything now? I'm assuming he doesn't have family."

Samuel Prichard looked up with trembling lips and chin. His face had turned ashen, pallid. "I do." He reached into his drawer and pulled out a business card. "This is the company lawyer. I will give him permission to speak with you. Chase drew this up five years ago. He doesn't have any family, and he wanted to make sure his company would keep going.

"He left specific instructions for me to carry out. And while I will get a substantial boost in my account, most of the money stays in trust for the company. He wants several monies donated to several charities, and he made provisions to help other less fortunate kids go to college. I will retain ownership. We were partners but he held the majority holdings."

Damien nodded as he took the card. "What exactly does Humphry Enterprises do?"

"We produce the nacelle for wind turbines. It's the box that holds all the inner workings of the turbine. We also manufacture the honeycomb interior used for the fiberglass blades. We have a manufacturing plant outside, La Porte Indiana."

"Was Chase from Indiana?"

"No. He was born in Springfield."

"Have you had any threats from environmentalists or threats from anyone opposed to the giant wind turbines going up across the states? Anything at all?" Damien asked.

"No. Nothing. We've gotten a few threatening letters or people showing up to say we are ruining the farmlands. We aren't the only game in town. We are one of the largest."

"Alright. Thank you for being upfront about the company holdings. We will contact your lawyer next week. If you could give him a heads up, I would appreciate it. Can you tell me what your movements have been since Thursday?" He noticed the man's color drained even more. "Routine question, Mr. Prichard."

Samuel Prichard took a deep breath and blew it out. "Sure. I understand. I left the office after seven. The security can verify. I had one of our company driver's pick me up, and I left my car here. I had an early morning appointment here in the city, so I stayed at the Ritz. You can check with the front desk. I stayed until this morning. I came in here about ten a.m. to finish up some work and get my car."

"Okay. We will check with the Ritz. The more people we can take off the list of suspects, the more we can concentrate on finding the killer." Damien stood. "If you think of anything else, please let me know. Oh, what is Jacey's last name and I'd like her phone number? I will have one of my detectives interview her to see if she knows anything. After you have had a chance to speak with her."

Mr. Prichard pulled out his cell phone. He wrote the information on a piece of paper and handed it to the detective. "Here. Umm, there is one thing."

"What's that?" Damien asked.

"I saw a letter to the lawyer. In it, Chase made it clear there were to be no more donations made to the home. Under no circumstances. I saw it on his desk and asked him about it. He closed the file and told me it was nothing to worry about. Then he changed the subject."

Damien nodded. "Thank you. Can you let the lawyer know today, he has permission to speak with us?"

"I will call him as soon as you leave."

"Can you show us to Mr. Humphry's office?"

"Absolutely. Follow me." Mr. Prichard led them down a narrow hallway. As they rounded the corner, an office sat at the end. It spanned an entire corner of the building. Mr. Prichard unlocked the door. He moved to the desk and unlocked it as well and turned on the desktop. He wrote down the login and passwords. "Here," he said, handing it to Damien. "I will print out a list of all our computer logins and passwords." He eyeballed the tall detective. "You will have your men come in and comb through everything?"

"We will. As a matter of fact, someone should be coming in soon. Please let the security know, and if you could get the list to me, I can pass it off to our techs." Damien smiled at the man. "I know this is hard. I appreciate your cooperation."

The tears Mr. Prichard fought hard to hold back, flowed freely down his cheeks. "Chase was my best friend and my business partner. I loved him like a brother. I want whoever killed him. If that means you tear my life and this company apart, then do it. I know I didn't kill him, and I know this company is above reproach. I don't have anything to hide." He turned to leave. "I will get the logins for you. I will be in my office until your men show up."

"Thank you." Damien watched as the man left the office. He walked over to the door and closed it. "What do you think?"

"I don't think he had anything to do with the murder. I believe him about the will." Joe began to rummage through some of the drawers and cabinets of the expansive wall unit. He kept looking out the window. "Some view, huh?" He nodded towards the lake. "We need a boat."

"We don't need a boat."

"We could go fishing every weekend." He wiggled his eyebrows at him. "Take our women out in bikinis...man, that would be awesome."

"Get back to searching." Damien sat at the computer. He opened several files scanning the data within. He quickly ran through documents. He did a search using the homes name. The document Prichard had mentioned popped up. "Hey, here is the letter to the lawyer Prichard mentioned." Damien read through it. "There isn't a whole lot here. It states he wanted a provision put in the trust, keeping the home from receiving any more monies." Damien continued reading. "Maybe the lawyer will share with us the reason for the letter."

Joe pulled out a file from one of the drawers. He thumbed through it. Closed it and replaced it. "We could be here for hours. Do we even know what we are looking for?"

Damien leaned back in the desk chair. "If I were Chase, I wouldn't keep anything in paper form. It would all be electronic." He opened the desk drawers. Went to the adjacent credenza. Searching those drawers. "He had to have one."

"What? Who had to have one what?" Joe asked.

"A laptop." Damien squinted at Joe. "What executive or business owner doesn't have a laptop?"

"Ask Prichard."

The door to the office opened, Mr. Prichard walked in, followed by one of the ECD detectives.

"Hey, Detective Todd," Joe said.

"Mr. Prichard, did Chase have a laptop?"

Mr. Prichard nodded. "He did. He had it with him Thursday night."

"Who is with you, Detective Todd?" Damien asked.

"Just me. Why?" Detective Todd asked.

"No reason. Who went to the house, do you know?" Damien asked.

"I think Detective Travis sent Detective Carson." He glanced at his watch. "He should be there by now."

"Okay. Do me a favor, text him and ask him to look for a laptop. Tell him if he doesn't find it in the house to check Chase's car in the garage."

"You got it." Detective Todd pulled his phone from his bag and texted the tech at the house. The detective set about his task of going through all the electronics. "Hey, Lieutenant Kaine?"

"Yeah?"

"I can copy all the drives, and do a search for hidden files. It would keep from taking all the computers."

"That sounds good. Make sure you sweep any of them for hidden files. I need to know if anyone from this company had anything to do with the murder."

"I can help," Mr. Prichard said from outside the office door. "I can call our IT guy. Everything on the computers is run through the cloud network. The employees get whatever files they need from the cloud. Outside of me, Chase, and our financial officer, Sean Weathers, no one can store anything on their drives. I don't have the network shit, only the passwords for the individual stations. I already gave your IT Detective the information."

"Where is the financial officer?" Damien asked.

"He and his wife left Friday morning for a three-week trip to Switzerland. I had a car take them to the airport. Their flight left at four a.m. Friday morning."

"Rules him out," Joe said.

"Umm, I don't want to call him and tell him. If at all possible. I want to wait until they get home. Sean's wife is in remission from breast cancer. That's why they're on this trip."

"That's fine. We won't need to speak with him until he gets back. No need to ruin their trip." Damien smiled at Prichard's relieved expression.

"Thank you. I'll call our IT guy." Mr. Prichard turned and walked back to his office.

Detective Todd's phone pinged. "Hey, Kaine. The ECD tech found the laptop in the car. Looks like the CSU is going over the car now."

"Okay, sounds good. Tell him to bring it into the ECD. I want Travis to go over it with a fine-tooth comb. Also, get the tapes for the garage security from Harold downstairs."

"You got it." Detective Todd tapped out the text to the other detective.

"Joe, you ready?" Damien said, glancing around the office.

"Hell, yeah. I need a snack." Joe rubbed his belly.

"A snack? You just ate lunch. Shit, you're going to be on one of those shows about overweight people before too long." Damien smirked at him.

"Fuck you. I'm a growing boy." Joe flexed his biceps. "I need to fuel these muscles." He continued to do bodybuilding poses.

"C'mon muscle man, let's get out of here." Damien turned towards

Detective Todd. "Keep me posted if you find anything. Grill the IT guy. Make him give you everything."

"I will. Although I'm already into the network, I really don't need him. I could test him and see if he's hiding anything."

"No, shit? You're already in?" Joe asked.

"Of course."

Damien nodded. "If we ever start our own detective agency, you might need to come work for us."

"Dude, I'm in. Just say when." He did some kind of dance.

"You can't come if that's how you dance." Joe frowned at him.

Damien laughed as he left the office. "Look who's talking. Your big butt can't dance."

Joe followed him. "Dude, the only dancing I need to be able to do is between the sheets. And I got that covered."

Damien shook his head, rolling his eyes. "That is a picture I don't want in my head."

CHAPTER SIXTEEN

Damien pulled away from Humphry Enterprise. "You want to go with me to eat dinner at my parent's house tomorrow?"

"Absolutely," Joe said. "Did you already talk to them?"

"No. The minute I do, I know my mother will insist I come eat with them tomorrow. Thought you might like to go. Since Taylor is staying at the farm."

"I love your mama's cooking." Joe pulled his phone from his back pocket. "Oh, fuck me."

"What?"

"I need to text Jenkins and make sure he isn't at my house. I don't want to go home and find him fucking someone in my bed."

"Isn't he dating Chanda, from Mulligan's?"

Joe snickered. "I wouldn't call it dating."

Damien laughed. "I see he has taken your spot as the Mulligan's whore."

Joe laughed. "I was not a whore. I was in demand." He batted his eyes. "I can't help it if all the women want a piece of me."

"You really should check into getting some medication. Your delusions are starting to worry me."

Joe's phone pinged. "Thank goodness. Jenkins is at her house. He said he would swing by and get his shit later, and give Muffin a kiss." Joe shook his head. "Fuck, he's trying to make me look bad."

Damien chuckled at Joe's dejected look. "Because he is being sweet to Muffin?"

"That fucking cat will wait to die when I'm on the clock watching her." Joe pointed at Damien. "You will help me if that ancient thing dies on me."

"I will help you, I promise. Knowing Taylor, she will want a big funeral. Then you have to get another cat."

Joe's expression softened. "I was thinking of getting her another one. It would help ease the blow when Muffin died."

Damien turned into the garage at Division Central. He pulled into his assigned parking spot. Turning off the motor, he glanced around. "I don't know if I'm ready for this part."

"I hear you. You've managed to piss off so many people, no telling who might punch you when we walk into the building."

"Fuck you. I'm talking about answering all the questions about Dillon."

"Tell anyone who asks, she's doing good. Leave it at that. You don't owe anyone any explanations about anything."

"You ready?"

"I guess," Joe said opening the door.

"We won't stay long. I want to check in with Detective Travis and see what he has if anything. I'm going to put in a call to the lawyer. I want to see him on Monday. I'm going to call Lieutenant Stevens and get an update on the VCU cases. Then we will get the hell out of here. You want to eat dinner with me?" he asked, exiting the vehicle.

"I'm going to go see my folks. Taylor talked to my mom, now she knows I'm home. She texted me earlier. Wants to see me before we get all bogged down in another case." He glanced at his watch. "Let's drag our feet here. I want to miss Mass."

"What, you don't want to go to Saturday Mass with your family?" Damien pulled open the door leading to the elevators.

"Shit, if you and I walk into church, we might spontaneously combust. We haven't been to church since—fuck—since Catherine killed all those priests." Joe stepped into the elevator. "Feels like a lifetime ago."

"Don't remind me. I'd like to forget that case." Damien exited the elevator. He and Joe walked past several empty offices on their way to the VCU pen. "Looks pretty dead for a Saturday."

"That's because we are the only ones who get the crap murders."

They walked around the corner to find Davidson at his desk.

"Hey, Davidson, I thought I told you to go home." Damien walked to the detective's desk.

"Hmm. The in-laws are still at the house. I decided this was the better place to be." Davidson smiled at his boss. "Don't get me wrong. I love them. After what I saw this morning, I'm not in the mood to be around them."

Damien patted him on the back. "I hear you. I'll be eating Sunday dinner with the family, and I roped Joe into going with me."

"I've been going through the logs. The guard went back a month. I haven't found any odd deliveries. I was going to contact each person who received a delivery of any kind and make sure they received it, but more important, that they ordered it."

"Good thinking. If anything pops up, let me know." He pulled Josey's information from his pocket. "This is Mr. Humphry's girlfriend's number. Call her on Monday. See if she knows anything. Wait until Monday though. Chase Humphry's business partner is going to let her know he is dead."

"No problem." Davidson put the number on his desk.

"Did Detective Travis get anywhere on the names of other residents from the group home?" Damien leaned against the desk.

"He's working on it." Davidson yawned. "I'll make Jenkins go through all the names when we get them."

Joe grabbed a piece of chocolate from his drawer. "I can help."

"Nah, I'll make Jenkins do it. He got today off. Detective Travis is trying to see if he can get the names or if the ADA will have to get him a warrant."

"I wouldn't think we need a warrant to see the roster of residents. It's a state-funded home as well as donations. It's not like we are asking for sealed juvie records." Damien held out his hand, waiting for a piece of candy.

Joe reluctantly handed him one. Throwing one to Davidson as well.

"I'm going to make some calls. Joe, let me know when we need to leave. I'll drop you at your parent's house." Damien headed to his office.

"I got a couple of hours. I don't want to go to Mass. My mom said they were eating after." Joe turned on his computer.

"Heathen." Damien strolled away, ignoring the names Joe called him. Entering his office, he felt like a stranger. Lieutenant Stevens had cleaned the clutter. Glancing around, he noticed a new shelving unit. "Shit I was gone for like ten days." All his files had been placed in a three-tier wire basket. It had three slots, open, closed, and pending. His desk was clean and organized. He wasn't sure he liked it. Sitting in his chair, it took Damien a few minutes to figure out where other things had been placed.

He turned towards the small digital case board hanging on the wall directly across from him. Jamal Harris and Mike Cooper had an open double murder case, and Hall and Sheila Alvarez were working a rape-murder case. "Crap let that be a one-off please," Damien said out loud as he picked up his desk phone and dialed Lieutenant Stevens' extension.

"Stevens here."

"Hey, it's Damien."

"Hey, Kaine. I heard they were reinstating you today. You shouldn't have been suspended in the first place."

"Thanks for the sentiment. I really appreciate the straightening up you did in my office. I can't find anything."

Stevens chuckled. "How you ever got work done before I will never know."

"Is there anything I need to handle, besides this case we got now?" Damien fidgeted with the cup holding his pens.

"No. nothing pressing. I'm working on a case chart for you. It will explain all the open cases. I'm sure you will want a rundown from your men, but this will give you some background on what they are working on."

"You don't have to go through all that trouble. Go home. Spend the weekend with your family."

"I'm actually on call today, filling in for Lieutenant Rodrigues. He had a family emergency. Plus, it gives me something to do."

"Well, I appreciate your help. I'll be here for a few hours before I head out."

"I'll shoot this report to you in about thirty."

"Thanks. You're a good man, Stevens. Hey, tell me about AD Reynolds. What was he looking for?"

"I'm not sure what his end game was. First, he asked if I had any of the files for one of the cases you worked on with them. I told him no. That all those files had been turned over. He said he needed to check some information to close the case. I thought his request was bogus as fuck, so I told him no."

"What happened then?"

"He went fucking ape shit. Saying we had to share our files with the FBI. Said they had jurisdiction. I told him to get the fuck out of the office. He went up to the captain and from what I heard, the captain told him to go fuck himself."

"Have you heard anything else?"

"Johnson has been saying he is going to sue you. Says he is fighting the bogus charge against him from Dillon. Although I think he referred to her as that bitch." Stevens laughed. "I think Detective Hall is in love with Dillon. He heard what Johnson said, and Hall was on his way out the door to beat the snot out of the guy."

Damien smiled to himself. "Hall would kick his fat ass all over this city. Okay. Listen if you hear anything, let me know. I think the AD is up to something."

"You have a lot more on your side than you think Damien. We watch out for our own. Trust me when I say, it may look like politics is winning out, it's not. Not now, not in this division."

"Thanks, Stevens." Damien disconnected the call. "I don't think I can handle this." He removed the pens from the cup and threw them in his desk drawer. He called Detective Travis.

"ECD, Detective Travis."

"Hey, it's Kaine."

"I thought I saw you through the glass. How you been buddy?"

"I enjoyed sleeping all day."

"I bet. Well, that's over. I don't have anything for you yet. Still going through everything."

"Hopefully, by Monday, you will have something. I have another name for you. This guy runs the home that our victim grew up in, Shamus MacDougal, aka Pops."

"What do you want on this guy?" Detective Travis asked.

"Everything. He's Scottish or at least has an accent. I want to know whatever you can find out about him and Sunshine Valley Home."

"You got it. I'll start on that next. By early Monday I should have something for you."

"Also, when you go through the video of Chandelier Heights entrance, I need you to see if anyone leaves on foot, bike, or motorcycle. I have to meet with the captain Monday morning, I would like to take something into the man. Keep me posted, Travis."

"You got it, boss."

Damien was about to head out to the pen when his desk phone rang again. "Kaine here."

"I almost called your cell phone," Dr. Forsythe said.

"Hey, Doc, what's up? You about to start on our dead guy?"

"Yes, I am. Do you two want to come over?"

Damien looked at his watch. "Sure, Joe and I will be right there. You don't have to wait on us. You can catch us up when we get there."

"That's good. I'll go ahead and start, let yourself in if no one is at the front desk."

"See you soon, Doc." Damien hung up the receiver. Glancing at the clock one last time as he headed towards the pen, almost five p.m. He groaned. It was going to be a long fucking week.

CHAPTER SEVENTEEN

"Joe," Damien said, walking towards him.

"Yes, old wise one." Joe laughed.

"I really hate you." Damien turned to Davidson. "Go home."

He stood stretching. "I hid out long enough. My wife sent me a text saying they were waiting on me for dinner." He put on his jacket.

Joe stood and put his on. "You left your coat in the SUV?"

"Yes. We're heading over to the ME's." Damien said as the three of them walked to the elevator.

"I'm glad I don't have to see old Chase again." Davidson stepped in first and pushed the button for the garage level.

"I'm not looking forward to this visit either," Joe piped up.

"You'll live." Damien led the way to the garage. "Enjoy your Sunday at home. If I need you and Jenkins, I'll call you, Davidson. Otherwise, see you on Monday."

"Thanks, Damien. It's good to have you both back." Davidson waved as he headed to his car.

Damien and Joe climbed into the SUV. "Shit it's cold," Damien said, cranking the heat.

Joe reached over and turned off the blower. "Wait till the engine warms up. Crap, it's blowing cold air."

"Baby." Damien pulled out into the early evening Saturday traffic. They were less than ten minutes from the morgue. "We won't stay for the full autopsy. I want to get a rundown of what the killer did."

"I bet the doc was spot on with his assessment. Doc Forsythe knows his shit."

"I want to see him all cleaned up. He was a fucking mess at the house." Damien pulled into the empty parking lot of the city morgue. He parked in the spot closest to the door. This time he grabbed his jacket from the back seat.

"Look who's the baby now," Joe said following him into the building.

"Man, it's cold. I dread sleeping alone tonight. At least you have Muffin."

Joe stuck out his bottom lip and pouted. "Poor baby."

"Shut the fuck up." Damien slid his ID through the key card slot unlocking the door leading to the lab area. He smiled at Joe. "I hear his music."

"Thank goodness it's not Doc McChuckles doing the autopsy. He listens to talk radio."

"Who the hell is Doc McChuckles?"

"Patterson, 'yuck, yuck'...he always does that thinking he's funny."

Damien laughed, walking into the autopsy room. "Hey, Doc."

Dr. Forsythe smiled at his two favorite detectives. "You haven't missed much. I just got him cleaned off."

"Well, the bath sure as shit didn't help." Joe stepped closer. "Damn, this guy had to be in some kind of pain."

"Our killer definitely hurt Chase." The doctor pointed to the stab wounds. "I was pretty close, there were twenty-five." He moved to the empty eye sockets. "The right was definitely taken out while alive, the left was not."

"That had to hurt," Damien said.

"I'm sure everything our killer did to Chase hurt." Dr. Forsythe pointed to his genitals. I was correct. Our guy made Chase eat his balls. Found some in what was left of his stomach. As well as in the vomit on his shirt."

"The eyes, the balls, they mean something. He didn't take them for the fun of it." Damien didn't think he could stand looking at this guy much longer. "Since you haven't gotten anywhere yet, you want to shoot me an email later? Or you can even call me at home."

"I can do that. I'm going to finish this up. Shouldn't take too long,"

"Great, let me know what you find." Damien smiled at his friend. "I'll talk to you later, Doc. Call me if you need me."

"Doc, don't spend all night here," Joe said.

"I don't plan on it. As soon as I'm done here, I'll be going home." He nodded at them as they left. "Have a good night, boys. It may be the last quiet weekend for a while."

"Thanks for reminding us," Damien said as he and Joe walked out to the SUV.

"You kind of ran out of there. Why?" Joe climbed up into the vehicle.

"I couldn't stand it anymore. We didn't need to see what we already know."

"What's up, Damien?"

He turned onto the main thoroughfare. "I ...I don't know. Man, I'm tired of this shit."

"You can't leave now. We need to finish this. Plus, we aren't ready for our bar yet."

Damien dragged a hand through his hair. "I'm just tired."

CHAPTER EIGHTEEN

Saturday evening

Damien pulled into his garage. His dashboard clock said seven p.m. His mind felt as if he'd been awake for days. He stayed in his truck as the garage door closed. He armed the security system using the remote. Exiting the truck, he frowned at the empty spot where Dillon's car usually sat. She was having the interior reupholstered. Now the empty spot was another reminder of how lonely this place was going to be.

Feeling sorry for himself, he entered his home, stopped inside the door and inhaled deeply. He could smell Dillon's perfume. At least he could spray his pillow tonight. "I'm a fucking wuss." He said to himself. He walked into the kitchen, praying there was still beer in the fridge. He smiled as he was rewarded with almost a full twelve-pack in front of him. He grabbed one, twisted off the cap, and guzzled most of the bottle. He grabbed two more and headed towards his office.

Placing the bottles on the desk, he pulled his cell phone from his pocket and called his mom.

"Damiano, *dove sie` figlio?*"

Damien's mom's voice filled his ear. The shrill of excitement almost busted his eardrum. "I'm at home, Mama."

"Where is Dillon? Is she there too?"

Damien could hear his mother speaking to his father in her native Italian tongue. "Tell Dad, she's fine. She and Taylor stayed at the farm. Joe and I have been reinstated."

"Oh, *è fantastico.* That is what you wanted, *si?*"

"It is."

Angelina repeated the news to her husband. "Your father is very excited."

"Look, Joe and I were going to come for dinner tomorrow." Damien held the phone away from his ear as his mother squealed in delight. "Mama, *calmati.*"

"I do not need to calm down. A mother can be excited to have her son for Sunday dinner."

"Well, we will be there around three p.m."

"*Fantistico.* We can't wait to see you. *Ti amo, figlio.*"

"I love you too, Mama." Damien disconnected the call before he had to answer any questions about why he was here and Dillon wasn't. He was sure he would get the third degree on Sunday. He checked his watch. He had placed an order for delivery when he dropped Joe off at his parent's house. His food should be showing up pretty damn quick. "I could actually starve by then." He shook his head. "I sound like Joe." He laughed at himself.

Sitting at his desk, waiting for his computer to boot up, his doorbell rang. "Yes." He jumped and ran to the door. Grabbing his wallet from his pocket as he pulled the door open. "Hey," his shoulders slumped. "Crap. What are you doing here?"

Camilla stood with her arms crossed. "After all the time we were together, that's how you greet me?"

"After all the men you fucked behind my back, you're lucky I don't punch you." He started to close the door when the Chinese delivery guy showed up. Damien's foot tapped against the metal plate spanning the length of the doorway. The clicking noise echoed in the dead space between him and Camilla as he waited for the man to come to him. Handing him the money, he started to close the door in Camilla's face once again.

She put out her hands. "I promise I'm not here to start a fight. I need your help."

Damien's eyes widened. "You can't be fucking serious. How could you ever think I would help you?"

"Please. Someone is stalking me." Camilla pleaded with him.

"Camilla, no one is stalking you. This is a ploy to weasel in between Dillon and me and cause more headache and drama."

"Damien, I promise it isn't. I really think someone is stalking me."

"Camilla, I suggest you have your company hire you some protection. It is probably one of your clients," he raised an eyebrow at her, "or one of their wives."

"I don't sleep with my clients," she huffed.

"Bullshit."

"Damien, please. I don't know who else to ask."

"Well, I'm not going to help you. Get your company to pay for security. Have them stake out your place. Hire someone yourself, but I am not going to help you." Damien closed the door in her face.

"Please, Damien. This isn't a ploy. I promise."

Damien cursed under his breath as he opened the door. "Camilla, I am not the only person who can help. There is no reason you have to ask me."

"You're the only one I trust. Damien, help me." Tears trickled down her cheeks.

"Hang on." He shut the door and set his food down on the small table next to the front door. He went into the office and pulled a card from his desk. Back at the front door, he calmed himself. "Here," he said, pulling the door open. "This guy is one of the best private detectives around. He can find out who it is, and he can also provide security. Call him."

Camilla took the card. She lowered her head, breaking eye contact. "I don't want anyone else." She stared at the card as she spoke.

"I know. That's part of the problem. Call him Camilla. He can help you. I need to go." He closed the door. He stood with his ear to it, listening for her car door and engine, feeling like a prisoner in his own home. After about two minutes he heard her car start. From the front window, he watched her little sports car drive away.

"I can't believe that fucking woman," he said to himself. He walked into the kitchen and filled a plate with food and headed back to his desk. Setting everything down, he sat staring at his computer. "Camilla you are a piece of work." Damien took a bite of an egg roll. Camilla would stop at nothing to break Dillon and him up. He never thought she would claim she was being stalked to do it. And yet, something in her expression had him second-guessing himself.

CHAPTER NINETEEN

Saturday evening at the farm

Taylor rounded the corner from the hallway. "I'm ready." She spun around. Dressed head to toe in pink sweats and pink snow boots.

"Really?" Dillon asked, looking her over. "You won't be noticed at all."

"It's all I have," she said shrugging.

"I reminded Agatha about our little adventure. She thinks we have lost our minds. She and Ralph will stay in their house." Dillon handed Taylor one of the IR flashlights, night vision goggles, and one of the mag lights. She walked over to the security control panel located behind a wall plate in the living room. She shut off all the floodlights situated around the farm. "All the lights are off. The farm is in total darkness," she said, putting on her jacket.

"Wait, what about the ear thingy's?" Taylor asked.

Dillon shook her head. "It's just us. We won't need them. Unless you want to separate?"

Taylor's eyes widened. "No way. Nope. Not going after the boogeyman by myself."

Gunner stood at the ready, eager to follow them out on the hunt.

"Gunner, baby, you're going to have to stay here." Dillon bent down and gave him a kiss on the nose.

The dog cocked his head to the side, whimpering in protest. Those whimpers turned into howls as they exited the house.

"Where are we starting?" Taylor asked as they walked on the pathway between the two pastures, heading towards the main barn.

"Based off what Joe said yesterday, I think we should hit the main barn and the area around the machine shop. After we cover that, we may need to venture out past the fence line."

As they exited the pathway onto the primary drive leading to all the buildings, they stopped glancing around.

"With the lights shut off, this place is dark." Taylor used her mag light to scan the area.

"The lights make a huge difference."

"Are there any buildings we can't see? I mean like something behind either the mechanic shop or the main barn?" Taylor asked, angling her light, allowing her to see Dillon's face in shadow and not blind her.

Dillon pooched out her lips as she thought for a moment. "Behind the mechanic shop, there used to be a storage shed. I remember Grandpa said once the mechanic shop was built, he was going to tear it down. It might still be there."

"Well, you lead the way." Taylor followed along next to Dillon. "Do you have a weapon?"

Dillon giggled. "I don't think we will need a weapon. Joe has gotten you spooked."

"That man watches too many horror movies." Taylor flashed the beam of light around the farm. "You have to admit this place is creepy at night. Especially with no lights on."

They came upon the mechanic shop first. "We'll start here. If we don't find anything, we will move to the main barn." Dillon stepped through the door into the dark shop.

"Do they leave this unlocked? Seems kind of stupid." Taylor asked.

"No. I asked the workers to leave it unlocked earlier. I'll lock it up when we leave." Dillon covered her lips with her finger. "Whisper."

Taylor nodded.

Using the mag light, Dillon set the beam on low and scanned the shop. A large plow sat in the center of the room, its massive size camouflaged by the darkness. Dillon checked over her shoulder to make sure Taylor was following her. She stopped abruptly, causing Taylor to run into her.

"Sorry," Taylor whispered. "Why did you stop?"

Dillon cocked her head to the side. A faint scratching noise drifted through the room. She couldn't discern what direction it was coming from, or if it was even in the shop. "Do you hear that?"

"Hear what?"

"That scratching noise?"

"No. Did your grandfather ever mention a rodent or mouse problem?"

"No. He was adamant about keeping this place as rodent-free as possible. Doesn't mean there aren't little creatures that live around here. But around the milking facility, you can't have that. Put on your infrared goggles," Dillon said to Taylor. She heard a slight giggle. "Stop."

"What? This is so much fun." Turning them on, she glanced around the machine shop. "Wow. These are cool."

Dillon shook her head. "You're such a dork." She reached out for her hand.

Taylor jumped doing some kind of dance as she brushed her hands down her arms. "Oh my gosh, something grabbed me..." she continued to squeal slightly. "There is someone in here with us." Her head swiveled from side to side, scanning the shop.

"Taylor, calm down."

"Don't tell me to calm down," she hissed. "Something grabbed my hand."

"Dude. That was me." Dillon reached out, taking hold of her hand. "I was reaching for you."

Taylor blew out a long breath. "Thank goodness." She wrapped her hand around Dillon's fingers, following her as she was led her towards the back of the shop. "Where are we going?"

Dillon turned towards her. "Sshh..." she continued towards the back wall. They stood in the middle of the room. She was sure she heard some kind of rustling. Looking from one end to the other, she saw nothing scurrying in the shadows.

At the far end to the right, there was a large metal cabinet containing several bins holding what Dillon assumed were supplies. As her eye traveled down the wall, she counted several tool carts of various sizes. At the same end, centered in one of the bays, was a lift. She headed towards it, dragging a trembling Taylor.

At the edge of the vehicle lift, she could see into the well where the hydraulics were located. As the lift rose, so did the sides where the mechanic could stand and work on whatever he needed to. "No way a critter would hang out down there."

Taylor peered over the edge. "They would be smashed."

Dillon led Taylor towards the other end of the building. Three more bays filled the vast shop, each allowing for large vehicles to be worked on. As they maneuvered their way towards the far-left end, Dillon stopped abruptly, covering Taylor's mouth with her hand. She pointed towards the corner and a back door.

CHAPTER TWENTY

Taylor stood next to Dillon. Peering at her through the night vision goggles. She heard something off to her left. Dillon had stepped a little ahead of her. As Taylor took a small step towards her, she felt something run across her foot. "Holy shit! There is something in here."

Dillon jumped tripping on the wheel of a cart resting near the back door. She hit the concrete floor with a thud. "What the hell is wrong with you?" She asked as she ripped off the goggles. "Take off your goggles Taylor, I need to turn on the mag light. I'll blind you if you don't."

Taylor did as instructed. "I didn't mean to make you fall. I swear something ran over my foot. It was probably a giant crazy man-eating rat."

"It couldn't have been that big." Dillon scanned the floor.

"It was huge," Taylor said panting.

Dillon continued to shine the light across the floor. Two tiny little eyes caught the light and beamed back at her. "There's your giant man-eating rat." She pointed in the direction of a tiny mouse.

Taylor crossed her arms. "I draw the line at mice, of any size, running up my pant leg." She said through gritted teeth.

"It didn't run up your leg. It ran over your foot, and it was the size of a turd." Dillon laughed at her as she stood. "Okay, enough of the mouse. I heard something in this area, and it wasn't a mouse." Dillon opened the back door and peered outside. She saw the old shed out back.

Taylor poked her head out, stepping up next to Dillon. "I suppose we are going to see what's in there?"

Dillon's brow wrinkled. "We're already here. Let's go."

"I won't freak out this time."

"Somehow I don't believe you," Dillon whispered as they walked towards the small barn-like structure. Dillon tried the doorknob. It opened with ease. As they stepped inside, both swept it with their lights. It looked like it had served as an oversized storage shed over the years. Things had been placed inside and forgotten. Dust covered most of the items located along the walls. The middle of the shed was open, and at the back, a small structure jutted out.

Dillon looked over at Taylor. "This was used as the original mechanic shop," she whispered.

Taylor shined her light towards the far-right corner. "There's a room back there," she said. "I don't see anywhere else for someone to hide."

As Dillon and Taylor crept towards the small office area, scurrying and shuffling could be heard from behind the frosted glass making up the office window and the top half of the door.

Dillon leaned into Taylor. "This is a tiny space. I'll go in first, you follow me." She placed both pairs of night vision goggles on a box near the office door.

"You got it." Taylor stepped up behind Dillon. "Wait, don't you think we should grab a weapon?"

Dillon shook her head. "I don't think we are dealing with a person."

Taylor's eyes bulged. "Then what the hell do you think we're dealing with?"

"Probably a giant man-eating rat."

"Then we need a weapon." Taylor looked around and found an old broom in the corner near the office. She retrieved it and came back to Dillon. "Okay. I'm ready."

"Unless we're attacked by a giant cobweb, I'm not sure the broom is the best weapon." Dillon twisted the knob and eased the office door open. They scanned the small enclosure with their lights. As the beams bounced off the metal surfaces casting shadows along the wall, something scurried from under the desk towards the back of the room.

"What the hell was that?" Taylor asked, taking a small step back, holding the broom out in front of her.

Dillon followed the creature with the beam of her light as it hid behind a wooden crate in the corner. Noises emanated from the crate. Hay lay strewn about the base of it. "I have no idea, but it was huge." She crept closer to the crate. Peering over the top, she could see maybe three feet of space between it and the back wall. Her angle kept her from seeing the bottom half of the crate and the corner of the building. "I'm going to pull the it out a little further from the wall. Shine your light towards it."

"It could be a rabid creature," Taylor said, balancing the broom handle and her mag light.

Dillon glanced over her shoulder. "Before I move the crate, shut the door. I don't want it getting out."

Taylor nodded as she pulled the door shut. "Great. Now you're locking us in here with some homicidal creature. We will probably be turned into zombies." Taylor stepped over to the right giving Dillon room to maneuver around the old desk.

"You sound like Joe," she said as she stepped to the crate. Dillon gauged its size to be about four feet long and three feet wide. She placed the mag light in the front pocket of her jeans and grabbed the corners of the wooden box.

Taylor took a half step back as Dillon pulled the box away from the wall.

A loud, hissing noise began as the box slid away from the corner.

Dillon paused, holding her breath. The hissing stopped. She began to slide the crate again. This time the hissing had a guttural sound. As the container swung around, a large hole in the wall became visible. Something thudded against the side of the crate. The noise echoed in the small room.

"What the hell?" Taylor asked.

Dillon stepped back. "Something is living in this box. The hole in the wall is its way in and out. I'm going to slide that corner towards us," she pointed to the upper right corner of the box. "Be ready." She took a deep breath as she grabbed the corner and started to swing the box around.

"Be ready for what?" Taylor panted.

"I don't know. Just be ready." Dillon slid the crate around. As it moved the weight inside the box shifted. The hissing turned into growls and snarling. At the very moment, the wooden crate's side came into view, Dillon could see a large jagged hole in the side of the box. In the dim light of Taylor's flashlight, two shiny eyes peered out at her. A large furry creature came out of its protected lair and stood on two feet snarling and holding its dagger-like claws up in a defensive stance.

Taylor jumped back when Dillon moved abruptly away. It took a few seconds for the shape of the creature to register.

"Looks like it's definitely a masked bandit," Dillon said as she blew a sharp breath out.

Taylor's hand flew to her chest. "Oh my gosh."

"Well, at least we know who the culprits are."

They both stared at the creature. A slightly plump and ominous looking raccoon stared back at them. The momma raccoon's stance had relaxed a bit as Dillon and Taylor stepped back. The creature scurried back into the comforts of its fort.

Dillon cocked her head to the side, listening. "I think her babies are in there."

Taylor stepped closer to the wall and shined her light through the jagged opening. The light reflected off several pairs of eyes. "I think you're right and I think we should step out and close the door. We can decide what to do. If she feels threatened, or thinks we're going to hurt her chitlins, she can become a nasty creature in a hurry."

Retreating from the office, Dillon pulled the door shut behind her. She made her way to the front of the shed, found the light switch, and flipped it on. The gloomy feeling quickly vanished, revealing old, un-used tools, and boxes of things long ago put in storage. "I don't even know if Grandpa..." her voice trailed off. "I don't know if Agatha or Ralph know what's in here."

She walked over to some of the boxes. Some were labeled some weren't. Brushing the dust off one, she could barely make out the words. "Looks like supplies they didn't take to the new shop." Dillon turned towards Taylor. "Tomorrow I will speak with Agatha. We can build a sanctuary for the raccoons. I'll make sure they're taken care of."

CHAPTER TWENTY-ONE

9 p.m. Saturday

Damien finished off his dinner, picking up his phone to call Dillon when it rang. "You must be psychic."

"Really? You expect me to believe you were about to call me?"

Dillon's breathy voice filled his ear. His pants tightened in the crotch. It still amazed him how much power she had over him. "Well, I'm hoping I can fool you. How's it going down there?"

"Pretty good. Taylor and I ate dinner over at Jethro's house. His wife made pot roast."

"Sounds much better than what I ate."

"Let me guess, MingHin Chinese."

"Yes. It was delicious, but I would've much rather have had pot roast. Actually, I would eat bark if you were with me."

"I miss you too. How's the case going?"

"You feel up to listening, giving me feedback? I could use your help."

"Absolutely. I'm itching to get back to work. I talked to Phillip today. I asked him if I could get back earlier. He said when the doctor releases me, he will think about office work, maybe local fieldwork. He doesn't want me traveling until I'm one hundred."

Damien nodded, realizing she couldn't see him. "I agree. I want you completely healed before you go back out in the field. I do think light duty would do you some good. Keep your mind working."

"Tell me about this case, but wait a second."

Damien heard shuffling. He heard the refrigerator, the ding of a wine glass, and the clicking of Gunner's paws on the hardwood floors. "Are you getting wine?"

"Yes, and a snack. Plus, I got a bone for Gunner. Give me another few seconds, I need to pee and get into bed."

"Seriously, you're going to pee with me on the phone?" Damien chuckled.

"Why not? You talk to me all the time when I pee at home. Why should a few hundred miles make any difference?"

He heard the flush of the toilet. "My gosh, are you almost done?"

"Shut-up," Dillon huffed into the phone. "Gunner, move your big butt over."

"Let me guess, he's taking his spot out of the middle?"

"Yes, him and Coach. Okay, I'm ready."

"Well hell, I'm ready for bed now."

"Listen, old man, tell me about the fucking case." She laughed.

"Alright. Chase Humphry was tortured. Our killer cut off his fingers, his hands, and feet, he then cauterized them."

"Wow!"

"Wait, there's more...he gouged out one eye, while he was alive. Cut off his balls and fed them to him. Sliced him up the middle, and finally took out the other eye. He put the eyes on skewers in front of a mirror. I know that means something, along with the balls, he didn't make him eat them for no reason. I need you to help me figure it out."

"Holy shit. What else?"

"Isn't that enough?" Damien chuckled into the phone.

"That's not what I meant. Dufus. Anything else you can tell me, to help me figure some things out?"

Damien leaned back in his chair, putting his feet on the desk. "Let's see, our guy abducted him from the office garage, used our victim's car to get him to his own house. Our victim lives in a gated community. I think the killer caused a false alarm, pulling the guards away from the gate. He then had to get out of the neighborhood without being seen or noticed."

"Our guy is smart and determined."

"What do you think the eyes and gonads mean?"

Dillon sighed into the phone. "Off the top of my head, I'd say the killer is pissed."

"Wow, what an Einstein. Hell, Joe came up with the same conclusion."

"I'm kidding. Let's think about this. I don't like to make assumptions; the evidence needs to unfold a little. Tell me about Chase's past."

"In a nutshell, our victim grew up in this home for kids, near Indiana Dunes. His business partner thinks Chase's father died in a drug deal and the mother was put in prison. She killed someone while she was there, don't know if it's true or not. He started this company which supplies parts for the wind turbine industry. That's all I know."

"Somewhere along the way, Chase was involved in something with this killer or at the least with someone associated with this killer. The amount of damage done to the body, especially while he was alive, indicates a huge amount of rage," Dillon said.

"My first thought was our killer wanted something from Chase. Whether it was business related or personal, I don't know yet. Although I lean more to personal." Damien took a sip of his beer.

"I tend to think you're right about the killer wanting something from Chase and I agree with it not relating to business. I also doubt he had to wait very long for whatever it was he wanted from Chase. I don't think your killer took the chance of being caught to just get information, though. I think his purpose was to torture and hurt. And if that is the case, I can't imagine Chase is the only one on this guy's radar. We won't know unless we have more victims. And they're all connected."

"Great. Why can't this be for business secrets? Why do we need another body? And what will he do to the next one? I can't even imagine."

"What evidence do you have?"

Damien sighed before taking a long pull on his beer. "Nothing much yet. ECD is going through all the security tapes and electronics. Davidson and Jenkins will go through all the names of residents during the time of Chase's stay at Sunshine Valley. We will track down as many as we can, at least for elimination purposes." Damien paused. "I need something on this guy. Something that will hopefully give me a clue as to how to find him. You got anything you can tell me about him?"

Dillon took a sip of her wine before she responded. "Okay, just using the crime scene, the fact this guy tortured his victim, and it was done in his home, tells me the killer wasn't worried about getting caught. This tells me the killer is detail orientated. He planned this down to the minute. I also don't think your victim was random. He was chosen for a reason."

"I think the damage done to Chase's eyes and gonads has to mean more than just torture."

"I think they do too. I believe both are symbolic for several things. Chase saw something he shouldn't have, he didn't react the way he should have, or do what he should have..."

"What do you mean?"

"In the case of the eyes, maybe something like, how can he look at himself in the mirror?"

"Okay, what about the balls? He took the time to cook them in the kitchen before he made him eat them. After Chase was dead, he ground his guts up in the blender."

"The first thing I think of is Chase was a coward." She paused for a moment. "If I take everything done to Chase, I'd say it this was more about punishment because Chase didn't do something or stop something. No idea what. Chase was personally involved in something that pissed the killer off."

"I can see that. Of course, all of this could be speculation. Our killer may have picked Chase because he cut him off on the road one day in his big fancy car."

"No. I don't think so. I said earlier, this wasn't random. I definitely don't' think Chase was killed over something trivial. And I'm pretty certain there is a very personal connection."

Damien sighed. "What a case to come back to." He paused, taking another sip of his beer. "How's it going on the farm?"

"It's going pretty well. Taylor and I figured out what has been stealing stuff around here."

"Really? What? And shouldn't that be who?" Damien asked.

"I guess it depends on how you look at it. It's a giant fat raccoon."

"Are you serious?"

"Yep. She made a home out of this crate in the old mechanic's shop. She's a klepto, too. We found her stash of all the stuff she has been taking."

Damien laughed into the phone. "Joe will be disappointed it isn't a crazed maniac. What are you going to do about her?"

"I'll call the wildlife preservation tomorrow. I'm sure they have someone they can send out here to help us come up with a plan."

"That's great. How are Coach and Gunner doing?"

"Both are fat and sassy. They think they own the bed. I barely get a sliver to sleep on."

"At least you have someone or something to sleep with. I'm all alone." Damien made a sniffling sound.

"You're pathetic. We will be back in a week tops. You'll live. What are you doing on Sunday?"

"I talked Joe into going over to my parent's house for dinner."

"Don't tell them about the money."

Damien heard the high pitch in her voice. "I won't baby, I promise.

Joe won't say anything either. It may come out some time. If someone does any research, they can find out what the farm is worth." An exasperated sigh filled his ear. "You need to be prepared, that's all I'm getting at."

"I know. I know. I don't like it. I never wanted money. I don't need it."

"Well, you have it now. Remember, I loved you when you were nothing more than a poor FBI Agent."

"Yes, you did." She laughed. "I miss you."

"I miss you too. And now I need to tell you something." For once, Damien was glad Dillon wasn't sitting next to him.

Dillon sighed into the phone. "Why is it I have a feeling this isn't going to be good?"

"Maybe you have psychic abilities you aren't aware of."

"Tell me what it is you have to tell me."

"It's not like it's super bad. I just want you to hear it from me."

"Damien, what's going on?"

"I had a visitor tonight." He held the phone away from his ear, waiting for a scream or a long series of curse words.

"Don't say that bitches name. I know that's who you're getting ready to say came by the house."

"Okay, a person I shall not name came by the house. You'll never believe what she said to me."

Dillon growled. "I can only imagine."

"She asked me for help."

"I bet she did. What is it she said was wrong this time?"

"She said someone was stalking her." There was an eerie silence on the phone. "Dillon? Hello? You still there?"

"I'm still here. Tell me you didn't believe her?"

"Well..."

"Are you kidding me?" Dillon huffed into the phone. "You can't be serious?"

"Hear me out first. Then you can crucify me." Damien guzzled the last of his beer, opening his third one. "She said someone was stalking her, I didn't ask for details. I didn't care about them."

"Right. She's using it to get close to you."

"Something tells me she isn't making this up. Yes, I believe she hoped it would get her close to me. But I didn't agree to help her. I gave her the card of a guy my father has used before. His name is Jeff Tinsdale. He is one of the best private investigators I know. Used to be a homicide cop back in the day. He can provide her with physical security."

"Okay. That I can swallow. I personally think Camilla is making it up to weasel her way back in."

"I thought the same thing. I mean I believe she hoped it would work to that effect. I don't know, Dillon. There was something in her expression, I think she really thinks she's in danger." Damien swallowed some of his beer. "I trust Jeff. He will find out if the threat is real or made up."

"Don't get involved in any way, Damien. I mean it. I don't have a problem with you giving her the name of someone else to help her. But I'm telling you, I'll walk if you're going to give any of your time to her."

Thankful Dillon couldn't see the pinched expression on his face, Damien could feel his jaw clenching. He twisted his head from side to side, hoping the movement would ease the stiffness in his shoulders. "I won't give her any of my time or resources. I tend to think she pissed off a wife somewhere. If anything, they're tailing her to see if their husband is with her."

"Might be a good guess. I don't believe it though. If your guy finds out it's a big fat ploy for attention, what an all-time low. Even for Camilla." Dillon grabbed Coach, who was snuggled between her and Gunner. She cradled him in her arms, setting off his purring.

"Is that Coach?"

"Yes."

"You're holding him like a baby, aren't you?"

Dillon laughed. "I'm snuggling him. You're jealous."

"I am. It's going to be lonely this week. You promise you'll come back to me?"

"Hmm. I'm not sure. I don't really need your money anymore. I could become a famous rancher. Raise the best cattle in this area. Have ranchers and other cattlemen after my herd. Restaurants charging fifty dollars a steak...man, I might stay here."

"Fine. I'll take you to court to get Coach back. He was my cat first. I will sue you." Damien sniggered on the other end of the phone.

"Well, others have been murdered for less. You might want to remember that."

CHAPTER TWENTY-TWO

Late Saturday night
Chicago

After three trips around the block, Maggie Newsome pulled into the vacant parking spot. She slammed the driver's side door, smashing her hip against it to get the latch to lock. "You may be a shit car, but you're my shit car," she said, repeatedly lifting the door handle. She wrapped her arms around her body. Hugging herself to keep as much of her body heat in as possible under her thin winter coat, as she walked the two blocks to her apartment.

"Fuck, I hate heels," she grumbled, catching the heel of her shoe in a crack in the sidewalk. She hurried the last few steps to her building on the balls of her feet. "If this heel is broken, I may shoot someone at the city," she mumbled as she climbed the five steps to the outer door of her apartment building.

"Hey Maggie, you have a good night?"

Maggie looked up to see her neighbor William looming outside his door. "Hey, William. No, shitty as usual. Better get inside before you catch the death of you."

"Had to take Little Missy for her nightly walk." William cradled the poodle-like dog in his arms.

"Did she walk or did you carry her?" Maggie asked wrestling with the lock on the metal door. She shimmied the key until it finally opened.

"A little of both I'd say." He laughed, juggling the dog as he unlocked his door. "Have a good night, Maggie."

"You too, William." She stepped inside to a dimly lit hallway. She pushed the button on the elevator and was immediately rewarded with a screeching sound. "No way. I'm not trusting this," Maggie said as she walked to the stairwell. She reached down to take off her shoes, deciding her health was more important. Her nose wrinkled at the dark brown stains littering the stairwell as if it were a skin of a leopard. "No telling what I'd be walking on."

Panting mildly by the time she reached the third floor, she yanked on the fire door. The hallway seemed to stretch out in front of her. She removed her shoes no longer worrying about the filth. With every step, she sighed in relief as her arches returned to their natural position. Unlocking the three deadbolts on her door, she walked inside to her little sanctuary. It wasn't much, but it was her home. And she only had to share it with Herman, her goldfish. A note on the counter said the exterminator had been there and had sprayed. She hoped this time around the bugs would be gone. At least for a few days longer than the last time.

To tell the truth, she would take bugs any day over not having to share her apartment with anyone. She dropped her shoes walking towards her bedroom, stripping, leaving a trail of clothes. She giggled to herself. "Don't leave your clothes lying around Maggie," she said in her best Scottish accent. "Well, fuck you Pops."

She turned on her hot water. Stepping inside the shower, she let it run over her. She shuddered at the memory of Pops. He had everyone fooled. They all thought he cared so much for the children. "If they only knew," she said under the flow of water. Tears welled in her eyes. "No," she lifted her face. She placed her hands on the wall in front of her. "I did what I needed to survive." She let the last of the hot water wash away the guilt.

CHAPTER TWENTY-THREE

Kerry watched as Maggie searched for a spot to park. He took note of the neighborhood. The last twelve years hadn't been as kind to Maggie as they had been to Chase. Her apartment building was situated on the edge of Hyde Park. A few neighborhoods over were some of the roughest neighborhoods in the city.

The old man and his dog were a nightly routine. Same time, same route. Which seemed to take about fifteen minutes. Maggie's schedule was fairly routine, with some variations here or there. Kerry wouldn't be given the luxury he had been afforded with Chase.

He looked down at the picture of the little girl. His eyes filled with tears. Had he known back then he could have protected her. His sadness quickly turned to boiling anger. "Sierra, I will make them pay for what they did to you. For what they let happen to other kids. I promise you." He wiped the wetness from his cheeks with the back of his hand. Placing the picture back in his wallet.

Focusing his attention on the front door of Maggie's building, he stepped away from his car. He checked the time on his watch as he pulled his baseball cap down low in front. Trotting across the street, he walked up the steps. Pretending to ring one of the bells, he glanced around as he picked the lock and entered the building. Scanning the lobby, he saw one camera. He wondered if it was even hooked up. He made a mental note to bring a jammer next time.

Walking down the deserted hallway, he made his way to the stairwell. He slipped in quietly, easing the door shut behind him. He jogged up the three flights of stairs. He placed his ear against the door, making sure there was no foot traffic and opened it slowly. Peering out, he walked casually down the hall. Kerry knew which apartment was hers. He had been there once before.

He frowned at the three locks on the door. Those are new, he thought. He could easily pick them, but he ran the chance of her hearing him. Glancing over his shoulder, then back towards the other end of the hall, he placed his ear against the door. He heard faint voices from the TV. If he could hear the TV, then the neighbors could hear it too.

The door to the stairwell opened up to the laughter of a couple of college kids. Keeping his head down, he nodded as he walked past them. He took the steps two at a time, running across the street to his car and glanced up and down the avenue one last time before he opened his car door. Once in his vehicle, he pulled out his cell and dialed a number.

"Dancing Dolls."

"Hey, when does Maggie work next?"

"Maggie is scheduled for Wednesday night. You want to leave her a message?"

"No thanks," he said as he drove off.

CHAPTER TWENTY-FOUR

Sunday morning at the farm

Taylor sat in the kitchen, looking at her phone. She had put on a pot of coffee and had placed the homemade biscuits in the oven. Checking the time, she had roughly ten minutes before she had to get the rest of the breakfast started. Her heart pounded in her chest when she received a text. "Oh no." She placed her hand over her mouth. "This can't be happening. Not now." She blocked the number and deleted the text.

"Hey, why are you up so early?" Dillon asked, wiping the sleep from her eyes. Gunner blasted past her, heading towards the front door. "Hang on, Gunner. I'll let you out."

Taylor turned her phone over face down on the table. "Hey," she said, getting up and checking on the biscuits. Her hands shook as she opened the oven. "They're almost done." She turned and jumped when she found Dillon right behind her. Her hand flew to her chest as she yelped.

"What the hell is wrong with you, Taylor? You look like you've seen a ghost." Dillon took a coffee mug from the cabinet and filled her cup. Adding way too much sugar and cream.

"I wasn't expecting you to be right there. I made homemade biscuits, and I'm getting ready to make eggs, bacon, and gravy. I hope you're hungry."

"No wonder Joe loves living with you." Dillon sat at the table where she could watch Taylor. She scrutinized her every movement. Something was off with her friend. She just wasn't sure what. "I can cook, I don't like it, but I can cook."

"I love cooking. Something about creating a dish that makes people drool and sigh with every bite." Taylor grabbed the eggs from the refrigerator. "Do you want scrambled or over medium?"

"Is there toast?"

"I made biscuits."

"But those will have gravy on them. I need toast with my eggs. I prefer over medium."

"I will make you some toast." Taylor placed two pieces in the toaster and set to work, turning the bacon. "Why don't you like to cook?"

Dillon sipped on her coffee before answering. She could hear Damien's voice in her head, *let her in.* "My mother and I used to cook. I was always in the kitchen with her. It was our time together. After she was murdered, my grandmother tried to get me to cook with her. I never wanted to after—after she died."

Taylor placed the bacon on a plate, then walked to Dillon. She took the seat next to her at the table. "I'm sorry you experienced what you did. Especially as a little girl. I can't begin to imagine how scary it was." She took Dillon's hand in hers. "Whenever you need someone to talk to about anything, your parents, your grandparents, all you have to do is call me. I know being here is hard. Remember, I'm here for you, always."

Dillon squeezed her hand. "You're such a good friend." Dillon laughed. "Umm, you are pretty much my only friend. I'm not the greatest at making those." She wiped the tear from her cheek.

"I'm always here for you. No matter what. You can try to push me away, but I'll always stay. I better get the biscuits."

"What do you need me to do?" Dillon asked, refilling her cup of coffee.

The toast popped up.

"You can butter your toast while I cook the eggs." She stirred the pepper gravy as she cracked eggs in a hot pan with one hand.

Dillon's jaw dropped open. "How do you do that?"

Taylor's brow wrinkled as she cracked the last egg in the pan. "Do what?"

Dillon pointed to the pan. "Crack an egg with one hand?"

Taylor giggled. "You have to practice. Once you do it a few times, you get the hang of it."

Dillon placed bacon on two plates and her toast on one. She watched Taylor skillfully flip the eggs without cracking the yolks. "Have you ever thought of opening a restaurant?"

"No. Not at all. Cooking wouldn't be fun anymore. It would be a job." Taylor placed eggs on the plates then sliced open two biscuits. Smothering each half with gravy. "Let's eat."

Dillon grabbed the plates, while Taylor took a pitcher of orange juice from the refrigerator and two glasses from the cabinet.

Taylor looked at the plates with all the food. "I think my eyes were definitely bigger than my stomach, but I'm going to eat as much as I can."

Dillon laughed. "It's a good thing the wildlife guy isn't' coming until later today. We're going to need a nap." She was about to take her first bite when Gunner barked at the door. "Dang, I forgot about Gunner."

Taylor filled Gunner's and Coach's bowls. The cat seemed to appear out of nowhere the minute she plated the food. Sitting back at the table, Taylor glanced up. "We can go through some of your grandparent's things later today. Pack up everything you don't want to be on display here."

Dillon nodded. "I would like get as much packed up as possible. I want to get back to Chicago."

Taylor ignored her phone as it vibrated next to her.

Dillon raised an eyebrow at her. "Don't you want to see if that's Joe?"

She shook her head. "I texted him earlier. It's probably work, someone asking me a question. I'm on vacation until next Monday. I don't want to talk to anyone from the office."

"I can't wait to get back to work."

"How are your injuries? Your cheek and nose don't look as swollen as they were a few days ago."

"They're healing. The achiness in my cheek is gone when I eat. I have to chew slowly. I couldn't stand wearing that nose brace thing," Dillon made a circle with her forefinger as she pointed at her nose. "It bugged the hell out of me. My removing it, probably won't help it heal."

"Broken noses take a long time to heal. Although the outward signs may go away. They can take well over a few months before they're fully healed."

"I know when I bend over or find myself being too active, my face pounds right behind my nose. I refuse to take the pain meds, though. They mess with my dreams and make me super groggy."

Taylor took her plate to the sink and rinsed it off. "I don't know what possessed me to make so many biscuits," she said, looking at the ten left on the cookie sheet.

Dillon grabbed the foil from the cabinet. "They will keep. I bet we end up snacking on those all throughout the day." She wrapped them in the foil and placed them at the back of the counter so Gunner couldn't get to them. She helped Taylor clean the rest of the kitchen. By the time they were done, it was barely ten a.m.

Taylor threw a log into the fireplace and started a fire. As if the flame was a beacon, both Gunner and Coach took their spots on Gunner's giant dog bed. She scratched Coach's head and gave Gunner a kiss before she stretched out on the sofa.

Walking in with a few boxes from the mudroom and a roll of tape, Dillon set about putting them together. She eyeballed Taylor, who looked like she had fallen asleep. "Did breakfast make you sleepy?"

"Mhmm. The fire is warm, and this is the most comfortable couch. I think you should keep it." She snuggled under a blanket she pulled from off the back, wrapping herself up like she was in a cocoon. She watched Dillon as she walked out the room. Closing her eyes, she relaxed and started to doze.

"I took many naps on that sofa," Dillon said, walking in carrying several hangers of clothes.

Taylor sat up. "Are you sure you're ready to do that?"

Dillon smiled at her as she set the pile down next to the sofa and sat down on the floor. "Yes. I have pulled a few things I want to hold onto. A couple of items from both of them with wonderful memories attached. Otherwise, the rest of the clothes can go. I spoke with Agatha yesterday; she said the city has a clothing pantry and could really use the clothes. I pulled out any worn items to throw away and the rest I'm boxing to send over there."

"Well, I can help." Taylor grabbed a shirt to go into the box. "Are you keeping the hangers?"

"I will keep some for the guests. No sense in buying new hangers. These work fine." Dillon said, placing several clothes into the box still attached to their hanger. "Plus, I bet the pantry could use them."

Taylor nodded and folded the garments into the box along with the hangers.

Feeling left out, Coach meandered over and sat on Dillon's lap.

"Coach? How do you expect me to do this with you right in the thick of things?"

The cat rolled over onto his back, baring his belly for a good scratch and rub.

"You're spoiled," Dillon said laughing as the cat purred, sounding like a Johnson outboard motor. She picked him up, smothering him in hugs and kisses. "I love you, Coach. Sometimes I think you're the best part of my relationship with Damien. Do you know that?"

As if on cue, the cat meowed and rubbed his face against hers.

She placed him on the floor, and he scampered back to his spot next to the dog.

Dillon rose and went to the bedroom to grab more clothes. The phone on the wall rang. "Hello?"

"Hey Dillon," Agatha said. "The Game and Wildlife Ranger is here. He came to our house instead of yours."

"Okay. Taylor and I will be right over. Give us about five minutes to get dressed and over there."

"Take your time. We'll be here."

Dillon hung up the phone. "Hey, get dressed. We need to go over to Agatha and Ralph's. The Ranger went there instead of here." She glanced at her watch. "And he is only two hours early."

Taylor jumped up from the floor, leaving the clothes there. "All I need are my boots and coat."

CHAPTER TWENTY-FIVE

Sunday afternoon

Damien pulled through the gate of his parent's house. He glanced over at Joe whose head rested against the window as he snored and smacked him on the arm. "Yo, sleeping beauty?"

Joe popped up. "Huh, what?"

"Did you sleep at all last night?"

"No. Muffin kept walking across me. Then she would lay down, then she would walk across to the other side. She seemed restless and agitated. Then I was worried something was wrong, so I kept waking up to check on her. The fucking cat is going to be the death of me."

Damien laughed. "Maybe you should buy her another kitten now."

Joe's forehead wrinkled. "Won't Muffin get jealous?"

Damien cocked his head to the side. "You're worried about the cat being jealous?"

"She might think we're going to replace her."

"Are you a cat psychologist now?"

"How would you feel if I started hanging out with another best friend? Always having him hanging with me..."

"Delighted I wouldn't have to spend as much time with you as I do now."

"Ha. You'd be crying like a baby."

"Actually, I've heard the opposite. When a new pet is brought in, it gives new life to the older one."

Joe frowned at him. "I'll call the vet and ask him."

"Don't trust me, huh?"

"Not in the least."

They exited the vehicle and headed towards the front door.

Damien grabbed him by the arm. "Remember, don't mention anything about the farm, or the money."

With his index finger and thumb touching, he moved his hand across his mouth, as though zipping his lips shut. "What money?"

Damien reached out for the doorknob when it flew open.

His mother stood there with an apron on and her arms outstretched.

"*Mio dolce figlio, ti stavo aspettando tutta la mattina.*" She kissed and hugged him. Then moved to Joe. "How is my second figlio? I have missed you both." She hugged and kissed him as she had done Damien.

"Hi Angelina," Joe said gasping as she wrapped her arms around his waist and squeezed.

"Momma, I told you we would be here about three." Damien walked into the foyer of the large home. Flowers had been placed on the round table greeting visitors with a burst of colors during the dreary Illinois winters.

"I waited with anticipation. I missed you." She hugged him one more time grabbing his cheeks to bring his face closer to hers. She studied his eyes. "You aren't resting well. You should stay here."

Damien headed for the kitchen. Before he could get there, his niece and littlest nephew bounded down the staircase from the second floor. They ran to him, wrapping their arms around him.

"Uncle Damien, Uncle Damien," they yelled in unison.

"Hey, guys." He hugged and kissed each one. "Lorenzo, you have gotten so big." He turned to Gia, the second oldest of his brother Nicky's kids. "You must have all the boys chasing you."

"Daddy says no boys. Ever."

"Si. No boys ever," little Lorenzo yelled, then did some kind of karate chop at Joe.

"Whoa," Joe said, backing up. "Don't hurt me."

Lorenzo lept into his arms. "We missed you, Uncle Joe."

Joe scooped up Gia as well. "I missed you too." He kissed both of them before placing them back on the floor.

Damien turned to his mother. "I can't stay here, Momma. I would be driving over an hour one way, every day. That would make my days too long. Where is Nicholas Jr.?"

"Well, one night here would do you some good. Be around your family. Nicholas Jr. is with his friend Adler. His family took a bunch of kids to the movies for Adler's birthday," Angelina said.

Entering the kitchen, Damien's father, Giovanni, brother Nicky and his wife Catherine, Damien's sister Daniella and her husband William, all turned their heads.

"It's about time," Damien's father said as he embraced him, kissing both cheeks. "Your mother and I have missed you. How is Dillon?"

Damien nodded glancing around at everyone. "She's doing better. She and Taylor are at the farm."

Catherine's eyes squinted at him. "Is she doing okay, really okay?"

"Yeah? Is she?" Daniella asked, looking at Joe.

"Why are you looking at me?" he asked her.

"Damien lies. We know you will tell us the truth." Daniella winked at Damien.

"*Sei il grande bugiardo grasso.*" Damien stuck his tongue out at his younger sister.

William laughed at his wife being called a big fat liar, only to receive a hard smack on the arm. "What did you hit me for?" he asked.

"You laughed at what he said." Daniella playfully swatted him again.

This time William was ready and took her in his arms. He kissed her neck. "Hit me again, and I will make you pay for it later."

"Ooh is that a promise?"

"For crying out loud. Can you two stop?" Damien laughed. "You guys are as bad as Joe and Taylor."

Joe scoffed. "He's turning into a crotchety old man. Don't listen to him." He gave Daniella, and Catherine kisses on the cheek and shook Nicky and William's hands. "It's good to see you guys."

Nicky hugged him. "No handshake, you're family. The ugliest member of the family, but still family."

"What are you a comedian now?" Joe asked.

Little Lorenzo came up to Joe, lifting his arms. "Pick me up," he said, jumping up and down. "Peeze."

Joe lifted the five-year-old, who quickly wrapped his arms around his neck, burying his face against him. "Lo, have you been enjoying preschool?"

The boy nodded not saying anything. He was content being held by his second favorite uncle.

Catherine ogled the big man as he rubbed her son's back. "He talks about you. After you were shot, he cried, worrying about you."

"He did?" Joe sneered at Damien. "At least I know who loves me."

The smell of freshly baked bread filled the kitchen when his mother opened one of the double ovens removing two loaves of Italian bread.

Joe inhaled through his nose, closing his eyes. "Smells like heaven." He tried to put Lorenzo down, but the boy tightened his grip around his neck. "Hey, buddy, what's up, huh?" Joe rubbed his back some more.

"Lorenzo?"

Catherine watched not interfering. As Nicky started to move towards Joe to take the baby, she stopped him, shaking her head.

"Lorenzo," Joe said, barely above a whisper. He set Lorenzo's butt on the edge of the kitchen island; the boy never let go of his neck. "Hey buddy, look at me." He peeled Lorenzo's arms from around his neck. Holding his hands in front of him with one hand, Joe lifted his chin. "Talk to me, buddy. I can't fix it if you don't talk to me."

Movement in the kitchen came to a standstill. No one wanted to interrupt.

Lorenzo lifted his tear-streaked face. "*Ti amo zio* Joe," was all he got out before the waterworks started.

"Hey, hey, I love you too, Lo. You know that. What else is going on? Do I need to beat someone up at school for you?"

Lorenzo giggled through his tears. "No. I was scared when you got hurt. I don't want anything to happen to you."

"Buddy, nothing is going to happen to me. Okay?" Little Lorenzo wrapped his arms around Joe's neck. "If you keep choking me though, I may pass out."

Nicky glanced at his wife and saw the waterworks about to start. "Hey Gia, Lorenzo, you guys go wash your hands. It's almost time to eat."

"Okay, Daddy." Gia grabbed her little brother's hand after Joe set him on the floor. "Let's go Lolo." The two trotted off to the bathroom.

Joe looked at the family. "What was that all about?"

Catherine carried some plates to the dining room located off the kitchen. She stopped and patted Joe on the back. "That little boy loves you. Worships you. And when you got shot, I think he needed to see and hug you. According to him, *tieni la luna e le stelle.*"

"Wow. I had no idea. I can't give him the moon and stars, but maybe one day, you and Nicky will let him spend the day with me."

Nicky smiled. "He would love that."

"You don't want him corrupting the kid, Nicky," Damien said.

"Pfft." Joe glared at Damien. He turned to Nicky with a big smile on his face. "Good, as soon as this case is done, I'll take him into the city. We can be tourists for a day." Joe carried the big tray of lasagna to the dining table.

The others followed with bowls of anti-pasta, salad, and grilled asparagus. They all sat at the table. Giovanni led everyone in the sign of the cross and a quick dinner prayer.

Joe lifted his glass of wine. "I'd like to make a toast."

Everyone joined in, raising their glasses.

"Family is not only the one you are born into. It is also the one that surrounds you. To my *famiglia Italiana*. Salute."

"Salute." Everyone said in chorus.

"You aren't getting into the will," Damien said, raising an eyebrow at him.

"Ha, you wait and see." Joe winked at his best friend.

CHAPTER TWENTY-SIX

Early Monday morning

He'd been following Maggie for the last few weeks and had seen a pattern. Whenever she had two days off, she always left her apartment on the morning of her first day off around eight a.m., she remained gone for approximately thirty minutes. Always returning with a large coffee and a bag of bagels or pastries. He wasn't sure which and it didn't really matter. And after the other night, he had decided this would be the way to deal with her.

Kerry watched her leave her apartment building. He pulled his ball cap down covering most of his face. He dressed in a nondescript maintenance outfit. Something no one would be able to recall with great detail if they were asked.

He grabbed the small tool kit from his back seat and removed two pair of black latex gloves from it, placing them in his pocket. Stepping out of his car, he strolled towards the building. When another person came out, he quickly thanked them for holding the door and stepped inside, disappearing before they could protest. He clicked the jammer in his pants pocket, giving him the time he needed to slip through the lobby area.

As he made his way up the stairwell, he put on the gloves, cautiously entering Maggie's floor. The time of morning afforded him little wiggle room. Hopefully, most day-trippers had already vacated the building heading to their jobs. Reaching into his back pocket, he removed the small pouch carrying his lock picking tools, making quick work of Maggie's three locks. Before he unlocked the third one, an elderly woman stepped out with her little yappy dog. He pretended to knock on the door. "Maintenance."

"She should be back in a few minutes. Always goes down to the corner shop for coffee and muffins," she said as she walked past him. "Pookie, let's go. I don't have all day, you know. The girls are expecting us."

He watched the older lady enter the elevator, as her voice trailed off. He quickly stepped inside Maggie's apartment, shutting the door. Locking the three deadbolts behind him, he walked around the small crappy abode. Little tchotchkes adorned several shelving units. Kerry thought back to the children's home they grew up in. Having anything of value was a risk. If it was left out in the open, it would be stolen. Anything of importance to him, or others, had to be carried in the state issued backpack.

He balled his hands into fists. Sierra never got the chance to have anything special. If only he had found out earlier who she was. He could've protected her. He could've gotten her out of Sunshine Valley before Pops got his hands on her.

Brought out of his memory, by the first lock clicking open, he had to think fast. He reached into his pocket for the chloroform laced cloth and pulled it from the small plastic baggy. Stepping behind the door, he placed his back up against the wall and made himself as skinny as he could.

Maggie unlocked the last bolt, balancing her coffee between her arm and chest and held the bag of muffins in the other hand as she opened her door. "Ugh," she said as she managed to step into her apartment. With her back to the wall, she used her hip and foot to close the door. She was about to turn around when she felt an arm around her waist. She managed a small scream before a rag covered her nose and mouth. Her coffee and muffins slipped from her hands. The last thought she had was what a mess she would have to clean up.

Kerry laid her down without making a sound. He bolted the door and walked to her small flat-screen TV. He turned it on with the volume high enough to drown out her screams.

He pulled the one dining room chair she had from the small table and placed it in the center of the room. Removing the ropes and gag from the small case, he put them on the floor next to the chair. Kerry moved back to the kitchen and picked up Maggie. He set her in the chair, bracing her with one hand as he tied her in place.

Once she was secured, he stuck a small ball gag in her mouth. If she did scream, it would come out as muffled cries. The TV should hide those. Chase had told him the part each person played in Sierra's death. And although Maggie's part was small compared to the other three, she was equally to blame.

On some level, Kerry felt sympathy for her. She too was victimized by Pops and the system. That didn't excuse her. She could've stopped it. She came before Sierra. All she had to do was tell one person. Instead, she took rewards for her silence and kept the secret. Now it was her time to pay.

CHAPTER TWENTY-SEVEN

Monday morning
Captain Mackey's office

Damien sat in front of Catherine, Captain Mackey's secretary. More like a guard dog, she came with him from the Marines. He remembered once the Captain had said his men were more afraid of her than him. Damien always felt like he was in the principal's office sitting in front of her. The buzzer on Catherine's phone made Damien jump. He saw the smirk on her face before she answered it.

"Yes, Captain?" She nodded. "I will." She hung up the phone and smiled at Damien. "He's ready for you."

"Thank you, Catherine." Damien reached for the door.

"Damien?"

He turned towards her. "Yes?"

"It's good to have you back."

"It's good to be back, Catherine." He winked at her and entered his captain's office.

Captain Gerald Mackey stood facing his window. He watched the traffic as it sped past the building, the Chicago city skyline in the background. He spoke without turning to his Lieutenant. "I love this city. I know it has its problems, like any other, but there is something about Chi-town. It gets in your blood, in your soul. The music, the food, the people." He turned around. His favorite detective stood waiting for permission to sit. He nodded to a chair in front of his desk. "Take a seat."

Damien sat, rubbing his palms on his jeans, before clasping his hands in his lap. His elbows rested on the arms of the chair, and he fought back the urge to let his knee bounce.

Captain Mackey hid a grin as he sat and opened a file on his desk. "Before we get to your case, I need to let you know AD Reynolds isn't very happy you're back."

"I might have heard something," Damien said relaxing into his seat. "Davidson?"

"He told me at the crime scene."

"I figured you would find out. Don't worry about it. I think it's all for show. From what I gather, he doesn't want it to look like you are receiving any kind of special treatment. At least that's my take."

Damien nodded but held his tongue.

"There is someone who wants your head on a platter. Well, yours and Dillon's."

"He's a slug. I'm not worried about Johnson."

"You might want to let your lawyer know he's coming for you. Says you and your girlfriend have a vendetta against him."

"He's an ass. I should've knocked his teeth out instead of breaking his nose."

Captain Mackey laughed. "I would've liked to have seen you two go through that glass window. Makes me think of the WWE matches I take my boys to."

Damien sighed. "I shouldn't have let him get to me." He smirked. "But it was worth it. Cost me a fortune to fix the damn thing."

"I know he's in a lot of trouble. His career is tanking. And although he would like to blame Dillon and you, he did it to himself." The captain leaned forward, placing his elbows on his desk. "Don't let this get around. I'm only telling you so you can be aware of it. He has been under investigation since the Cartel case. All those incidents with Dillon buried him even more. He doesn't know about the investigation."

"He's dirty, isn't he?" Damien squinted at his captain.

Captain Mackey nodded. "Yes. How dirty is yet to be determined."

"Are there others in it with him?"

"I think so. I haven't been told about the others. But from my talks with Director Sherman, I get the impression there are a few others, one other FBI agent, low level. And two other DEA agents."

Damien cocked his head to the side. "Anyone from Division Central?"

Captain Mackey shrugged. "I don't want to believe one of our own is dirty. The FBI is staying tight-lipped about it."

Damien leaned his head to the side. "Is that why AD Reynolds is looking like an ass when it comes to me and my investigations?"

The captain narrowed his eyes at his lieutenant. "I don't know for sure. Like I said earlier, I think his outbursts were for show. He may be wanting to throw whoever he thinks is involved here at Division Central, if anyone is involved, off the scent."

"I wonder if that is why Phillip hasn't mentioned this to Dillon."

"No, I don't think so. He let me know when I called you back in. He plans on telling her when she gets back." He tipped his head down, before meeting Damien's stare. "You are not to say anything. Do you understand? I know it isn't my place to step into your relationship with her, but I'm telling you this so you can be prepared. Phillip will tell her. Am I clear?"

Damien's fingers curled around the arms of the chair. The veins in his forearms pulsed as he squeezed tight. "Fuck. I kept secrets from her before, look at the trouble I got into."

"This is different. She needs to hear it from her boss. Her Director. Not you. I think shit will hit the fan when Johnson finds out he is under investigation. He will direct his anger at you and her. This was a courtesy, Damien. Don't make me regret it."

Damien's nostrils flared.

"Reel in the dragon, son. I'm on your side. The chief knows about this. You have us in your corner. Johnson can't touch you, not professionally anyway."

"He won't touch me in any fashion. I'll make sure of that."

Captain Mackey leaned back in his chair. "This stays here. Between us. I will keep you in the loop as to what happens. When Director Sherman tells Dillon, then you two can talk about anything I tell you. I'm not asking you to keep this secret forever. But the initial information must come from her superior. Are we clear?"

Damien nodded. His right knee bounced up and down. "I understand."

Captain Mackey smiled, trying not to laugh. "You're so mad at this moment your hair is about to catch on fire. It's going to be okay. Keep your eyes open when you're around Johnson. He still has his job, albeit in a limited capacity." He sighed. "Now, let's get to this case." He glanced down at the open file on his desk. "Our killer did a number on his victim." He read through the ME's report. "The Medical Examiner had a heck of job processing the body."

"It was a fucking mess. This guy is pissed. And he took it all out on Chase."

"What do you have so far?"

"Not a hell of a lot. I'm waiting for a shit ton of information. We're looking into the state home where Chase grew up. I'm waiting on the names of other kids who were at the home during the time Chase was there. We will go through that list and run down those residents. After that, we will look at any business associates. I'm still waiting to hear back from Humphry Enterprises' lawyer."

"You think it's personal or business related?"

Damien frowned. "The scene had a lot of rage. Hate. It didn't read as business. It felt personal. Very personal. I think he tortured Chase for information. Then the anger and rage took over. If the killer got what he wanted, he could've killed Chase. But he didn't. He took his time and hurt him. That screams personal."

"Put Officer Baker and Officer Ivansky on the list of business associates. Let them question them, get any background. Keep Davidson and ECD on the list of residents. If you think it's personal, let's concentrate there."

Damien raised an eyebrow at his boss.

"I'm not running your unit." The captain laughed. "I see the look in your eyes."

Damien chuckled. "Not at all, Captain. I was going to put one of the officers on that list. I don't think it will pan out. But I would be remiss not to look at every option. Isn't Officer Baker testing for detective?"

Captain Mackey nodded. "She is. It's the reason I want you to give it to her and Ivansky. I also want you to make her the lead on it. Then watch her. See how she runs with it. I know she has the smarts to pass the test, but I want to see how she will handle this."

Damien shimmied in his seat. "No problem. I think this case will be a good test."

The captain leaned back, laughing.

"What?" Damien asked.

"She makes you nervous. You, of all men."

"She looks at me funny. She's so young." Damien relaxed. "She is one of the best cops I've ever worked with."

"But she looks at you funny?"

Damien chuckled. "Joe used to call it googly eyes. She would blush and couldn't look me in the eye when she first started in the VCU."

"Ah, she had a crush on you. No wonder she makes you so nervous."

"She's past that now. I'm not. But she is."

"She'll do fine. Don't go easy on her, though."

"Never. Is there anything else?" Damien asked.

"I know it's none of my business, but I care about Dillon. And you. How is she? How are you doing?"

Damien's chest tightened. He shrugged. "We're getting past it." He dragged a hand through his hair.

"Talk to me, Damien. It stays here."

"I trust you, Captain. I do. I ...I feel like... I...I don't know."

"Damien, I would have done the same thing. If my wife had been abducted by a hitman, especially the son of the man who killed her family, I wouldn't have hesitated to save her. The FBI was playing politics and Dillon would've been killed had you not gotten to her when you did. Did you break a hell of a lot of rules doing it, yes. But I would've done the same thing."

"Thanks." Damien looked down at his hands. "Do you think your wife would blame you for everything?"

"Ah, you think Dillon blames you for her grandparents' murders?"

"Wouldn't you?"

"Hell yeah. But I would get over it. She will too. It won't take long. She is a smart woman and knows no matter what you would've done, David was going to kill her family to hurt her. They were dead the minute David Allen Parker's father was put to death by the State of Arkansas. David had every intention of hurting Dillon, nothing anyone could've done to stop him."

Damien shook his head. "I hope you're right Captain. I hope she forgives me."

"Maybe it's not her forgiveness you need. Maybe you need to forgive yourself. You made mistakes, Damien. I won't sugarcoat the situation or blow smoke up your ass. But take it from this old Marine, you make decisions affecting people all the time. People you care about. Sometimes shit doesn't go as planned, and you're left with a mess. But at the end of the day, you trusted your gut, and it paid off. You brought Dillon home. Don't second guess yourself."

Damien stood to leave. Sweat beaded down his back, and his skin prickled. He had to get out of there. "If there is nothing else, I'll get going on this investigation." He took a step towards the door.

Captain Mackey stood. "You may go, Lieutenant."

Damien nodded and all but ran out the door.

Captain Mackey moved to stand in front of his window again. He knew bringing back his lieutenant was the best thing for this case and this department. He wasn't sure if it was the best thing for Damien.

CHAPTER TWENTY-EIGHT

Damien stepped into his office and shut the door. Moving to a window a quarter the size of Captain Mackey's, he leaned his head against the cool glass and stared at the top of the parking garage. He closed his eyes and forced his chest to take in a full breath. He knew the captain cared about him, more than a captain and his subordinate. Normally he welcomed his wisdom. But he wasn't ready. He had to block out as much of the last few week's events as he could. He needed to focus on this case.

His head pounded out a beat that bounced around his skull. Damien rubbed his temples stretching to relieve the tension in his shoulders and neck. He turned his focus to the small blank murder board. Going to his desktop computer, he ordered up several prints of the crime scene. Within a few minutes one large picture of Chase dead in the chair, and several smaller ones of the entire scene printed. He pinned the pictures to the board, making a few scribble notes under each one when a knock sounded on his door before it opened.

"Yo, boss," Joe said, entering. "What you doing, trying to hide out? Playing a little touchy-feely with yourself?"

Damien laughed. "You got me. How's Muffin?"

"Still alive. Looks like you know what you're talking about when it comes to pets. The vet said it would help her. He also said she was in great health, even though she looks like a bag of bones, she should live a while longer." Joe took a handful of jelly beans from the jar on Damien's desk. "Where did you learn that anyway?"

"Mrs. C. When Gunner came to live with us, she told me. Said being around Coach will help him heal. She went on about how animals thrive when other pets are brought in. She knows everything." He glanced at his board. "Maybe I should get her help with this case. I don't know shit about this killer."

"How is Mrs. C.? She in town?" Joe popped all the green jelly beans into his mouth.

"Yup." Damien watched his partner. His brow wrinkled. "Why do you do that?"

Joe looked up, his hand stopping halfway to his mouth. "Do what?"

"Eat only one color at a time? When did you start eating them that way? Can't you eat them like normal people?"

"I do eat them like normal people. Everyone else eats them wrong. You have to eat them one color at a time. That way, you get an explosion of flavor. And I started eating them this way sometime after you made lieutenant." He threw a handful of pink ones in his mouth. "I could've waited to see Chase's crime scene again." Joe nodded in the direction of the board.

Damien stepped back and stared at the murder scene. He coked his head from side to side. "What you got? Anything from ECD? Davidson? Or have you been farting around out there?"

"Farting. Farting is so much fun." Joe raised his right butt cheek and farted and giggled.

"Jesus man, did you shit your pants?" Damien fanned his hand in front of his face.

Joe laughed. "It's your mom's food. Got to be the sausage and tomato sauce." He rubbed his belly. "I'm eating the leftovers tonight. She sent enough home with me to feed five people. She must think I'm the most inept person at caring for myself."

"That's the Italian way. She made an extra lasagna for leftovers for everyone." Damien snapped his fingers. "I almost forgot." He opened up the bottom drawer of his desk. "Mrs. C. made these for you and me. This is your container. But you might want to leave it in here. Those vultures out in the pen will gobble them up."

Joe took the container. "Are these fudge brownies?" He lifted the lid and sniffed. "I love these." He took one out an ate half of the square in one bite." He sighed, sinking into his chair. "This is so good," he stuffed the remaining brownie into his mouth.

"She brought over a cake too. Later you can come by and help me eat it."

"You better save me a piece." Joe took the soda can from Damien's hand. He watched as Damien grabbed a second one from the small fridge in the corner of his office. "When did you get a fridge?"

Damien shrugged. "I guess Lieutenant Stevens requested it. He has one in his office. I'll take it. Hopefully, no one will come take it back."

"Hide it."

"Hide it how? It's a big ass square."

"Put a table cloth over it."

"Jesus, how the fuck do you function in the real world?" Damien ducked as Joe threw a wadded-up piece of paper at him.

"You're an ass."

Another knock had both looking towards the door.

Davidson entered taking the vacant seat next to Joe, setting the file folder he carried on the edge of Damien's desk. "Hey are those brownies?" He reached over to the open container.

Joe swatted his hand. "Touch, and you die." His eyes narrowed in on Davidson, daring him to take a brownie.

Detective Davidson laughed and took one. Licking the top before Joe could take it from him.

Damien laughed as Joe cringed. "He got you on that one."

"Man, that's gross." Joe handed the container to Damien. "Lock these in your drawer until it's time to go."

Davidson laughed. "This is how you claim shit in a house full of kids. Those fuckers take all the good snacks if you don't act fast." He moaned as he chewed the brownie. "These are fantastic."

Damien took a sip of his soda. "Mrs. C. made them."

"How is she doing?" Davidson asked. "I haven't seen her since the Christmas party. She has to be the sweetest little old lady ever."

Damien smiled. "She is, and she is doing great. Making sure I'm okay while Dillon is still at the farm. Evidently, I can't care for myself anymore. At least, according to my mother and Mrs. C."

"Nah, that's moms. It's what they do." Davidson swallowed the last of his brownie. "Okay, you ready for an update on the case?"

Damien leaned back in his chair. "You got something? Besides the dumbass tie you're wearing?"

Joe peered over at Davidson. "That is an ugly tie. Who bought it for you?"

"Shit, wait till you have kids. This is what you'll get for Father's Day. And if you don't wear it, they cry. Plus wearing stuff like this throws people off when you're questioning them. Makes it easier to put them at ease. As for the case...I think we are about to go down a rabbit hole."

He opened the folder he brought with him. "First, I spoke with Humphry's girlfriend this morning. She's a mess and doesn't know anything. Second, Detective Travis in ECD managed to get a list of all the residents during the time Chase Humphry was at Sunshine Valley. The

ADA pulled it for him since it was directly related to the case. Not sure what we have to do to get other names but this is a start. There was a total of 155 kids there during the same time our victim was there. Not all were there for the whole time, but that's how many Chase may have come in contact with."

"That's a lot of names, he was only there for what, two years?" Damien asked.

Davidson nodded. "Actually, three years, from the ages of fifteen to eighteen. Then he left for college. There are roughly forty to fifty full-time residents now. They stay at least six months. If a kid is there that long, they're more than likely staying." He handed an aerial picture of the grounds to Damien. "I pulled this off the Internet. You can see the grounds have a main house and two barrack-like buildings. According to the website, twenty boys and twenty girls live in the barracks. The main house has several bedrooms, which are reserved for the non-permanent residents.

"If you look at the website, it looks like a nice place. The kids learn about gardening and shit like that. They have classes and workshops. There is a mechanics garage allowing them to learn about small engines. You know, stuff to keep the kids busy and out of trouble."

Damien flipped through the photos Davidson had given him. "Did you get a bunch of names for business associates as well?"

Davidson nodded as he took a handful of jelly beans. "About twenty-five, not counting everyone in the company."

"Let's start small, then branch out as we need to." Damien rubbed the sides of his head. "Give me the list of names from the business end. I've been instructed to give Officer Baker those." He paused glancing between the two detectives. "She's going to be taking the next detectives test. Captain wants her to take the lead on those names."

"I like that. Less for me to do." Davidson shuffled the papers in the file. "Here," he said, handing the list to Damien. "I'm not seeing anything leading me to think this is some kind of bad business deal."

"I'm not either." Joe pointed to the pictures on the murder board. "Chase was tortured because of something he did, didn't do, or knew about."

"I agree. But we still need to check out everything. This will be good for Baker." Damien set the paper on his desk. "What else you got?" he asked Davidson.

Thumbing through his file, he shrugged. "Not a bunch yet. I've got Travis running a background check on the names from the home. He set up some kind of computer program to pull in their information. Well, the new kid, Detective Todd did it."

Joe slapped his leg. "I'm telling you, between Travis and Todd, those two can bring down the country if they wanted to."

"No, shit. Todd can write a program for anything. The kid's brain is like a computer. And you should see him and Detective Travis when they speak geek. You know they have boners."

Joe and Damien laughed.

"I don't even know if they're dating anyone. I never see them with women." Davidson adjusted his tie. Staring at the ugly black cat with big yellow sunglasses.

"I bet they're dating supermodels." Joe threw his empty soda can into the trash bin.

"Enough about their dating habits. Once you get the backgrounds, divide up the names between you, Jenkins, and Joe." Damien scoffed at Joe's huff. "You have to do work once in a while."

Joe sank in the chair. "Damn, I hope most of these people are dead."

"I can't believe you said that." Davidson shook his head.

"You know you do, too. Man...what else we got going?"

Damien leaned back in his chair, placing his hands on the top of his head. "At some point, we need to go to Sunshine Valley."

"Let's do it tomorrow. Leave early and catch ole Shamus by surprise. See how he reacts to the news of Chase's death."

"He probably already knows he's dead," Davidson said.

"The news has only been given limited details of Chase Humphry's death. He won't know he was murdered until we tell him." Damien glanced at his watch and the clock wall. Ten a.m. "Let's go now." He stood and grabbed his jacket.

Joe sulked. "I knew you were going to make us go down there. Grab my brownies. If I got to ride to The Dunes now, I want some comfort food. Plus, your buying lunch."

Damien handed him the container of brownies, and grabbed the list of business associates for Officer Baker, and followed Joe and Davidson out into the almost empty pen. Jenkins sat at his desk, writing a report. A quick glance at the case board showed all his detectives out in the field. He scanned the area but didn't see Baker. "Jenkins, have you seen Officer Baker recently?"

Jenkins looked up and shook his head. "Not this morning, no."

Damien handed the sheet to Davidson. "You're in charge till I get back. You know what to do on this case. Tell Baker what she needs to do, and tell her Ivansky is working with her on this. Also, tell her she is lead on it, as well."

Davidson saluted Damien. "You got it, boss." He turned towards his desk and his partner Jenkins. "You hear that, Jenks? I'm in charge. You're buying lunch."

"Fuck you, Davidson."

Damien walked out, followed by Joe. "C'mon, pouty face. This gets us out of here. There's a great seafood place at The Dunes. We'll get lunch after we talk to Shamus MacDougal."

"That's the only good part of this little trip. It's going to be damn cold down there."

"It's fucking Illinois, it's cold everywhere."

CHAPTER TWENTY-NINE

Late Monday morning

Maggie's head hurt. She squeezed her eyes tight. The haze surrounding her brain began to fade. She tried swallowing but something in her mouth kept her from doing it. Her body shook uncontrollably as her hands clenched into fists then unclenched. "No, no, no, this isn't happening. Oh my gosh, what's happening?" The mantra played over and over in her head. She whimpered struggling against her restraints.

Maggie's gaze darted around the room. She realized she was in her home, but that brought little comfort. She hyperventilated as her chest tightened and she had the sensation of not being able to get enough oxygen. Vomit hovered at the back of her throat. Not wanting to choke she concentrated on the sound of her breaths, slowing her pulse down. The last thing she remembered was getting her coffee earlier that morning. She tried to focus on the clock sitting on her TV stand. She blinked, squinting at it but she couldn't make out the time.

Kerry walked out of the bathroom, whistling. "Well, nice of you to wake up, Maggie."

She pushed back against the chair. Her eyes widened as the stranger came closer to her.

Kerry smiled at her. "I'm sure you don't remember me. Chase didn't either." He walked over to his case and removed a straight edge razor and small self-locking forceps. When he turned towards her, Maggie's eyes bulged as she shook, sinking into the back of the chair. "I will give you the courtesy of explaining who I am and why I'm here."

He squatted in front of her. "My name is Kerry. Kerry Landon. I spent about two years at Sunshine Valley." He giggled. "I see you remember the place. Kind of hard to forget it, huh?" He opened the straight edge razor and dragged the blade across the meaty part of her thigh. She tried to scream, but it came out as a muffled howl. Kerry sneered at her. "Nice and sharp."

Tears flooded her eyes. Maggie sniffled as snot dripped from her nose. Her head shook, her eyes pleaded with him.

"I know what Pops did to you. I am sorry you suffered. I promise, if it is any consolation, Pops will suffer greatly for what he did to you and the other

girls at that house of horrors. But, Maggie, you are here for your own actions."

Maggie squirmed against her restraints.

"No point in trying to argue with me, or convince me otherwise. See, Maggie, you had the opportunity to tell someone about Pops. When he started to hurt little Sierra, you did nothing." He dragged the blade across her other thigh.

Maggie's garbled scream caused her body to tremble.

"You had the chance to help her. You chose not to. And, in exchange for your silence, Pops left you alone." Kerry stood; he dragged the blade across her right forearm in three quick slashes. He watched as the tears flowed down her cheeks. Drops spattered on her blouse and chest.

"You were rewarded while Sierra suffered. Then, after her death, you still said nothing. You knew what he continued to do to other girls. Yet, you chose to say and do nothing." Kerry dragged the edge of the blade across her left forearm, slicing it to the bone. Blood poured from the open wound.

Maggie whimpered gagging on the snot filling her nasal passage trickling down the back of her throat. Unable to expel the sticky phlegm, she had to swallow it. At one point, the thick mucus felt as if it stuck in her throat. Her body shook as a cold chill swept over her.

"Hmm. The last cut was a little deep. So, listen," he waited for her to look at him. "Hey, Maggie?" He slapped her face.

She lifted her head, sweat beaded along her hairline.

"These are simple, yes or no answers. If you answer them, I will show you mercy and let you live. Do you understand?"

She nodded. Her head dropping back down to her chest.

"Did Pops ever bring any outside men into the fold?"

She shook her head.

"Is there a special room in the main house where he took the girls?"

She nodded. Maggie stared at him.

Kerry saw the fatigue wanting to take over. "Maggie, I need some more answers from you. I told you I would show you mercy, but I need you to answer my questions, okay?"

Maggie nodded.

He reached out and lifted her face. He caressed her cheek. "I am sorry Pops hurt you. I will make him pay." Kerry released the gag on one side.

She swallowed but made no attempt to scream.

"I need to know somethings. Tell me about Sierra and Pops?"

She tried to speak, but her raw throat caused her to cough spewing droplets of saliva. "I know he took a special liking to Sierra."

Kerry gritted his teeth. "Tell me."

Maggie had to slow her breathing as the threat of vomit tickled the back of her throat. "He took her to the room in the basement. Almost every day."

"How did he keep everyone quiet? Surely they knew what he was doing."

Maggie nodded. "None of the kids knew. Except those of us he hurt. I think some of the staff knew, but you have to understand. If you said anything, you disappeared."

Kerry's nostrils flared. "I don't understand. Who disappeared?"

"Other kids. Mostly girls. I think all girls. One staff lady who questioned Shamus once. He made it look like she was stealing. I overheard the conversation." Maggie inhaled deeply breathing out slowly. "I was listening at the door of his office. He threatened if she said anything, he would make sure she went to prison for theft and a bunch of other charges. The next day she was gone."

"Do you know what happened to her?"

"No. We all assumed she quit." Maggie stared at the man before her. She didn't recognize him.

"Maggie, you have to know something else. How does Pops hide the girls' information? How is it no one has found out what he's doing?"

Maggie shook her head. "I'm not sure. I was a kid. I don't know. But I think someone higher up knew."

"Higher up?"

"There was always this suit who came to the home. He never touched the girls. But he made Shamus nervous."

"Why didn't you say anything to someone?" Kerry asked.

Her eyes filled with tears. "I did. No one listened. Then I noticed girls going missing. I kept my mouth shut after that. I turned fourteen, and the abuse stopped. Shamus gave me special privileges. It kept me sane in there." She glanced up. "You have to believe me. I didn't mean for anything to happen to Sierra."

"I believe you, Maggie." He smiled at her. He watched as Maggie's eyes filled with a glimmer of hope. Kerry ran his fingers through her long hair. Brushing it out of her face. "But you had a chance, and had you said something, Sierra would still be here." He clasped the forceps in his left hand. He used his right to squeeze open her mouth. Using the forceps, he grabbed her

tongue. "All you had to do was say something. Tell someone. And you might have saved her."

The whites of Maggie's eyes glistened. What little color had filled her cheeks, drained.

Kerry took a half step to his right side. His nostrils flared, as he pulled her tongue out of her mouth. He bent down and placed his mouth next to her ear. "I said I would show you mercy and let you live," he slowly dragged the razor across the meaty part of the back of her tongue, slicing it in half, "I lied."

CHAPTER THIRTY

Joe grabbed his phone from the middle console, glancing around the road leading up to the home. "Not a bad area. Seems semi-isolated. Neighbors aren't too close," he said as he searched the Internet on his phone.

Damien drove through the gates of Sunshine Valley. He parked under the massive porte-cochère. "Wow, some entrance for a state home."

Joe looked up. "According to this, this place was donated by the Chandler family back in the 1970s. They had adopted several children and made provisions for this place to run as a home for kids. Most of the monies used to run this facility comes from a trust the estate established."

"Does it say anything about Shamus?"

"Not much. Other than he was once a renowned psychologist who specialized in working with kids. He was hired on in the early nineties after the last administrator retired."

Damien read through an email from Detective Travis. "I asked ECD to send me what they had on Shamus MacDougal. Originally from Scotland, he became famous for working with some of Hollywood's troubled youth. He had several complaints against him for inappropriate behavior with female patients."

"How the fuck did this guy get this job then?" Joe asked as he looked out the window at the front door of the mansion. "We got eyes on us."

Damien leaned forward glancing in the same direction as Joe. "Good. Let them wonder who we are." He went back to reading the email. "It seems all the complaints were dropped. Either by the parents or the girls recanted their stories. In an interview, Shamus said the types of teens he deals with have deep issues, and he holds no animosity towards the girls. He wants to help them."

He quickly scanned the rest of the file. "It'd be nice if we could get those files." Damien tapped out a quick message. "I'm going to have ECD check on it." He turned off the engine. "Let's go meet this Scotsman."

They exited the vehicle. About to ring the bell, the front door flew open.

"Who are you?" A boy about fifteen stood with his arms crossed.

"We're detectives. Who are you?" Damien asked.

"I'm Rondel. Rondel Spears. What are you detecting?"

"Why aren't you in school, Rondel?" Joe asked, meeting the young man's stare.

"I got here today. I start school tomorrow."

"Is Shamus MacDougal here?" Damien leaned towards the young boy. "This is official police business."

The boy's eyes widened then narrowed. "You didn't say you were the police."

"Well, I'm saying it now. We need to speak to Shamus or whoever is in charge. Now. Please." Damien said as he rested his hand on his weapon.

The boy was unmoved. "I need to see your IDs before I let you in."

Joe smirked at Damien. "He's a smart kid."

Damien raised an eyebrow at him. "Not smart enough to ask us for those before he opened the door to two strangers." He reached for his ID in his front pocket.

Rondel stepped back. His early bravado gone at the realization of his mistake.

Damien and Joe showed their IDs and hid their laughs when the boy finally breathed.

"Go get whoever is in charge." Damien stepped into the spacious entryway, followed by Joe.

Rondel ran from the room. "Pops, the police are here."

"Nice place." Joe stepped to the side and peered around a corner. The room had been made into some kind of art studio. Several unfinished drawings, paintings, and pottery lay scattered about shelving units. Another hallway jutted off, but Joe didn't follow it.

Damien glanced up the double curved stairway. The left side of the rounded banister drew the eye upward. A large balcony area continued to lead the eye to the far wall adorned with pictures of the prior estate owner's family. As his view followed along the opposite stairway, smaller pictures of some of the residents adorned the lower half of the wall.

"As nice as this place looks, I don't think it's a very nice place to live," Joe said.

Damien started to respond when a tall, slender man approached them.

"May I help you, detectives? I'm Shamus MacDougal. I run this facility." He held out his hand.

Smiling, Damien shook it. He was struck by the contrasting light blue eyes with medium brown hair color. He knew Shamus MacDougal was in his early sixties, but he looked barely fifty. And for some reason Damien expected a short red-headed freckled man. "I'm Lieutenant Kaine and this is Detective Hagan, we're with the Vicious Crimes Unit out of Chicago."

Shamus MacDougal took a small step backward. "I'm not sure why Chicago cops would need to speak with me." He stuck his hands in his front pants pockets.

Damien heard some noise above and glanced up to see a few young children coming down the stairs with an older lady leading the way. "We need to speak with you about a sensitive matter. Is there a private office we can go to?"

Shamus offered the two men a flash of a smile. "I suppose. Martha?" he called out to the older woman with the kids.

"Yes, Mr. MacDougal?"

"I'll need some privacy. I'll be in my office."

"I'll cover everything." Martha scooted the train of kids off down another hallway.

"Please, follow me." Shamus led the men through the kitchen and up a small flight of stairs located at the back of the house. At a small landing, Shamus turned to the right and led them into a cozy office. Two chairs faced a small love seat, and a large desk sat in front of a window overlooking the back of the property. "Have a seat," said Shamus as he sat on the loveseat.

"Thank you for seeing us. Can you tell me about your relationship with Chase Humphry?" Damien watched as Shamus' eyes widened for a split second before he recovered.

Shamus readied himself on the sofa. "He used to be a resident here. One of the few who seem to have made something of themselves." He tugged on the sleeves of his shirt. Picking a small piece of lent from his chest. "He recently gave a rather large donation to the home. That's about all I have to offer."

Damien scrutinized the Scot. "Are you aware Mr. Humphry was murdered the other night?" He noticed Shamus' skin flushed.

Shamus wiped his brow. "I—I hadn't heard. Can you tell me anything?" His sentence came out choppy.

"It's an active investigation. We can't give you any details. I can tell you it seems to be someone with a possible grudge. Can you tell me about the other children who might have been here when Chase was a resident?"

Shamus opened and closed his fists, trying to alleviate the tingling in his fingers. "It's public record who was here. I would have to check with our lawyer to make sure I wouldn't be violating any privacy issues. But I can tell you I don't remember there being anyone Chase had a problem with. I mean no one sticks out in my head." He glanced between the two men in front of him.

"You don't remember any kind of incident which may have led to Chase and another kid not getting along? Even the smallest incident could be important."

Shamus shook his head. "No. Nothing comes to mind."

"Can you tell us what kind of kid Chase was?" Damien asked as he scribbled in the little notebook he had removed from his back pocket.

The Scotsman leaned back, crossing his legs. "Chase was your typical kid. I don't think I would be violating anything telling you this. Chase came from a severely broken home. His father was murdered in a drug deal, and his mother went to prison shortly thereafter. He had a hard time. Didn't have any other relatives. Came here. He was your typical teen boy."

"What do you mean?" Joe asked.

Shamus shrugged. "You know."

"No, I don't. Explain it to me," Joe said.

"C'mon. We were all teen boys at one time. Girls were more important than anything else." He grinned at Joe. "You sound like an Irishman. Where do you hale from?"

"Dublin. Can you elaborate on Chase? Please." Joe flashed him a brilliant smile.

"All I meant by it was Chase came from not the greatest of circumstances. He did well in school." Shamus walked to his filing cabinet behind his desk. "I'm sure it would be okay for me to let you look at his school records. Or my copies at least." He dug through a file until he found what he was looking for. He glanced inside before walking back to the sofa. "Here," he said, handing the file over. "Chase received good grades. I think he planned to do something different with his life from the start."

Damien looked through the file. "Do you guys keep any kind of discipline files?"

"Not sure I understand what you're asking," Shamus said frowning.

"Do the kids get written up if they mess-up too many times, or if they step out of line? You must have a system in place for discipline." Damien nodded to Joe. "Can't imagine there would be this many teen boys in one place and not have some discipline problems."

"Sure. If the children don't do their chores or their school work, they lose privileges," Shamus said.

"What kind of privileges?" Damien asked.

"Working out in the shop for one. Most of the young men love working in there. Art classes or gym time. You get the drift."

"Could we see the grounds?" Joe asked. "I would love to see what the living conditions look like."

Shamus sat up straight. "I would have to get permission from our attorney before I could let you walk around. Unless you have a warrant."

"No. I didn't realize we needed one," Damien said.

Shamus rose. "I think it would be best if you guys returned after I got clarification from the home's attorney."

"Who is the attorney?" Damien asked.

Shamus retrieved a business card from his desk drawer. "Martin Escobar." He handed the card to Damien. "He has been the attorney for the estate since before I was hired. You can ask him for relevant records you may need."

Damien nodded as he and Joe followed the man back to the front door. He waited until Shamus MacDougal turned towards them. "When did you take over the residence?"

"In 1994. I left a very lucrative practice in Hollywood to come here." He lifted his chin.

"Why would you leave so much money and prestige on the table to come run a state home in Illinois?" Damien asked.

"I thought I could make a difference here. I had become bored with the Hollywood elite, and I wanted to change the lives of less fortunate kids," Shamus said.

"Mr. MacDougal, can you tell us about the incidents in California?"

Damien asked.

Shamus MacDougal flinched back with an audible intake of breath. "What are you implying?"

Damien glanced at Joe. "I don't think I implied anything. I was simply wondering if you could tell us about those charges some of your former patients leveled against you."

"I don't like the tone you're taking with me. It feels very accusatory." Shamus crossed his arms.

"You had three accusations of unwanted sexual encounters with young girls you were counseling. I have read about the case. I thought you might like to expound on it for us. Give us the information that isn't in the reports."

"No. You are accusing me of misbehavior. I haven't had any complaints against me here at this home."

Joe noticed movement out of the corner of his eye. The lady from earlier stood at the top of the stairs. When Joe caught her eye, she nodded at him, before disappearing around the corner. Joe smiled at Shamus. "Mr. MacDougal, we aren't accusing you of anything. We are merely trying to see if there is a connection between Chase's murder and this home. Surely you would want to know if there was any danger to any other residents or employees?"

"I don't understand. Why would there be any danger to employees of this home? I thought you said it looked like Chase was murdered by someone he knew?"

"Chase was murdered in a way which leads us to suspect someone was settling a score. We hope it wasn't anything that might have occurred while Chase was here," Damien said. "Or, that could mean the killer wasn't done. We're trying to get ahead of the situation. Surely you can appreciate what we are doing." He nodded in Joe's direction. "Thank you for your time, Mr. MacDougal." He handed a card to Shamus. "Once you get clearance, we would like to come back and have that tour."

Joe led the way out the door. "You're not seriously going to wait for MacDougal to get clearance for us to have a tour, are you?"

"Not on your life. I'm going to call the lawyer myself. Let him know we need a tour. I think Shamus is not very excited about us snooping around the property."

"I can't imagine a lawyer for the estate would want anything like a murder to ruin the reputation of the home." Entering the vehicle, Joe noticed Martha standing at the edge of the building. "Hey drive slowly and stop in front of her." He pointed to the older woman.

"Why?" Damien asked, even though he followed Joe's instruction.

Lowering the window, Joe nodded to the woman. She didn't say a word but handed him a note, then turned and walked away, back to the gaggle of kids playing on an adjacent playground. Joe opened the carefully folded note.

"What did she give you?" Damien asked as he pulled down the semicircular drive to the main road.

Joe raised an eyebrow at his partner. "It has three names on it."

Damien pulled onto the main highway. "What are the names?"

"Nancy Milligan, Maggie Newsome, and Clara Rogers." Joe stared at the names. "Why would she hand us this?" he waved the note in the air. "She's obviously too scared to talk to us."

"You got to wonder why." Damien used his Bluetooth to call Detective Travis back at ECD.

"Detective Todd, ECD."

"Hey it's Damien, where's Travis?"

"He stepped out for a second. Can I help you with something?"

"Joe is going to text you three names. Find out everything you can on these women. If there are sealed records, get them unsealed. Contact ADA Flowers to help you."

"You got it, Lieutenant. Anything else?" Detective Todd's voice trailed off as a door in the background opened and closed.

"Did you guys get anywhere on the surveillance at Humphry's business?"

"Nothing but static Thursday night. Looks like the cameras went down for about thirty minutes."

"I doubt that's a coincidence. What about Chase's home? Anything from the front gate, or anyone leaving by bike, motorcycle, or anything else?"

"Nothing much. The only thing we have is at the back of the property is a maintenance and construction entrance. There are cameras, but they aren't working. Usually it is locked up tight, but at some point during the weekend Chase was murdered, the locks had been cut. I bet that's how your killer got in and out."

"Crap. Okay. There's nothing else. Get on those names as quickly as you can. Thanks, Detective Todd." Damien was about to hang up. "Hey, actually there is one more thing."

"Sure Lieutenant, what do you need?"

"See if you can find out what happens to the trust set up to run Sunshine Valley if the home is closed. The family set it up as a home for kids, but there must be a provision if something happens and the State closes the place."

"I will look into it. See what I can find."

"Thanks, Detective." Damien disconnected the call. "This case is kicking our butt."

"Great. We got nothing." Joe texted the names. He folded the note and put it in his pocket. "You owe me lunch."

Damien rolled his eyes. "You're always fucking hungry."

"So?"

"So? So—you're going to get fat." Damien followed a road off the main highway. The sign said the seafood restaurant was two miles ahead.

Joe leaned his head back. "I don't get fat. I have a very active metabolism."

"You have a very active and delusional imagination."

CHAPTER THIRTY-ONE

Monday evening at the farm

Dillon stared at the boxes in the living room, which Taylor had obsessively put into groups: donation, keep, and after remodel. The biggest portion in the keep section. "I'm going to have to go back through those boxes."

"Go through what boxes?" Taylor asked, entering the living room. She plopped down on the sofa, setting her phone next to her, and grabbed Coach from the end, snuggling him in her arms.

Dillon pointed at the keep section. "Those. I can't keep all that stuff."

"You can for now. Put it in storage. And when you aren't so attached, you will be able to whittle it down. But you don't need to do it right now. You kept all those things because they mean something to you. That's what you're supposed to do." Taylor's phone pinged. She lifted it glancing at the screen. She froze, rooted to the sofa. She gripped Coach tighter in her arms, causing a small squeak to bubble out of him.

Dillon's eyebrows drew together. "What's going on?" she asked, waiting for an answer. "Hello? Taylor?"

Taylor looked up at her friend but looked right through her. "Huh?"

Dillon noticed the glassy mirrored look in her eyes. "Taylor? What the hell is going on?"

"I—I don't know how to explain it." She scratched Coach's head. "No one knows."

Walking over to the sofa, Dillon sat crisscross on the end once occupied by the fat cat. "No one knows what?" Again, no answer. "Taylor, I have seen your reaction to some texts the last few days. You glance at your phone and the color in your cheeks fades away, you shake, you act like nothing is going on, but I know something isn't right. Come clean."

"It's my problem. No one else's."

"Don't give me that shit. You made me tell you all my secrets and my problems, even when I didn't like you."

Taylor giggled. "There was never a time you didn't like me, bitch."

"Ha. I had you fooled. Now tell me what the hell is going on."

Taylor kissed Coach's nose and set him on the floor. She let out a ragged breath and picked up her phone. Tapping on it, she handed it to Dillon. "I guess it would be easier to let you read the texts."

Dillon's forehead wrinkled. She took the phone from Taylor's hand. As she read through a series of texts, rants actually. It didn't take a rocket scientist to see the downward spiral the correspondence was starting to take. She scrolled through until she got to the end. Looking up, her eyebrow raised, "Who is this?"

Taylor's lips pressed together in a slight grimace. Her gaze ping-ponged between Dillon and Gunner who laid on the floor at her feet.

"Taylor? Who is this?"

Taylor opened her mouth to respond, immediately closing it. She squeezed her eyes shut and sighed. "Joe doesn't know any of this. No one does."

"I'm not going to say anything. Unless your life is in danger. Otherwise, I won't tell anyone, not even Damien."

Taylor sighed as she turned and put her back against the arm of the sofa and faced her friend. Her best friend. "My family has some archaic traditions."

"Archaic?" Dillon asked.

Nodding Taylor continued. "My father is of Indian descent. He was born here, like third generation too, but he held the traditions of his relatives from India more staunchly than his parents ever did." Taylor smiled. "My grandparents were wonderful. They told me I could be whatever I wanted, do whatever I wanted, marry whoever I wanted."

"I'm guessing, your father wasn't like that."

She shook her head. "Not in the least. My mother was from the south. Deep South. When she met my father, she was in college, and he was older than her. He had a lot of money." Taylor looked up. "A lot. And because of that, my mother went along with whatever my father said. My brother got off easy. He was older than me by five years. He wasn't held to the same standard my father held me to."

"Your father expected you to marry someone he picked out for you?"

"Pretty much right out of high school. But I got a scholarship to college. Best thing to ever happen to me. It paid for everything. So, I left."

Dillon leaned her head to the side. "You left? Like in the middle of the night?"

Taylor laughed. "Almost. I didn't tell my parents about my scholarship. I was eighteen, I didn't need their permission. I had money in my account. Enough I wouldn't have to work for a while. I transferred everything into another account. And when my parents were out of the house, I packed everything into my car and drove away."

Coach jumped onto Dillon's lap, maneuvering himself until he was in the right position before settling down. "Couldn't he track you via the car?"

"The title was in my name; the insurance was in theirs. Once I got outside Atlanta, I traded it for an older model truck from this old mechanic. I didn't know what to do, so I told him the truth. He checked the car and saw that it wasn't stolen and the papers were intact, so he did an even swap for his old ford. And promised he wouldn't tell my parents if they ever came asking. He said he could get rid of it and get the money for it. He helped me get some tags in my new name and register the car. He helped get me a new driver's license. I stayed with him and his wife for about a week.

"I'm pretty sure this guy was into stolen cars, but he was a good man. He told me what I needed to do when I got to school to keep my scholarships and use my new name. Even gave me papers showing my name change. I never would've been able to escape had it not been for them." She wiped the tears from her cheeks.

"What's your real name?"

"Taylor is my real name. Reese..." She trailed off.

"Reese was their name, wasn't it?"

She nodded. "That's why it was easy to get the paperwork done. It was the woman's maiden name. Harris was her husband, he sold my car, that was all done on the up and up. That way, he didn't get in any trouble. He had the title nothing illegal about that sale. But when I drove away from there a week later, I was Taylor Reese. Taylor Hunjan died that day."

"Whatever happened to Harris and his wife?"

"They're still alive. They moved to Florida to be near their grandkids. They don't contact me. I contact them, and they respond with a quick note. I do it for their protection."

Dillon sat quietly for a few moments. She watched as Taylor fidgeted with her hands in her lap. Her shoulder's drooped as if she carried a heavy weight on them. "This Adnon dude, is he the guy you were supposed to marry?"

Taylor shook her head. "No."

"I don't understand."

"That guy didn't care. He moved on, married another girl."

"Who is the guy texting you?"

Taylor lifted her eyes. "He's my brother."

Dillon pushed out a harsh breath. "Oh shit."

"I don't know how he found me."

"The news reports."

"What news...oh shit! I never even considered that." Taylor pulled her knees up to her chest and buried her face. She rocked slightly as she tried to catch her breath. "Oh man, oh man, oh man..."

"Hey, don't worry."

"Don't worry?" she asked with wide eyes. "Are you kidding me?" Taylor's stomach hardened. She gulped in gasps of air. "How can you say, don't worry? He knows where I am. Probably where I work and live."

"Taylor."

Taylor continued to rock with her head buried between her knees. "This isn't good. This isn't good." Her breathing was no longer gasps, but full on pants.

"Taylor."

Taylor's head snapped up. Her mantra stopped mid-sentence.

"I can help you. But we need to tell Joe and Damien."

Taylor's head swiveled from side to side, almost spinning completely around. "No way. Uh-huh. No."

"Yes."

"Are you fucking kidding me? I knew I shouldn't have said anything." She swung her legs over the side of the sofa and held her head in her hands.

The movement startled Coach. He jumped down hissing and scowling as he made his way to the fireplace.

"Taylor." Dillon reached out, touching her shoulder. "Taylor, you know we have to do this. Joe isn't going to judge you. He isn't going to leave you. He loves you and will protect you. But we need to let your work know, they need to know this guy might show up."

Taylor shook her head as she stood and paced. "No. They have a case going on. He doesn't need the distraction."

Dillon rose and stood in front of her friend. She placed her hands on her shoulders. "Listen to me. Do you have any idea why he would be so concerned now? Has something happened to make him want to find you now?"

Taylor's shoulders sagged. "I haven't looked up my family since the day I left Georgia. I never checked on them, I never wanted to know anything about them."

"Okay. But something must have happened. Were you close to your brother?"

"Not really. He was five years older than me. He was in college when I was in high school. By the time I left for college, he was working in New York City. He came home occasionally for holidays."

Dillon's brow furrowed. "That doesn't make sense. Why would he text you—those texts? You can see he is furious. He threatens to make you pay. He is blaming you for something. Do you have any idea what it is?"

"No! I told you. I don't know!" Taylor stood and tried to leave the room.

Dillon wrapped her arms around her. "It's okay. It will be okay. I know you're scared. But let's take a deep breath. Let me get my laptop. I still have access to the FBI database. Let's do some research and see if we get some answers."

Taylor nodded into her shoulder, but she didn't say anything. When Dillon tried to pull away, she held on tighter.

Dillon let her friend hold onto her. Taylor's body trembled. "Hey," Dillon said as she lifted her friends face. "Look at me."

Taylor glanced up.

"I promise. We'll get ahead of this guy. We'll find out what is going on. Don't act out of fear. Once we have all the facts, we will sit down together with Damien and Joe, and we will come up with a game plan, okay?"

Taylor barely nodded.

"Do you trust me?"

"Yeah. Yeah, I do."

"Okay, then. Let me get my computer." She glanced at her watch. "You get us a couple glasses of wine. Are you hungry? It's almost dinner time."

Taylor laughed at Coach and Gunner. Both sat up from their perch in front of the fireplace at the word dinner. "I could eat. And judging by their reaction, they're hungry too." She walked into the kitchen. "C'mon you two. I'll get you fed first."

The cat and dog ran past her. They both spun around in the kitchen. Coach meowed while Gunner whimpered nudging his bowl.

Taylor fed the pets. "What are you hungry for?"

Dillon set her computer on the table. "Something easy. Don't we have leftover chili?"

"Tons. I froze it so it wouldn't go bad." Taylor set to work getting some warmed up in a container. Within minutes she had two bowls filled. Both she and Dillon added corn chips, sour cream, and cheese before sitting down at the table with two beers instead of wine.

Dillon logged into the FBI database and searched Taylor's parent's names and last known addresses. "It will take a moment for it to generate a file on them. This program scans everywhere and everything for any information. I'll do a deeper search once this is done. Once I go deeper, it will register on the system. I want to see if we can get what we need here first." She took a bite of her chili. "We can have Damien run a deeper search. Where no one will know what we are doing."

Taylor raised an eyebrow at her. "You're so quick to go off the grid these days."

"Haha. Don't tell Damien."

They ate in silence for a few minutes. The cat and dog stared at them, waiting for scraps.

Dillon checked her computer, her spoon stopped midway to her mouth. "Umm..."

Taylor's spoon clanked against her bowl. "Umm—what? That doesn't sound good."

"I might have an idea what is making your brother so irate." She turned her computer towards Taylor, who sat next to her.

The screen showed several local articles about her parents. It mentioned Taylor and her disappearance on her way to college years ago. But it was the last article that caught Taylor's eyes. Her gaze shifted from the computer to Dillon and back again. "Oh, no!"

"Mhmm."

"He blames me. But I didn't have anything to do with what my mother did. Our mother."

"He wants to place the blame on someone. Was your father abusive?"

"I never saw marks on my mother's face. But he was controlling. My mother had a job, but he took her to and from work. He went with her to the store. He pretty much shadowed her. He did it to me too, but I was involved in school stuff, giving me a little more freedom." Taylor sat back. "I remember one conversation before I graduated from high school. It was one of the rare times, my mother and I got some time alone. I had to go for my annual girly appointment. We were in the car. She had said my appointment was like at ten. We left and went to breakfast."

"Could you guys not even spend time alone together?"

"It was very rare. My father was always with us. This particular time, she told me she lied to father. My appointment wasn't until later. We spent the morning at a café talking. It was one of the last times we spent time like that together. My mother told me she would protect me, but there was only so much she could do." Taylor sighed. "The conversation felt cryptic. Like my mother was telling me to go, to make a life for myself. But not really saying it. Looking back over the years, I know my mother wanted more for me than what she had. Granted, she had money, but she was trapped. I see that now."

"Well, it sounds like she had enough and took matters into her own hands." Dillon read through one of the articles. She pointed towards the screen. "Look, it says the last few years she was in the hospital for broken bones. She always said it was accidents, but it looks like he was abusing her more and more."

Taylor read on. "I had no idea." Tears began to flow down her face. "I should've helped her."

"No, no, no! You are not going down that road. You wouldn't have been able to do anything."

Taylor walked into the kitchen. She needed to process this. She was flooded with emotions. The loss of her parents. But more than that, the way they died. "I can't imagine what my mother was going through. I'm heartbroken." She leaned against the counter. She couldn't hold back the sobs as they flooded out.

Dillon came to her and wrapped her arms around her. "I know that loss. It's overwhelming." She hugged her. Taylor shuddered in her arms. "But hear me. This isn't your fault. Mourn the loss of your parents. As bad as your father was, he was still your father. Your mother did what she had to do."

"All those years, I thought my mother was weak for not standing up to my father, or doing what she wanted. Not letting him control her every movement. I now realize she did everything for me. She gave me as much freedom as she could by taking the brunt for me."

"It's clear how much she loved you."

Taylor stepped back and grabbed the rag the sat on the counter. She wiped her face and blew her nose. "She killed herself. She could've faced the courts. She wouldn't have been given a long sentence, if any." Taylor sunk to the floor, leaning her back against the cabinets. "I know I didn't speak to them anymore, but I never wanted anything to happen to them. Especially my mother."

"Your mother shot your father. From the note she left and from what I could gather from the articles, your father had beat her pretty badly. She didn't want to face a trial or the shame of what she allowed him to do to her." Dillon sank down next Taylor as she spoke. "I'm sure she felt some remorse for not helping you more."

"Now, my fucking crazy brother is pissed at me." She turned towards Dillon. "He's coming for me."

Dillon stood, got her computer, and came back to their spot on the floor. She scrolled through pages of information. "It looks like your brother inherits fifty percent and you get the other fifty."

"I don't want their money. He can have it all. I'll sign it over to him." Taylor blew her nose again. Her body shook. She crossed her arms and curled into herself.

"He isn't motivated by money. I tend to think he shares your father's archaic views of the place of a woman. Your mother killed his father, then herself. Without allowing the courts to punish her. Then, he sees you, a woman, head of a crime lab. And, he blames you. For everything. Signing over the money won't stop him."

"Well, I'm going to find a lawyer and get him to do it anyway. Can't I make my brother sign something saying he will leave me alone to get the money?"

Dillon shrugged. "You can. But I'm telling you it won't help. I think you should claim your inheritance. I will get Andrew to handle it for you. I think you need to stand up to your brother. We can protect you if we face this head on." Dillon pulled her phone from her the back pocket of her jeans.

"Who are you calling?" she exclaimed, making flighty hand movements.

"Calm down. I'm calling my lawyer. He can get your side of the estate handled."

"No. this is too soon. Too soon. I need some time."

"Quit babbling. Your brother has already found you. At least your phone number. Everything else too, I'm sure. We need to attack this, not run from it, not hide from it." Dillon stopped short of dialing her lawyer. She grabbed one of Taylor's trembling hands. "Taylor, you carry a fucking pink gun. You shot David in the back of the head to save Damien and Joe. Don't let this asshole scare you. You have faced scarier shit than this. Hell, you had a serial killer stalking you. Quit acting a like a fucking girl. You're a badass. You got this. We got this."

Taylor tried to smile at the words of encouragement. She squeezed Dillon's hand. "Thank you for this. It makes it easier knowing I'm not alone."

"You're not alone. Joe and Damien will do whatever needs to be done to keep you safe. Your asshole brother isn't going to hurt you. I will guarantee that." Dillon stood as she spoke with her lawyer.

Taylor remained on the floor. Gunner had made his way to her and rested the upper half of his body in her lap, his big brown eyes trying to reassure her it would be okay. But she wasn't convinced. She rubbed the big dog's ears. "Gunner, I know one thing for sure. Adnon is like Dad. He won't stop until he kills me."

CHAPTER THIRTY-TWO

Tuesday morning 7:45

"Maggie?" Mrs. Cromwell shouted through the door. "Maggie, are you in there." She held a plastic container with some muffins she had baked earlier that morning. Rap, rap, rap...she tapped on the door.

Maggie's next-door neighbor stepped out. "I doubt she can hear you with her TV blaring. It's been going since early yesterday morning."

Mrs. Cromwell looked at the young man. "There was a maintenance man here yesterday."

The young man stopped as he walked past the old lady. "We don't have a maintenance man. He was fired the other day for stealing."

"No. You must be mistaken. They must have hired another one. I saw him here yesterday morning. He had case and everything." She smiled at him.

Chad pulled his phone out. He called the management office. "Hey, this is Chad Winters; I live on the third floor. Did you guys hire a new maintenance guy?" He nodded into the phone. "Okay. My next-door neighbor has had her TV turned on since yesterday. Mrs. Cromwell says she saw a maintenance man here yesterday. You may want to check on her."

Mrs. Cromwell quit knocking on the door. Her lips and chin trembled. "He wasn't a maintenance man, was he?"

Chad shook his head. "I don't think so, Mrs. Cromwell." Her face went ashen, and she stumbled a bit. "Let me help you back to your apartment. I will wait for the office people to show up." He escorted her down the hall and made sure she got into her home okay. As he pulled the door shut one of the ladies from the office exited the elevator.

"Did you call in the TV noise?"

He pointed to Maggie's door. "Here."

The young lady sighed at the site of the locks. "I hope I grabbed the right keys." She found the master lock for the bottom door lock. "Keep your fingers crossed," she said as she twisted the key. As she pulled the key out and was about to unlock the first of the deadbolts, the door eased open. She glanced at Chad. "It's unlocked." She pushed the door open. "Mrs. Newsome? Maggie?" The office lady stepped over the spilt coffee on the floor. "Maggie, is everything okay?" She swung the door open a little more. "What's that smell?" The metallic taste hit the back of her throat before she saw Maggie in the living room. "Hey, Maggie," she said as she walked into the small kitchen heading to the living room.

Chad stepped over the mess on the floor, not paying attention to what the lady from the office was doing. He was about to look up when a terrified scream stopped him in his tracks. Before he could step out of the way, the office lady ran past with hand over her mouth, almost knocking him over. Confused, he took a few steps into the living room. "Holy shit!" Chad yelled as he backed out of the apartment, retracing his steps.

CHAPTER THIRTY-THREE

Damien walked into the VCU at six-thirty a.m. He carried two twelve packs of soda, to restock his new fridge. The nights without Dillon or the pets were making it hard for him to sleep. Twice he had to remind himself it was Tuesday. The jolts of caffeine throughout the day would help keep him somewhat alert.

He didn't have to be there until eight, but he had been awake for several hours and was bored. The electronic case board that hung on the wall was updated every morning at seven. "Not even the technology is working this early," he mumbled as he walked into his office. He placed the soda in the fridge, taking one.

Sitting, he thumbed through all the many notes and mail adorning his desk since he and Joe were gone the entire day before. "This shit is never-ending." He jumped at the loud knock on his door. "Hey, Detective Travis what the hell you doing here this early?"

"Couldn't sleep. Came in. I checked with my boss, he said I could get the overtime, why not get paid if I can't sleep. I'd be lying at home doing nothing." He took a seat in front of Damien. "Why are you here so early?"

"Same reason. Dillon and the pets are still at her grandparent's farm. Fucking house is too damn quiet. Can't stand it. Plus, I have the whole bed to myself. Used to sharing it with the dog, cat, and Dillon."

Detective Travis laughed. "I hear you."

"Why are you in my office. Eating my jelly beans?" Damien asked as Detective Travis grabbed a second handful from the jar.

"I need the sugar rush." He stuffed them into his mouth, then held up his finger as he chewed them. "Okay...those names you texted Detective Todd," he handed a file to Damien. "I pulled everything I could on them. First, Nancy Milligan. She went into foster care when she was nine years old. I wasn't sure why you wanted her in the search, she didn't come up as ever being in Sunshine Valley."

Damien shook his head. "Are you sure?"

"Yup. I went ahead and ran her anyway." Detective Travis thought for a moment. "It's in the file, but I think she was placed in foster care in another state. That was in the records. She thrived and later went on to college. Looks like she got a degree in chemistry. Works for a small lab outside of Gary Indiana.

"Next, we have Maggie Newsome. She entered the home in 2005 and was at Sunshine Valley from the age of eleven until fifteen when she, too, ran away. She was never put back in foster care, though. Ended up living with an aunt until age eighteen. She now lives here in the city, Hyde Park to be exact. And last but not least, Clara Rogers." Detective Travis paused.

"What is it, Detective?"

"This is heartbreaking. Clara Rogers was eleven when she entered Sunshine Valley in 2014. She was there for about eight months before she was moved to a state hospital. Had some kind of breakdown. She was in the hospital for about five months. The home couldn't provide the care for her she needed once she left the hospital. She ended up being released into the custody of another foster home, and ultimately killed herself when she was sixteen, almost seventeen."

Damien glanced through the file on Clara. "Were there any charges ever brought against the last foster care family?"

Detective Travis shook his head. "No. This is one of those rare families that care about the kids they have. They tried to work with her. The notes I gathered," he pointed to the file, "said that Clara seemed to be improving. She had started going to therapy and was making progress. She had started to talk about an incident that happened when she was younger. She said someone sexually molested her. But she wouldn't talk about it."

"Nothing to indicate she was suicidal?"

"Not that I could find. Jeff and Sandy Moreno, they live here in Chicago. North of the city. They have a small farm that is used as a therapy farm. I think that's why Clara thrived with them. You might get more from them. As for Sunshine Valley, in regards to what happens if it ceases to be a state home, then all remaining monies will be donated to various charities."

"What about all the Chandler kids?"

"The Chandlers were billionaires. Each child has a very hefty trust. The monies left over were placed in a separate trust to run the home."

"What about the property?"

"It would revert to the children. They could sell it, and the proceeds shared between the siblings. According to the public information regarding the home, the siblings agreed to those terms when the house was donated as property to the state."

"Then, it would be in the State's interest to keep the home."

Detective Travis shrugged. "I guess. The state doesn't control the money. They actually have no say in the money other than what is needed to run the home. The trust set up for the home has all the power."

"Who is listed as the trustee?" Damien asked.

Detective Travis frowned. "I don't rightly know. I can hunt it down for you."

Damien shook his head. "I can find that out. Were you able to find anything on Shamus?

"I did. He was a big wig therapist to the Hollywood elite. There seems to be a few girls who complained about him. When he was questioned, he told the authorities the girls had a lot of issues. Looks like he spun it back on them. Out of the blue, they dropped their complaints against him."

Damien leaned forward resting his forearms on his desk. "Was there any explanation of why they dropped them?"

Detective Travis shook his head. "Because the girls were minors at the time, and under Dr. patient privilege, I couldn't get their records. I did speak with a detective listed on the reports. He said over the span of maybe four days, the parents called in and withdrew the complaints."

"That reeks of foulness." Damien took a sip of his soda.

"The detective thinks someone threatened them. Probably something like telling their little girls secrets.

"Okay. Thanks for hunting down the information for me," Damien said.

Detective Travis took another handful of jelly beans as he stood. "Need anything else, you know where to find me."

Damien smiled at him. "You ever think of leaving this job? Going into private investigations?"

"Sure. If the right job came around or I could start my own business. I would like to be in a place I can do more for people." Detective Travis glanced over his shoulder, turning back to Damien. "I would like to be where I don't have to abide by so many rules. The criminals sure as shit don't care about rules. Sometimes I wonder why we do."

"I hear ya on that." Damien nodded at him. "If I hear of anything I think you might do well at, I'll let you know."

"Please do." He turned to go out of the office. "Let me know if I need to get you any more information on those ladies. I can do a deeper search with a warrant."

"Thanks."

"Hey, Detective Travis," Joe said as he entered Damien's office. "How long you been here?" he asked squinting at Damien before looking at his watch. "It's like barely seven fifteen."

"Since about six-thirty. Why are you here this early?" Damien asked as he took two soda pops from the little fridge in the corner of his office.

"Couldn't sleep. Muffin."

Damien's soda stopped before it hit his lips. "Is something wrong?"

"No. I worried all night about her. She slept on the bed next to me. She snores. Every time she quit snoring, I would wake up and check her."

Damien laughed. "What are you going to do if you ever have a baby?"

"Ah, hell. Fuck that shit. I don't want kids. Can you imagine me dealing with a little me?" Joe shook his head. "No. No kids."

Damien laughed. "You look like you just shat your pants."

"You're such a hoot." Joe scowled at him as he finished off his soda.

Damien was about to say something else when his desk phone rang. He glanced at the clock. "Shit it isn't even eight a.m. This can't be good. Kaine here," he said, picking up the phone. "Alright. Send me the address. Do you have a name? Crap. No, I got this one. Detective Joe Hagan is with me. We got this covered."

"What's up boss?"

"You know those three names the lady gave you yesterday?"

Joe nodded as he stood to follow him out of the office. "Yeah, why?"

"Our latest dead body is one of those names, Maggie Newsome." He handed Joe the file Detective Travis had given him earlier. "Read this while I drive us over there."

Joe grabbed his jacket as they walked past his desk.

Officer Baker walked in. "Hey Lieutenant Kaine, you got a minute?"

He shook his head. "Not right now. Is this about the case you're on?"

"Yes, Sir."

"Talk with Davidson when he gets in. Let him know we got another dead body that looks to be associated with this case. Tell him he's in charge and he needs to get going on all the names from the home. Also, tell Davidson to get the Moreno's phone number and get everything he can on Clara Rogers." His voice trailed off as he and Joe ran down the seven flights of stairs.

CHAPTER THIRTY-FOUR

Kerry walked into his company late Tuesday morning, and it was still the hustle and bustle of activity. Owning a building in the heart of Chicago was no small feat. He rented out what space his IT company didn't use, and made enough to pay the note on the building.

He didn't need to be here, his executive officer and finance officer had everything running smoothly. But it was his company, and he needed an untraceable, secure connection. He walked through the lobby to the express elevator to the twenty-fifth floor. His company occupied the top five floors of the building with his office and the rest of the executive level and human resources on the top floor.

Exiting the elevator, he stopped by the XO's office. Kerry stood at the doorway, watching his colleague obsess over a computer file. From where he stood, it looked like Bob was going over the latest data on the network. His XO was more than capable of running this company in Kerry's absence. He held two degrees, one in software engineering and one in big business analytics. But the man had no sense of humor. "Hey Bob, what's up today?"

Bob Stacey glanced up from his desk. "Hey, where you been? You take an extended weekend?"

"Sorry. I should've let you know. I had a meeting out of the city and didn't get back until late Sunday evening, I took Monday off. My bad." Kerry sat in one of the oversized chairs in front of his desk. "Did I miss anything?"

Bob removed his glasses, rubbing his eyes. "No. Not really. Banks twenty through twenty-five went down. Looks like there was a spike from the advertising agency on the fifth floor."

"What kind of spike? What would cause the outage?" Kerry asked.

"Those dumb assholes ran a special contest on the main page of their website. Had they taken the time to tell us what they wanted to do, we could've set up a designated landing page for the contest and routed all traffic to one node. The system was slammed with like 4k hits in under two minutes. Damn near shut the whole system down."

"Did you guys reroute it through block forty?"

"Yes. Managed to spread the hits out over ten nodes. But the entire site went down for about thirty minutes before anyone recognized the backup. I told them next time, give us the parameters of anything like that, and we'll

have the system up and ready to go with a dedicated server. They won't have those same problems again."

"How long total was the section down?"

"Two hours tops." Bob typed out something on his screen. "To be safe, I rerouted their system for a day or two." He put his glasses back on and checked the screen. "That quadrant is running fine now."

"Sounds good. That's why you are my right-hand man. Couldn't run this company without you." Kerry stood and stepped towards the door. "Hey, I have some personal stuff to attend to this week. Don't be surprised if I'm out of the office more than I'm in. Make the decisions you need to. I trust your judgment on things."

"Thanks for letting me know. I will operate under the assumption this will be the last day I see you then." He chuckled at his attempt at humor.

"I'll be here for a while. Later." Kerry headed towards his office. He walked past the HR department and his numbers guy, who was nowhere to be found. Which meant he was probably grilling someone about an expense.

Kerry entered his office, closing the door. The glass front automatically frosted when he locked it. Sitting at his desk, he logged in. Using a secure VPN and browser, he hacked into the State of Illinois' employee database.

"Let's see what you have been up to Pops." Kerry searched for Shamus MacDougal. He read through the man's files. Prior records of sexual complaints were listed but were found to be deemed unreliable. "I don't think so. You buried it somewhere, Pops. And I will find it."

The State's site had a link to Sunshine Valley's website, but it didn't host it. "Well now, had your site custom-built huh, Shamus? Wrong move." Kerry assumed Pops wanted to keep the State out of his business. But that leaves open a possible entry into the castle.

His fingertips flew across the keyboard. Searching for an unrestricted file upload vulnerability. "Gotcha." He continued hacking into Sunshine Valley's network by uploading a random digital file, helping him gain access to a low privilege shell. This let him see all the computers on the home's network.

Once in the Sunshine Valley's network, Kerry had little trouble finding the man's secret files. "You couldn't do better than this?" Shamus MacDougal had disguised his filthy porn habit as a masked file of Illinois State legislation. "Oh, you stupid man." Kerry cracked the file open like an egg.

He scrolled through endless pictures of young girls in various levels of dress. Some were naked, and the fear in their eyes made Kerry's stomach churn. He seethed with hate. He could take all this and slowly leak it to the police, the State, and the press, but that would keep Shamus MacDougal from being punished. Severely punished. "No. You are not getting off with a jail sentence."

Leaving the photos in place, he copied all the man's files and email correspondence. Before he exacted revenge for what Shamus did to Sierra, Kerry decided he would have a little fun with him. He set up an email blast from an untraceable account. Shamus would get a few surprises delivered right to his inbox.

Kerry chuckled as he downloaded the man's passwords and logins to all his accounts. "If you're going to keep a password manager on your computer people, make sure no one can get into your computer," he couldn't stop the maniacal laugh from escaping. He had to stop for a moment to regain himself. "Besides a pervert and pedophile, you are a fucking moron, Shamus."

Remembering what Maggie had told him, Kerry searched the man's hard drive for a connection to the Suit. It had to be someone associated with the home, but he had no idea in what capacity. Opening Shamus' emails, he scrolled through them. Correspondence with several board members about the home's expansion. Over the years Shamus had new buildings put up. Things listed as enrichment facilities for the youth. "Right. Enrichment my ass," Kerry said as he scrolled through endless messages.

"There's no way you have this in your regular email." Kerry searched the man's password manager for another email provider. He found what he was looking for. He logged in to the email service. He checked the time and decided he would read through them later. He downloaded the messages and closed the program.

He started his search for any information regarding the building Chase had told him about. He found receipts for the work on the small steel building. According to Chase, Patrick, and one of his buddies laid the concrete. Chase didn't have the other guy's name. Kerry might have to let that one go.

A knock at Kerry's door prompted him to darken the screen. "Come in." He pressed a button under his desk, remotely unlocking the door. He glanced up to find his finance officer storming towards him.

Frank Peters waved a number of pages in the air. "Kerry, did you give acquisitions permission to purchase new cable testers?"

"Yes, Frank, I did." Kerry raised an eyebrow at him when he slapped the invoices down on his desk. "$4,800.00 bucks worth? Seriously what the hell

are we testing?"

Kerry loved Frank. He was the best damn accountant anywhere. Knew every loophole the IRS had and knew how to use them, too. But he didn't know a damn thing about IT. *"Frank, this is a tiny amount to pay. Trust me on this."*

"They only got five. Five for that amount. Please explain this." Frank flopped down in a chair and took a piece of candy from the bowl on the desk.

"Listen. They could've spent triple if they bought one for each category of testing. These particular testers enable one unit to test all levels. I okayed it. I should've sent you a note. I'm sorry I didn't." Kerry sat back and smiled, his attention shared between Frank and his previous task at hand.

Frank sighed. *"Okay. I'm sorry. It's tax season. I'm going over the expenditures from last year, and I shouldn't have reacted the way I did. But from now on, you need to shoot me an email. I know everyone goes through you for their purchases. However, you tend to forget to tell me, and then I'm blindsided. Like last week, I got a requisition from HR regarding new desktop computers. No one bothered to tell me."*

Kerry snickered. *"Actually, I did. I sent you an email. Right after Bob and I left the meeting."*

Frank grimaced. *"Um, you sent me an email?"* he asked, rubbing his neck. *"Are you sure?"*

Kerry nodded. *"Yes. Frank, why don't you hire an assistant? He or she could do this menial stuff. They could be in the loop for all purchase meetings or requests, and you can handle the major stuff, like our taxes. I brought you in because you're a CPA-Attorney, but sometimes, I think you get too wrapped up in the small shit. Hire an accountant."*

Frank's eyes lit up. *"I will do that. I got someone in mind. She's one of the accountants I have used. I'd be stealing her from Youngston and Youngston accountants."*

"Shoot me the details of what she wants for pay and compensation. We'll see what we can do. Is there anything else?" Kerry's fingers tapped his desktop.

Frank all but ran from the office. *"Nope. I got this covered. I'll let you know about the accountant."*

Kerry waited for the man to walk past his office window before he locked his door again. He quickly pulled back up the home's website. He doubled checked to make sure he had what he needed downloaded and left open a backdoor into the network for later access. He scanned Pops' files one last *time before exiting. Something caught his eye. "What the hell..." his voice trailed off as he opened a file labeled security. Inside there were several correspondences between Pops and someone he never expected. "Well, now. This makes my life a little easier."*

His last line of business was to find information on Patrick Weinsted. Chase had explained the lengths Patrick had gone through to please Pops. According to Chase, Patrick was Shamus' right-hand man, and according to this file, Patrick was still Shamus' right-hand man. "Looks like you're still on the payroll Patrick." Kerry opened Pops' bank account using the password manager. He found regular payments to Patrick Weinsted. "Oh Patrick, you're so going to pay," he said, laughing.

CHAPTER THIRTY-FIVE

Tuesday 8:45 a.m.

Damien filled Joe in on the information regarding how the family set up the home and what Detective Travis had told him as he drove to Maggie Newsome's home.

"Why did that lady give us Nancy's name if it doesn't show she was at the home?"

"I don't know. But we will interview her and find out."

"Do you think any of the Chandler kids have anything to do with this?" Joe asked.

"Anything is possible. But it doesn't feel like that. From what I gathered, each child is a millionaire in their own right. If the property is no longer used as a state-run home for kids, then the children will sell the property and split the proceeds."

"I can't see why one of them would want to murder Humphry. The kids have been long gone from the home for almost two decades. Unless a greedy grandchild is looking to take over the Chandler empire."

Damien laughed. "I bet that's exactly what it is." Driving onto the street, he took notice of the neighborhood. Not the worst part of town, not the greatest.

"Have you heard back from Humphry's lawyer?"

"I got an email from his secretary. She has been instructed to answer any questions. He said he got called out on a deposition. He mentioned his partner could help with anything. I sent her a list of questions. I figure that's the easiest way to get answers. To tell the truth, I don't see a connection to Chase's death and anything having to do with his company. After I get the answers, if I think I need to speak with the lawyer, I'll call him."

Damien parked between two police cars. Yellow crime scene tape surrounded Maggie's stoop and the entryway to her building. He grabbed his ID and clipped it onto his belt after showing it to the officers guarding the front doors.

"I'm not seeing anything implicating anyone from the company either." Joe almost bumped into Damien when he stopped mid-stride.

Damien pointed to the security camera in the corner. "You think that works?"

"Not a chance," Joe said.

"Our victim is on the third floor. Let's take the stairs." Damien pushed the door open.

Entering the dimly lit stairwell, Joe put his hands in his pockets. "This building is on the cuff of being a crappy place to live. Better than some, but I sure as hell don't trust this railing."

Damien stepped into the third-floor hallway. "It's nicer than most I've seen in this area, especially a few blocks over." Walking up to Maggie Newsome's door, a little old lady stood down the hallway clutching a small dog. Damien nodded to Officer Talon, who stood like a century outside the victim's door. "Why is she standing there?"

"She insists on speaking with the detective in charge. She won't go back into her apartment until then." Officer smirked at Damien. "She hasn't budged either."

Damien sighed. "You know her name?"

"Mrs. June Cromwell."

Damien looked at Joe. "Hang on." He walked to the elderly lady. "Mrs. Cromwell?"

"Are you in charge?"

"Yes, Ma'am, I am. I'm Lieutenant Damien Kaine. I will come back to your apartment in a little bit and ask you some questions. Until then, can I get you to wait inside?"

Her eyes narrowed into slits. "I saw the man."

Damien cocked his head to the side. "What man?"

"The man that hurt Maggie." She adjusted her little dog, who eyed Damien with caution and a few snarls.

"You saw a man enter Maggie's apartment?" Damien asked.

"Yes, I did." She lifted her chin. "I'm not a crazy old woman."

"I don't think you're even remotely a crazy old woman. My partner and I will be back in a little bit. Please don't speak with anyone until you speak to us. Can you do that for me?"

"I will. I will be waiting inside for you to come and speak with me." She turned in a huff and closed her door in Damien's face.

He heard several locks engage as he turned back to Joe. "She said she saw the man who entered Maggie's apartment."

Joe raised an eyebrow at him. "Really?"

"That's what she said. We will talk to her after we talk to the ME." Damien started to walk into the apartment when Officer Talon grabbed his arm.

"It's good to have you back, Lieutenant," Officer Talon said, smiling at Joe. "You too, Detective."

"Thank you. Hey, do you know if the security camera in the entryway works?"

"No, I don't. I can find out for you."

"That's okay. I'll get the CST to do it," Damien said as he entered the apartment. He cleared his throat as the metallic taste hit the back of it. He noticed the dried spilled coffee and bag from a local pastry shop on the floor. Both had been tagged by the CST. He continued into the small living room and stopped at the site before him.

"Motherfucker," Joe exclaimed at the site of the young girl.

Damien stepped up next to Dr. Forsythe and lead Crime Scene Tech, Roger Newberry. "Hey, guys."

Roger Newberry was removing a small ball gag that seemed to be caught on Maggie Newsome's hair. "Hey, Damien. Good to see you, man," he looked at Joe, "you too."

"Same," Joe said as he moved to the side of the girl.

Dr. Forsythe nodded at the two detectives. "Hello. How's the return to work been for you?"

"Ehh," Damien said as he shrugged. "Not bad. Except for this case."

Dr. Forsythe pushed his magnifying glasses down his nose. "You think this is connected to Chase Humphry?"

"I know it is." He met the doctor's stare. "I got a piece of information directly associated with the Sunshine Valley home and Maggie Newsome."

"Well, that may explain her death." Dr. Forsythe moved to the body and tilted the young girl's head back. "The killer cut out her tongue."

"That's what killed her?" Joe asked. "No way. Really?" he bit down on his bottom lip. His eyes narrowed in on the doc. "The mob cuts out tongues all the time, they don't die."

Dr. Forsythe smirked. "If you know what you're doing, you can kill someone by cutting out their tongue. And this killer knew what he was doing." The doctor pried open the young girl's jaw. Shining a small pen-light into her mouth. "Our killer made sure to cut the lingual artery feeding the tongue with blood. If she had immediate help, she might have survived. But not likely."

"Wouldn't be much of a life if she did," Joe said.

"No. Probably not." The doctor pointed to the cuts on her legs and arms. "A few of these are very deep. He made sure not to cut an artery, but she may have bled out slowly from these cuts. They are just too deep."

"How long ago was she murdered?" Damien asked.

"From the state of the body and what the officers gathered from the office worker and the other resident who found her, the last time she was seen was Monday morning." Dr. Forsythe rubbed his chin. "I can hazard a guess she died somewhere between ten a.m. and one p.m. on Monday. I will narrow it down back at autopsy."

Damien studied the apartment. He glanced back towards the door. "This isn't a very big place. Not many areas to hide." He stepped back, giving him a clear view of the door and the living room. "I'd say he got into her apartment and waited for her. That would account for the coffee on the kitchen floor." He looked at Newberry. "Did you find any other signs this guy was here?"

Newberry stood and walked into the small bedroom and bathroom. "I found the closet doors open and a towel on the bathroom sink." He pointed to the items in question. "I can't imagine our killer was stupid enough to use it, but I plan on bagging it."

"Do you know if the security camera downstairs works?"

"I can check on it when I'm done here. If it does, I'll call ECD for you."

"That'd be great." Damien glanced around. "I don't think he took anything. I mean, what does she have to take?"

"He took one thing," Dr. Forsythe yelled from the living room.

Damien walked back. "I can't wait to hear this."

Joe smiled. "Trophy."

Damien's brow wrinkled. "Oh, hell."

Dr. Forsythe nodded. "He took the tongue."

Damien shook his head. "What does he want with the fucking tongue?"

Joe shrugged. "I got no clue. He didn't take Maggie's eyes or anything else for that matter."

Damien motioned towards the door. "Let's go talk to the lady down the hall. Doc, email me your findings."

"You got it, Damien." Dr. Forsythe went back to collecting evidence.

CHAPTER THIRTY-SIX

Joe followed Damien out of the apartment. "He didn't spend as much time with Maggie."

"I noticed. This building doesn't offer much in the way of privacy. I would imagine there are times of the day there is more traffic than others." Damien stood in front of Mrs. Cromwell's residence. "Makes me think he watched Maggie," he said, knocking on the door.

Two locks and the jangle of a door chain preceded the opening of the door. Mrs. Cromwell stood with her dog in her arms. "Come in please."

Damien wondered if the dog ever walked anywhere. "Mrs. Cromwell, this is my partner Detective Hagan. Thank you for waiting to speak with us."

She shut the door behind them, locking them in. Only then did she put the dog on the floor, who stayed right at her feet. "Sit." She motioned to the small dining table with three chairs, in the corner of the kitchen. "Been here for twenty-five years. Never had anything like this happen before."

Mrs. Cromwell didn't ask. She just set three cups and a pot of coffee on the table. She set three plates out and put a huge blueberry muffin on each plate. "Eat."

Joe's grin filled his face. "Did you make these muffins?" He asked, putting sugar in his coffee. He wasn't about to tell her he didn't drink it, and he hoped the sugar and milk would make it taste better.

"Of course, I did," she responded. "Now," she squinted at them, "don't you need a notebook or something?"

Damien smiled as he removed his small notebook from his back pocket. "Yes, thank you for reminding me. Can you tell me what you witnessed?"

Mrs. Cromwell opened her own small notebook. "I walk Pookie every morning at eight thirty. I stepped out of my apartment on Monday morning and saw a young man at Maggie's door."

"Can you describe him?" Damien asked swallowing the bite of his muffin.

"I'll get to that." She took a sip of her coffee.

Damien squeezed his lips together to hide his smile. He didn't dare look at Joe, who he could see from the corner of his eye grinning in his direction.

"Now. The man was carrying a case, like a toolbox but plastic. And not very big. I'd say the size of a fishing tackle box. He was knocking on her door and saying he was maintenance. When I approached him, I told him Maggie stepped out. She always does on her days off." She nodded at Damien. "You'll want to write this down, son."

She gave him a few minutes to finish his bite. "Maggie had off every Monday and Tuesday. Occasionally those days would change. She was a dancer down at Dancing Dolls. She could've done more with her life. But she seemed to like what she did and she did what she needed to in order to get by. Anyway, she always got a coffee and bagel from Snickers Deli, down the block.

"Now, I told the man she wasn't home, and he said he was the maintenance and he would come back in a few minutes. I went on to walk Pookie. He was still standing there when I entered the elevator. I came back by nine a.m. he wasn't there. I assumed he would be returning."

"When did you first realize something was wrong?" Damien asked. He peered over at Joe, who beamed a smile at Mrs. Cromwell when she put another muffin on his plate.

"Not until this morning. Monday, when I came back from my walk, Maggie's apartment was quiet. I didn't see Maggie while I walked Pookie. Sometimes I run into her coming back from the coffee shop. I went on about my daily business. I left my apartment Monday afternoon, around two p.m. I heard the TV from inside Maggie's home."

"What time did you get back Monday morning?"

She paused her coffee cup mere inches from her mouth before taking her sip. Replacing it on the saucer, she replied. "It was nine fifteen."

"That's an exact time." Damien took a sip of the cold coffee.

"I know my time, young man. I usually get back at nine sharp, for my morning shows. But this time Pookie decided it was more important to sniff every post before going to the bathroom."

Damien nodded. "But nothing made you suspect anything was wrong at that time?"

"Not at all."

"What tipped you off this morning, what made you realize something had happened?" Damien asked.

"I knocked on Maggie's door this morning after my walk. I had some baked goods for her. Chad, the young man who found her with the office lady, came out of his apartment. He lives across the hall next to Maggie. He mentioned the TV had been on all night. I told him about the maintenance man. He said there was no maintenance man. Ours had been fired. He called the office. You know the rest."

Damien made some notes. "Can you describe the man you saw at Maggie's door?"

"He was tall. Wore a dark pair of overalls and a baseball hat. He never looked at me. Kept his head down. There was one odd thing."

"What was that Mrs. Cromwell?" Damien asked.

"He wore gloves," she said.

"Like winter gloves?" Joe asked, finishing the last bite of his muffin.

She shook her head. "No. Like surgical gloves. And they were black."

Damien scribbled in his notebook. "Is there anything else you can think of? Do you know if Maggie had any friends, or family who came to see her?"

"No. None. I never even saw her dating anyone." Mrs. Cromwell rose and went to the kitchen counter. She placed two more muffins in a small brown paper sack and carried it and a piece of paper back to the table. "If you need anything else from me, call me." She handed Damien the piece of paper. "This is my phone number." She handed Joe the paper sack. "These are for you."

He rose and took the bag from her. "Thank you."

Damien walked to the door. "One more thing, do you know if the security camera works, the one in the entryway?"

"That thing hasn't worked for years. They've gotten it fixed a few times, but it keeps breaking. Or someone breaks it," Mrs. Cromwell said.

"Thank you for your help. You have given us a lot of useful information."

She stepped up to Damien and patted his cheek. "You're very welcome." She turned to Joe. "My husband was an Irishman. He loved those muffins."

Joe bent down and kissed her damp cheek. "He was a lucky man, Mrs. Cromwell." He handed her his card. "If you ever need anything, you call me."

Damien made sure he heard Mrs. Cromwell lock her door before he stepped across the hall to Chad's apartment. Knocking on the door, he waited. No answer. "Let's check with Officer Talon, maybe someone got his information." As he walked away from Mrs. Cromwell's door, he looked at Joe. "She practically confirmed the ME's time frame for the murder."

"I was thinking the same thing. Our guy had to know Maggie's schedule," Joe said. He opened the bag and sniffed.

Damien shook his head. "You ate two big muffins, aren't you full?"

"Yes. But they smell so good." He inhaled one last time before rolling the bag shut.

"I can see you at the retirement community, you're going to be the fattest guy in the geriatric ward."

"And the most popular. While you'll be the old grumpy Italian."

CHAPTER THIRTY-SEVEN

Damien looked at the clock on the wall of his office, then his watch as if to make sure the time was right, three p.m. He glanced at his calendar; it was still Tuesday. "Shit," he hissed out. He'd texted Dillon earlier but hadn't heard from her. Picking up his desktop phone, he pulled the card for the lawyer for Sunshine Valley from his desk drawer.

"The law office of Martin Escobar, how may I direct your call?"

"This is Lieutenant Kaine with Division Central, I'd like to speak with Mr. Escobar if possible."

"Um, one moment, Lieutenant."

Damien found himself tapping his fingers to the beat of the music filling the line. He reached in his desk for a pen and notepad.

"Hello, this is Martin Escobar."

"Mr. Escobar, this is Lieutenant Kaine."

"Yes, Lieutenant, what can I do for you?"

"I'm investigating the murder of Chase Humphry. I was hoping you could help me with a few things."

"I heard from Shamus that Chase had been murdered. I'm sorry to hear about his death. He was a fine young man."

Damien scribbled on his notepad. "How long have you been the lawyer for Sunshine Valley?"

"Technically I'm not the lawyer for the home. I've been the liaison between the trust and the State since around 1999."

"I'm confused. Who do you work for, the State or the trust?" Damien asked.

"I specialize in estate planning. I was hired by the State and the trustee to act as an advocate for Sunshine Valley. In that role, I act as an auditor, ensuring both parties are complying with the terms of the trust."

"I didn't know such a thing existed."

"In this case, it was warranted. There were questions as to what the State could do and what the trust wanted. The Chandler family contacted me. After I gave them my opinion, they asked me to be the liaison and arbiter between the two entities."

"Very interesting. Who is listed as the trustee, or who actually has access to the money?"

"The Chandler children are listed the board of trustees. However, for small things that I deem the home needs, I have been giving leeway to right the checks. If it is a substantial amount of money, I have to get the board's approval."

"Okay. That clears up a few things. I'm actually calling to ask if we could take a tour of the facility?"

"Of course, you can. All you have to do is schedule it with Shamus."

Damien tapped the pen on his notepad. "So... we don't need your permission?"

There was a pause on the phone. "I don't know why you would need my permission for a tour."

"According to Mr. MacDougal, we needed your permission or a warrant; which I can get if need be. However, I hate to go through that much trouble."

"No need for a warrant. I can instruct Shamus to give you a tour. What else can I do for you, Lieutenant?"

"I could use the records for a few of the residents who were there during the time when Chase Humphry was a resident of the home."

Another long pause.

Damien waited for an answer. "Mr. Escobar?"

"I'm sorry. What records are you looking for, Lieutenant? I'm not sure how records from over ten years ago can help you with a murder now."

"We believe there is a connection to Sunshine Valley. We would like to see records for kids who were there during the same time Chase Humphry lived in the home."

"Do you think one of those kids is responsible for the murder?"

"I'm sorry I can't tell you anything other than what I have already. We want to cover the bases. It would help us to know who was there and when they left the home. It may help us learn more about our victim."

"What information do you want, exactly?"

"Disciplinary reports, school reports, who lived in the home at the same time. Those three things would go a long way to helping us and our investigation."

"I think you might have me confused with the actual State attorney. He would be the one to grant permission for the personal files. I do have a list of residents. Something I regularly get when kids enter or leave the facility. The attorney for the State is required to send me a copy each month of any residency changes. It is the State's lawyer that will have to give you the records you seek."

"How about this, can you at least give me a list of the names of the residents during the years in question, along with how long they lived at the home and when they left the home? I can't imagine that would be violating any privacy laws."

"I think that would be doable. I will put in a call to the State attorney that handles the home along with the Secretary of Human Services. I think I can get the information for you quickly. And I think my input will keep you from having to get a warrant. But it will take a few days. In the meantime, I will have my secretary send you the names of the residents."

"Thank you. I will call our ADA and see if a warrant would help ease the State's worries about privacy issues. But the list will help us immediately. How quickly can you get that for me?"

"I should be able to get you a list fairly quickly. A day tops."

"Thank you. You can send it to LTDKaine@DivsionCentral225.com."

"I will have my secretary send you a file."

"Again, thank you, Mr. Escobar. Please let me know when you find out about the other issue."

"I will, Lieutenant."

Damien frowned at the phone when the line went dead. He stared at the receiver. "Goodbye to you too." He turned and focused on his murder board with the latest victim, Maggie Newsome. He'd read through the information Davidson had hunted down while he and Joe were at the crime scene. Most of it matched what Detective Travis had given him earlier.

She didn't have the money or the connections Humphry had. She was connected to the home. That's what connected both these victims. "Shit," he huffed out as he yanked on his hair. "I got two dead, more on the way, and no fucking clue who the killer is or why he is killing."

"Um, who are you talking to?" Officer Baker asked as she stepped into the office.

Damien jumped, pushing his chair back. "Myself. This case is kicking my butt. You got something for me?"

"I'm not sure." She pointed to the seat in front of him.

"You don't have to ask to sit down, Baker. What are you not sure of?" Damien set his elbows on his desk.

"Officer Ivansky and I went through the list of business associates. We didn't find any connections there. Anyone on the list was either out of town, lives out of town, or had an alibi for the weekend in question. So, I got some of the names from Detective Davidson."

"The ones from the home?" Damien asked.

She nodded. "Yes. He had cleared a bunch of them. However, I found one name that came up on both the list from home and in a correspondence with Chase Humphry."

"I don't think I understand. You said everyone was cleared from the business list?"

"Let me explain better. While I was going through the business list. I found a bunch of emails. Scanned them quickly and made sure there was no overlap from the list. One was in regard to the donation made to the home, by Chase Humphry."

"Okay," Damien said.

"Davidson said you guys already knew about the donation. I set it off to the side. When I was going through the partial list I got from Davidson, regarding residents of the home when Chase was there, I saw a name. The same name on the correspondence regarding the donation."

Damien shook his head. Either he wasn't seeing the connection or Baker was high.

"I can see you're aren't getting this." She opened a file, handing him a piece of paper. "This is the email regarding the donation. You can see the first time the email is sent, Chase sends it to Shamus MacDougal. On the response back to Chase, Shamus has copied, Patrick Weinsted." Baker paused for a moment waiting for Damien to look up from the email. "This is Patrick Weinsted." She handed him an article showing Shamus MacDougal with three kids."

She pointed to the boy on the end. "That is Patrick." She pointed to the other two people in the picture. "I'll give you two guesses who the other two kids are."

Damien looked at the photo then Baker. "You're shitting me."

"Nope. When I found Patrick's name had been added to the email, I didn't think anything of it. But when I found his name on the list of kids from the home, I did some research. In that photo, Patrick is seventeen. He was older than Chase and Maggie. I found out Patrick is currently employed as an independent contractor. Want to guess where?"

Damien smiled. "Sunshine Valley?"

"Bingo." Baker sat back in her chair. "I couldn't find any connection between Chase and Patrick via his business. The email clearly indicates Shamus added Patrick to the email. I had Detective Todd search the network files of Chase's company for any correspondence to Patrick Weinsted. Nothing."

Damien stared at the sheets. He looked up at the doe-eyed Baker. She was young and yet had a sharp mind for details, like a seasoned officer. He rocked back in his chair. "Tell me what you think the connection is?"

She sat up. "I think Shamus and Patrick have had a relationship since he was in the home. When I researched Patrick's job history, he has had one employer, Sunshine Valley. When he left the home, at eighteen, he went to a tech school, while still being paid by the home. Since then, he has been listed as part of the security. At least on the website."

Officer Baker leaned forward. "While I'm not certain they had anything to do with Chase's murder, their relationship is more than a legal line of work, I believe they know why Chase was killed. Everything I found on Patrick showed he had a troubled childhood. He was abused by his father, and when his father killed his mother, then himself, Patrick found his way to Shamus."

"This is damn good work, Baker." Damien rolled his chair to the side of his desk. "Davidson...get in here."

Davidson walked in wearing a bright yellow shirt. "Yeah?"

Damien squeezed his eyes together. "My gosh man, you're going to blind us all. Have a seat."

"Hey, Baker." Davidson shifted his eyes between the two. "What's going on?"

"First, did you get ahold of Jeffrey and Sandy Moreno?"

"No. I had to leave a message. The lady who worked there said they were due back tomorrow. I told her to let them know it was in regards to Clara and gave her your name and number."

"Okay, that will work. What else have you got?" Damien leaned in on his desk.

"Well, I ran Maggie Newsome after she became the latest victim. You have that already. On the names that I have, out of fifty kids so far, thirty are either dead or incarcerated. There is a disturbing pattern, but I need a little more time to flush it out."

"What's the pattern?" Damien asked.

"I have come across a lot of girls who were at the home during Chase's time there. While most of them have gone on to become very productive business women or members of society, a handful haven't."

"Explain," Damien said.

"Girls who entered the home after the age of fourteen seemed to be the most productive. The girls who entered between the ages of nine and thirteen those are the ones who are in my pattern."

"What's the pattern?" Damien asked.

"Suicide and something I'm not sure about," Davidson said.

Damien's eyes blinked as he tried to process what he heard. He opened his mouth, then closed it. Shaking his head, he closed his eyes. "Okay," he opened his eyes and stared at Davidson. "Start with the suicides. How many girls are we talking about?"

"Total? I don't have the exact number yet. Roughly over three years, I've tracked down fifteen girls who committed suicide—well the records indicate suicide—while at the home. There is also an enormous number of girls who ran away from the home."

"How many runaways?"

"Over fifty."

"And that's from the time Chase was in the home?" Damien asked.

"Yes," Davidson said.

"What about what you aren't sure of?" Damien asked, rocking in his chair.

Davidson blew out a breath. "There have been a few boys, but it's mostly girls who seem to run away not too long after they move to the home. The records show several had been transferred because they weren't a good fit for the home. I can't get anything else without a warrant for the personal files."

"This is so crazy," Damien said as he threw a pen across the room.

"Care to elaborate?" Davidson asked.

Damien did some quick math in his head. "You realize in a three-year span, more than fifteen percent of the girls who went through the home, committed suicide or ran away?"

Davidson nodded. "I know it's a lot of girls."

Damien's gaze fell on Baker. "Do you have any thoughts on this?"

Baker flinched, holding her breath. "I don't...."

"Think about it, Baker." Damien waited.

Davidson's brow wrinkled as he waited for her to respond.

"I'm not sure I have any..." Baker's eyes widened. "Oh, no," she gasped.

Davidson's head swiveled between the two. "What the hell am I missing?"

Damien nodded to Baker. "You want to tell him?"

She turned towards the detective. "Shamus MacDougal is a pedophile."

Davidson's brow furrowed a split second before his shoulders sagged. "Mothereffer." He dragged a hand down his face. "Why didn't I see that?"

"You were focused on the pattern of suicides. You would've seen it when you stepped back from the case. We found out McDougal had a few complaints levied against him a long time ago by some girl patients he had. And even with that, I didn't come to a conclusion that he was abusing girls. But if you take what you found and what Baker found, it's kind of hard not to see it now. If there was abuse, that would explain all the runaways and a reason for suicide. Although, it's still a large amount of girls." Damien went to his board. He looked out into the pen. "Joe?"

"What?" Joe asked without looking up.

"Get in here." Damien went back to the board.

Joe sauntered in to find Baker and Davidson. He rubbed his eyebrows. "What the heck, you got a party going on?"

"Baker found a connection, Davidson found a pattern, and Pops is a pedophile." Damien slid the dry erase board over, covering the pictures of the murder victims. "Okay, I'll explain later," he said to Joe. "Baker found a connection between Pops, Patrick, Maggie, and Chase. Two of these people are dead." Using a marker, Damien drew a triangle with Pops at the top, Patrick in the middle, then Maggie and Chase on the bottom. "Davidson found a pattern around many of the girls who spent time at the home."

"What's that pattern?" Joe asked.

"Suicides and runaways or disappearances," Davidson said.

"Well, hell." Joe sat in Damien's desk chair.

"Baker, I want you to take the lead on finding everything Shamus and Patrick have been involved in. Start with the home, see if there are any public stories linking them together. Get Detective Todd from ECD to help. We will need a heck of a lot more than we have now to get us warrants. I haven't seen any reports from girls that were in the home claiming abuse."

Damien glanced around at his detectives. "Doesn't mean they weren't buried or destroyed. But to get in deeper into the records we need to prove these murders have something to do with abuse. At a minimum, I want Sunshine Valley's business records, including bank transactions and ADA Flowers won't give us squat on what we have now."

Damien narrowed in on Davidson. "Follow up on the girls. Start with the missing ones. See if they have been found, dead or alive anywhere. Any girl that set foot in the home—track her down. I should be getting a list of residents from a lawyer associated with the home, I will forward that to you. I want it crossed-referenced with the list Detective Travis gave you, the one you have been working off of. Let's make sure these lists match up. The list from the lawyer will go back to 1999. That may help you in figuring out more of a pattern.

"Baker's connection tells me the killer is making this group pay for something. I bet it has to do with another girl or possibly girls. Check the missing girls, and see if any of them have a brother, uncle, or cousin. I need all the years of abuse. I imagine this started pretty close to when Shamus MacDougal took over."

Joe crossed his arms. "What do you want me to do?"

"You and I are going to Gary, Indiana."

"Oh, boy. I've always wanted to go there. Why?" Joe asked

"The third girl on the list we got from Martha at the home, lives there. I'm hoping she can give us some information." Damien pointed to Davidson. "You get Jenkins on this. Make sure the other detectives are doing okay with the other cases. If you need to pull anyone in, grab a few uniforms. They can do searches with you. I want as many girls tracked down as we can. If we can lay out a connection between them and abuse, I think I can get ADA Flowers to give me my warrant."

"You got it." Davidson and Baker left the office.

"Give me a few minutes. I need to make a phone call," Damien said to Joe.

Joe raised his brow. "You want the door shut?"

"Yes."

"Grab two sodas from your fridge before you leave," Joe said as he closed the office door.

Once his door was shut, Damien called his brother Nicky using a virtual private network.

"Yo, *fratello. Come sei stato?*

"I'm good. I need a favor."

"Hmm. I'm guessing this is a secret favor."

"It is. I need everything on every girl who spent time at the Sunshine Valley Home located down at The Dunes."

"Jesus, you don't ask for much."

"You can keep it to the years of 1995 to present. Make a separate file focusing on the years 2004 to 2008. And limit your search to nine to twelve-year olds. After that, run a separate search for girls thirteen to fifteen."

"This sounds bad. Do I even want to know?"

"No. But I also need you to do a deep run for me on Patrick Weinsted and Shamus MacDougal. Cover the run. I need all their history."

"Damien, are you sure you want to do this? You can't use anything you find. I mean shit, you can't even tell anyone you've done this. You and me, we're breaking tons of laws."

"I don't plan on using it, except to narrow in on a killer. And bring some justice to some young girls who need it. I also need you to run Martin Escobar, he's a lawyer."

"Man, so you want me to lasso the moon too?"

"Can you do it?"

"I can do it."

"Remember, Nicky, no tracks."

"Call me Casper."

CHAPTER THIRTY-EIGHT

Road to Gary, Indiana

Damien's phone rang through the speakers of the car. He pushed the Bluetooth control on his steering wheel. "Hey, baby. I was beginning to wonder about you and Taylor."

"Yeah," Joe said. "I was starting to think you and she had taken all the money and left for a private island somewhere."

"Hey Joe," Dillon said.

"Hi, Honey. I miss you," Taylor yelled through the phone.

"Seriously, that was my ear," Dillon said.

Damien turned to Joe frowning. "Where are you guys?"

"We are on our way home," Dillon said.

"We sure are," Taylor butted in. "We got everything done, and we missed you guys."

"Nice," Joe said. "How far away are you?"

"We are about three hours out. We rented a pickup truck," Dillon said.

"Okay. Joe and I are headed to Gary, Indiana. We should be back before you guys get to the house. We'll meet up there." Damien nodded at Joe, waiting for confirmation.

"That'll work," Joe said. "Can't wait to see you, baby."

"Me too." Taylor made kissy sounds through the phone.

"For crying out loud! You two are sickening," Dillon said. "We will be home soon. Love you."

Before Damien could respond the call was disconnected. His brows squished together. "Well, I love you too," he mumbled.

Joe had a big grin on his face.

"What the hell are you smiling at?" Damien sniped at him.

"Hey, don't take out your frustrations on me. And I'm smiling because I don't have to sleep alone. Now quit pouting and tell me what you are having Nicky look up."

"How do you know I'm having him look up anything?"

"Cause I know you."

"I'm making sure we get all the information we need on Shamus and

186 Victoria M. Patton

Patrick."

Joe shook his head. "Information we can't use in any court of law."

"This won't be used in court. But it might help us frame the information we do get in a better, easier to understand light." Damien blinked his eyes at Joe.

Joe rolled his eyes. "Oh, brother."

"I'm also asking him to search for girls who went through the home. Davidson uncovered hundreds who either ran away or disappeared, then a handful during Chase's time at the home who committed suicide. At the fucking home. How does this shit not raise a red flag? Nicky can find them a lot faster, and then I can cross-check whatever Davidson finds, and I can use the list Martin Escobar is going to give me." Damien hit the lights on his truck as soon as they cleared the Chicago traffic. "Don't tell anyone."

Joe glared at Damien. "When the fuck have I ever told anyone the shit you do?"

Damien snorted at his reaction. "I wanted to say it out loud, that's all. I trust you more than anyone in my life, Joe. You know that."

"I know. You're still an ass for saying it, though." Joe munched on a bag of chips he grabbed from a machine before he and Damien left Division Central. "Have you called this lady?"

"No. I don't want to give her a chance to run and not tell us anything. Right now, she is the only one who can tell us about the inner workings of the home." Damien checked his watch. "Gary is thirty minutes away. We should be there in roughly twenty."

"Why do you think the girls are coming back now? I thought for sure Dillon would stay at least to the end of the week?" Joe asked before drinking the last of his soda.

Damien reached out and tapped his phone before he answered. "I don't know. I was surprised to hear they're coming home. I think something is up." He checked Google Maps on his phone. "Our exit is ten miles ahead."

"What do you mean you think something is up?"

"I don't know. I got a feeling."

"I don't like your feelings. They always get our asses into trouble." Joe crossed his arms.

Damien smirked. "My feelings don't always get us into trouble.

That's a very broad statement."

"Broad my ass." Joe remained quiet for a few moments. "Back to this case, possibly our last case as law enforcement the way it seems to be going, how could Shamus "Pops" MacDougal molest all these girls over the last twenty-five fucking years and no one finds out?"

"Think about it. Most of the kids who go into these homes come from horrible situations. Most have disciplinary problems. If they accuse someone, especially someone like Shamus who has credentials out the fucking wazoo, who are they going to believe?" He glanced over at Joe. "Right?"

"True."

"And I bet old Pops could make them look crazy too. If any young girl accused him of inappropriate behavior, I bet he either made them leave, shipped them off saying they were nothing but trouble, or..."

"Or the missing ones are the one's Shamus and Patrick took care of," Joe said.

"Yup. I'm betting that's the case exactly. And unless we can find proof, I have no idea how we will prove it."

CHAPTER THIRTY-NINE

Tuesday 4:15 p.m.

Damien parked along the curb in front of Nancy Milligan's house. "It's four thirty. She may not be home yet."

"I don't know why you rushed down here in the first place." Joe unbuckled his seat belt but made no effort to exit the vehicle.

"I wanted to get out of the city before the rush hour traffic started." Damien turned towards Joe. "I would much rather sit here for a bit, than in the middle of traffic."

"You got me there." Joe looked up and down the street. "Are we going to go knock on the door, or what?"

"What the hell, you in a rush or something?"

"As a matter of fact, I am. My woman is coming home, and I want to see her."

"They are at least two and a half hours away. We got plenty of time." Damien reached for his door handle. "Let's go see if Nancy is home. If she isn't, we'll hang out in the truck for a bit."

Joe nodded. "You got it, boss man." He laughed at Damien's snarl. "Gets you every time."

Damien rang the bell. A dog barked from the other side of the door. He waited a few minutes before ringing the bell again. This time he knocked on the door as well. The dog barked and growled. "I guess we will wait in the truck."

As they stepped off the porch, a car pulled into the driveway. Two teens and a woman stepped out, heading towards them.

"May I help you, gentlemen?" the lady inquired. "Justin?"

"Yeah Mom?" the boy responded, stopping at the foot of the steps.

"Unlock the door for you and your brother. Get a snack, and get going on your homework," she said, tossing the keys to her son. "Put the dog in the backyard."

"Yes, Ma'am."

The attractive lady turned back to Damien and Joe. "Nancy Milligan?"

"Yes. Who are you?" Nancy asked.

"I'm Lieutenant Kaine, and this is my partner Detective Joe Hagan. We would like to ask you a few questions about the Sunshine Valley Home."

Nancy Milligan's posture stiffened. Her breathing quickened, and she wiped the palms of her hands on her pants. "Why do you need to ask about that?"

"We are investigating a case, a murder case, and we think you may be able to help us with some details."

"I don't see how I can help you. I was only there for a short time in the 1990s. I couldn't possibly have anything that will help you with a current murder." Nancy shifted from foot to foot.

Damien glanced at Joe. "Mrs. Milligan, is there someplace we can sit down? I think you would be more comfortable than standing in your front yard."

Nancy looked at the front door and back to the two detectives in front of her. Glancing around the street, she didn't want her neighbors wondering who she was speaking with. "I guess. Follow me."

She led them through the front door. "Boys?" Nancy called out.

"Yeah, Mom?" a young boy called down from the top of the stairs.

"You two stay upstairs and get your homework done."

"Okay, Mom."

Damien heard a door close from the second floor. He smiled at Nancy. "Thank you for taking the time to speak with us."

Nancy led them into the kitchen. "Please have a seat." She pointed to the kitchen table. "Can I get either of you a drink?"

"No, thanks." Damien took a seat with his back to the window and pulled out the chair next to him for Joe. "Mrs. Milligan, can you tell me about the time you spent at the home?"

Nancy Milligan grabbed a bottle of water from the refrigerator. She took a long sip as she sat down across from the two men. "I don't like to talk about my time there."

"I realize this is hard. But we need your help." Damien pulled out his small notebook from his back pocket.

Nancy began to peel the label from the front of her water bottle. "I went there right after I turned twelve." She squared her shoulders. "My parents died when I was nine. I didn't have any other family members who would take me in. After I bounced around, in and out of foster homes, the State sent me to that horrible place."

Damien laid his pen on the table. "What made it so horrible?"

Her shoulders curled over her chest. Nancy's hands gripped her water bottle. She closed her eyes and took a deep breath. "Shamus MacDougal raped me while I was there."

"I'm sorry, Nancy," Damien said.

"No. No need. I got past it. I'm not about to let that asshole take any more of my life."

"Can you tell about what happened afterward?" Damien asked.

"I told my school counselor. Because I had a few behavior problems, no one believed me. And that stupid counselor called Shamus. Told him what I said, and because he was this famous psychologist, she took whatever he said as golden."

"What happened when you got back to the home?" Damien scribbled in his notebook.

"I ran away like three days later." Nancy took a drink of her water.

Damien raised an eyebrow at Joe.

"Did something else happen? Something that made you run? Not that what happened wouldn't be enough," Joe said.

Nancy nodded. "When I came home that afternoon, Shamus met me at the door. He took me to his office. Told me if I ever told anyone else about what happened, he would make sure I disappeared, and make it look like I ran away."

Damien looked over at Joe, turning back to Nancy. "Did he assault you at the home?"

"Yes. There is a storage room in the basement. He semi-renovated it, making it look like a storage room from the outside, but when you walk in, it's a bedroom."

"Did he keep it locked? Did only he have access?" Damien asked.

"He had the only key. Some of the women workers knew of it. I think some of them went down there with him." Nancy looked down at her hands. The label for the water bottle lay in a tattered mess around the bottle. Her brow wrinkled. "When did I do that?" she whispered to herself.

"Mrs. Milligan?" Damien waited. "Nancy?"

She looked up. Her eyes filling with tears. "I'm sorry. When I left, I ended up a few states over in another foster home. Those people treated me like their daughter. I went to counseling. I left that part of my life behind." Her eyes shifted between the two detectives. "Can you tell me what this is about? Why are you here, asking me questions about an incident from twenty plus years ago?"

Joe shook his head at Damien.

"I'm sorry. I can't discuss this with you. I can say it has nothing to do with you and the incident that you went through." Damien smiled at Nancy. "Mrs. Milligan, I promise you no one will know about what happened to you."

Her nostrils flared as her stare shifted between the two detectives. "I'm not ashamed of what happened." Nancy stood and went to her purse located on the counter. She removed a pen and a business card from her wallet. "Here's the odd thing. When I ran away, I never told anyone what home I was in. I was afraid they would tell Shamus, and he would come after me. I gave them my name. And when the DHS counselor checked my records, she said couldn't find any record of me."

Damien turned to Joe and then back to Nancy. "You mean in the system?"

"No. She found me in the system as a runaway. But there was no record of me being at Sunshine Valley. I never corrected it either." She handed Damien the card. "This is my information. If you need someone to stand up in court against Shamus MacDougal, I will. I know the statute of limitations in my case is long past over." She scribbled on the back of the card. "This is the school I went to and the name of the counselor. I don't know where she is, but if you need me to sign anything to release my records, let me know. I know I named him in my session. I don't know if they kept any records or not." She held out the card.

Damien took the card. "I appreciate that offer. If we find we need your information we will contact you." He and Joe walked to the front door. Damien turned to Nancy Milligan. "Do you know if any other girls ever complained during the time that you were there?"

She leaned against the hallway wall. "I kept to myself. But there was this one girl. Her name was Brittney...Brittney," she closed her eyes. "Give me a minute...Lewis, Brittney Lewis. She was there before me. She was really quiet. I saw Shamus take her to the basement." Nancy's eyes narrowed in on Damien. "A few days later, Brittney was gone. Shamus had a house meeting and said that she had been placed with a relative. But after what he had said to me, I realized that she didn't go with a relative. I think he hurt her. That's why I ran."

Nancy thought for a few minutes. Her head hung low as her shoulders rounded. I spent a few weeks at that home. Maybe two months. Besides Brittney, I don't remember anyone else. But I was there for a very short time."

"Thank you, Nancy. What you have told us will help us with our investigation." He handed her a card. "If you need anything, don't hesitate to call on me." He stepped out the door but turned around. "I'm sorry the system let you down all those years ago."

"No need, Lieutenant. I used it to make sure I didn't turn out like Brittney or other girls who had the same thing happen to them. In the end, it made me who I am."

Both Damien and Joe nodded as they left the house. Once in the car, Damien looked at Joe. "We need to find out everything we can about Brittney Lewis. I think Shamus made sure she didn't tell anyone what he did to her." He texted the name to Detective Travis, with a quick explanation of what he needed.

"The information in the records isn't matching up. Nancy says she was there. But there is no record of her ever being there," Joe said.

"I know. Something is really wrong with this. I don't even know how to prove there is anything wrong."

"My head is spinning." Joe tapped the dash clock. "Let's get the hell back to Division Central. I need to get my truck. Then head to your house." He rubbed his hands together like a child. "I can't wait to have my woman home."

Damien rolled his eyes at him. "You sound retarded."

"You sound jealous."

CHAPTER FORTY

Mrs. C. watched as the headlights from Damien's SUV filled the driveway she shared with the man she thought of as a grandson. She watched as Damien pulled into his garage, Joe followed right behind him parking in the circular driveway. "Come Mr. Pickles. Let's go see Damien."

The dog ran around in circles, waiting for his coat to be buckled and his leash to be put on.

Mrs. C. grabbed the new ID tag and walked out the front door.

Damien walked to the edge of the garage. "Come in through here."

"Are you too lazy to walk to the front door?"

"Why should I walk to the front door, when there is a perfectly placed door right here?"

At the sound of a door closing, they both turned towards the noise. Mrs. C. approached them with Mr. Pickles in tow.

Joe swallowed the giggle bubbling up at the sight of the little dog. "What the hell is he wearing?" he muttered out of the side of his mouth to Damien.

"I don't know." He snorted as the dog came closer.

Joe tilted his head down to hide the smile and the laughter.

"Hey, Mrs. C.," Damien said. "Is Mr. Pickles wearing a new coat?" He too had to look away to gain his composure. The last thing he wanted to do was hurt Mrs. C.'s feelings.

"Yes, he is. I ordered it the other day. The poor thing shivered so much whenever I took him for his walks. She bent down and picked him up. Twisting him from side to side so the two men could see the full view of the coat.

"Is that fur?" Joe asked.

She waved him off, shaking her head. "Of course not. Its faux fur." She held out Pickles. "Here, feel it."

Joe and Damien reached out to stroke the coat.

"Soft. Must be warm," Damien said.

"Mr. Pickles gets so excited when we go out. He also likes to stay out longer." Mrs. C. reached into her coat pocket and pulled out the new tag.

"I need your help with something." She held it up.

"Sure. Let's go inside." Damien led Mrs. C. and Joe into the house. He closed the garage door behind them. "What do you need me to do?"

Mrs. C. put Mr. Pickles on the floor who scampered around looking for Coach and Gunner. He whimpered when he couldn't find them.

"Don't worry Mr. Pickles, your pals will be back soon enough." She removed her coat. "When will Dillon and the pets return?" Her lips puckered slightly as her brow lifted.

"They are expected back tonight." Damien lifted his wrist, checking his watch. "I am expecting them within the next hour."

"Good." She sat on the sofa.

Damien took the package Mrs. C. held out.

Joe sat next to her. "What did you bring over Mrs. C.?"

"I bought one of those fancy trackers. I can put it on the dog's collar and then all I have to do is connect it to my phone. But I don't know how. I was hoping you can do it for me."

Damien opened the package and read through the directions. "Do you have your phone?"

"Yes." She handed it to him.

Before he added the app to the phone, he made sure the tracking software he had placed on her phone was still working like it should. It ran in the background, keeping Mrs. C. from knowing it was there.

"Mrs. C., when are you going to make me a cake?" Joe asked.

She frowned at the handsome Irish cop. "Didn't I just make you brownies?"

"Yes, ma'am. And they were delicious. You could always make more of those."

Her eyes widened. "You ate them all, didn't you?"

Joe laughed. "Of course. How long were they supposed to last?"

"Longer than a day." She shook her head. "I don't know what to do with you two."

"Okay, Mrs. C. I have it linked to the app." Damien sat on the other side of her holding her phone where she could see it. "This red dot is Mr. Pickles. You can narrow the map or broaden it simply by pinching the screen." He showed her how to do it.

"Oh, that's fantastic. Usually, Mr. Pickles stays right next to me, but sometimes he gets away from me. This way, I can find him." She put back on her coat. "I need to walk him. He ate dinner. He always has to poop right after eating." She hooked the lead back onto the dog's harness after securing his collar around his neck. "Mr. Pickles, are you ready to do your walkabout?"

Mr. Pickles wagged his tail barking.

"You know Mrs. C., I can enclose your backyard like I did mine. It's a pretty large area, and it would allow you to let him out when it's raining. Or just too cold."

Her eyes lit up. "Ooh, I would love that. When?"

Damien smiled at her excitement. "I'll text the fence guy tonight. He will get it up as soon as he can." He tapped out the message to his buddy. Within a moment, he responded. "Looks like he can do it this weekend."

"That's perfect. I'll be gone, just do what you need to." Mrs. C. hugged Damien and Joe. "Thank you for your help," she said as she patted Damien's cheek. "I hope you two are staying out of trouble." She walked towards the front door.

"Not a chance, Mrs. C.," Joe said, opening if for her.

Mrs. C. leaned back looking up at him. His beautiful, emerald green eyes took her breath away. "I bet you were hell on wheels for your parents."

Joe feigned disgust. His hand covered his open mouth. Before the corners turned down into a pout. "I'm hurt. You think I would be a troublesome kid."

She rolled her eyes at him as she patted his arm. "You're so full of crap." She smiled at his widened eyes. "I love you, boys. Try not to get hurt." She waved as she walked away with Mr. Pickles in his fancy fur coat.

CHAPTER FORTY-ONE

Late Tuesday evening
Sunshine Valley Home

Shamus MacDougal sat at his computer in his little office. He pushed the day's mail to the side, including the padded envelope that had arrived earlier that day. His desk clock read ten thirty p.m. His eyes shifted to the office door. He pushed his glasses down his nose as he squinted at the lock. He smiled and turned back to his computer. "Okay, Google, tell me what I need to know."

He searched for any information on Chase Humphry's death. "I know there has to be something here." Shamus skimmed a few articles, but they had few details. He picked up his cell phone.

"What?"

"I need you to find out some information for me," Shamus said.

"Alright. What do you need?"

"Find out everything you can on Chase's death. I can't get any details."

Patrick chuckled on the other end of the phone.

"What the hell is so funny?"

"You lost your cash cow. Must be driving you insane."

Shamus' head pounded as his pulse increased. The muscles in his neck tensed, causing his jaw to clench. "I don't need him. I have plenty of money. I knew it wasn't going to last; I made provisions," he said through gritted teeth. He leaned back in his chair. A sneer filled his face. "You're the one who will miss his contributions."

"I don't think so. If you want to keep me quiet, you'll find some way to pay my fee."

Shamus flexed his fingers before making a fist. His blood rushed to his ears. "Don't threaten me, Patrick. I have covered my tracks. Have you?" He picked up a pencil from his desk, twirling it between his fingers.

"Shamus, nothing can be tied to me, other than I work for the home. Don't forget, I'm one of your mighty success stories. But if you think I didn't take out a security net, you obviously underestimated me. Let's cut the crap."

Shamus' jaw tightened. The snap of the pencil echoed through the office. "You forget about the other girl. She knows what you did for me."

"Last I checked, she was working in a strip club. She was having a hard time paying her rent. She isn't going to say shit. Especially when she hears about Chase."

"Did you kill Chase, Patrick?" Shamus asked.

"Fuck you. I didn't kill anyone. You're the one who should be worried."

Shamus regretted ever bringing Patrick into the fold. "Well, you should remember I can take care of you if I have to." Shamus waited for a response. Silence filled the line. "Listen, find me any details you can on Chase's death. Those detectives wouldn't tell me anything, but they made it sound like it was associated with the home."

"Did you talk with the lawyer?" Patrick asked.

"Yes. He said they wanted me to cooperate with them. But I'm not going to let those two dicks know about it. I'm going to make them jump through as many damn hoops as I can. The last thing I need is for them to snoop around this property."

"Can't the lawyer keep them from doing that?"

"He said if we give the police grief, it will look like we are hiding shit."

"He has protected the operation this long. He will keep it going. It brings in a lot of money." Patrick sighed into the phone. "Don't worry. They won't find them. We made sure to hide them. And the lawyer covered the records."

"Well, you better hope so. I'm not going down alone, Patrick. If it comes down to it, you're right there with me."

"You're the one who killed them. If you weren't a disgusting bastard and could keep your dick in your pants, this never would have happened."

"You like young girls too. Quit acting like you're high and fucking mighty." Shamus wiped his brow with his sleeve.

Patrick roared in laughter. "I may like them barely legal, but I don't dip into the kiddy pool. You couldn't keep your hands off them. You would think you would've learned not to play with the merchandise even all these years later."

"Get me the information." Shamus hung up. "Fucking bastard." He opened his special file. As he scrolled through the pictures, pleasure aches flooded his body. The tingling sensation that overtook him turned into shivering as his desire blanketed him. His body broke out in a light sheen of sweat.

Shamus' desire overwhelmed him. He loosened his belt and slid his hand down his pants. He softly stroked himself as he closed his eyes and thought of the young girl on his screen. His heart rate sped up. He was almost there when a ding of an incoming message stopped his fantasy.

He tried to finish, but he was distracted, wondering if Patrick had found out some information for him. He would finish later. He opened his email. He scanned the several unopened messages looking for the latest one. It had an email address he didn't recognize, but the subject line more than intrigued him. It had one word, *SURPRISE*. "Now, what do we have here?"

Shamus' heightened senses brought back the tingling sensation. He opened up the email to find several files attached. He opened the first one. It contained four photos of a young girl; a girl who looked familiar. His brow furrowed as he opened the second file attachment. It too had a few pictures in it. These pictures were date stamped with today's date. They were screen captures from the live feed he had in the basement. "What—what the hell?" He tapped the mouse, advancing each photo. His pulse roared in his ears. The lumps at the back of his throat had him struggling to swallow. "No!" His breathing coming in rapid pants.

He fumbled with the keyboard, trying to get back to his main screen. He hit the wrong button. "Fuck!" Shamus opened the file and scanned his photos. The pictures of the girls were still there. "I—I don't understand." He opened a subfolder within the current file. The feed from his surveillance camera showed no one in the basement. "What the fuck is going on?" he scrolled through all his personal photos.

The dryness of his mouth made his lips stick to his teeth. He used his tongue to moisten them, but the sandpaper-like feel made them worse. "No, this can't be happening. How could anyone get these files? Someone is playing a joke on me."

Shamus went back to the email and opened the last file. It too contained a series of photos. These photos stopped his breathing. The ache in his chest forced him to inhale. The breath burned as it entered his lungs. He swallowed hard, wiping the sweat from his brow. "Holy shit!"

Chase Humphry, or what was left of him, filled his screen. The empty eye sockets and gaping wound in the stomach made Shamus heave.

He grabbed his garbage can from the side of his desk and emptied his stomach. He grabbed the day-old half empty bottle of water from his desk and washed out his mouth, spitting the nasty water into the trash can. Another wave of nausea crested over him when he saw what was done to Chase's hands and feet. "My God," fluttered out of his mouth. The hair on the neck and arms stood on end. He lifted a trembling hand to his mouth, as he read the one caption on the last photo.

He didn't keep your secrets.

CHAPTER FORTY-TWO

Dillon drove up the driveway to her home. She looked in the rear-view to see Gunner sound asleep on the backseat. "Crap. It's only eight p.m., but it feels like we've been driving for days."

Taylor yawned. "I hear that. I don't think Gunner stirred after the last stop."

Gunner sat up at the mention of his name.

"I spoke too soon." Taylor stretched one last time before they began to unload the vehicle. "Let's get inside."

"I want to get Gunner and Coach into the house first. We can sweet talk the boys into helping us." Dillon opened the rear driver's side door and grabbed Coach's carrier. He meowed and head-butted the door of the crate. "I know baby. It's going to be good to be home. C'mon Gunner."

The dog jumped out of the rental truck and ran around the front yard area. He barked, sniffed, and peed on everything.

"Okay, Gunner. Everyone in the neighborhood will know this is your property," Dillon said.

He stopped mid-run when the front door of the house opened up. Gunner took half a second to barrel towards Damien and Joe as they stepped onto the porch.

"Hey buddy," Damien said as he reached down to scratch his ears. He smiled at Dillon as she walked towards him. "It's about time. We were beginning to wonder where the hell you two were." He wrapped his arms around her waist. He buried his face in her neck and inhaled. "Damn, I missed you."

Dillon sank into him. His hot breath on her neck made her body shiver. She kissed him softly at first only to lose herself in the moistness of his mouth. Coach mewed, breaking the spell. She leaned her head against his chest. "I missed you too." She lifted the carrier. "I think he did, as well."

Taylor squealed as she ran to Joe. "I missed you!" She jumped leaping into his arms. His hands found her butt as she wrapped her legs around his waist. She smothered him in kisses.

"Okay, babe," he laughed as she tickled his ears. "Man, it's been like three days. Maybe I need to go on a month-long undercover case."

She leaned back and glared at him. "You better not."

Damien took the cat from Dillon and led her by the hand into the living room. "We picked up Chinese on the way home tonight. And we made sure to leave you two some." He set the carrier on the coffee table and opened the door. "Joe even managed to leave a few pieces of cake."

"Cake from Mrs. C.?" Dillon asked.

Coach scampered out and ran to the kitchen. Not finding his food, he came running back into the living room. His meowing started as short squeaks, escalating into long howls.

"Of course." Damien looked at Taylor and Joe as they walked through the door. "Taylor, please tell me that bag has his food."

Taylor laughed. "It does." She walked into the kitchen almost tripping over Coach. Gunner ran in and spun her around. She grabbed the edge of the doorway to balance herself. "Holy shit. You guys trying to kill me?"

Damien walked to the window. "Looks like the back of the truck is full of boxes."

"It is. It's stuff I need to go through, but I'm not ready yet." Dillon sat on the sofa. She nodded to Taylor as she entered the living room to sit next to her.

They exchanged glances.

Damien squinted at the two women. "What's up?" He sat on the coffee table across from them.

Joe stood behind him. "Why did you guys come home today? We thought you would stay longer."

Taylor wouldn't look up.

Joe pushed Damien over and sat next to him. "What gives girls?"

"You want me to tell him or you?" Dillon asked her.

She sighed. "I'll tell him."

Joe's heart rate sped up. "Tell me what, Taylor?"

A smile crested her face. "I need to tell you something about my family."

Joe started to say something, but Damien tapped his knee against him, barely shaking his head. Joe tried to relax, breathing in slow, exhaling slower. "Talk to me, baby."

Taylor went on to tell him about what she and Dillon had discovered. She explained how she met the family and what they had done for her.

By the time she finished, tears had run down her cheeks.

"Taylor, I'm so sorry about your parents. I can't imagine what you're going through." Joe took her hands in his.

"I wasn't honest with you. I lied about my family and hid things from you." She wiped her cheeks. "I'm sorry, Joe."

Joe lifted her hand and kissed her fingers. "Listen, you would've told me in your own time. I'm not mad. I'm worried about your brother, Adnon." He looked between Dillon and Taylor. "Do you think this guy is going to come after you or do you think he is angry and looking for someone to blame?"

Dillon leaned back taking a deep breath. "Give him your phone."

Taylor opened up her text app. "Here are all the texts. At least the ones from the last few days. I quit deleting them after I told Dillon about what was going on."

Joe angled the phone, allowing Damien to read the messages too. Neither said anything as they read through them.

Damien dragged a hand through his hair, glancing at Joe. "This isn't good."

Joe shook his head. "No, it isn't." He turned to Damien. "We need to get ahead of this guy."

"I'll get my Dad on it." Damien studied Taylor. "Taylor, we will deal with this head-on. My Dad can gather all the intel on your parents and what happened there, and he can find out what your brother has been up to."

"I don't want to be a bother. You guys have this case. You don't need me and this drama adding to it." Taylor pulled her knees up under her.

"Babe," Joe said, standing and pulling her off the sofa. "This is nothing. Between Damien's Dad, and us," he waved towards Dillon and Damien, "we got you covered. We will get all the information we need, and then we will take care of it." He lifted her chin. "Do you understand how important you are to me?"

She nodded, sniffling.

Joe brushed her hair out of her face. "Hey."

She let out a hard sigh and closed her eyes. She made no attempt to wipe the loose tears away.

"Look at me Taylor," Joe said, cupping her face in his hands. "I am not mad you didn't tell me about your family. I know the kind of woman you are. You would've told me when you were ready. However, from this point forward, don't be afraid to tell me anything. Between the four of us, we will hit this head-on and take care of it. Okay?"

"Okay," she said, burying her face in his chest. It was the first time in several weeks she felt a small bit of relief. "I'm sorry, Joe. I wasn't hiding it from you. I hoped I would never have to go back to that part of my life."

"No worries, baby." He kissed the top of her head. Glancing at Damien, "You'll bring your Dad in on this tomorrow?"

"I will call him before I get to work." Damien ogled Dillon. She sat on the sofa hugging Coach. "Is this the reason you guys came home early?"

Dillon smiled at him. "That and we missed you guys."

He cocked his head, raising an eyebrow at her.

She laughed. "I promise. It was time to come home. The farm is in great hands. I wanted them to get started on the renovations, and it was time the farm got back to normal operations. It will help everyone heal. The next time I go down, it will be to see the house. I told Agatha we wanted to be the first people to stay in it."

The corners of Damien's mouth pulled upward. "Did you get the raccoons settled in?"

"What raccoons?" Joe asked, still holding Taylor in his arms.

Dillon's brow wrinkled. "You didn't tell him yet?"

"Tell me what?" Joe asked.

"I haven't had a chance," Damien said.

"Dude, tell me what?" Joe said with a bite to his tone.

Taylor stepped back and wiped the last of the tears away. "We did our own little investigation."

Joe's eyes shifted from Taylor to Dillon. "Are you telling me..." Joe rubbed his chin. "Racoons?"

"Yep," Dillon said. "Racoons made a home in the old mechanic's shop. A very large fat raccoon."

"And her babies," Taylor said.

"And her babies." Dillon stood.

"Are you sure?" Joe asked.

Dillon tilted her head, looking at Taylor then back at Joe. "Yes. We saw them with our own eyes."

Joe's brow wrinkled. "I can't believe it. It has to be more than—raccoons."

"I'm sure Jason will show up eventually, and you will get your chance to kill him," Dillon said.

"Is the wildlife ranger setting something up?" Damien asked.

"He is. He will set up a sanctuary. We are going to use the shop, the old shop. I told Agatha to let them do what they think will work best. He told us how to keep everything raccoon proof. We will provide food for them too." Dillon stood. "I also named the colt."

Taylor giggled.

Joe squinted at Dillon. "What did you name him?"

"Ringtail."

Joe glared at her. "You did that on purpose."

"Not really. Maybe a little. It does seem perfect though." She laughed at Joe's dejected look. "Let's get these boxes loaded up in storage before it gets too late." She patted Joe on the shoulder. "Let's go big boy."

CHAPTER FORTY-THREE

Wednesday morning 5:00 a.m.

Kerry sat in his home office. He used a VPN and searched for Patrick Winsted's information. Shamus' graciously provided Patrick's social security number in one of the files downloaded earlier. Using it in a program to cull Patrick's financials and credit history from the web, he sorted through other files. Shamus was dumb enough to keep records of every penny he paid to Patrick. While most of the payments were paid for work-related items, there were several payments originating from another account.

Digging deeper into Shamus' files, Kerry noticed payments going back to when Patrick was nineteen and listed as a full-time employee of the home. The payments amounted to thousands of dollars. Whenever a donation was made to the home, deposits were made into the home's business account, then into Shamus' personal account and finally some into Patrick's account.

"I can only imagine what you have been paying Patrick for," Kerry said out loud as he read through the file. His program pinged notifying him the search was complete. Opening the program, he read through years of Patrick's financials. Every purchase or bill he paid.

Reading through the information, Kerry laughed at how much porn the man paid for. "Damn, Patrick. You're a horny bastard, aren't you? Running a search on the porn sites, Kerry was surprised there was no kiddie porn. "It seems you don't share the same love of little girl's your boss does," Kerry muttered as he searched the man's downloaded porn videos. It didn't make Patrick less repulsive. The man seemed to have an affinity for gang bangs and rough sex.

Kerry's heart ached for the young girls in the video. Although they were of legal age, he couldn't imagine this was the lifestyle they dreamed of as a girl. He couldn't stand the sex videos any longer. He checked other files to see where else Patrick was making money.

"Well, I'll be damned." Kerry found regular payments to some very high interest-bearing accounts and investment accounts. "Patrick seems you know how to make your money grow. And grow fast." Several account balances showed a combined total of over one million dollars. "Not a bad nest egg, Patrick. Too bad, you won't be around to enjoy it." Kerry made sure to

make a note of all the account numbers. He would put the money to good use. He had several charities needing a boost in their bottom line.

Continuing his research, Kerry shifted his attention to Shamus. Using the usernames and passwords from the file, Kerry opened Shamus' accounts. There were several open and active bank accounts. The man was skimming money from donations and putting the stolen monies into them. As he scrolled through them, one caught his eye.

Kerry found the account in the password manager and used the username and password. Payment after payment filled his screen. Every payment was posted to an offshore account. Every payment was for tens of thousands of dollars. They went back as far as the nineties. His heart pounded in his chest as he scanned the deposits.

His gut tightened as he slowly yet forcibly expelled the breath he held. His brain processed the amount of money made over the last twenty plus years. Kerry poured over his memories of the home. He never saw this. And why would he? He was a kid.

But it all made sense now. During his two years at the home, before Sierra showed up, young girls would come and go so quickly. Shamus explained it all away by stating the girls had been adopted or moved to another home better suiting their needs.

"How could this go on, and no one see it?" Kerry asked out loud as he opened the cloud drive and searched the files of emails he had downloaded the other day at work. Maggie had mentioned a Suit would show up to the home periodically. That had to be whoever was helping Shamus hide the records of the girls.

"Son of a bitch," Kerry said as he read the emails. The parties had been careful to use secure nontraceable email accounts, and even though Shamus was arrogant enough to keep the emails, there was nothing pointing Kerry to the Suit. His stomach rolled at the callousness of these two men. He tightened his fists. Then flexed his fingers. His lips flattened as he ground his teeth.

He picked up his desk phone and dialed. "Hey Bob, it's me."

"Where you at? Is something wrong?"

"Listen, I'm sorry I'm calling this early. We don't have anything pressing going on at the office the rest of this week, do we?" Kerry continued to scan the emails between Shamus and the man he thought was actually pulling the strings.

"I guess not. We have the meeting with DataComp. But that's to go over what they need with their new security software. I can handle the meeting. I'll take Frank from IT with me. He knows everything."

"Okay. I know this is short notice, but I need to take care of something. I may not be back until next week."

"No worries Kerry. I got the office taken care of."

"Thanks, man." Kerry hung up. He reread a few of the emails. They didn't give away the name of the other man, the man Maggie referred to as the Suit. However, there were two people who knew the man's name, and Kerry was determined to get it.

CHAPTER FORTY-FOUR

Damien struggled to breathe, yet his chest rumbled. Something brushed against his face, tickling his nose and cheek. He swatted whatever it was away. A minute later, the annoying itch returned. Groggy and still half asleep, he tried to roll over, but something weighed him down.

"What the hell...," he trailed off as his heavy cat's tail brushed against his face. "Coach, why can't you sleep on the bed and not on me?"

At the sound of his name, Coach stood and spun around. Rubbing his nose and head against Damien's face.

He blinked rapidly. "Stop." He turned his head towards Dillon, only to be greeted by Gunner's wet nose. "For crying out loud." He lifted his head, craning his neck. Dillon had half the bed, with no pets. He had a sliver of covers, and the left side of his body was at the edge of the bed. "I don't believe you two." His head flopped back against his pillow.

Gunner nuzzled him, and Coach pawed at his chin.

"Stop." Damien waved his hand at them, in a shooing motion. Not understanding the signal, Gunner moved closer, draping his paw over him, and Coach rubbed his head against Damien's face. He reached over and poked Dillon in the back. "Wake up!"

She stirred and moaned in disagreement.

"Dillon, wake up!"

She languidly stretched and rolled over facing him. Her eyes blinked open. "Why are you waking me up? I didn't hear the alarm go off."

"If I'm awake, you're awake."

Her brow wrinkled together. "Why?"

"How is it I get a teeny tiny portion of the bed which I have to share with these two lard asses and you get all that space?" He pointed to her side of the bed.

Dillon giggled as she wiped the sleep out of her eyes. "I'm not responsible for what these two guys do at night. Maybe they like sleeping with you more." She stretched, looking at the clock on Damien's nightstand. "Shit, it's like five thirty." She poked Gunner in the back, then wrapped her arm around him and rubbed his belly. "Why you sleeping here? Your bed is on the floor."

Gunner stretched his front legs over his head as he bared his belly for more rubs.

"I'll let Gunner out in the back. C'mon Gunner let's go potty." Damien pushed Coach off his chest and grabbed a pair of shorts from the floor next to the bed.

As Damien exited the bedroom with Gunner in tow, Dillon decided a shower would help her wake up. She walked into the bathroom and turned on a classic rock channel. Music blared from the speakers in the ceiling. She programmed the shower to pump out 101-degree water. She removed her t-shirt and panties, stepping in, letting the multiple water heads sooth her still sore body.

Dillon lifted her face to the large shower head in the ceiling. "Shit," she hissed out the minute the pelting drops hit her still broken nose and cheek. She placed the palms of her hands against the wall to steady herself as the rippling pain subsided. Memories of the moment when David tried to beat her into a pulp, filled her head.

She had to slow her breathing, reminding herself it was over and David was dead. Hopefully, in hell with his father. Dillon squeezed her eyes shut, but the tears flowed out anyway. She stepped under the main shower head this time shielding her face. The clicking noise of the shower door made her turn around. "Did I say you could join me?"

"It is my shower." Damien moved to the center. "It feels like it's been forever since we took a shower together." Damien pumped out a few dollops of shampoo from the dispenser on the wall and rubbed it into Dillon's hair.

"Mhmm, that feels very nice." She turned around, allowing him to reach the back of her head. She swayed gently to his touch and the music.

Damien pulled her under the rain head letting all the shampoo rinse out before he applied the conditioner. He inhaled through his nose. Citrus and vanilla. "I love this smell. I remember the first time we met. I think I fell in love with the way you smelled."

She turned around, grabbing the shower sponge from the nearby shelf and slathered it in his favorite body soap. Dillon scrubbed his chest and arms, purposely avoiding his lower half. She then spun him around as she did the same to his back. "I remember the way you smelled. I leaned into you and smelled woods and pine trees."

Dillon slowly caressed his ass then moved down his legs. She spun him around, as she started to wash the front of his legs, moving slowly upward, when she lost her balance.

Damien grabbed her helping her stand. "Dizzy?"

She clung to him, wrapping her arms around his waist. "I keep forgetting about this damn broken nose. Every time I bend forward the blood rushing to my face feels like a jackhammer." She leaned back gazing into his sapphire blue eyes, her legs felt rubbery. Dillon reached up, taking two handfuls of his jet-black hair and pulled his head to hers, devouring his lips.

The warmth of his mouth ignited a fire within her. Something Dillon hadn't felt since she left the hospital several weeks ago. She moaned as their tongues dueled for supremacy, sinking into him as his hands roamed her body.

Damien moved her towards the wall, lifting her left leg, resting her foot on the bench. He trailed his finger down her chest between her breast while he maintained eye contact. His hand caressed each breast and moved slowly down her hips.

She lifted her arms, draping them over his shoulders.

Damien watched as the amber color in her eyes ignited with a fiery glow. His gaze was drawn to her lips as they parted, and her tongue licked them slowly. He bent down and kissed her as he teased her with his fingers. Damien placed his right hand under her raised knee, lifting it slightly as he entered her, swallowing her moan.

She broke the kiss, panting. Dillon tipped her head back, closing her eyes, focusing on the intensifying sensation. The fluttering in her chest and stomach made her shiver from the onslaught of pleasure. Her fingers dug into his back. Her leg bearing most of her weight quivered, barely keeping her steady.

Damien wrapped one arm around her waist. "I got you baby. I won't let you fall."

She opened her eyes, locking on his as she tightened her grip on his shoulders. The usual sapphire blue now dark indigo. Her body shuddered under the weight of his stare. Dillon's climax hovered torturing her with release then receding slightly. Only to build back up again.

Damien felt her body tremble. He knew she was close. He increased the movement of his hips, rotating slightly. His eyes never breaking contact. "I love you, Dillon."

She brought his mouth to hers. Hunger and passion made her greedy. She relished in the gentleness of his movements. Slow and fulfilling. Her eyes remained locked on his. "I love you more." Ecstasy overtook her as her supporting leg quivered.

"Let it all go, baby."

Damien's soft voice filled her ears. She closed her eyes and followed his command. Letting go everything from the last few weeks. Her breath hitched as the tears stung her eyes. As her orgasm raged a flood of emotions erupted. She buried her face in Damien's neck. She heard the soft grunts as he came inside her.

When finished they stood there, clinging to each other.

Damien leaned back and lifted her chin. Out of the line of the water, he knew the moisture on her cheeks wasn't from the showerhead. "Baby," he said as he kissed her lips, gently wiping away the tears. "Talk to me."

She buried her face against him. "I miss them so much. I see them and smell them. I feel like this is all my fault. Like somehow who I became, brought David to my grandparents."

"No, no baby. None of this is your fault. It's David's. It's his father's. None of this is yours." Damien placed his hands on the side of her face. Her soft cries tore Damien's heart to shreds. "You have to let go of guilt. It will begin to consume you if you don't."

She wrapped her arms around him. Not wanting to see his face and the pity staring back at her. "I'll be fine. I guess, I don't know. Everything welled up. It was like a giant damn broke." She squeezed him tighter. "I couldn't get through all this without you. I love you more than I can put into words."

"Dillon," he whispered as he kissed her neck. "I'm not going anywhere."

"You promise? No matter how bad it gets, you won't leave me?"

"I promise, Dillon. No matter what happens, I will never leave you."

CHAPTER FORTY-FIVE

Damien sat at the kitchen table. Several times he asked Dillon if he could help her, but she insisted on making breakfast on her own. "You're looking kind of wifey."

She stopped flipping pancakes and turned to look at him. "I could kill you for saying that."

He laughed. "Why does it make you so angry?"

"The wifey part. It makes me think you want a barefoot and pregnant wife running around the house."

"And what is wrong with that?" Damien's mouth watered as she placed a plate of pancakes, eggs, and bacon in front of him. "I could get spoiled with breakfasts like this."

"Don't get to use to it. Tomorrow I'm sleeping in." She sat across from him and slathered her pancakes with butter and syrup.

Damien raised an eyebrow at her. "Really?"

"What? I like a lot on my pancakes." Dillon looked at Coach, who sat in an empty chair at the table. Gunner sat right next to him on the floor. "You guys have to wait."

Damien shook his head. "That cat thinks he's a person."

She took a bite of her food, washing it down with a big gulp of orange juice. "What do you plan on doing regarding your case today?"

Damien shrugged. "I don't know what the hell I'm doing in this case."

"Explain."

Damien filled her in on what Baker and Davidson came up with regarding the girls at the home. Along with what happened at the home and the lady with the note.

Dillon stopped eating. "Let me get this straight. Since the mid ninety's this guy MacDougal has been sexually assaulting girls, possibly boys and no one in the state has caught on?"

"That's what it looks like."

"How the fuck does that happen? What about the suicides, how many do you have?"

Damien pushed out a sharp breath. "I have to pull the numbers; it's looking like about fifteen. Just during a three-year period. But I'm not sure how many occurred at the home or off the property. Davidson is tracking that down. Let's assume for argument sake, a few of those occurred at the home, you would think it would raise a red flag with someone."

"What about the worker who gave you the note, maybe you can get her to help you."

"She handed us the note as we were leaving. It's clear she is scared." Damien gave Coach and Gunner a piece of bacon. "Her name was Martha. I bet I could find her last name from employee records. Maybe she would speak to us."

Dillon's brow furrowed. "Something isn't adding up. If he is molesting girls, one of them had to complain, or tell someone." She swallowed a bite of food. "I know most won't, but over that many years someone had to say something."

"Someone did. Nancy Milligan. She spent some time at the home. She was raped by Shamus; she told her counselor at school. When she spoke with Shamus, he convinced her Nancy was a very troubled young girl. The counselor dismissed her. But when Detective Travis ran her, there was no record of her ever being at Sunshine Valley."

"How?"

Damien shrugged. "I have no fucking idea."

"What happened after Nancy spoke with the counselor?"

"She told us when she got home from school, Shamus threatened her. Said if she told anyone else, he would make sure no one heard from her again. Told her no one would miss her either. She said there was a girl who had disappeared prior to her and when Shamus threatened her, she ran away." Damien's fork stopped midflight to his mouth. "Wait."

"Wait, what?" Dillon asked.

"Nancy told us she was there, but the records showed she was never at the home. She also told us that when the DHS worker looked her up, she wasn't in the DHS system except as a runaway."

Dillon raised an eyebrow at him. "The official record says she was never there?"

"Yes. At some point, someone had to remove her from the entire system. I can't imagine that Shamus has the know how to do that."

"You think someone higher up might be helping him?"

"Seems logical."

Dillon sat back. "I want to help with this."

Damien frowned. "You can't work until you're cleared."

She shook her head. "I'm calling Phillip, I mean Director Sherman, I mean Phillip."

"Why don't you call him Phillip?"

"He's still my boss."

"Okay, when you have to talk to him as an employee, then call him Director Sherman. When you aren't, call him Phillip. He's more than a boss."

"I know that. I—I need time to sort that out." She pushed the remaining eggs to one side of her plate. She gave Gunner the bacon and placed the plate in front of Coach.

Damien's stomach tightened. He wanted to tell her everything the captain had told him. *Fuck, I hate this.* He was about to blurt out the entire conversation with Captain Mackey when Dillon's cell rang.

Her eyes widened. "It's Phillip. Is he psychic now?" She took a deep breath answering using the speakerphone. "Hey Phillip, I mean, Director." She placed a finger over her lips, looking at Damien.

"Good morning Agent McGrath. How are you feeling?"

"Great. Aside from my nose and cheek. I'm healing."

"Do you think you can go to the office today? AD Reynolds needs to speak with you about Agent Johnson. There are some situations that have developed, and I think it's imperative that you are in the loop."

Dillon sat up. Her eyes brightened. "Absolutely. I could use the distraction."

"Don't get excited, I don't want you working on any cases yet."

"Umm, about that."

"What have you gotten yourself into?"

"What, why do I have to have gotten myself into anything?"

"I know you. What? What are you about to ask me?"

Dillon squirmed around in her chair. "Damien is working this case. I want to help them. It wouldn't require me going anywhere. I would help track down some information. Things the Feds can get that they can't."

"Is this in regards to the Chase Humphry case?"

"Yes. He was called back in for it."

Silence filled the air.

"Hello? Director?" Dillon frowned at Damien who shrugged. He started to clean, but she waved at him to stop, again placing her finger over her lips.

He rolled his eyes at her folding his arms across his chest.

"I don't think you're ready for work."

"I'm not some wallflower. I can handle the shit I've been through. What I can't handle is sitting around doing nothing. All I do is fill my head with scenario after scenario. I need a distraction."

Director Sherman sighed heavily. "Dillon..."

"Phillip, I know you and Laura worry about me. I know how much you care for me. I also know I couldn't have gotten through those first few days without her here. She cared for me and sat with me, between her and Damien's mother, I didn't want or need for anything. And I needed that, from both of you. But right now, I need to do something. I can't sit around being little miss homemaker. Please. It's this case. I won't do anything in the field. I want to help Damien narrow in on a suspect."

"Okay. Okay. I will let AD Reynolds know. You can work with Damien. But, if you get tired or it becomes too much, I need you to step back. Before you get involved with this case, you need to take care of the situation with Johnson. AD Reynolds will fill you in. I'll tell him to expect you this morning."

Dillon silently danced around the kitchen. "Yes, I promise. I won't overdo it. I'll be in the office by eight a.m."

"I want updates on how you're feeling. Remember, whatever you need Dillon, Laura and I are here for you."

"Thank you, Phillip. I mean, Director."

"I'm sure I'll speak with you later."

Dillon glanced at her phone when the line went dead. "I hate it when he just hangs up. No goodbye, just hangs up." She sat in the chair then stood back up. "I'm too excited to sit." She began cleaning up the breakfast dishes.

"I know you're excited. But you have to take this slow. I can drive you into your office," Damien said as he helped load the dishwasher.

"Why would I need you to drive me?"

"You don't have a car."

Her lips puckered. "I have the rental truck. I'll call them and let them know I will keep it for a few more days."

"I guess that'll work. Wouldn't you rather turn it in and get a smaller car to drive around?"

"I don't care. I guess I could. There's a rental place on the way into work. I could trade it out." She tilted her head to the side. "The truck is a double cab. Kind of big."

Damien looked at his watch. "How about you call me when you are done with AD Reynolds, and you can come to Division Central. I know the guys would love to see you."

A smile pushed her cheeks up as her eyes shimmered. "I bet Hall misses me."

Damien pinched his nose. "I think he is in love with you. Which normally I would be mad at, but there's something about the way he looks at you. I'm not threatened or worried, but the man worships the ground you walk on. And he doesn't hide it. I guess it's why I'm not jealous."

She wrapped her arms around his waist and bit his bottom lip. "Are you sure you aren't a tad bit jealous another man has googly eyes for your woman?"

"If it was anyone but Detective Hall, the man would be dead and buried somewhere."

"Now that I'm a wealthy woman, I don't need you." She winked at him as she turned to leave the kitchen.

"Oh, really?"

His eyes darkened and narrowed in on her. Dillon's stomach fluttered. She giggled as she took off running towards the stairs.

Damien caught her before she reached them. He scooped her up in his arms and trotted up to the master bedroom. "I'll show you how much you need me."

CHAPTER FORTY-SIX

Wednesday 6:15 a.m.
Indiana Dunes

Kerry sat outside Patrick's house. He removed the leather driving gloves. Folding them, he placed them in the interior pocket of his jacket. Making sure not to touch any part of the car, he quickly put on the pair of black rubber latex gloves he carried in another pocket.

The drive had taken under thirty minutes with no early morning traffic. He had no idea if the man was home, the lights were still off in the residence. He looked back over his shoulder. The street was deserted. The middle-class neighborhood had small houses but bigger lots. Placing the nearest neighbor at least fifty feet away from either side of the house. Patrick's street had an alley in the back, allowing for off-street parking.

Kerry had rented a car at the airport, using false ID and credit card. He also switched out the plates with another one he had taken earlier from a different car lot. He had placed the original license plate in the glove box, allowing him to replace it when he returned the car. He had booked the car online, and all he had to do was pick his car from the row and go. No interaction with personnel.

He drove the car around the block and down the alleyway. There was a house for sale directly across from Patrick's home. A sign said 'shown by appointment only'. He parked in the small driveway. Before exiting the car, he removed a jammer from his pocket. Not wanting to take a chance if there were camera's anywhere, he jammed any RF signals within a twenty to thirty-meter range. He grabbed a small bag from the passenger seat and trotted to Patrick's back door. He crept around the house; no lights could be seen through the windows. Neither neighbor was awake.

Kerry stepped up on the small back stoop and made quick work of the locked door. Once inside, he used a penlight and made his way through the one-story cottage-style home. Beer bottles lined the counters and the table in the dining room. A twinge ran through his body. He hoped a late-night party didn't mean someone had slept over. The living room was empty.

Inching his way down the narrow hallway, Kerry heard heavy snoring from the room at the end directly in front of him. Placing his back against the wall, he peeked around the corner. Patrick was passed out face down on his bed, alone.

Kerry moved to the side of the bed, pulling a small syringe from his jacket pocket. He probably didn't need it, but he didn't want to get into a fight with the big man. He plunged the needle into Patrick's thick neck. The man twitched for a few moments then fell back asleep.

Looking at his watch, Kerry figured he had thirty minutes before the small dose of ketamine wore off. Doing some quick calculations in his head, he added some extra time due to the after-effects of the alcohol. And it looked like Patrick may have consumed quite a bit.

"Holy shit," Kerry said as he struggled with the dead weight of the large man. "Fuck, you weigh a ton." He managed to roll Patrick onto his back. Unable to move the man closer to the head of the bed, Kerry used the comforter the man rested on pulling the corners of it until he positioned him where he could tie him to the bed.

"Not the most ideal but this will have to work." Kerry had brought a coil of rope and removed it from his bag. Using a boning knife he brought, he cut the rope and tied Patrick's arms and legs to the legs of the bed. There was no head or footboard. Checking to make sure Patrick was secured, Kerry hauled a chair from the dining room and set it at the foot of the bed.

He waited.

CHAPTER FORTY-SEVEN

Wednesday 8:15 a.m.

Dillon parked the new sports car she traded the truck for, in her parking spot at the FBI offices. She sat in the driver's seat with her eyes closed. The last time she was here, David had chloroformed her and abducted her. She swallowed the bile trying to creep up her throat. "Push it down, Dillon. He's dead. It's over. Let it go." She inhaled a deep breath through her nose, exhaling through her mouth. Forcing herself to breathe slowly.

Exiting the car, she entered the office building and headed for the elevator. Harrison, the security guard manning the desk, greeted her with a big toothy grin.

"Well, well, well. Look who's back." He came around the edge of the security desk and gave her a big hug. "Damn you look good, Agent."

She smiled at the reaction of the big man. "I missed you too, Harrison." Dillon adjusted her weapon on the side of her hip. "I think you got even more handsome since I've been gone."

"What can I say." He pulled out a sheet. "Are you in your car?"

"No. I have a rental. It's parked in my spot." Dillon was mesmerized by the man's golden hazel eyes. They had a hint of green. She knew from prior conversations with Harrison that his mother was Korean and his father was black, blessing the man with the most gorgeous skin tone she had ever seen. He was more muscular than Damien, but not quite as tall.

"I'll go get the information and have a tag for you to put in the window. When will your car be done?"

"I'm hoping in the next two weeks. The interior is taking a little longer than they thought." Dillon headed towards the elevator.

"What car did you rent?" Harrison asked her.

Dillon smiled as she stepped into the lift. "A Corvette." She heard Harrison laugh as the doors shut. She readied herself for the stares and hugs she was about to receive, as it climbed to the FBI offices. When the doors opened, Dillon exhaled the searing breath she had been holding.

Margaret, the longtime receptionist and guard dog, didn't look up from whatever occupied her attention when she spoke. "May I help you?"

"I would think you might look up when speaking with someone." Dillon stood at the edge of the chest high desk.

Margaret glanced up and squealed as she came around and hugged Dillon. "It's good to see you." She squeezed the agent, not letting go.

"I can't breathe, Margaret."

She stepped back only to hug Dillon again. "I don't care. I was worried about you. I have missed seeing you." When she stepped back, tears wetted her cheeks.

"I missed you too. How have things been here?" Dillon asked as she handed Margaret a tissue from the box on the counter.

"Same as usual." Margaret glanced around making sure no one was behind her. "Have you heard about Agent Johnson? I mean I'm guessing that's why you're here."

Dillon cocked her head to the side. "Yes, I'm here to speak with AD Reynolds about Johnson. But I haven't heard anything. Why? What should I know before I walk in there?"

Margaret sat at her desk. "He's in a lot of trouble. He got in another fight with another Agent from the DEA over some missing evidence."

"Hmm. I can't imagine I have anything to do with missing evidence." Dillon walked to the frosted glass door. She was about to key in her code when Margaret buzzed her in.

"I'm glad you're back, Dillon." Margaret smiled at her.

"Me too." Dillon braced herself as she walked through the FBI offices. As she moved down the hallway, several Agents in their offices stopped and smiled at her. She stopped at her desk to drop her jacket on her chair.

"Hey Dillon," Agent Carmelo said, spinning around in his chair. "Man, it's nice to have you back."

"I have to say it's nice to be back." She nodded at a case file on his desk. "What you working on?"

"Two armed robberies at two banks in the last two months."

"You got any suspects? Any clues?" she asked, leaning against her desk.

"Nothing much to go on. Working with some detectives at one of the precincts in the area."

Dillon stood and headed towards the AD's office. "I guess I better see the AD. He's expecting me."

"I'm glad you're okay." Carmelo smiled at her. "It isn't the same without your sweet and kind personality filling the room."

She laughed as she walked out. "Fuck you, Carmelo."

"That's my girl." He waved her off as she left.

Dillon adjusted her shirt, calming her nerves before she knocked on the AD's door.

"Come in."

His booming voice made her jump. "Jesus, Dillon. Get a fucking grip," she said under her breath. Opening the door, she stepped in. "Hey, AD Reynolds."

The AD stopped what he was doing. "Agent McGrath. Shut the door behind you. Have a seat. How are you doing?"

She took the chair in front of his desk. "Pretty good. Glad to be out of the house."

"I spoke with Director Sherman. He said you were going to help Damien with the Chase Humphry case. You sure you feel up to it?"

"Yes, Sir. I need the change. I'm going crazy sitting at home."

The AD had been instructed to fill her in on everything. He hoped she was mentally ready for the shit about to hit the fan. But if anyone could compartmentalize and keep her shit separate, it was Dillon. "I need to bring you up to speed. What I'm about to tell you, stays here. You can share it with Damien. But no one else."

"Why would I need to share anything with Damien about my work?"

"It involves him. Actually, it involves someone at Division Central." The AD opened a file laying on his desk.

"I don't understand. Does it involve Damien or not?" she asked.

"Not really. Has Damien said anything to you?"

"About what? I was at the farm until last night. He and Joe have been working the Humphry case. To be honest, we haven't had much time to talk. Why? What should he have told me?"

AD Reynolds laughed. "It's not like that." He leaned forward in his chair, placing his elbows on his desk. "Okay, where to start. First, you're here so I can fill you in on a meeting you will be having with Internal regarding your complaint against Johnson. Nothing bad. They are going to ask you questions. Answer them honestly. They will only ask you questions about the incident with Johnson here in the hallway. If they ask you anything about Damien and Johnson, reply you can't give them any information, they have to ask Damien."

"I don't understand. Why would they even inquire about Damien and Johnson? Other than the fight which took place here, and I wasn't even present."

"Johnson is running his mouth. He's going after Damien with a civil suit..."

Dillon burst out laughing. "Good luck with that. Damien's family has some of the best lawyers in the country on their payroll. He won't get far."

"Look while you were gone some shit has bubbled up to the surface. I made a big deal of going to Division Central and making it look like I wanted all of Damien's investigations."

"Why? What am I missing?" Dillon bristled in the chair.

AD Reynolds held up his finger. "Hang on." He dialed a number. "Hey, you got a minute? Dillon is in my office." He nodded into the phone. "Okay. Call me back when you have it set up... Phillip is going to call me back." He didn't say anything else, as he returned the handset to the cradle. "How's the nose and cheek?"

She crossed her arms over her chest. "Seriously? Small talk?"

He laughed. "It will be easier to explain when we are all on the phone."

"We. Who is we?" Dillon asked.

The phone rang. "Reynolds. Alright, I'm putting you on speaker." He pushed a button on his phone. "Phillip you there?"

"Yes. Hey Agent McGrath," Director Sherman said.

"Hi." She peered at AD Reynolds. "What's going on?"

"One sec, Dillon," Director Sherman said.

She heard a few clicks.

"Are you there, Damien, Captain Mackey, and Chief Rosenthal?"

Dillon's eyebrows squished together as her hands gripped the arm-rests of the chair. "Uh, would someone tell me what's going on?"

"Me too," Damien said.

"Let me start," Director Sherman. "Damien, I know you have become aware of AD Reynolds and his inquiry into your past cases."

"Yes, a few people here at DC have told me," Damien said.

"Why are you interested in Damien's cases?" Dillon asked.

"I'm not," AD Reynolds responded.

"He's not. After the incident with Dillon and Agent Johnson and she pressed charges against him, we have learned Johnson and two other DEA agents and someone at Division Central are on the take. The problem is, we aren't sure who it is at DC. The two agents have agreed to assist us. They have told us Agent Johnson has someone high ranking at DC that has been funneling him information on cases that the DEA have been involved in."

"The Metacruze Cartel case?" Damien asked.

"Yes," Captain Mackey chimed in.

"When AD Reynolds came looking for all my files on Dillon's abduction, he was looking for the Metacruze Cartel?" Damien asked.

"Exactly," Director Sherman said.

"Damien, Dillon, it has nothing to do with either of you," Chief Rosenthal said. "And if it seems to others around you we are allowing the Feds to come after Damien, you need to be aware that it is all for show. If the person involved thinks we were looking at that case specifically, then we lose the upper hand."

"Chief Rosenthal was brought in shortly after the case went down. When Johnson had so many issues with Damien, it made us wonder if the person on the inside of DC works near or has some kind of connection with Damien or his unit," AD Reynolds said.

"I guess you want me to make a big stink about AD Reynolds picking on me?" Damien asked.

"Yes. I don't want you digging into why the AD is doing what he's doing. You can make a big deal about it. You can complain about it, but don't bring anyone in to help you look for why," Captain Mackey said.

"Listen, Dillon," Director Sherman said, "Johnson is dirty. We are operating under the assumption he has not figured out we are on to him. We also believe he will use his argument with you and Damien to deflect attention from him. Go about your day. Don't change anything about the way you would interact with him."

"I'm glad you guys decided to bring Dillon and me in on this. I was beginning to wonder what you guys were up to," Damien said.

"Dillon, you've been awfully quiet. What are your thoughts on this?" Director Sherman asked.

AD Reynolds leaned into her. "What are you thinking, Dillon?" he asked.

Dillon rubbed her broken cheek. Opening her jaw and closing it. "Do you have any idea who or at least what department this dirty cop is out of at DC?"

"This stays between everyone on this call," Director Sherman said. "Captain Mackey and Chief Rosenthal are the only ones from DC brought in on this investigation. To be honest, they are the only ones I trust at this point. Preliminary reports indicate three departments in question. Narcotics, Vice, and Robbery. We aren't sure if it is a detective or a lieutenant. Everyone in these departments are being investigated."

"Excuse me," Damien interrupted. "I can't imagine Lieutenant Diego would be involved in anything illegal. I've known the man for almost five years. I've never seen any kind of questionable behavior."

"That's all well and good, Damien. But he was directly involved in the Metacruze case," AD Reynolds said.

"I must be confused. Why does this center around the Metacruze case? Wasn't that closed, except pending the court cases for the traffickers?"

"Evidence has gone missing. Over fifteen kilos from the evidence locker," Chief Rosenthal said.

"How did you keep that hidden? I haven't heard one leak about this," Damien said.

"Only the ADA knows. She went to check something in the locker and found the missing kilos. She notified the chief and me," Captain Mackey paused, "she didn't tell anyone else. Not even her boss. She wasn't sure who to trust. As of now, she is the only outside person who knows it's been stolen. And whoever stole it has no idea we even know."

"This is a mess." Dillon leaned forward, placing her elbows on her knees. "Whatever you need from me, and I'm sure I speak for Damien as well, we will do."

"Absolutely, whatever you guys need," Damien said.

"Go about your business. If Johnson comes after you, proceed like you normally would, barring throwing him through any more glass windows," AD Reynolds said.

Light laughter filled the lines.

"I won't, I promise. My father has instructed me to let the lawyers handle everything and not touch a hair on the ugly troll's head. Unless he touches me first," Damien said.

"That's it. As more information comes across, I will disperse it as necessary. Agent McGrath and Lieutenant Kaine, you were brought into the fold because of your association with the main suspect, DEA Agent Johnson. But you two are to do nothing. I don't want you investigating or researching Johnson in any way. Do I make myself clear?" Director Sherman asked in an authoritarian tone.

"Yes, Sir. I understand," Damien said.

"I don't want any part of this investigation. The less I have to deal with that asshole Johnson, the happier I am. You said I could help Damien on this case. If it's alright, I will help from my home or Damien's office. I'd like to keep my distance from Johnson as much as possible. At least until I am reinstated to full duty." Dillon searched AD Reynolds expression, not sure what she saw there.

"I think that's a good idea, Phillip," AD Reynolds said.

"I do too. Captain Mackey, Chief Rosenthal, you two will be kept abreast of any developments. That's it for now." Director Sherman hung up.

The other lines disconnected and Dillon and AD Reynolds were left in silence.

"Is there any paperwork for me to sign?" Dillon asked, shifting in her chair.

"No. I made a big deal about this to keep Johnson from being surprised if he bumped into you here. If you were here for any other reasons, he might become suspicious."

"Okay. Then I can go?" Dillon stood.

"Yes. Internal will contact me with a time for the meeting. I will let you know when. I think it is a great idea for you to help Damien. From what I hear, he and Joe could use the help. Doesn't seem to be a shred of evidence leading to anyone." AD Reynolds smiled at her. "I'm glad you're doing better. I hope you know, I'm here for you, too, Dillon. If I can ever assist you or help you, all you have to do is ask."

Dillon took a step closer to the door. "Thank you, Sir."

"Go on, Agent."

She reached out and opened the door.

He rose as he spoke, elevating his voice. "I will let you know if there is any other paperwork I need you to sign."

"Yes, Sir." Dillon headed towards her desk. She picked up her coat from the back of her chair. "Hey, I'm outta here," she said to Agent Carmelo.

"It was good to see you, Agent." He turned back to his desk.

"You too, Agent Carmelo." Dillon headed down the hall and nodded to other agents as she walked past their offices. She heard someone laugh and glanced over her shoulder. When she turned back, DEA Agent Johnson was coming towards her. She locked eyes on him but didn't say anything.

"Fill out your bogus complaint against me?" he asked as he slowed his pace.

"You know it." Dillon walked past.

"You're a bitch McGrath."

"You're a big fat asshole," she replied as she walked out into the reception area.

CHAPTER FORTY-EIGHT

Patrick's head pounded. He tried to open his eyes, but they felt as if someone had glued them together. Blinking several times his ceiling came into focus. "Holy shit," he mumbled. He tried to lift his hand to his face. "What the fuck?" He yanked on his left arm, then his right. "Fuck!" He struggled to move his legs. He angled his head and looked towards the foot of the bed.

Kerry smiled. "Hi, Patrick. How's it been going?"

"Who the fuck are you?"

"Is that any way to treat a visitor?"

"Visitor my fucking ass. Untie me, you motherfucker." He yanked on his limbs. "Why did you tie me up, asshole?"

Kerry reached into the bag next to his chair and removed a boning knife. He walked casually towards the side of the bed. "Now, now. I don't like being called names."

Patrick's eyes widened. "Whoa, hey now. Let's talk about this." His stare shifted between the blade and the man before him. "Dude, I don't even know who you are. What do you want from me?" He tried to scoot across the bed. Stretching his right arm as far as he could. "Please, man. Tell me what you want."

Kerry grabbed Patrick by his hair. He dragged the blade from his temple down his cheek. Not cutting too deep but deep enough. "You'll remember soon enough who I am. Until then, we need to have a chat."

Patrick yelled out. He tried to turn his head, but the man's grip was too strong. Bile crept up his throat. He gagged, breathing deep to keep from vomiting.

"I have some questions for you. If you want to get out with minimal damage, you're going to answer my questions. Understood?"

"Yes. Yes, I understand. Whatever man. Whatever you want." The metallic smell of blood wafted around him. He rubbed his face on his shoulder. Repeating this only made his face sticky and his shirt wet.

Kerry stepped back to the foot of the bed and checked the bindings around Patrick's ankles. He began untying each shoe.

Patrick tried to move his foot, but the man tightened his restraints. "What are you doing? Stop, man. C'mon."

Kerry continued his task of removing the shoes and the socks. "Patrick, I'm going to ask you some questions. If I think you're lying to me, I'm going to punish you. If you answer, truthfully, I will show you some mercy. And I will let you go. Understand?"

Patrick nodded. "Yeah, sure."

Kerry sat, pulling the chair closer to the foot of the bed. "Tell me about what you do at Sunshine Valley."

"Um, tell you about my job?"

"Yes, Patrick. That was my question." Kerry dragged the tip of the blade along the bottom of Patrick's foot. "Now, answer me."

"Okay, okay. What do you want to know?"

"Everything. When did you actually start working for Shamus MacDougal?"

"Uh, shortly after my eighteenth birthday. I didn't have anywhere to go, and during the time I lived there, I got to be pretty good at handyman work. The ancient guy who used to run the maintenance department was getting too old, and he was really sick. Shamus gave me the job."

"Was there another reason you got the job?"

Patrick bit his bottom lip as he shook his head. "I don't think I understand what you're asking me."

"You want me to believe at eighteen you were wise enough and seasoned enough to run the maintenance portion of that home?"

"Hey, I'm not stupid. While I lived there, I qualified for tech classes at the community center while I was in high school. I learned a few various trades. How to fix things, concrete work, things like that."

"When did you start procuring little girls for Shamus, or should we call him Pops?"

Patrick's eyes widened. "I—I don't know what you're talking about."

Kerry's mouth pulled up into an evil sneer. "What did I tell you at the start of this conversation?" He asked, grabbing Patrick's left foot. In a swift movement, Kerry sliced off the tip of his big toe.

Patrick screamed, writhing on the bed. "Are you fucking crazy? My toe, oh God my toe," he cried out. "You sliced my fucking toe in half." Patrick's screams turned into groans. He panted spewing spit as he gritted his teeth.

"Technically, I only cut the tip-off. Now answer my fucking question."

"It started shortly after I got there. I was fifteen when I landed at that fucking place. I saw Pops take a girl down to the basement. I started paying

attention. He caught me one night." Patrick glared at the man. "I knew men like Pops. I told him what I knew. I explained he could help me and I would help him. That's how our relationship began."

"But you could have stopped it. Why didn't you?"

"You can't be serious? I was looking out for myself. Pops didn't care about me; he would have killed me like he did others. I wasn't about to be a statistic."

Kerry stepped closer to the bed. "You don't expect me to actually believe you? All you had to do was tell someone what you saw. You chose not to." He reached out with the knife and sliced off the rest of Patrick's toe beneath the nail.

Shrill screams filled the bedroom. "Why?" He whined. "Why did you do that? I answered your questions." Patrick gagged as a rush of blood flooded down his foot. He lifted his head and turned to his left, spewing vomit across the bed.

"Tell me what happened to Sierra."

"Who?" Patrick coughed. Spittle dribbled from the corners of his mouth. Kerry lifted the knife, squinting at him.

"Wait! Wait, please."

"I'm waiting," Kerry said as the knife rested against the second toe on Patrick's foot. "Twenty seconds."

"She came in about two years after me. I guess I was about seventeen. She was young. Maybe nine." Patrick lifted his head to look at the man. "I don't know anything else about her."

Kerry watched Patrick's eyes. He couldn't maintain contact. His breathing had increased, and sweat beaded along his forehead. He took the edge of the knife and sliced through the rest of his toes.

Patrick wailed. "You fucking asshole." He yanked on his restraints. He shimmied from side to side, trying to free himself. He lifted his head and looked at his toeless foot and passed out.

Kerry pulled the chair closer and sat down. He laid the knife on the edge of the bed and picked a small hand-held blow torch from his bag. Several times he paused to swallow the anger. He walked to the head of the bed and smacked Patrick on the side of his face. "Hey, sleeping beauty?" He smacked his cheek several more times. "Dumbass, wake up!"

Patrick blinked rapidly. He raised his head and caught a glimpse of his foot. "Mhmm, my foot. You cut all my toes off." He whimpered as he began to gag again at the sight of his bloody stump.

"Patrick, I still need some answers."

"Go away. Let me go." Patrick ogled the man. "How do you know about Pops and me?"

Kerry sneered at him. "I'll explain everything later." He crossed his heart. "I promise. First, you said Pops could kill you like he did others. Who else did he kill?" Kerry lifted the small blow torch and lit it.

"Dude, please don't use that on me. Please." Patrick's eyes filled with tears. "Pops killed this lady who worked for him. It happened before I ever got there. He told me about it. He killed a couple of the girls too."

"Was Sierra one of them?"

Patrick hesitated.

Kerry took the torch and held the flame an inch from his good foot.

Patrick screamed and tried to move his foot. "Stop! Please!" Tears streamed down his cheeks. The screams turned into guttural moans.

Kerry removed the torch and turned it off. "I can't understand why you don't want to tell me what I want to know." He picked up his knife and used the tip to slice through the freshly burnt skin.

"Motherfucker," Patrick screamed, "Okay, I'll tell you everything."

"You're going to start with telling me what happened to Sierra."

"Pops liked her. I don't know why. He abused her, took her to the basement several times a week. One night, she tried to get away by sneaking out of the home. Pops caught her." Patrick closed his eyes. "I had never seen him so angry. He grabbed her and threw her down the basement stairs, telling her, he was going to punish her. I tried to stop him. I ran down the stairs, and she was lying there limp, barely breathing."

"What did Shamus do next?"

"He was scared. He ordered me to help him get rid of her."

Kerry's pulse sped up. The vein in his neck bulge as his jaw clenched. "What did you do with her? Was she still breathing?"

Patrick trembled. "I swear, I don't know. I don't know if she was dead or not. He had me load her into the trunk of his car. He left right after."

Picking the knife up from the edge of the bed, and placed it against Patrick's little toe and sliced it off.

"No!" he yelled. "My God, please stop. Okay. After he left with her in the car, I didn't see him until the next afternoon. He had marked out a new area in front of the shop where he planned to extend the concrete slab."

"Did you ever see Sierra again?"

Patrick shook his head. "No."

Kerry picked up the bag from the floor and carried it, the blow torch, and knife to the right side of the bed.

Patrick's eyes bulged. "Man, please don't kill me."

"You still don't know who I am, do you?" Kerry asking standing over the man.

"No, should I?"

"Don't you remember the kids you tortured while you were at the home? I can't imagine I was the only one. Surely you must think about those kids once in a while?"

"I was a teen, man, I was fifteen. Some of the stuff I did was for survival, some for fun, you know, what stupid kids do to their friends."

"I don't remember ever being your friend. And you were seventeen when Shamus hurt Sierra. You could've stopped him."

"No. As a kid, I had no power against Shamus. He made people disappear. I didn't want to be one of them. I wanted to survive there."

"And yet all these years later, you still stay there. As a grown man. You know he is still hurting girls, and you do nothing," Kerry said. "But after the way you treated me, and some of the other kids, even at fifteen, I think this is who you are. And I think you like what you are."

Patrick squinted at him. "You keep talking like I know you. I don't know who you are." He shook his head. "I've never seen you before."

"How about this, do you remember a kid you pissed on out behind the shop?" Kerry lit the blow torch.

Patrick's gaze drifted towards the ceiling, searching for any memory of the event. "I don't remember." He squeezed his eyes shut. His breathing came in rapid pants. "I'm sorry, man. I'm really sorry about it, though."

"Who else is helping Pops?"

Patrick's body shook. "I don't know."

Kerry took the blow torch and held the flame against Patrick's thigh. His jeans bubbled and then melted onto Patrick's skin. Kerry repeated this, two more times.

Patrick's screams of agony filled the bedroom. "Stop! Please!" he cried. The caustic smell of burnt denim and skin filled the bedroom. Patrick coughed, then vomited. He turned his head to the side to keep from choking. "Maggie always called him the Suit. I only found out after Sierra went missing."

"What do you mean, after Sierra went missing?"

"*After I helped put her in the car, I heard him on the phone in the office. He called someone. He only ever referred to him as Boss. He's got a lot of power. He's been helping cover up the disappearances of the girls.*"

Kerry turned off the torch. "*How? How can someone change the records and make someone disappear, and no one question it?*"

"*His job. Gives him all the power. In my drawer,*" Patrick nodded towards the tall dresser in the corner. I have tapes, videos, and recordings. I also have private emails between him and pops. I have been collecting everything I could, for insurance. I've seen firsthand what this man is capable of. Pops is a sick bastard, but as long as he provides girls, and the money flows in, the Suit doesn't care. But I know one day, he's going to close the operation down and I don't want to go down with it.*"

"*Everything is in this drawer?*" Kerry walked towards the dresser. Inside he found a large leather satchel filled with tapes and cd's, as well as a file of printed emails and several jump drives.

"*Everything you need to hang Pops and the Suit is in there. I uploaded all the recordings and video to a cloud account. The password is in there.*"

Kerry walked back to the bed. He removed a ball gag from the bag he'd brought with him.

"*No, man. No, no, no! You said you would let me go!*" He squirmed and writhed on the bed. Screaming at the top of his lungs.

Kerry laughed. He grabbed Patrick's hair with one hand and stuffed the gag deep into his mouth. Fighting to hold his head still, Kerry secured the strap. He patted the man's chest. "*I know what I said. And I am truly sorry. I seem to have a problem with lying.*"

CHAPTER FORTY-NINE

Wednesday morning 9:30 a.m.
Sunshine Valley Home

Shamus read through his appointments for the day. He had a meeting at the school with the new guidance counselor. He had a meeting with the Board of Trustees later that afternoon. "I wish I could run this house and the trust. It would sure make my life easier."

He rummaged through yesterday's mail. After seeing the pictures of Chase on his computer, he had to get out of the house. He wasn't sure who was messing with him, but he had a pretty good idea, it was Patrick. This would be something he would do. If for nothing else to make sure he knew Patrick had the goods on him.

"Damn, I should have gotten rid of him long ago." He pulled the padded envelope from the stack. It had been sent overnight from a law firm in Chicago. "What's this?" he said with the excitement of a little kid.

He opened the package and pulled out a pretty blue box. "Well, this looks like a nice surprise." He removed the ribbon from the box and lifted the lid. A little note card sat on top of neatly folded pink tissue paper. Blocking him from seeing what lay beneath. The scripted note had two lines on it.

Maggie Newsome told me all about you.
I wanted you to have something to remember her by.

"Maggie?" Shamus had to think for a minute. When it dawned on him who she was, his hands shook. His raspy breaths echoed in the quiet office. He glanced at the open door. Rising, he quickly shut and locked it.

His first thought was to throw it away. But he had to know what was in the box. He blew out a deep breath as he lifted the delicate paper. "What the hell?" The first layer of tissue lifted easy. The second layer was stained with something red and sticky.

As he peeled the second layer back, he gasped. Bulging eyes kept him from blinking as he bolted backward. The wheel of his rolling desk chair caught a cable, sending him flying. He smacked the back of his head on the file cabinet.

In an unsteady movement, he stood and crept towards his desk. Inside the box, a bloody tongue stared back at him. "Maggie. Maggie, you stupid bitch. I know you told." He paced his office, trying to slow his breathing. "Who, Maggie? Who the fuck did you tell?"

Shamus picked up his phone and called Patrick's cell. "Answer, you fucker, answer." It switched over to voicemail. "Listen, I need you to call me. Now!" Shamus slammed his phone onto his desk. "Son of a bitch."

He had to make one more call. He picked up his phone. His fingers trembled. He had difficulty pushing the correct numbers and had to start over several times. He swallowed, hard. It rang once.

"I thought I told you not to call me on this line ever."

"We have a big problem." Shamus rubbed his forehead.

"What is the problem?"

"Maggie is dead."

CHAPTER FIFTY

Wednesday morning 10:30 a.m.
Division Central

Damien looked over the list Mr. Martin Escobar's secretary had emailed him. He scanned the names searching for the ones he could recognize right off the bat. He was about to call Davidson into his office when his cell phone rang. "Kaine."

"Lieutenant Kaine, this is Jeffrey Moreno."

Damien sat up straight. "Mr. Moreno, thank you for calling me back so quickly."

"As soon as we heard someone was investigating Clara's death, we cut our trip short."

Damien's brow wrinkled. He held in the exasperated sigh. "I'm sorry, I think there is a misunderstanding. I thought Clara committed suicide?"

"That's what the report said, but my wife and I have been trying to get someone to investigate it."

Damien opened his desk drawer, rummaging through it, he removed a pad and pen. "Okay, let's take this from the beginning, but before we do, would you mind if I called in a few of my detectives working on this case with me?"

"Not at all, Lieutenant. We need your help."

"One second, I'm going to put you on hold for a moment." Damien laid his phone on the desk and walked to his door. "Joe, Davidson, you two come in here, please."

He sat back at his desk and picked up his phone. "Davidson, where is Baker?"

"She's at a court hearing for an unrelated case." He glanced at his watch. "I expect her back pretty quick."

Damien nodded. "She told me. I forgot. I have Mr. Moreno on hold. Mr. Moreno?"

"Yes, I'm here."

"I'm going to put you on speakerphone," Damien said as he waved his detectives into his office. "Mr. Moreno, can you hear me okay?"

"Yes, Lieutenant. My wife is with me, as well."

Damien nodded to Davidson and Joe. "I have Detective Hagan and Detective Davidson with me. Can you start from the beginning and tell us about Clara?"

They heard a shuffling sound and some inaudible whispering.

"I'm sorry, Lieutenant Kaine, my wife insisted on me putting the phone on speaker."

"Hi, I'm Sandy. Clara was wonderful. By the time she came here, she was damaged. We knew something had happened to her, but she refused to tell us."

"We decided to have her see a counselor, and we told her when she was ready to talk, we would be here. She had asked to be homeschooled, and we agreed. She seemed to thrive," Mr. Moreno said.

"You said you don't think Clara killed herself, can you tell us about that?" Damien asked.

"She had begun to open up to the counselor," said Mr. Moreno.

Davidson leaned into the desk. "Mr. and Mrs. Moreno, I'm Detective Davidson. Can you tell us who the counselor was?"

"Dr. Jane Freeman," Mr. Moreno said.

"Do you know what Clara told the counselor?" Damien asked.

"No. She wouldn't violate patient confidentiality with us. Legally we are—were not her parents but..."

"Clara was like a daughter to us." Mrs. Moreno interrupted her husband. "We didn't need a piece of paper. We still thought of her as our daughter. The state was reluctant to move forward with the adoption."

"Why?" Joe asked.

"Clara was going to be seventeen the year she died. The state said they thought it best to get the okay from her therapist before she went through the stress of adoption hearings."

Damien scribbled on his note pad. "Why do you think Clara didn't kill herself?"

"Tell him, Jeffrey," Mrs. Moreno whispered into the phone.

"Listen, they said she took a bunch of pills and alcohol. They found a suicide note. But when we read the note, it didn't sound like Clara. The note said she was sorry for putting us through all this trouble, and she couldn't take the depression anymore. I'm telling you, Clara wasn't depressed, not enough to commit suicide."

Damien's gaze shifted between Davidson and Joe. He squinted at them both. "Where was she found?" he asked.

"In her car. She had left her therapy appointment Thursday evening, around seven thirty. When the therapist left her last appointment at nine-thirty, she found Clara in her car," Mr. Moreno stated.

"Dr. Freeman had said the appointment had been emotional, but even she felt Clara wasn't depressed enough to hurt herself. The ME found nothing suspicious and ruled it a suicide. We have been trying ever since to get the ruling changed and get it reopened as a homicide," said Sandy Moreno.

"Or at the least an unsolved death. But to pin it as a suicide...it seemed like no one but us cared enough to investigate," Mr. Moreno said.

"Mr. and Mrs. Moreno, we didn't set out to investigate Clara's death. We are, however, working on a murder investigation of someone who was at the home after Clara had been there. We will do our best to give you guys some answers."

"Thank you. Thank you so much." Mrs. Moreno squealed on the other end of the phone.

"Sandy, don't get your hopes up," her husband said.

"Yes, please don't. I can't guarantee we will find anything to contradict the answers you already have. But I will do my best to get all the facts for you. Can you send me a copy of her death certificate and any other information you have for her?" Damien asked.

"Mr. Moreno," Joe said, "do you know if Clara kept a diary?"

"Yes. She did. She didn't have much in it. But the therapist had told her it may help her come to terms with what she experienced," Sandy Moreno said.

Damien and the others heard a muffled sound.

"No, I think we should tell them," Sandy Moreno whispered.

"Mr. and Mrs. Moreno, tell us what?" Damien asked.

"We never turned the diary over to the police. I know it was wrong. But when we figured out they weren't going to look any further than suicide, we didn't want to lose the book to an evidence locker," Mr. Moreno stated.

"We know it wasn't the right thing to do. But it was all we had left of Clara," Sandy Moreno said between the sniffles.

"I'm not concerned with her diary, but I would like to read it. If I sent an officer to your home, would you let us borrow it? I promise to return it as soon as we are done with it," Damien said.

"That would be fine with us. We will expect someone today." There was a pause. "Thank you, Lieutenant. You have given us some hope."

"As soon as we have any information, I will contact you. Thank you again, and I will have an officer there in the next few hours," Damien said.

"We will be waiting." Mr. Moreno disconnected the call.

"What do you think?" Damien asked.

Davidson swallowed his mouthful of jellybeans. "I think someone wanted her dead. It makes sense with what I have found so far."

"What have you got?" Damien asked, grabbing three sodas from his little fridge. As he turned around, Dillon walked through the door. He stood and moved towards her. "Hey, babe. We got some information. Davidson was going to fill us in on what he has come up with. I can bring you up to speed afterward."

She raised her hand in a half-wave, before sticking it back in the front pocket of her jeans. "Cool."

"Take my seat," Damien said.

Dillon sat and opened the soda can sitting on his desk. "What you got?"

Davidson scrutinized her. "You get to help us with this case?"

"Is that a problem?" she asked, raising an eyebrow at him.

"Hell no. With your help, we should have this solved in a hot minute," Davidson replied smirking at Damien.

"You're hilarious. Soon to be Sergeant Davidson, was about to tell us what he has found out."

Davidson laughed. "I went back over the names of the missing girls. Out of all the girls who were listed as suicides, their records indicate overdose on pills or hanging. Most of the girls overdosed. A handful hung themselves somewhere on the property."

"Medical records?" Damien asked.

"All the medical records were signed by the ME.

"Dr. Morgan?"

Detective Davidson shook his head. "No. A doctor Theodore Osgood."

"Who is that?" Damien asked.

"A doctor the city employs. I guess he fills in for Dr. Morgan."

Damien turned to Dillon. "Can you pull any records on this doctor and make sure he's a real doctor?"

"Sure." She turned towards Damien's computer. "Unlock this and I will log in from here and check."

Damien unlocked his desktop for her. He turned towards Davidson. "When you're done here, check with Travis and see how and when Osgood filled in for Dr. Morgan."

"Dr. Osgood is a retired ME. He often fills in for various jurisdictions in Indiana. From the records, he seems to be on the up and up," Dillon said.

Davidson made some notes. "Back to what I was saying. There was very little in the way of investigations. By the time the police or authorities were called, Shamus or a worker had tried to perform CPR on the girls leaving the scenes trampled. But the ME reports that nothing seemed out of the ordinary, and they were ruled a suicide. Now, as for the runaways. I couldn't find one girl. Not one."

Dillon glanced around the room. "I know I need to be brought up to speed, but what I'm hearing is you have a shit ton of girls you can't find, who left the home at some point, never to be heard from again."

"Yes, that pretty much sums it up," Davidson said.

"We got off a phone call with foster parents who took in a girl who ran away from the Sunshine Valley. They said she was doing well and was close to telling her therapist what had happened to her. she left an appointment and was found dead in her car hours later. From a drug overdose."

"Was she suicidal?" Dillon asked.

"Not according to her foster parents. They wanted to adopt her, but the state dragged their feet on it. Saying something about she didn't need to go through the stress of an adoption hearing until she got a release from the therapist."

Dillon leaned back in Damien's chair. "That doesn't make sense. The State wants these kids adopted. Especially if the foster parents are in good standing. I can't imagine the State of Illinois would balk at an adoption. It relieves them of any responsibility for the child moving forward."

Joe nodded. "Then why would they contest an adoption?"

Dillon looked at Damien. "Who did the Moreno's file their request for adoption with?"

"I will find out." He pulled his cell phone from his pocket and called

ECD.

"ECD, Detective Travis."

"Hey, it's Damien. Can you tell me who Jeffrey and Sandy Moreno filed their petition of adoption with? I need to know who might have been informed of the request."

"Sure Kaine, give me some time, I'll run it down."

"Thanks. Oh, and one more thing. I need you to check out...hang on." Damien dug through his desk until he found the business card. "I need you to see if a Freda Marksman is still alive and where she might be."

"Who's this?" Detective Travis asked.

"A high school guidance counselor from 1994. The high school is the one in The Dunes. And sorry one more thing, pull the records on Clara's suicide from the police," Damien said.

"No problem. I'll get back with you."

Damien disconnected the call. Looking around his office, he continued. "Okay let's assume, for argument's sake, the State did tell them. That doesn't stop anything else from continuing. Clara would've continued her counseling. Then at the age of eighteen, she would be released from state custody. The Morenos indicated they would've adopted her then. One year wouldn't make a difference to them. They treated her like their daughter anyway."

"Then who would benefit from the adoption not going through?" Joe asked.

"If you think, like the Morenos, Clara wouldn't have committed suicide, then the better question to ask would be, who would benefit from Clara's silence." Dillon looked up at Damien. "I think this would be a good time to fill me in on where you guys are at."

Damien, Joe, and Davidson explained what had been uncovered thus far.

Dillon sat quietly as she listened. She took the pad from the corner of Damien's desk and scribbled several lines of something. She crossed out lines and rewrote lines. She mumbled to herself. When she had finally finished, she looked up and found everyone staring at her. "What?" she asked, squinting at them.

Joe smirked, trying to hide his giggle.

Dillon glared at him. "What is so damn funny?"

"You and your quirky habit. It makes me laugh," Joe said.

She glanced at Damien, giving him an evil eye. "This is not a quirky habit. It helps me think and organize."

He chuckled. "Why are you giving me a dirty look? Joe is the one who opened his big mouth."

"Because I know you two always laugh at me." She glanced at her notes.

"What did your beautiful mind come up with?" Davidson asked.

Joe smacked him on the arm. "Suck up."

"Hey, I'm not stupid enough to piss her off," Davidson said.

Baker walked up to the door of the office. "Hey, Lieutenant, I'm back." She nodded at the crowded room and smiled at Dillon. "Hey Agent McGrath, it's great to see you."

"You too, Baker," Dillon replied before taking a sip of her soda.

"Baker, I need you and Ivansky to run out the Moreno's farm. It's north of the city." Damien used the GPS on his phone and retrieved the address. He scribbled it on a piece of paper and handed it to her. "They are going to give you a diary. Do not put it into evidence. Understand?"

"Yes, Sir."

"When you get back if I'm not here, you sit and read it. If you need a quiet place, use my office. Let Davidson know where you are," Damien said.

Her eyes lit up. She had to pinch her lips together to keep from smiling. "I can do that. Thank you, Lieutenant." She turned and left.

Damien caught Dillon's wrinkled brow. "She's up for the Detective exam."

"Makes sense." Dillon nodded.

"Plus, she was the one who found the connection between Patrick and Shamus. I want to get her take on the diary." Damien turned to Joe. "I think we need to go down to The Dunes and question Patrick." He looked at Dillon. "You can go with us, right?"

She paused for a second. "I'm not supposed to do any fieldwork, but I think I can go and be part of the questioning of a person of interest." She rose, "I'll call my AD and make sure." Dillon walked out of the office. "I'll be right back."

Damien turned to Davidson. "I need to know who the last person to come in contact with the missing girls was. I have a feeling it's going to be Sunshine Valley. And if that is the case, I can use it to get a warrant for their records."

Davidson stood. "I'm pretty sure you're right. But I will find the paper trail."

Damien reached into his desk and pulled out the file Mr. Escobar's secretary had sent him. "Make a copy of this and give it back to me. This is a list of names from Escobar's secretary. It is all the residents since he took over in 1995. Start with concentrating on the time of Chase's stay. He was willing to give me this but not any discipline records until he checked with the State's lawyer. Cross-check this with whatever you find."

Davidson took the list. "I'll get right on this."

"One more thing. Look for a Britney Lewis. See if she is on the list you got from Detective Travis, or on this list from Escobar. If not, see if Detective Travis can find her in the DHS system."

"You got it." As Davidson walked out, Dillon walked in.

"Hey, all clear?" Damien asked.

"As long as I don't shoot anyone, I should be good." Dillon opened the little fridge. "When did you get this?" She took another soda from it.

"When Lieutenant Stevens filled in for me, he brought it in. No one has come to take it back, yet." Damien grabbed his jacket. "You ready, Joe?"

He nodded. "Let me get my shit." He walked out of the office.

Damien moved to stand in front of Dillon. He rubbed her arms before embracing her. "How did the rest of the meeting with your AD go?"

"I learned everything in our phone call." She glared at him. "How much did you know before the phone call?"

He laughed. "Captain Mackey pulled me into his office early Monday, he didn't tell me much, but enough to keep me from wanting to punch AD Reynolds. The rest I learned with you during the call." He kissed her softly. "We need to get going."

"Hmm. I think you knew more. But I get why he had to tell you what he did. I know you were stewing about AD Reynolds looking into your cases. Now we know Johnson is a dirty cop," Dillon said following him out.

"I have a feeling this is going to get a hell of a lot worse before it gets better." Damien walked over to Hall and Alverez's desks. "Where's Hall?" he asked Alverez. The only woman detective in his unit. He couldn't help but stare at her. She came in from Vice, and still had a hard edge.

Alverez smiled at Dillon, squealing as she stood to give her a hug. "Girl you are looking fantastic." She wrapped her arms around her and kissed her cheek. "How you been?"

Dillon's eyes widened at the show of affection. "I've been good. How's it been here?"

"Not bad. Better since our fearless leader is back." Alverez looked at Damien. "Although Lieutenant Stevens was a pretty good substitute. If we ever have to have a new leader, I hope you can put him in your chair."

"I'm gone for a few weeks, and you're already trying to replace me." Damien shook his head. "Where's Hall?"

She recoiled, placing her hands on her hips. "Didn't he tell you?"

Damien looked at Joe, who shrugged.

"Don't look at me," Joe said.

Alverez laughed. "He had an early morning doctor's appointment. He thinks he is dying. Has a cough he can't get rid of. He's sure it's cancer. I told him it was allergies." An evil grin filled her face. "I made a bet if it is allergies, he has to buy me lunch for a week."

"Easy money right there." Joe laughed.

"You know it." Alverez lifted her fist until Joe bumped it. "I plan on making him pay for my favorite restaurants all week."

"Keep me posted about your case." Damien turned to Davidson. "Let me know what you come up with. I doubt we will make it back before you leave. If anything needs my attention, call me."

"Roger that." Davidson went back to reading over the names.

CHAPTER FIFTY-ONE

Wednesday 1:00 p.m.
The Dunes
Friendly's Diner

Kerry sat at a table in the back of the diner with his laptop open. He read through the file he took from Patrick's house. Everything he needs to nail Shamus and his partner is here. As he read, his anger boiled. Shamus has used his position as a therapist to take advantage of young girls. He raped girl after girl over the years at Sunshine Valley. He used his prominence as a psychiatrist to manipulate the system.

The files show when and how girls were taken. If a young girl came in and Shamus liked her, he slowly began to isolate the girl. Keeping her away from the rest of the girls in the home. Patrick had notes of how he would do this.

"You weren't as stupid as I thought you were, Patrick." Kerry smiled at the waitress as she came by and refilled his ice tea.

"You want a piece of pie?" she asked.

"Sure. What you got?" Kerry asked.

"Pecan, chocolate cream, and lemon meringue."

"Chocolate cream."

"Coming up," she said as she walked away.

Kerry opened his phone, connected his mobile hotspot, then logged on to his computer, and looked up Chase Humphry. He wanted to see if the news was reporting anything about the home in association with his murder. He couldn't find much. However, he did find the two investigators who were on the case. He read about Lieutenant Damien Kaine and Detective Joe Hagan. Kerry made some notes on the two men. He found himself drawn to Lieutenant Damien Kaine.

As he sat in the diner waiting for Shamus to go out, Kerry researched the lieutenant. He found he liked the man. From what he could gather, Damien was a man who sought justice and often blurred the lines to find it. He read about his suspension after the last case he handled where his live-in girlfriend, an FBI agent, was abducted and almost killed.

"Honey, this pie is really good with a cup of coffee. I brought one for you."

She winked at him. "It's on the house."

He smiled at the petite waitress. "Thank you. I could do with a cup of coffee. You must be a mind reader."

"Well if I was, I sure as shit wouldn't be working here. I would've bought a winning lottery ticket." She laughed as she walked away.

Kerry glanced at his watch. He had a few hours before Shamus would go to the local bar for his Wednesday night dinner. Patrick had told him it was a regular occurrence. The bar was about twenty minutes from the home. Close enough Shamus could get back to the house if needed. But far enough away no one would bother him.

Searching maps on his computer, he saw a few different routes he could take to get there. Kerry didn't look anything like he did fifteen years ago. He knew Shamus wouldn't recognize him. His plan rested on that fact.

He sat with the file from Patrick's home opened on the table. His first bite of pie, made him stop and sigh. It was delicious. Kerry took a sip of the hot black coffee and savored the flavors. "Chocolate and coffee do go well together," he said as he took another bite of pie.

He watched a family enter the diner. They had two young girls with them. He thought of Sierra. He pinched the bridge of his nose to stymie the tears. Kerry wondered what she might look like now. She would've been in her twenties. Six years younger than himself.

From what he had been able to learn over the years, he left the home shortly after Sierra came there. Within days. Kerry was seventeen when he got a special scholarship to MIT. He took the opportunity and never looked back. He knows he had no idea Sierra existed until after the fact, but that didn't keep him from carrying the guilt with him.

Turning back to the file again, he decided what he wanted to do. There was clearly one person who allowed Shamus to get away with what he did in order to line his pockets. He used little girls like a commodity. Death would be too easy for this person. No, Kerry planned something worse. He had to make sure the information fell into the right hands.

CHAPTER FIFTY-TWO

Wednesday 12:30 p.m.

Mr. Martin Escobar sat in the office of the Secretary of Human Services. The round table had been gathered the moment he requested information be released to the appropriate authorities regarding the files of the kids who had stayed in Sunshine Valley. The Secretary of Human Services and the State's lawyer had requested an immediate meeting.

"I still don't understand why this is such a big deal." Martin Escobar said as he tapped the conference table. The lawyer for the Secretary peered at him over his wire-rimmed glasses. He wore his short salt and pepper hair in a style more for a man of thirty, not one in his late fifties. Martin didn't trust the man. Never had.

He trusted Shamus less, but he had no control over what happened at the house. Unless it had to deal with the estate only. His loyalties laid with the family first, even though the state paid part of his way. Martin spent time in Sunshine Valley long before Shamus took it over. *Thank God for small favors*, he thought as he listened to the lame excuses the State's attorney rattled off.

"Mr. Escobar, I know we retained your services to bridge the gap between ourselves and the trust..." Mr. Roger Franklin started.

"You didn't hire me. The family did. But to maintain an equal representation, you and the trust pay my bill." Martin Escobar's nose flared. "I don't represent anyone but the family and the home and the family's wishes when they granted you the use of their property. I think that fact should be remembered."

The lawyer dismissed him and his statement off with a wave of his hand. "Either way," Roger Franklin turned to face Mr. Tristan Rinehart, the Secretary of Human Services, "Tristan, I don't think turning over the records is a wise thing."

Mr. Rinehart shook his head. "I'm not sure I understand why you are so resistant, Roger. It doesn't seem like this lieutenant wants the information for anything other than to solve the murder—of one of our residents, nonetheless."

Martin had to hide his laughter of Roger's pinched expression. He coughed, clearing his throat. "Excuse me," he said as he poured a drink of water from the pitcher in the middle of the table into one of the glasses sitting on the same tray.

Roger's eyes narrowed in on Martin before he swatted the air as if to remove an annoying gnat. "Mr. Secretary, I see no connection between kids in a home from fifteen years ago, to a murder now. And I think to open said door would be a detriment."

Tristan Rinehart rubbed his chin. When he took this job, he had no idea shit could get so complicated. "Roger, you're the lawyer representing the State's interest, is there any privacy issue that would be broken?"

"No. But I don't..."

Mr. Rinehart cut him off. "I don't care what you think. You have made your position on this matter very clear, but I think if some information about our former residents will help solve a brutal murder, I think we should give it to them."

Roger Franklin made an audible sigh. "I think this is a mistake."

"Duly noted." The Secretary looked at Martin. "Do you know if there are certain kids the Lieutenant wants or all of them from the time in question?"

"Lieutenant Kaine wanted the records for that time frame. By my calculations, it is roughly two hundred. I looked before the meeting and the records for those residents are now in digital form in the online file system. The information can be easily culled with the parameters of years."

Tristan Rinehart leaned back in his chair, spinning in the direction of Roger Franklin. "Do it. Send it to Mr. Escobar. Since he has been in contact with the Lieutenant, he can pass the information on to him."

"But..." Mr. Franklin was about to interject.

The Secretary held his hand up. "Quit bitching and do it. Today." Mr. Rinehart smiled at Martin Escobar. "You will have the information by the end of the day. If you don't, you call me." He stood. "I'm sorry you had to come all the way down here for this."

Martin stood, shaking the man's hand. "I didn't mind. I'm glad you and this office are going to help." He nodded in the direction of Roger Franklin. "Good day, Gentlemen."

Roger Franklin watched the man leave. He turned back to his boss. "I think this is a bad idea."

Tristan sat behind his desk. "What's a bad idea is you trying to hide this."

"I only did it to help you. I thought I could handle it."

"You're the lawyer for the State. One of many I might add. Don't let this happen again. Make sure this lieutenant gets the information he asked for. The last thing I need is to be part of a scandal."

CHAPTER FIFTY-THREE

Wednesday 1:30 p.m.

"Did you give everything to your dad? About Taylor's family?" Joe asked as Damien exited the freeway.

"I did. He will search everything and let us know what he comes up with. He has Daniella's husband, William, in touch with someone at the State Department."

"Okay. That sounds good. Very good." Joe stared out the window.

"Hey, don't worry. Between my dad and Dillon, we will find out everything."

Joe nodded but didn't say anything.

Damien drove into The Dunes and followed the GPS directions to Patrick Weinsted's home. As he rounded the corner of the street, several police cars and the ME's van were parked in front of the home. Damien looked over at Joe in the passenger seat then glanced back over his shoulder to Dillon. "This doesn't look good."

As they exited the SUV, a police officer came over to them. "I'm sorry, but you are going to have to leave the area."

"Who's in charge?" Damien asked as he produced his badge.

"Let me get Detective Thomas." The officer jogged to the front of the house.

Within a few minutes, an older lanky man walked out of Patrick's house. He stepped up to Damien and frowned. "Who are you?"

Damien showed him his ID. "I'm Lieutenant Kaine from Division Central. This is my partner Detective Joe Hagan and FBI Agent Dillon McGrath. Your victim is now our victim. We're down here investigating two murders occurring in Chicago, and Patrick Weinsted was a suspect."

Detective Thomas shook his head. "Listen, you want this case you can have it. Come on in. Our ME got here about ten minutes ago." At the door, he handed each of them a pair of disposable booties. You're going to want to wear these. It's a fucking mess in there."

Detective Thomas sighed, leaning his head back and closing his eyes. "Let me tell you what I got. We got a phone call from one of Patrick's neighbors. She heard screaming, then it stopped. She didn't think much of it. Went to the store, ran some errands. When she came home, she said she had a feeling something wasn't right."

Dillon raised an eyebrow at him. "What kind of feeling?"

Detective Thomas shrugged. "How the hell should I know, Agent? She explained she usually saw Patrick by this time of day and he hadn't been out to get his mail. I got the impression she was a little nosy. She came over, found the front door unlocked, and stepped inside. She said she called out his name and made her way back to here. When she peeked into the room, she ran out screaming. That's when her niece, who is visiting, found her and called us. That was all we got out of her before the paramedics took the old woman to the hospital. They were worried about her high blood pressure."

"What time did the neighbor hear the screams?" Damien asked.

"Around eight thirty," Detective Thomas said.

Damien caught Dillon's glance. He turned to Detective Thomas. "Has your ME started anything yet?"

"No, actually. He isn't sure where to start." Detective Thomas yelled into the home. "Dr. Morgan?"

Five minutes later, a short fat man rounded the corner. "What the hell. I was about to start. What do you need Detective?"

"This is Lieutenant Damien Kaine..." Detective Thomas paused. "Where are you from again?"

Dr. Morgan waived Detective Thomas off. "No need to introduce him. I'm a college friend of Dr. Forsythe. I know all about you." He smiled at the other two standing with Damien. "And you two as well. You must be Joe and Dillon."

They both nodded.

Dr. Morgan smiled. "I bet this is about Chase Humphry, huh?"

"It is. Would you mind if we called in Dr. Forsythe? We have two other murders connected to Patrick and the Sunshine Valley Home."

Removing his gloves, Dr. Morgan reached into his pants pocket and pulled out his phone. He grinned at the three standing before him. "Hello, Bernard. Guess who is standing in front of me? No, it isn't Elvis. It's Damien. Looks like the dead guy we got is related to one of your current cases, Chase Humphry." He held up his finger to the three detectives. "Okay. I will do it. See you soon."

He replaced his phone. "It looks like you are stuck with me until Bernard gets here. He has asked me not to remove our victim, but he wants me to give you any information I can on what happened first." He chuckled at Damien and Joe's reaction. "He said you would understand what he meant."

"Unfortunately, we do," Joe said, taking the gloves the ME held out to all of them.

"Let's see what your killer has left us, shall we?" Dr. Morgan led the way to the back of the home and the master bedroom. "This is where the magic happened."

Dillon looked around. She hadn't yet seen the pictures of the other crime scenes, but Damien had described them to her. "Wow. This is one brutal guy."

Damien blew out a breath. Patrick's arms and legs were still tied to the bed. However, they had been removed, no longer attached to the torso. "Jesus," he said as he made the sign of the cross.

Joe walked around Detective Thomas to the end of the bed. He pointed to his feet. "Looks like he moved from fingers to toes," he said.

Detective Thomas raised an eyebrow at him. "What do you mean?"

"Our killer took the fingers of his first victim. We think he was after information." Joe bent down and looked at the bottom of Patrick's feet. "I'd say he used Patrick's feet to get whatever information he had."

Damien studied the body. Patrick's torso had been sliced open. His head was still attached. Looking over at the ME, he nodded at the doctor. "Can you tell me what was done first?"

Dr. Morgan put on a pair of overalls. Zipping up the front, he put on a fresh pair of gloves over his original pair. He smiled at the handsome detective. "Let's see if I can tell you something." He stepped up to the body and used a pair of magnifying lenses to inspect the wounds where the legs and arms were dissected.

The doctor moved around the bed. He looked at the feet. "The toes were removed while he was alive." He stood and cocked his head towards the side. "The right arm was also dissected while Patrick was alive." There is vomit on that side of the bed," he said, pointing towards the side closest to the window.

"I can hazard a guess. I'd say he started with the toes. I mean, if I was going to torture someone that's where I would start. Most shock value, least amount of deadly damage. But very effective when it comes to pain." Doctor Morgan pointed to the left leg. "This was dissected while he was alive, but I would guess he died shortly after."

Damien pulled on his hair. "I imagine Patrick vomited sometime during the torture session."

Dr. Morgan pointed to the right side of Patrick's torso. There looks to be vomit on the shirt, at least I think it's vomit. Looks like it from here. I'm sure Dr. Forsythe will test it to make sure."

Dillon slowly walked around the room. She opened a few drawers in the tall dresser. She opened the bottom ones and came back to the top. Walking slowly to the bedside tables she checked the drawers, then came back to the upright dresser.

Damien watched her every movement. "Dillon, what are you seeing?"

"All the other drawers are full of stuff, but this top one." She pointed to the up-right dresser. "I can't be sure, but it looks like something was in here. There's a void."

"If we keep with the assumption our killer is after information, then I bet that drawer had something he wanted." Damien rubbed his chin with the back of his hand. "Dr. Morgan, what did Dr. Forsythe tell you to do with the body?"

"He said he was on his way. To leave the body and he and I would do the autopsy at my house. No sense in transporting him all the way to Chicago. But he wants to be in on it since this is related to your case." Dr. Morgan smiled. "He also said I had to buy him dinner at the seafood restaurant."

Damien laughed. "Sounds like him. I'm going to leave and head over to Sunshine Valley. Ask Dr. Forsythe to call with his findings."

"I can do that. I'm sure Bernard knows what you guys will need. If you need anything, you can call my office, and they will get ahold of me." Dr. Morgan lifted his bloody hand. "I will shake hands with you later. It was great to finally put a face to someone Bernard talks about regularly."

Damien nodded. "It was nice to meet you too. I really appreciate your help." He turned to leave then turned back. "Dr. Morgan, do you know a Theodore Osgood?"

Dr. Morgan snorted. "Yes. Unfortunately. He is an old doctor the state gets to fill in when other ME's go on vacation or needs help. He used to be the ME over in Indianapolis."

"Sounds like you don't like him," Damien said.

Dr. Morgan waved his hand. "No not at all. He is a very nice man. Just very old. Isn't as thorough as I would like. There is a paper sack at the front door. Place your booties and gloves in it. We will dispose of those at the lab."

"Okay. Thank you." Damien led the way out of the house, they climbed into the SUV. He turned to face Joe in the passenger seat and glanced at Dillon in the back seat.

"I bet, whoever is helping Shamus makes sure Dr. Osgood is working when they need a less thorough ME." Damien pulled on the ends of his hair. "Just another circumstantial piece we can't prove. I want to head over to the home. I want to deliver the news to Shamus MacDougal and see his reaction."

Joe squinted at him. "You think we can get on the property?"

"According to Martin Escobar," Damien said. He started the car and headed towards the home. "What did you think of the crime scene, Dillon?"

Dillon sat back and looked out the window. "Your killer is methodical yet very mean. He inflicts the pain not only to get the information he wants, but it is done from a place of controlled rage. The dismemberment occurred a relatively short time prior to Patrick's death. If so, then the killer did the bulk of his damage after he got his information. Shows a rage fueled by something very personal and something he feels he has to hold these people accountable for."

"Like a modern-day vigilante?" Joe asked.

"Yeah, he's righting a wrong. Whether it directly involves him or someone he knows, it really doesn't matter. The only thing I know for sure, he won't stop until all those responsible are dead."

CHAPTER FIFTY-FOUR

Damien drove under the portico of Sunshine Valley Home. "Let's see if Shamus is a little more forthcoming regarding a tour after we tell him about Patrick's death."

They walked to the door which opened before they stepped up to it.

"Hello, Lieutenant Kaine." Shamus nodded at the other detective but zeroed in on the pretty blonde lady. "I don't think I have had the pleasure of meeting you." He held out his hand.

Dillon shook his hand at the same time she showed her credentials. "I'm FBI Agent Dillon McGrath."

Shamus had a dazed look on his face as he jerked his hand back. His posture stiffened with rigid muscles. He shook off the sudden coldness at his core. "Now if it's about the tour, Martin called me." He stepped back and waved them in. "I'd be more than happy to show you around."

Dillon's eyes shifted towards Damien as her head gave an indiscriminate nod in his direction. "I think that would be great. I would love to see this facility."

Joe raised an eyebrow at her, then smiled at Damien. "Me too."

"Thank you for taking the time, Mr. MacDougal," Damien said.

"I didn't mean to be rude the last time. I was caught off guard." Shamus led the way through the house. "Here is our art room. The kids are taught by volunteer art teachers who come in and spend time with them." He turned towards the three. "We even had one of our residents win an art scholarship in the late '90s."

"That's impressive." Joe glanced around into other rooms as they passed by. "Do you have classes here?" he asked, pointing into one of two rooms where there were several desks and chairs.

"No, but we do have tutoring. If one of our residents has trouble with classwork, we provide tutoring," Shamus responded.

"Does the State pay for this?" Dillon asked.

"The trust does. We have to submit the child's school records and then a signed document from the student's teacher or teachers." Shamus climbed the rounded staircase to the second floor. "There has been a little remodeling on this floor to accommodate some of the children. The ones who are here for a short time, less than a month," he said as he opened one of the bedroom doors. "They stay up here."

"What do you do with the children who stay longer?" Joe asked.

"Up here, the little ones stay, even if they are longer than a month. The others stay in an annexed building off the back of the kitchen. We have two barracks for the girls and the boys." Shamus led the way back down the stairs to the kitchen and through the back door.

They walked under a covered archway leading to a large building. In the middle was a common area with games and a pool table. Along with a few video game consoles.

Shamus pointed to the set of double doors on each side of them. "You need a key card to get into these areas. One is for boys, and the other is for girls. Each one has a house parent. Unless the resident has a job, curfew is ten. Lights out are at eleven." He opened the doors to the boys' residents. "Everyone is at school." He glanced at his watch.

Shamus continued leading them through the grounds of the home. After he took them through the last building, the mechanic shop, he stood outside and locked the doors. "We keep it locked because of the tools inside." His gaze lingered on the concrete slab.

Damien peered around looking at the expanding property. He turned his focus back to Shamus. "Can you tell me about your relationship with Patrick Weinsted?" Shamus' gaze turned challenging and full of judgment. "Mr. MacDougal, I'd appreciate knowing how you employed Patrick."

"Patrick works for Sunshine Valley. He handles maintenance and odd jobs. He has been working here ever since he turned eighteen." Shamus crossed his arms and squinted at Damien. "I understand how you may have questions in regards to Chase Humphry's death, but your line of inquiry is getting a little questionable."

Dillon stepped back, looking at the concrete surrounding the shop. As Damien questioned Shamus MacDougal, she extracted herself from the conversation and walked around the building. She wasn't a construction person by any stretch of the imagination, but she knew enough to know this slab had been added well after this building was erected.

Damien watched out of the corner of his eye as Dillon moved away from them. His main focus was Shamus. "Do you know if Patrick has had any trouble lately?"

"I think it's time for you to leave. I have given you a tour." He turned at a sound behind him and watched Agent McGrath walk back to them.

"What were you doing?" Again, his gaze landed on the concrete slab.

Dillon watched him stare at the concrete. She smiled at him as he lifted his eyes to hers. "Admiring your shop. When was this outer slab added?"

The Agent's honey blonde hair sparkled as it caught the afternoon rays of the sun. Shamus licked his lips before glancing down at the 20X12 pad. "I think this was added around 2008 maybe 2007. I would have to look it up. Why?" he asked, facing her.

"Curiosity." Dillon gave him her best smile. "When was the building built?"

"Around the same time as the art studio. Late 90's or early 2000's." He turned back to the Lieutenant and his partner. "Why are you here, with an FBI Agent?" Shamus wiped the sheen of sweat from his brow.

"Mr. MacDougal, when was the last time you spoke with or saw Patrick Weinsted?" Damien asked.

Shamus swallowed the excessive saliva pooling in his mouth. Feeling overheated, even though the temperature was a balmy forty degrees. "I don't know. Maybe, a day or so ago. He did some work here two days ago. I know he had to run a few errands and pick up some supplies for a project." He twisted his wristwatch on his left hand. "I expect him today at some point."

Damien gave Dillon and Joe a side glance. "I'm sorry to have to tell you this, but Patrick was found murdered this morning in his home."

Shaking his head in denial, his muscles tensed, causing his posture to go rigid. Shamus' heartbeat thrashed in his ears. "How? I don't understand."

"I can't tell you the circumstances of his death. We do think the killer was after some information." Damien scribbled in his notepad he had pulled from his back pocket. "Do you know who might have wanted Patrick dead?"

Shamus pushed his shoulders back and jutted out his chest. "How would I know who wanted Patrick dead? I have no idea what Patrick did in his own time. For all I know, he was involved in less savory things."

"How about Maggie Newsome?" Joe asked.

"What about Maggie Newsome?"

"When did you last speak with her?" Damien asked.

Shamus shrugged. "I haven't spoken with Maggie since she left this facility."

"Do you know who might have wanted to kill her?" Joe asked.

Rolling his eyes, Shamus gave the Detective a dismissive nod. "No, I don't know who wanted Maggie dead. I didn't know Maggie was dead." Shamus' eyes shifted left before meeting the detective's stare. "As I have already stated, I haven't spoken to or seen Maggie since she left here years ago."

Damien lowered his head, staring at Shamus. He shot a quick glance at Dillon, who raised an eyebrow at him. "Mr. MacDougal, can you tell me about Clara Rogers?"

Shamus' breath quickened as he glared at the Lieutenant. His brow wrinkled as he rubbed his chin. "I'm not sure if I remember Clara Rogers." He wrung his hands.

"She was hospitalized, after being here for roughly eight months." Damien zeroed in on the man. He squinted at him. "I find it hard you wouldn't remember her. I can't imagine you have many girls hospitalized."

Shamus snapped his fingers. "Yes, now I remember. Sad case. She had a lot of mental issues. The poor girl ultimately killed herself."

Joe raised an eyebrow at Dillon and Damien.

Dillon stepped in closer to Shamus. "How do you know what happened to her?"

Shamus blustered. "The State must have let me know."

Damien rocked on his heels. "Why would the State notify you about the death of a girl who was no longer in your care?"

Shamus waved both his hands in the air. "I don't know. But I am sure either the Department of Human Services or the attorney for the home notified me. How else would I have found out?"

"Do you mean Martin Escobar?" Damien asked.

Shamus shook his head. "No. No. Roger Franklin. He works for Tristan Rinehart, the Secretary for the Department of Human Services."

Damien's eyebrows squished together. He turned towards Joe, started to say something, then turned back to Shamus. "Why did you make me think Martin Escobar was the attorney for the State?"

Shamus' eyes widened, showing the white around the entire iris. His skin flushed as a bead of sweat lined his hairline. "I—I don't know what you mean?"

"You said we had to get permission for a tour from the attorney.

Then you pointed us in the direction of Martin Escobar."

Shamus paced around. "No. You misunderstood. Mr. Escobar is the liaison between the Department of Human Services and the trust. If I said speak with Martin Escobar, it was because he deals with the property on a daily basis." Shamus lifted his hands. "You know, uhm, whenever we need things or to upgrade buildings, I have to submit the request to him."

Joe stepped in front of Shamus MacDougal, impeding his pacing. "Mr. MacDougal, what exactly does Roger Franklin do for the State in regards to the home?"

"Huh?" Shamus asked as he ran a hand through his hair.

"What does Mr. Franklin do for the home?" Joe asked again.

"He handles all the records or requests for information on the home or the residents," Shamus responded.

"Can we see the basement of the main house?" Damien asked.

Adrenaline shot through Shamus' system. His chest tightened, and the sensation of not being able to get enough oxygen brought on a sudden feeling of dizziness. "No. I'm sorry. We had a leak in the basement a few days ago and the workers repairing the pipes have everything a mess. It's hazardous down there." A sudden overwhelming sensation of dread flooded Shamus. "I need to get ready for the kids." He started towards the front lawn. Walking around the main house, he stopped outside the front door. "Is there anything else?"

"Yes, actually there is. Do you know a Nancy Milligan?" Damien asked.

Shamus wiped his brow. "No. That name doesn't sound familiar to me. Sorry. I need to go." He opened the door and stepped over the threshold. He turned to the three detectives. "I think the next time you need to speak with me, you need to call Roger Franklin."

Joe whistled as they walked back to the SUV. "I don't think I have ever seen someone try to get us out of someplace so fast."

Damien glanced over his shoulder at Dillon. "You were quiet in there. Any reasons?"

"I was watching Mr. MacDougal. He has a lot to hide. He lied about Nancy Milligan, and several other things," Dillon said. "But I was more interested in his reaction to you asking to see the basement."

Damien dialed Mr. Escobar's number.

"Martin Escobar, here." His voice boomed through the Bluetooth.

"Mr. Escobar, I was expecting your secretary, this is Lieutenant Damien Kaine."

"I wanted to speak to you, great timing."

Damien shot a side glance to Joe. "Why is that?"

"When I put in a request for all the records regarding the children who were at the home during the time when Chase Humphry was there, I was called into a meeting with Tristan Rinehart, the Secretary for the Department of Human Services and Roger Franklin, the lawyer. Mr. Franklin fought the release, quite vehemently."

"Do you have any idea why?" Damien asked.

"To be honest, at first I thought he was being a prick. He's been the lawyer for DHS since the beginning of time. I figured he didn't like me stepping in on his territory. But going over the records he sent me, I'm finding some inaccuracies.

"The list of names I sent you was what Roger gave me at the end of every month. That started shortly after I took over in 1995. However, the latest list Roger sent me, has a lot more names on it. I went back and compared the two lists."

The rustling of papers came through the Bluetooth. "Mr. Escobar?"

"I'm sorry, Lieutenant. I wanted to double-check something. There is a huge discrepancy. I think I need to get you these records."

Damien glanced at Joe then at Dillon in the rearview. "Are they paper or electronic?"

"They are all electronic. Look, I have a program which allows me to take electronic lists or data and find all the matching items in each document. I can highlight the items that don't have a match. My kid developed this program. He's trying to sell it. To be honest detective, I never thought the software would work, but it did."

Damien pulled into The Dunes ME's parking lot. "Mr. Escobar, I don't think I'm following you. Could you explain it better for me?"

"I ran the software on the two different files. There are a couple of hundred girls that are in this new list from Roger Franklin, that aren't in the original lists from him over the years."

"Mr. Escobar, I need those files as quickly as you can send them to me. Can you send me the list of names that your software filtered out? It will save me a lot of work." Damien turned off the engine.

"I have compressed the files into a zip file and emailed it to you. If you need anything else from me, let me know."

"I have one question. Did any pipes burst in the basement requiring a major renovation?" Damien asked as he removed his phone from the cradle on the dash, immediately switching the call to private. He nodded into the phone. "Okay. Yes. Thank you. I will contact you if I need anything else. Thank you again." He slid his phone into his back pocket as they exited the SUV.

"Well?" Dillon asked as they entered into the ME's building.

"I'm sorry, do you want to know what he said?" Damien smirked.

"Dude, you better spill the goods," Joe said, stepping up to the reception desk.

"Not one pipe has burst. No construction, no workers." Damien leaned over and told the receptionist who they wanted to see.

"They're expecting you. Follow the yellow line, and you will come to Dr. Morgan's office."

"Looks like Shamus is a big fat liar," Dillon said.

Joe pointed to the yellow line. "And this is the yellow brick road. Which tells me we aren't in Kansas anymore."

CHAPTER FIFTY-FIVE

Wednesday late afternoon

Kerry drove his car into the parking lot of the restaurant and bar where Shamus usually spent his Wednesday evenings. Scoping out the property, he could see no cameras on the building. He had left the diner shortly after eating. Not wanting to bring attention to himself, he didn't want to sit there for too long. The bar Shamus frequented was on the main strip of downtown Indiana Dunes.

He parked in the back line of parking spaces, placing the rear of his car up against a brick wall and his driver side next to a row of bushes. Kerry bent over and retrieved the plastic bag from under the front seat. He removed the small needle and put it in his coat pocket. Placing the remaining item in the front pocket of his jeans.

Picking up his laptop off the passenger seat, he used his mobile hotspot to again get on the Internet. He researched Kainetorri Securities. From what Kerry could tell, Damien had a pretty nice family. He glanced up as a few cars pulled into the lot. Two couples exited and made their way into the building.

He logged into the secure browser via a virtual private network. Kerry used his phone and scanned in the files he had taken from Patrick's home. He used the back door he had created a few days ago and uploaded them to Shamus' computer. While he was in there, he removed the photos of Chase he had sent earlier and replaced them with child porn pictures. He put a few of the more incriminating emails Patrick had on Shamus's drive and then removed the back-door access. He erased any trace of him being on the man's computer or network.

He opened the box of padded envelopes he had purchased earlier in the day along with shipping tape. Kerry found the closest Fed-Ex store on his computer and was filling out the address on the envelope when he saw Shamus MacDougal pull into the parking lot. He watched as Shamus parked in a spot towards the back of the building. A sneer crept across his face. "Perfect," he said as he closed his laptop and placed it and the file, along with the envelope, under the front seat of his car. He pulled a pair of glasses from the glove box and checked his looks in the rearview. The glasses were fake, *but they would provide an extra layer to keeping his identity a secret.*

CHAPTER FIFTY-SIX

Wednesday 5:00 p.m.
Division Central

Damien parked in his spot in the DC garage, glancing over at Joe, he noticed him texting on his phone. "Taylor?"

Joe nodded. "She has a late evening meeting. She said she would meet me at the house around eight. She's picking up something to eat."

As they exited the vehicle, he grabbed Dillon by the hand. "Hey, you need to go home? Rest?"

She smirked at him. "What, am I an invalid?"

"No. I know you haven't put in a full day of fieldwork." He opened the door for all of them to enter the building.

"I'm good. Let's go up and look at those files. I'm anxious to see what's going on," Dillon said.

"Joe," Damien said. "You can go on home if you want."

He shook his head. "Nah, I want to see what's going on too. I'll head home before Taylor is going to be there."

"I'm hoping Detective Travis has found something on the school counselor. I would like to ask her a few questions."

"I'm going to the bathroom," Dillon said, walking away.

"Me too," Joe said.

Damien walked into the VCU pen. Detective Jamal Harris sat at his desk. His partner, Mike Cooper, sat at his desk as well, henpecking his keyboard. "Hey Harris, Cooper how's your case coming along?"

"Pretty good," Harris replied. "Coop and I are about to go over and interview some of our victims' co-workers."

"You got any leads on it yet?" He turned and smiled as Dillon walked towards them. Turning back to Harris, he waited for his answer.

Harris read through his notes. "These two worked together at the law firm, and some of the neighbors for victim number one, Jesse Fowler, said he was dating some girl for a while before they started seeing him hanging out with victim number two, Patricia Mariner."

Damien narrowed in Cooper. "You thinking this is a jealous ex?"

"Not sure. That's why we are heading to the firm. We arranged for the employees to hang out and be interviewed all at once." Cooper stood checking the time on his watch. "We need to get over there." He nodded in the direction of his partner.

"Oh crap, we do." Harris put on his coat. "It's good to see you back, Agent McGrath."

Dillon, who stepped up next to Damien, smiled. "Call me Dillon. How many times do I need to tell you?"

Detective Harris laughed. "I will. Sorry. Good to see you, Dillon," he said as he and Detective Cooper raced out of the pen.

Damien studied the case board. He had Davidson and Jenkins helping him, but they also had an unsolved murder at a local bar. "I don't see Davidson or Jenkins; they must be on their other case." He glanced over his desk. "Or they cut out."

Joe walked over to his desk. "Got anything from Travis?"

"Let's go to my office and find out." Damien led the way. He grabbed a few sodas from the fridge and placed them on the desk. Joe was already digging through his handful of jellybeans when Damien's desk phone rang. "Kaine here."

"Hey, Kaine," Detective Travis said.

"Are you psychic now?" Damien asked, gulping down half his soda. "I'm putting this on speaker."

Detective Travis laughed. "No. I saw you out in the pen. I'm in the middle of taking apart a computer for Vice; I called you instead of leaving ECD. I got some information on the counselor."

"Please tell me it's good."

"No. It's not. She died a few years back."

Joe shook his head and sighed.

"Shit. You got anything on Clara's adoption?" Damien asked as he opened a folder Davidson had left on his desk.

"Yes. When the Morenos filed for adoption, they filed with their local Department of Human Services. The petition was kicked up to the Secretary, Tristan Rinehart. From there, it looks like the lawyer for the State and the DHS shut down the adoption. He cited since Clara was still actually a ward of the state and in counseling, she had to be cleared by her current counselor in order to be eligible for adoption."

"Anything from the therapist in the file?" Damien asked, reading through Davidson's notes.

"No. I can see the correspondence from the lawyer to the family was dated shortly before Clara's death."

"How did you get all this?" Damien raised an eyebrow at Dillon and Joe.

"He hacked in," Joe blurted out.

Detective Travis laughed. "Not this time. Called in a favor. I got an IT buddy who works at the State Capitol in Springfield. He pulled the records for me. It's the same place the ADA got the names of the residents for us, I just skipped going through her."

"Hmm, sounds fishy to me. But I'll take it." Damien leaned back in his chair. "Can you pull the crime scene photos from when Clara was found in her car?"

Detective Travis could be heard typing on a keyboard. "I think I can get those. I will shoot them to your email as soon as I do. I gotta run, this computer I'm working on is giving me shit."

The line went dead.

Damien laughed. "You know if Travis is rattled, it has to be kicking his butt."

"Open the file from Martin Escobar." Dillon reached in front of Joe and took a handful of jellybeans. "Damn, I'm hungry," she mumbled as she put them all in her mouth.

Joe's jaw dropped. "How can you do that?"

"Hmm?" She held up a finger as she washed the candy down with a sip of soda. "Do what?"

"Eat them like that?" Joe asked.

Her eyebrows pinched together. "What the hell are you talking about?"

"The jellybeans dude. You don't eat them like that. One flavor at a time." He shook his head, muttering. "I can't believe I have to put up with this."

Damien roared back in laughter. "They're jellybeans. You need medication."

"You definitely need meds." Dillon popped another handful in her mouth as she batted her eyes at Joe.

"I hate you right now," Joe said, turning his back to her.

"Okay, children," Damien said, opening the file from Martin Escobar on his computer. He printed out the new list. He held it up. "This is the list Escobar said contains names he has never seen before. Give me a minute and let me look at these names." As he ran through the list and quickly compared it to the one from Davidson, Damien couldn't believe what he was seeing. "Holy shit! Listen, when we started this investigation, the ADA got us our list of names of children that were in the house during the years Chase was there. Davidson has been working off that list. He found that several girls were gone, just vanished, and some had committed suicide.

"A few days into the investigation, I received another list from Martin Escobar. I asked Davidson to compare the two lists. He found there were names on the ADA's list that were not on Escobar's list." Damien glanced at Dillon and Joe. "You two with me so far?"

They nodded.

"Today, Martin Escobar gets a brand-new list from Roger Franklin. Only this list goes back the entire time that Martin has been working for the family and the trust, since 1995. He realizes there are way more names than there should be. He checks all the months and years he received monthly updates about the children who came into the home."

Damien holds up a list with highlighted names. "These are all the names Martin Escobar has never seen. It has Nancy Milligan, Maggie Newsome, and Britney Lewis on it. We know Nancy was in the home, she saw Britney. We know Maggie was in the home. Shamus even admitted to it. How do you account for these three names, let alone the several hundred others on this list?"

Dillon shook her head. "If I'm hearing you right, for the last twenty some odd years, Martin Escobar has received names monthly. And now he finds out that he hasn't been getting the full list of names?"

"Yes," Damien replied.

Joe leaned in, putting his elbows on his knees. "I got to think, that was a mistake. I'm not sure it was intentional and I'm not sure who made the mistake, but I can't imagine whoever went to great lengths to hide those names wanted them to come out."

Damien leaned back in his chair. "Nancy Milligan said when the local DHS office searched for her record, they couldn't find she had even stayed in the home at all. Her record of time there had been erased. Why?"

Dillon straightened up. Her skin tingled.

Damien held the list from Davidson. "I had asked Davidson to go through the names from the time Chase was at the home." He held up a second list. "These are names of girls he can't find anywhere. No record of them being dead or alive. They are gone. Vanished. But, they are on today's list from Roger Franklin. How do you explain that?"

Dillon cursed. "They're trafficking girls."

Joe sat back. His nostrils flared. "Wait, wait. This can't be happening. No way Shamus and whoever is helping him could get away with 'losing girls'."

"They could, and they have." Damien went to his murder board. He erased his earlier notes and grabbed a marker. He put a question mark at the top. He then wrote Shamus, and underneath Shamus, he wrote Patrick. Below Patrick, he wrote Chase and Maggie's name. "Okay—Martin Escobar takes over the trust of the home in 1995.

"We know he is getting monthly reports from Roger, concerning the number of children who come into the home. From what we have learned, we know Shamus is abusing girls. We also know Patrick had some kind of working relationship with Shamus dating back to when he was placed in the home. It has also come out Patrick has been working exclusively for the home. He has held no other job."

Dillon pointed to the board. "You can't be suggesting Chase and Maggie had something to do with the abuse or the trafficking?"

Damien shook his head. "Not at all. I don't think they had any part in it. I think they knew about the abuse, but not the whole extent. I'm willing to bet Maggie was abused. We know she ran away after she turned fourteen. According to Davidson, Shamus likes them young."

Joe grabbed some more jellybeans. "Our killer was there. Our killer was at the home."

"Yes. That's what I think." Damien sat back down.

Dillon crossed her legs. "I don't think the killer is part of this."

"I don't either. But you said in one of our conversations, you thought the killer was personally involved, he had been wronged. I think the two are connected."

Dillon stared at the board. "Who, besides the lawyer, would have the ability to manipulate records? And who would benefit from trafficking girls?"

A long sigh drew Damien's shoulders down. "You got Roger Franklin, Tristan Rhinehart, or anyone else in the DHS office."

"Aw hell." Joe sat back and crossed his arms. "And, how the hell are we going to prove who?"

Damien nodded at Joe. "I'm going to check on what I asked Nicky to get for me. As soon as I get home, I'll run a check on Roger Franklin and Tristan Rinehart. Maybe we can find out who works in both offices who may have access to the records and the means to pull this off."

Dillon used her phone to look up something. "According to the state website, Tristan Rinehart is only thirty-eight years old. He was only fifteen when all this started in 1995. That eliminates him. And according to the website, Roger Franklin was thirty years old when he started working for the State. He came over from private practice as a defense lawyer. He is quoted in an interview as saying he needed a change from working for crooks." She continued to read. "He gained a lot of notoriety for handling some of the bigger criminal cases. Made a lot of money and connections over the year."

Damien clasped his hands on top of his head, and closed his eyes as he leaned back in his chair. "Then it has to be Roger Franklin or someone he is working with inside the department. Fuck. We have nothing but discrepancies in records. Something anyone could say was an oversight. We have missing girls, who have records as being trouble makers or having mental problems, making it hard to argue that something happened to them, other than they used drugs or got involved with the wrong people."

Joe stood. "I'm going home." He turned to leave. "We need to figure out how we are going to approach this. We can't get a warrant or anything else to get us into the actual records of the State. No one in their right mind would believe us if we took what we have right now to anyone. Captain Mackey would fire us and kick us into the psych ward. We are fucked." Joe stared at his partner. "I need a break. Let's meet at your house in the morning. Say eight? We can strategize then."

Damien nodded as he stood. He grabbed all the paperwork and the files from Davidson. "I agree. I have a headache forming at the base of my skull. I need to find out what Nicky got for me. Maybe if I can compile this in a format that wouldn't make your head spin, we could go to the chief and the captain." He followed Joe out, holding Dillon's hand.

"When we get home, I will get on the FBI database and pull all the records I can for Mr. Roger Franklin. If we can find a connection to him or someone in the office of Secretary of DHS, we might be able to wrangle a federal warrant." Dillon let go of Damien's hand as they entered the elevator.

"Baker should have something from the Morenos as well. If we get lucky maybe we can tie Clara's death to someone, get the case reopened and that might be the domino we need to fall," Damien said.

Joe waved as he walked to his truck. "See you in the morning."

"Eight. Don't be late." He and Dillon climbed into the SUV. "What are you hungry for?"

She leaned her head back on the seat. "Any good leftovers at the house?"

Damien shook his head. "Nah. Let's get Chinese. I have a feeling I am going to be up late tonight. I need to get something to take to the captain in the morning. The faster we move on this, the faster we can narrow in on a suspect."

CHAPTER FIFTY-SEVEN

Kerry stepped into the tavern-like restaurant. The smoke in the bar hung heavily, coating his lungs. He resisted the urge to cough, hoping his lungs would acclimate quickly. He spotted Shamus at the bar, talking to the old bartender and he made his way to the empty seat next to him.

He nodded at the old man. "Can I get a draft beer?"

"Sure thing." The bartender filled a mug, setting it in front of him. "You want a menu?"

"Sure," Kerry said, taking a sip of his beer. Shamus glanced at him, but didn't speak. "Can you recommend anything?" Kerry asked him.

Shamus swallowed his bite of food. "You can't go wrong with anything on the menu here." He took a drink of his beer. "You're not from here?"

Kerry shook his head. "No. Down from Chicago on business. You?"

"I run the Sunshine Valley Home." He turned and held out his hand. "Shamus MacDougal."

"Mark Rodgers." Kerry smiled at him. "I bet your accent charms all the ladies."

Shamus laughed. "That it does."

Kerry cocked his head to the side. "Didn't I hear about a guy who was murdered in Chicago who was associated with your home?"

Shamus nodded. The corners of his mouth turned downward. "Yes. It was one of our former residents. I was pretty devastated. The man was one of our success stories."

Kerry handed the menu to the bartender. "I'll take an order of potato skins."

"You got it," the bartender replied.

Kerry watched Shamus. His predatory stare followed a young lady across the room. Kerry smiled at the Scotsman when Shamus squinted at him. "She's a looker," Kerry said taking a sip of his beer.

Shamus wiggled his eyebrows. "Looks like a handful too."

"Aren't all women?" Kerry chuckled.

"Don't I know it. I spend all day with young teenage girls. The hormones running through them. Moody little creatures, all of them." Shamus took a swig of beer.

A few minutes later, the bartender set a plate of potato skins in front of

Kerry. "I can't imagine being responsible for kids. Are they all runaways, or orphans?" He took a bite, washing it down with a swig of beer.

"We get all kinds. Some have nowhere to go, some are abused. I'm the house therapist as well as the caretaker." Shamus tapped the top of his beer.

Kerry watched as the bartender replaced Shamus' empty bottle with a new one. "Are you married?" he asked taking another bite of his food.

"No. Never wanted to go down that road. I like what little freedom I have. Plus, there are way too many young girls who need attention." Shamus winked at his barstool buddy.

"I agree." Kerry feigned interest in the basketball game playing on the television in front of him.

Shamus' head swiveled every time a young woman walked by.

Kerry swallowed hard, pinching his lips together, stuffing his outrage down deep. A sour taste filled his mouth. Taking a sip of his beer, he gripped the mug, one step away from smashing it against the man's head.

The bartender walked by.

"You can ring up the check when you get a chance," Kerry said catching the man's attention.

Shamus was finishing his dinner.

Kerry quickly paid his bill and stood. "I have an appointment I need to get to. It was a pleasure meeting you."

"You too, mate." Shamus waved as Kerry exited the bar.

Sitting in his car, Kerry waited patiently for Shamus to leave, scanning the parking lot every time someone drove in.

The psychiatrist exited the building about twenty minutes later.

Kerry got out and banged on his hood. "Shit," he said loudly.

Shamus looked up as he unlocked his car. "Hey, you got a problem?" He walked to his new friend.

"Stupid rental. I'm having problems with it," Kerry said as he pretended to remove one of his winter gloves.

"I can drop you somewhere." Shamus nodded at him.

"I would very much appreciate it. I can get a ride back here after my meeting, but I really need to get there." Kerry followed Shamus to his car. As he walked behind him, he reached into his pocket and flicked off the protective cap on the needle. As he opened the passenger door, he removed the needle from his coat pocket. Once Shamus got in and started to put the car keys in the ignition, Kerry jabbed the needle into the man's neck.

There was a quick moment where Shamus' brow wrinkled before his eyes rolled back in his head and he slumped against the window.

"Sorry Shamus. I had hoped I would be able to make you suffer for your sins."

Shamus moaned.

Reaching into his jean pocket, Kerry removed the baggie and the small vile from within. He had purchased the solution earlier in the week from the dark web. The synthetic drug in the vile would pop up in a toxicology screening as an overdose of Fentanyl.

Kerry smacked Shamus. "Hey, Pops." He didn't want him fully awake, but he wanted him to feel the pain this drug would cause before he took his last breath. "I need you to be a little more awake...you there?"

Shamus moaned again. He tried to move his hands and arms.

"You can't move. The drug I injected you with is a paralyzing drug. It will wear off in about..." he checked his watch, "...ooh, in about five minutes. I have to time this right." He smacked him again. "You hurt Sierra. Do you remember her?"

Shamus moved his mouth, all that came out was a whisper. "You...it's you."

"Well, I'll be damned. Kind of ruined my surprise." Kerry noticed the man was squeezing his hands into fists. He acted fast. He removed the lid of the small vile. Using his left hand, he squeezed Shamus' jaw open and emptied the vile into his mouth. He forced his chin closed and pinched his nose shut, forcing the man to swallow the liquid.

Shamus began to cough. His wheezing turned into raspy gurgles from the back of his throat.

"Listen, sorry about this. You won't get to enjoy the high. This is way too potent." Kerry watched as Shamus struggled to breathe. "I bet you feel like you're drowning, huh? It's only going to get worse."

Shamus' body seized as the drug started to shut down his major organs. He foamed at the mouth.

"I bet your chest feels like it's going to explode right about now. It might. I think this dose is enough to bring down an elephant." Kerry scooted towards the passenger door. "Shamus," he said as he waved his hand in front of his nose. "I think you shat your pants. Shameful." He opened the door as Shamus turned towards him, but Kerry didn't think he could see him. "I hope hell has a special place for you."

Kerry exited the car locking the doors as Shamus' body spasms became worse. He watched through the window as blood ran from his nose and the corners of this mouth. He quickly walked back to his car. He drove off the lot and followed his phone's GPS to the nearest Fed-Ex.

CHAPTER FIFTY-EIGHT

Damien drove into the garage, waiting for the door to close. He watched as Dillon snored softly. She had fallen asleep within minutes of picking up the Chinese food. "Hey babe?" he rubbed her arm.

"What? Huh?" She sat up. "Why did you let me fall asleep?" she asked yawning.

"I figured you needed the catnap." He grabbed the bags of food and walked to the door leading to the living room. He glanced over his shoulder. "C'mon, let's get our food, and I will call Nicky and see what he has for me."

Entering the house, Coach stood fashionably angry. His scowl had his whiskers drooping. His eyes were black slivers.

Gunner bounded towards them, barking and spinning in circles.

Coach huffed at him then focused his attention on the other two. His meow started at a high pitch, rumbling into a guttural moan.

Gunner stopped his dancing and slinked away from the cat hiding behind Damien.

"Really?" Damien asked, looking at the coward. "You could eat him."

"Coach, why are you being so mean? We brought you a treat." Dillon carried one of the bags into the kitchen.

At the mere mention of the word treat, the cat raced around almost tripping Damien as he tried to maneuver around the big brown four-legged oaf.

"For crying out loud. You two want to kill us. I think you secretly want to watch us fall and break something." He placed the food on the table and lifted everything out of the bags as Dillon grabbed beer from the refrigerator and two plates.

Damien removed his phone from his back pocket and typed out a message. "I texted Nicky. Hopefully, he has something for us."

Dillon turned towards him. "What did you ask him to get for you?"

"When Davidson first noticed the girls from the home either disappearing or having committed suicide, I had Nicky get me all the names of girls who were in Sunshine Valley. I also had him give me everything he could find on Shamus, Patrick, and Martin Escobar."

"Did you suspect Martin Escobar of something inappropriate?"

"Those were the names I had to work with. I figured I'd start with them. Now I know that Escobar is on our side." Damien grabbed a few pieces of beef and fed them to Gunner and Coach.

Dillon doled out some of their food into their bowls. Both ate as if they hadn't had anything for the last two days. "You two aren't starving. You'd think we never feed them the way they act." She followed Damien into their office and set her plate on the desk. She took a long sip of beer, set it down, then disappeared into the kitchen. When she returned, she had two more beers. "Once I sit down, I don't want to get up again. And that first beer tasted way too good to stop at one." She handed one to Damien.

Damien fired up his laptop. His phone pinged. "Nicky says he sent me a file." He opened his secure email and downloaded it. "Okay, he sent me a list of every kid who has gone through Sunshine Valley since the home opened, in the early 80s."

Dillon shook her head. "I don't even want to know how he got the information."

"No, you don't. I don't plan on using it. But I need to see what we're missing. I'm only concerned with the home since Roger Franklin became involved, and that would be 1993. These reports tell me my hunches were correct. But my hunch won't get me shit these days."

"Except suspensions."

"Haha. You're real funny." Damien accessed his work email and downloaded the file from Martin Escobar. "I don't have the program Escobar used to separate these names, but I have something similar. I think it will give me what I need." He took a bite of an egg roll. "I have the printed file from work, but it would take to long for me to read through it and match names." He took a swig of beer. "I know I can't figure out the who the killer is from this list."

"What are you going to use it for?"

"To start, I can cross-check and see if the latest list from Roger has all the names. Then maybe I can use what Nicky has found on Shamus and Patrick to have some idea on how to stop what is going on at the home."

"Does he have anything on those two yet?"

Damien scanned the rest of the email. "Looks like we have some accounts under Shamus with a lot of money. It seems our boy is siphoning money from the home. But..."

"But without a warrant, you don't even know those accounts exist."

"Such a stickler for rules." Damien scrolled down. "Patrick has over a million dollars in a couple of accounts."

Dillon looked up. "How does a maintenance man make that kind of money?"

Damien looked at what financials Nicky had gathered. "I can see deposits made into Patrick's account came from Shamus' account. That establishes a money trail."

"A money trail you can't use."

"Yes, but I can have Travis pull Patrick's financials. The guy is dead and part of our investigation. That will get us Patrick's end of the money trail. We could leverage that to get Shamus's records, if he can't prove what he paid Patrick for."

"I like that thinking." Dillon took a bite.

"Wait, listen to this. Patrick was in Chicago the day Clara died."

Dillon sat up. "That could get us somewhere. Does it look like something Travis will find when he runs his financials?"

"I believe so." Damien wiggled his brow at her. "You are becoming so diabolical." He laughed at her glare. He looked back at the file from his brother. "Looks like our Martin Escobar spent time at the home."

"When?"

Damien read the information. "Back in the mid-80s."

"Anything else?" Dillon guzzled her beer.

"Nope. He is squeaky clean."

Coach jumped up on his desk and sat ogling him.

Damien pointed at him. "Don't even think of stealing from me."

Coach huffed but didn't move.

Feeling the weight of the massive fur ball's stare, he relented. "Here." He placed a piece of chicken in front of Coach. He flung another piece to Gunner, who looked as if he was about to cry. "You two are pathetic."

Focusing back on the computer program, he input the original file from Martin. He then added the file from Nicky and the file from the DHS lawyer. Setting some parameters, all he could do was wait. "It may take a few minutes to get a list of names. I'm running the two lists from Martin Escobar against the list from Nicky. I know my brother's list is way more comprehensive. This way I can cross-reference them against the list Martin says he never received."

Damien scrolled through some emails. "It looks like I got a response back from Humphry Enterprise's lawyer. I had asked him to tell me why Chase made a point of sending him a letter, making sure Shamus didn't receive any more money from him."

"What does he say?"

"Just that Chase was adamant should anything happen to him, no further money was to go to the Sunshine Valley Home," Damien said.

"That doesn't help us at all." Dillon typed out something on her computer. "I logged into the FBI database. Since I have clearance to help you, I don't have to be sneaky." She stuck her tongue out at him.

"You're such a goody-two-shoes." Eating while he waited for results, he watched her as she took a bite, typed, then took a drink of beer. He thought she looked tired, yet at the same time, she looked like she had new energy. He would bet some of her money, she was glad she had something to do.

"Hey," he said to her. "I was thinking about getting Nicky to give Taylor a phone like what you have."

She looked at him without raising her head. "One of the spy phones?"

He chuckled. "Yes. A spy phone. That way, we can track the calls from her brother. We may be able to find where he is."

"I think that's a good idea. I know she wouldn't mind." Dillon tilted her head to the side. "For gosh sakes, make sure she knows you guys can read her texts. You won't believe what she and Joe text to each other."

Damien laughed. "X-rated, huh?"

"Try triple X." Her computer pinged. "I got something."

"Who did you run first?"

"Roger Franklin. Seemed like the most logical place to start. We know it can't be Tristan if it started in 1995." She scrolled through the reports. "It looks like our Roger has a lot of questionable friends."

Swallowing another bite of egg roll, Damien washed it down with the last of his first beer. "What do you mean?" As he waited for her to respond, his computer beeped. "I got some results."

"Roger has ties through business to the Mancusso family."

Damien sat up. "That alone could be the tie to trafficking. I know you guys and the ATF have been trying to get the Mancusso family on a lot of stuff."

"Human trafficking being one of them." Dillon printed out the list of other known associates. "He has business deals with some other lower-level criminals and some legitimate people too."

"How did he get a job with the State with those kinds of associations?" Damien asked.

"Money greases a lot of wheels."

Damien lifted the sheets of paper from the printer. He quickly added up the names on each page. He scanned the electronic file. "I have about fifty girls unaccounted for from Nicky's list to the list Martin gave us."

"The list his son's software ran?"

"Yes. Hang on." Damien ran another data file. This time he put in all three lists. He set parameters for the software to compile a list of names fitting the age group of the abused girls. As he waited for the list to generate his knee bounced under his desk. When the list populated, a slight gasp escaped.

"What? What did you find?" Dillon asked as she stepped up behind him to look over his shoulder.

"I'm narrowing the list to girls who fell into the nine to thirteen range." He pointed to the list. "That's a lot of fucking girls." He scrolled through the pages. "We are looking at hundreds. Over the years since 1995, over three hundred girls have gone missing."

Dillon stared at the endless list of names. "We have nothing to prove this. We can't even get a search warrant." She leaned against his desk. "If we use the lists from Davidson and the two from Martin what do you get?"

"Let me get the list from Davidson. He sent an electronic copy to my email." Damien ran a new data search. "Okay. With what we have through proper channels, we get 125 girls who are missing. Now, remember. These are being run against the master list from the attorney."

Dillon cocked an eyebrow at him. "That could work in our benefit."

"How you figure?"

"Let's simplify this for Captain Mackey. Leave out everything from your brother. We know there are more, and once we get into the records of the home, we can figure out a way to get that information brought in."

Damien flinched back. "Who are you?"

"What the hell does that mean?"

Damien giggled as he recoiled from the swat on his arm. "You're trying to figure out a way to bring in illegal information to help a case."

She laughed as she went back to her desk. "It's clear this lawyer, at least I think it's the lawyer, and Shamus are trafficking young girls. I want to stop that, and this may be one of those times it needs to be done any way possible." She zeroed in on him. "You've corrupted me."

"You can't blame me." He did some stuff on his computer and printed a few things. "Alright. Using what we have received legally, I compiled a list of names of girls that have either committed suicide or disappeared. I personally think the suicides are a cover-up for the disappearances. I think whoever is putting the information into the girl's files randomly switches between suicide, runaways, disappearances." He stapled the sheets together. "I have 172 in total. That should be enough to get the captain to go to bat for us to get a warrant for the grounds and the records of the home."

Dillon nodded. "I want to know what's under that slab."

Damien frowned at her. "Why?"

"Did you not notice the way he kept staring at it?"

Damien shook his head as he ate the last of his food. Coach weaved in between his legs. Gunner sat next to him, eyeballing every bite that entered his mouth. "How come they aren't bugging you? You have more food than I do."

She laughed. "I think they know how much it bugs the hell out of you. Anyway, back to the perv. Shamus kept glancing at the slab. If it didn't have any meaning to him, he wouldn't look at it."

"Like a treasure?" he guzzled his beer. "You think he hid some money down there?"

She shook her head. "No. Think about it. He said the slab was added in either 2007 or 2008, that puts its construction there during the time when Chase and Maggie both lived at the home."

Damien stared at her. "What do you think is buried down under the slab?"

Dillon put her beer on the desk. "I think he buried a body under it. And if I'm right in my assumption. I think it's the key to who the killer is, or at least why he may be killing."

CHAPTER FIFTY-NINE

Dillon gripped the edge of the cliff. Her fingers digging into the rocks. She placed the tips of her toes against the edge of the mountain, but she couldn't get a toe hold. Her breathing labored. She winced at the tearing sensation in her shoulders, as if the muscles were ripping slowly from the bone. "Someone help me, please," she called out as she attempted to pull herself up and over the edge.

"Let go already."

Dillon looked up at the sound of the familiar voice. "Grandfather, help me." Dillon continued to claw at the mountain.

"You have to let go, Dillon. It's the only way to save yourself," her grandfather said.

"What? No. If I let go, I'll die." Dillon managed to pull herself up a bit as she reached for a vine growing out of the top of the cliff. "Help me, grandfather, please."

"You don't understand, Dillon. I can't help you. You have to do this on your own."

"Why? You're right there. Help me. I need you to help me. I don't want to die." Her fingers started to slip. She glanced over her shoulder at the blackness beneath her.

"You're already dead, Dillon."

She heard laughter. But it wasn't her grandfather's. Dillon looked back up. David stood there. Her breath caught in her throat. "You're dead."

He laughed at her bulging eyes. "You didn't think I would go away that easy, did you?" He stepped up to her fingers. He dug the heel of his shoe into them.

She heard the snapping sound of the bones breaking. Dillon cried out as she let go of the cliff's edge. As she plunged to her death, the last thing she saw was David waving at her.

"Dillon?" Damien struggled to wake her. "Dillon? Wake up!" He could hear her moaning, but he couldn't wake her. He reached for the light on his nightstand, just as his phone rang. Dillon stirred while he fumbled for his phone. "Damn." He glanced at the clock, three a.m.

"Hello?"

"Kaine, Lieutenant Kaine?"

"Yeah, this is Kaine. Who is this?"

"Detective Thomas from The Dunes. We have a problem. I think you need to get down here."

Damien sat up, swinging his legs over the side. Gunner, who had been laying between his legs, moved up and took his spot.

"What's going on?" Dillon asked.

He covered the mouthpiece. "It's Detective Thomas." He put the phone on speaker. "What's going on, Detective?"

"Shamus MacDougal has been found dead in his car."

Dillon shot up out of bed and started to get dressed.

"Where?" Damien asked.

"His car was parked in the parking lot of a bar he goes to regularly."

Damien heard a muffled conversation before the detective came back on the line.

"Listen, Dr. Morgan is on his way. I don't know how long we can hold the body."

"We will be there within an hour or an hour and a half. If you have to move the body, take as many photos of the scene as you can. I will call you when we're almost in town, you can let me know then where the body is. I'm guessing Dr. Morgan has contacted Dr. Forsythe."

"Yes, he has. He told me not two minutes ago to tell you. He said he will have all the information for you."

"Can you interview anyone around the bar for me? Ask them if they remember anyone being at the bar. Anyone they had never seen before?" Damien asked as he walked to the closet.

"I will handle it. It's going to be a shit storm down here when the State gets wind of this."

"Detective Thomas, if you could keep from saying anything to the powers that be, I would greatly appreciate it." Damien took the jeans and shirt Dillon held out to him.

"I'll stall and dodge as much as I can. I'll text you the address of where we are now. If we leave before you get here, I'll let you know."

"Thanks, Detective." Damien hung up and dialed Joe.

"Unless you're about to give me some money, I don't want to talk to you."

"Get your fat ass up. I'll be over in about twenty to pick you up. Shamus is dead."

"Fuck. I hate this case. See you in twenty."

Damien stuck the phone in his back pocket. Dillon was letting the dog in and feeding them. "I'll call Mrs. C. in a few hours and ask her to come over and let Gunner out."

"He'll be fine until then." She followed him out the door after grabbing her credentials and her gun.

"Are you supposed to be carrying?"

She frowned at him. "Like I would go anywhere without my weapon."

Damien searched her face for any sign of the nightmare she had. "Do you remember the dream?" He backed out of the garage waiting for her to reply.

Dillon stared out the passenger window. "Yeah." That was all she offered.

Damien left it alone for now. "If Shamus was killed in his car. That's a big change in MO for our killer."

"I was thinking that." Dillon pulled her hair into a loose bun. "Makes me wonder what the end game is."

Damien texted Joe when he stopped in front of his house. He watched as the big guy bounded the steps.

Dillon got out and got into the backseat. "Take the front. I know your legs are longer."

"You love me, don't you?" Joe said, kissing her cheek.

"No. I don't want your knee bumping into the back of my seat every chance you get."

Joe climbed into the front. "What's up? Got any details?"

"Only Shamus was found in his car outside a bar." Damien headed towards the freeway.

Joe glanced back at Dillon. "What does that mean to you?"

Dillon scooted towards the other side of the back seat, keeping Joe from turning around to see her. "If we are operating under the assumption the killer is exacting revenge on these few people, I would have thought he would've wanted to make Shamus pay the most. Since it seems he has strayed from that, I have to think during this killing spree something has happened making him change his end goal."

Joe turned and stared at her. "I don't think I understand. What could he be after now?"

"I don't know for sure," Dillon said.

Damien flipped on his lights as he entered the freeway. "What if he has learned something from the torturing, that made him change the end goal?"

Dillon looked through the windshield at the empty highway. There was little traffic and the dark black sky made for an eerie setting. "I can see that being a probability. If we have figured out that there may be possible human trafficking going on just based off what little evidence we have, I can only imagine what our killer has gotten from torturing his victims."

They rode in silence.

Joe's head rested against the window. His soft snores filled the cabin.

Damien peered in the rearview at Dillon. She looked as if she was trying to figure out a puzzle. "Talk to me about your dream," he said.

She met his eyes in the mirror. "I was hanging off a cliff. I heard my grandfather's voice telling me to let go. When I looked up, it was David. He stepped on my hands and broke my fingers. As I fell backward, I saw him laughing at me."

Damien concentrated on the road. His heart raced. "Do you have any ideas about what it means?"

"It means he is still fucking with me. That's what it means." She looked out the window at the blackness. "My grandfather said let it go, but David said I couldn't get rid of him that easily."

"Follow your grandfather's voice. Let it go. I'll do whatever you need me to, in order to help you," Damien said.

Dillon was about to comment when Damien's phone rang. "Kaine here."

"Kaine, it's Detective Thomas. Dr. Morgan is taking the body to the morgue. He said to meet him there, and he will fill you in on what he has. I'll meet you there as well, and I'll give you my interview notes."

"See you there in about twenty-five minutes." Damien disconnected the call.

CHAPTER SIXTY

Thursday 4:00 a.m.
The Dunes

Damien parked in the ME's parking lot. Several police milled about. Nodding in one of the officer's directions Damien got his attention. "I'm Lieutenant Kaine, do we go on in?"

"The doors are open."

They entered the morgue, following the raised voices to the back.

"I don't care what you want, no one is getting into the home. There are kids we need to take care of first."

Damien didn't recognize the voice. As he entered the autopsy room, he saw Dr. Morgan, Detective Thomas, and some high dollar suit. He winked at Dillon. "Hello, Dr. Morgan."

Dr. Morgan's face softened with relief. "Lieutenant Kaine, I'm glad you are here."

Damien shook Detective Thomas' hand. "Hey, Detective. Thanks for all your assistance."

"My pleasure. This is Roger Franklin. The attorney for the State of Illinois DHS."

Damien held out his hand. The distinguished older gentleman shook it. "Nice to meet you, Mr. Franklin. This is my partner Detective Hagan and this is FBI Agent McGrath."

Roger's eyes narrowed in on the three of them. He spun on Detective Thomas. "Why are they here?"

"This is my case." Damien stepped closer to the man.

"No. This is a case occurring here. You aren't needed here." Roger Franklin crossed his arms.

"Mr. Franklin, this case started with a murder, two actually in Chicago. Both were people associated with the Sunshine Valley Home. I'm with the Vicious Crimes Unit out of Division Central, we have absolute jurisdiction in this matter. This is FBI Agent McGrath. She has been assigned to help us with this investigation."

"I don't care who you work for. You aren't getting into the home until I say so. I've already been in contact with the Secretary of DHS,

Tristan Rinehart. I will have the home ready for you to enter, but not until I feel the kids at the house are adequately taken care of. I was explaining this to Detective Thomas." Roger Franklin tugged on his coat.

"We need to get into the home and look at Mr. MacDougal's personal effects and see if we can ascertain if anyone killed him." Damien stepped closer to the man. Roger Franklin looked young for a man in his late fifties. He wasn't too tall. Roger used his fancy suit and position to wear his authority like some men wore cologne.

"You will have to wait." Roger puffed out his chest.

Dillon took a half step towards the man. "You do realize the FBI has Federal jurisdiction here?"

"I still don't have to let you in. He didn't die in the home. If you can't wait until I give you the okay, then try and get a warrant. You won't get one from any judge in this town." He buttoned up his coat.

"I will get a Federal warrant. And when I do, I will make sure to include you, your office, and home as well." Dillon smiled at him.

"Are you threatening me, Agent?"

She glanced around the room. "I don't think I made any such thing. I was simply making sure you are aware of what is to come. That's all."

Roger Franklin turned towards Damien. "I will contact you, Lieutenant, later today with a time you can come into the home. Good day," he said as he stormed out and down the hall.

Damien shot a glance to the detective.

He raised his hands. "I didn't say a word. We rolled up here, and he popped up two minutes later." Detective Thomas leaned against the wall. "He's an ass. I don't know if you have ever had the pleasure of dealing with him, but you will end up hating him."

"How do you think he found out?" Damien asked.

Detective Thomas shrugged. "I bet it was one of the cops. Could've been someone from the bar. Roger has a lot of pull in this town."

Dillon stepped up to the body. "Hi, Dr. Morgan. Nice to see you again."

Dr. Morgan lifted his gloved hands. "I would shake your hand, but I have started preparing the body for autopsy. My hands are icky. However, it's a pleasure to see you again."

"I understand. Do you have anything on how he died?" Dillon asked.

Damien, Joe, and Detective Thomas stepped to the table.

Dr. Morgan pointed to Shamus MacDougal's face. "I won't know for sure until I have results back from Toxicology, but I'm sure he ingested or was injected with something. The foaming around the mouth, mixed with blood and the blood from his nose, tells me it was highly toxic whatever it was."

Damien turned to Detective Thomas. "Do you have anything from witnesses?"

Detective Thomas removed his notepad from his pocket. "The bartender said he came out of the bar after closing and cleaning the place and found Shamus' car parked in the lot. He knocked on the window then peered through the glass and saw the blood on him. He went back into the bar and called the police." He flipped through a few pages. "The bartender, along with several waitresses, said there was a guy at the bar talking to him. But no one had a real description of the man."

Damien frowned. "Do they have surveillance around the bar?"

"Outside, but not inside the bar," Detective Thomas said. "However, before you get excited, there seemed to be a malfunction with the cameras throughout the evening. At several points in the recording, there was interference. All you see is static."

"Damn. This guy is so far ahead of us." Damien looked at Joe and Dillon, then turned back to the detective. "Do you have a guy you trust in the department?"

Detective Thomas flinched back raising an eyebrow at him. "Yes, but for what?"

"I need someone to sit on Roger Franklin," Damien said.

"Why?" asked Detective Thomas.

"I need someone to tell me what he does and where he goes. But I don't want anyone to know." He turned to Dillon. "You think you can get a warrant faster than us?"

She nodded. "I can call AD Reynolds. See if he can help. I don't want to call my Director. I'll let the AD do that." She stepped out into the hallway to make the call.

Damien looked at Joe. "We have to get into the house."

"I agree. We need to stop him from removing anything from the office." Joe crossed his arms as he leaned against the wall.

"I got someone. But he isn't a cop. I trust him with my life. I'll call him." Detective Thomas stepped out as Dillon walked in.

"I got AD Reynolds putting in a call to Director Sherman. He thinks he can get one pretty fast. Especially since the FBI is on a joint task force with Division Central to solve these murders."

Damien raised an eyebrow at her. "Joint taskforce? I didn't even know there was a task force."

"Amazingly enough, it was put together, in time for the request of a warrant." Dillon chuckled.

"I called Dr. Forsythe before I showed up on the scene. I will have all the results sent to him, and he's going to do the autopsy with me via telecom." Dr. Morgan looked at the clock on the wall. "I have approximately ten minutes until he comes on the line with me. I thought it would be best since this case started with him in Chicago."

"Thanks, that will help us out a lot." Damien smiled at the doctor. "I appreciate how cooperative and helpful you have been, Dr. Morgan."

"Dr. Forsythe has been a long-time friend and colleague. I wouldn't think of doing it any other way," Dr. Morgan said.

Detective Thomas stepped back into the autopsy room. "I got a hold of my buddy. He's making a few calls and seeing where Roger Franklin is now. He'll find him and follow him. He'll keep me updated, and I'll keep you updated," he said nodding towards Damien.

"I appreciate this," Damien said.

Dillon's phone rang. She held up her index finger as she answered it. "Yes, AD? Okay...We will head there now. Send me the warrant. I can get it printed." She nodded as she continued to listen. "I will. We have a local detective here with us. Yes, it was. Okay. Thank you."

She hung up and turned towards Detective Thomas. "Can we print this over at your station?"

"Absolutely. You guys want to follow me over there? It's down the road. Literally."

Damien's brow wrinkled. "Why do you need a printed warrant?"

"Roger Franklin has already called DC to complain about you. Captain Mackey was called at home and the phone call was put through. He then called AD Reynolds. The AD wants to make sure Mr. Franklin doesn't use the digital warrant as a means to deny us entry."

"Detective Thomas, lead the way." Damien glanced over at the doctor. "Let us know what you find, please."

"I will Lieutenant Kaine," Doctor Morgan responded.

CHAPTER SIXTY-ONE

Thursday 6:30 a.m.

Damien pulled into a parking spot next to Detective Thomas. As they exited the car, Detective Thomas was on the phone walking towards them.

Joe raised an eyebrow at Damien. "This doesn't feel like it's going to be good news." He pointed to the Detective.

"Damn. Stay on him and tell me where he goes." Detective Thomas waved them to follow him. "That was my buddy. He said Roger left Sunshine Valley. He said it didn't look like he was carrying anything. And he doesn't know how much time he spent in the home. He only found out because the bartender at the place where Shamus was killed is a friend of his. He overheard a part of a phone call, Roger mentioned he was heading to the home as soon as he left the coroners."

Dillon shook her head. "He has a lead on us. He could take anything from the home or download incriminating evidence off the computer." She reached out and touched the detective's arm. "Do you have an office out of the way?"

He grinned at her. "That's why we are entering through this door. I'm taking you guys to our computer guru. He's my brother-in-law. Got him the job here." He opened a double door as they entered a long sparsely populated hallway. "No one comes down here if they can help it."

Detective Thomas led them through a dimly lit corridor, to an unmarked door. "Jimmy, he likes it down here. He's a little odd. But I would trust him with any secret." Opening the door ice-cool air rushed at them. "Yo, Jimmy?"

A man rolled a chair from around a stack of shelves. "Hey, Garth. Who did you bring with you? And why are you here?"

"I need your help. Can you print something from her phone for me?" Detective Garth Thomas leaned against a desk resembling something out of a *Star Trek* set. "This is FBI Agent Dillon McGrath, Detective Joe Hagan, and Lieutenant Damien Kaine. They are from Division Central."

Jimmy held out his hand to the three visitors. "Nice to meet you guys." He nodded at Dillon. "You got the file pulled up on your phone?"

She fiddled with her screen before handing it to him. "I need this. Two copies would be great."

He took her phone and hooked it to a USB cable. Jimmy sat at his desk. He copied the file from the phone and transferred it to his desktop. After he printed it, he smiled at the pretty FBI agent. "I will not only delete this, but I will also erase this from my printer and print driver." He handed her the two copies. Jimmy squinted at Garth. "This about the murders associated with the home, huh?"

"It is," Detective Thomas said.

Damien caught both Joe and Dillon's eyes. "Detective Thomas, how much trouble would Jimmy get in if he went with us to the home. I need someone we can trust to tell me if anything was taking off Shamus' computer."

"And not leave a trace," Dillon said.

Joe laughed. "I knew we would get you to the dark side sooner or later."

She smacked his arm, turning back to Detective Thomas and Damien. "If Roger is already making moves to get us out of his hair. I don't want anyone knowing what we know. Until they have to. I'm not planning on hiding anything from anyone. I want to delay the disbursement of information."

Joe cracked up. "That sounds so—official."

Jimmy's eyes widened. "I'd love to. I leave this office regularly. I came in early to finish some files." He glanced at his watch. "I think I'm hungry." He retrieved a jump drive from his desk drawer. "You hungry brother?" he smiled at Detective Thomas.

"Why, yes I am." Detective Thomas headed to the cars. As they stepped into the hallway, he led them down a corridor towards a different door from the one they had entered. Before pushing the door open, he hit a small button on the wall.

Joe glanced around the garage, then at the door. No handles. "What was that? A secret escape?"

Detective Thomas chuckled. "You're not supposed to use it. I disabled the alarm before we walked through it. You guys follow me. I know a shortcut to get us to the home in half the time."

Damien pulled out behind the detective. He glanced back at Dillon. "Do you think this will get you in trouble?"

She shook her head. "No. Maybe. I don't know. Roger Franklin is up to something. I don't know what. But I'm betting he took something from that home." She looked over the warrant. "This gives us permission to search Shamus' residence at the home and his office, as well as any common areas of the house. But not the grounds. Or the buildings the kids sleep in, or any of the other buildings. If we find anything, we can get a warrant to search the entire facility."

Joe turned towards her. "I think we need to hit the basement, while Jimmy searches the computer." He peered over at Damien. "Why didn't you go through the computer?"

"I know a lot, but I don't know everything about computers. I would've had Detective Travis go through it, but we don't have time. Plus having an independent agent looking at it will keep Roger Franklin from claiming we're harassing him."

"Ah, good thinking." Joe smiled. "I'm amazed every day at how smart you are."

"And I'm amazed every day I haven't killed you and buried you somewhere." Damien laughed at Joe, flipping him the bird.

CHAPTER SIXTY-TWO

Thursday 7:45 a.m.

Damien led the team to the front door of the Sunshine Valley Home. He was about to knock on the door when a school bus pulled up. The door opened as a hoard of kids ran out. They all stepped to the side as the kids boarded the bus. Damien turned back to the door to see a security guard standing there.

"What can I do for you guys?" he asked.

Damien looked at Detective Thomas, who shrugged. Turning back to the guard, he nodded to Dillon. "This is FBI Agent Dillon McGrath, I'm Lieutenant Damien Kaine. We have a warrant to search the premises."

The guard shook his head. "I've been instructed by Roger Franklin to not let anyone in."

Dillon stepped up and produced a copy of the warrant and handed it to him. "You have two choices. You can either abide by that Federal warrant, or you will be arrested."

His eyes got wide. He quickly scanned the paper, handing it back to her. "I don't want to go to jail. I'm not paid enough. Mr. Franklin said no one would be able to get a warrant and all I had to do was make sure no one entered." He stepped back. "You can search whatever you want."

Joe leaned into the man, towering over him. "Do you have a cell phone?"

The man nodded slowly. "I do."

"Do not call Roger Franklin or anyone else. Or you will be arrested for obstruction." Joe leered at him. "Do I make myself clear?"

"Yes, Sir. Very clear."

"Good. If anyone comes to that door, call out for us, but do not let them in. You work for us now." Damien smiled at him and patted him on the shoulder. "I appreciate your help." He led the way through the home to Shamus' office. Once inside, he pointed to Jimmy. "Start on the computer. I have no idea if it is password protected. We could ask one of the workers here if they know."

Jimmy pulled out the jump drive he had brought with him. "Let me see something first. If his password is starred out, I can use this program to retrieve it." He sat down at the desk and plugged the drive into the computer. He then turned on the desktop. As it roared to life, he tapped away on the keyboard.

"Let's hit the basement," Damien said. "Detective Thomas, you want to rifle through everything in here?"

"I can do that." Detective Thomas moved towards the file cabinet. "This looks as good a place to start."

"What's the meaning of this? Who are you?" A lady stood in the doorway with her sweater tied tight around her waist. Her scowl feigned authority.

Damien didn't recognize her as the lady who gave them the slip of paper days earlier. "We have a search warrant to search Shamus' residence and his office, as well as all common areas." He reached out for the warrant from Dillon. He handed it to her.

She read the warrant only shaking her head. She thrust it back into his hand. "I don't know what that means. Shouldn't I call the lawyer?"

"Mrs.?" Damien asked.

"I'm Sheila Grant. I'm one of the house mothers."

"Mrs. Grant, I'm going to ask you not to call anyone. We're hoping to keep the kids from knowing what's going on until it's necessary." Damien smiled at her.

She crossed her arms. "I don't know what you mean. Where is Shamus? He never came home last night."

Dillon leaned into Joe and whispered something into his ear. She stepped up to the woman as Joe walked out of the office. Dillon made eye contact with Damien who excused himself and followed Joe down the hallway. "Mrs. Grant, is there somewhere we can talk?"

Sheila Grant fidgeted with her sleeves. "I think you should tell me what's going on. Is Shamus in some kind of trouble?"

Dillon placed her hand on her shoulder. "Let's go to the kitchen. I need to tell you and the other workers something. How many are still on the premises?"

Sheila Grant headed towards the tall counter in the kitchen and poured a cup of coffee. "Would you like one?"

"Yes, thank you." Dillon sat at the large dining table. The kitchen was a large spacious room. The table barely filled half of the space, and it sat ten. "Is there anyone else here?"

Sheila shook her head, sitting across from her guest. "No. When the kids leave several of us go shopping. Today they left before the kids did. I was still in the kitchen. I let Damon, the security guard, get them on the bus for me."

"Does he work here often?" Dillon put two cubes of sugar into her coffee.

"Once in a while. Roger called me early this morning and said he was sending him over, but he didn't say why. Then when Roger showed up an hour later, he went right to the office and locked the door. He left about thirty minutes later without saying anything." Sheila stirred her coffee. Staring at the swirls of cream. "Please tell me what is going on."

"I'm sorry to tell you this, but Shamus died last night."

Sheila blinked, covering her mouth with her hand. "Oh my gosh!" Her hands and voice trembled. "I don't believe you." She stood and paced the kitchen. "How? When?"

"Mrs. Grant, I can't give you many details, this is an ongoing investigation. But I can tell you, we believe he was murdered."

"What? No! I don't understand. Who would want to murder Shamus?" Sheila fell into the chair she had earlier vacated. Tears flowed down her cheeks. "I don't understand."

"I know this is hard," Dillon said. "Maybe you can answer a few questions for me." She waited a moment, giving Sheila a chance to catch her breath. "Sheila?"

The young woman sniffled and wiped her face with her sleeve.

"Sheila, how long have you worked here?" Dillon asked.

Sheila continued crying. Using the bottom of her shirt, she wiped her eyes. "Umm, over three years. I have a room in the girl's barracks. I'm their house mother."

"Have you ever noticed Shamus acting inappropriately with any of the residents?"

"What? No. Of course not. Shamus was a good man. He loved these kids." Sheila shook her head with intensity. "Shamus was a good man."

Sheila's body language disagreed with her words. Her lack of eye contact had Dillon wondering how much she knew of her former boss' activities. "Sheila, have you ever been to the basement?"

Her hands shook. "Why are you asking me this?"

Dillon leaned across the table, she was about to say something when Damien and Joe ran into the kitchen.

"You need to come to the basement." Damien motioned for her to follow.

"Sheila, stay here. I need to ask you some more questions." Dillon waited for her to respond. "Sheila?"

She waved her off. "Yes, yes. I will stay here."

Dillon followed Joe and Damien down the stairs located off the back of the kitchen. "What did you guys find?"

"You'll see," Joe said as they rounded the corner at the bottom of the stairs.

She stood and looked around the large space. At first glance, it looked like a normal basement. There were storage shelves along one wall, filled with household supplies. Another series of shelves were filled with canned goods and dry foods. Dillon walked further into the space. She glanced around. "What's that?"

Damien cocked an eyebrow at her. "See for yourself." He pointed to a door. "This space was added some time ago. Just like Nancy Milligan described it."

She tilted her head to the side. "Was the lock broken when you came down here?"

Joe looked at Damien, then back to Dillon. "Yes."

Damien bit his bottom lip, nodding. "Mhmm."

Dillon placed her hands on her hips. "I guess Roger Franklin was looking for something."

Damien smiled at her. "Someone was." He pointed to a rather large screwdriver laying on the floor next to the wall. "Looks like someone used it to pry off the lock. I don't think it took much effort."

"Well, a kid could have come snooping down here. You never know." Dillon moved to the door. It was cracked open. She used her foot to push the door open wider. She gasped as the door swung easily open. "Oh, no."

"A part of me hoped Nancy was wrong." Damien followed her into the small room.

It had been decorated to look like a young adolescent kid's room. A full-size bed with a frilly bedspread and one white end table sat in the center of the room. Stuffed animals lined a small shelving unit as well as other little girl décor and playthings.

"I don't even want to think about what that man did down here to these girls." Dillon walked around the room careful not to touch anything. "You two kept your hands in your pockets, right?"

"We aren't stupid. Of course, we did." Damien smirked at Joe.

"It's a good thing the lock was broken, or we would've had to wait for a warrant." Joe rocked back on his heels. "This should give us enough to get a warrant for the entire premises."

Dillon pulled her phone out and snapped a few photos. "I'll send these to AD Reynolds. I bet he gets us what we need."

Damien pointed to the corner. "There is a camera. Looks like it picks up this entire room. I don't see any wires; I'm betting it's remotely connected to his computer. Let's go see what Jimmy found."

Back in the kitchen, Dillon motioned for them to head on up to the office. "Sheila?"

Sheila looked up with puffy eyes and a tear streaked face. "I'm sorry. We never said anything. He threatened anyone who ventured into the basement. There was another woman who used to work here. She disappeared." She broke down crying.

Dillon sat across from her. "How long?"

"Years. One of the ladies, Terra Vans. She worked here for several years. She suspected something was going on, but she couldn't prove it. Girls went missing, she said something to Patrick, next thing she was fired." Sheila lifted her eyes and met Dillon's. "I knew her. She got me this job. She went missing after she left that day. I tried calling her, she was gone, disappeared. Left everything. No one believed me when I said she wouldn't do that. I tried to tell him, but no one would listen to me."

Dillon's brow furrowed. "I don't understand. Him who? Shamus?"

"What? No. Shamus fired her; said she was caught stealing. She would never steal."

"Sheila, I don't understand. Who did you tell Terra had vanished?"

"Mr. Franklin. I tried to tell him something was wrong and I asked him to help find Terra. He said he would speak to the police, but I needed to let it go." She sniffled into a napkin she took from the holder on the table.

"Did you ever see Mr. Franklin go into the basement?" Dillon asked.

Sheila didn't look up.

"Sheila?"

"He's very powerful. You have to know that. I tried to protect the girls as much as I could. If I quit, no one would be here to protect them. When a new girl came in, I made sure to never leave her alone. I kept such a close eye on them. But I couldn't be here all the time." Sheila couldn't contain the emotions any longer.

Dillon fumed on the inside. They should have said something. "Did Mr. Franklin or Shamus ever threaten you? Specifically, threaten you?"

"No. But Patrick did."

"What do you mean?" Dillon scooted a little closer to her.

"After I spoke to Mr. Franklin about Terra, a week later, Patrick followed me into the laundry room. He closed the door behind us and blocked me up against the dryer. He was really close to me, he said if I keep looking for Terra, I'll end up like her. Missing."

"Sheila, you're going to need to stay here. When will the others be back?" Dillon looked at her watch.

She shook her head. "I don't know. Probably in the next hour. I can call them."

"No. Don't do that. I need you to stay off your phone. If you use it, I will slap an obstruction charge on you. Do you understand?"

Sheila began crying again. "Yes. I understand."

Dillon started to move away when Sheila grabbed her arm.

"Am I going to jail?"

"I don't know. You should've said something to someone, but I can see how you didn't know who to trust. And you were scared. I think any prosecutor will give you leniency for your testimony against Roger Franklin."

She nodded. "I'll do whatever I need to. I'm sorry I didn't help more. I'm so sorry." She hung her head and wept.

Dillon headed up the stairs to the office. She wondered how many girls would've been saved had even one person spoken up.

CHAPTER SIXTY-THREE

Damien turned around at the sound of the office door opening. "Hey, what did Sheila say?"

"She tried to protect the girls as much as possible. She was too scared to say anything. Patrick threatened her after she spoke to Roger Franklin about a lady named Terra who used to work here."

Joe glanced up from a file. "Wait, a worker went missing from here?"

Dillon shrugged. "It seems so."

"I bet that's why Martha slipped us the note." Joe leaned against the desk.

Detective Thomas stood with his mouth gaping open as he stared at the computer. "This is so wrong!"

Jimmy glanced at everyone. "This is all I could find on the computer. One file. Everything else had been erased. Looks like with a program that targets specific files. All the home's business files were left untouched."

Everyone moved behind Jimmy and stared at the screen. Several video files were open in front of them. It showed Shamus hurting several girls. The videos looked to go back several years if the date stamp was correct.

Dillon cringed and walked away. She didn't need to see any more.

Damien pulled his phone out. "Shut that off." He said to Jimmy as they moved back in front of the desk. "Captain, we have a serious situation." Damien stepped out into the hallway.

Joe stared at Detective Thomas. "Your buddy, did he say how long Franklin was in here?"

"No longer than twenty minutes," the detective said.

"He wouldn't have needed more than five minutes to wipe the files off the drive," Jimmy said as Damien walked back into the room.

"What did the Captain say?" Joe asked.

"He is sending Travis down here, along with a few of our officers. Along with two CSU crews. As soon as either Dillon gets a warrant or we get a warrant we will search the home." He turned towards Dillon. "Everywhere. I specifically told him about your ideas on the slab."

Detective Thomas slammed the file drawer shut. "There's nothing here. What Jimmy has found only points to Shamus who is conveniently dead."

"We need something to point to Roger." Dillon stood and paced. "Sheila's testimony won't provide anything."

Jimmy pulled a USB drive from the computer. "I cloned the hard drive onto this. All of the files as they stand now. Including the videos. In case they go missing. They are coded, so there is no mistaking where the files came from." He handed the USB to Dillon. "I will testify I retrieved the files."

Detective Thomas squinted at the crew. "My buddy will testify he saw Roger Franklin here, but it won't do any good. Roger can say as the lawyer for the State, he had every right to be here after learning of Shamus' death."

"We need more. Shit," Joe dragged a hand through his hair. "Roger is going to spin this against Shamus. Say he hid everything. You know Roger has to be involved somehow."

"Listen, we need to go over and see if we can speak to Roger or Mr. Tristan Rhinehart. I have a feeling we will come up against a wall. Until we have something in the way of proof." Damien nodded towards Detective Thomas. "Do you have some officers you trust who won't tell Roger or anyone else anything, who can stand guard over this place. Making sure nothing goes missing?"

"Do we have that authority?" Detective Thomas asked.

Damien turned towards Dillon. "Do we?"

"Fuck. Probably not. Right now, we have a search warrant for the common areas and this office. That's the only reason we could get into the basement." She pulled her phone from her pocket. "AD Reynolds said getting a warrant for the rest of the home is going to be hard-pressed. Roger Franklin has already put up a roadblock."

"What do you mean?" asked Joe.

Dillon read through an email. "It looks like he has an injunction against anyone searching the home. Some crap about ensuring the safety of the kids. Which is crap."

Detective Thomas' phone rang. "Yeah. No shit. Okay, thanks." He motioned to the door. "We're about to get company. That was my buddy, he said Roger and several officers are on their way here."

Damien glanced around the room. "Did you get all you could off the computer?" he asked Jimmy.

"Everything that was on there. If I had more time, I might be able to run a program to retrieve the deleted files. But I can't do it here," Jimmy said.

He looked at Joe and Dillon. "Nothing was in the files. I bet everything we needed was once on that computer."

A commotion could be heard from downstairs.

"Looks like they're here." Damien led the way out of the office.

Sheila and the other workers had been gathered in the main living room. Shopping bags filled with groceries littered the floor. Roger Franklin stood with several patrol officers and several other suits.

"What's the meaning of this?" Roger Franklin stepped towards Damien. "You do not have the authority to be here."

Dillon smiled at the disgusting man. "Actually, we have all the authority we need." She handed him the search warrant.

He yanked it from her hand. He glared at her. "You have no right being here. You're way out of your jurisdiction."

She stepped a half step closer to him. She stood face to face with him. "The Federal government has jurisdiction everywhere. You're a lawyer Mr. Franklin, I'm pretty sure they covered that in your law classes."

Roger Franklin huffed. "You had no authority to secure a search warrant."

"We had every authority. This case links directly to a murder case out of Chicago. Along with the murder of Patrick Weinsted and Shamus MacDougal. Which all seem to be connected to this home." Dillon took the warrant from him. "I also think we need to look into the disappearance of Terra Vans."

Roger Franklin blinked rapidly as he rubbed his chin. "Did you find anything in the home?"

"Yes. Can you explain the basement to us?" Damien asked.

"No. What's in the basement?" Roger's stomach churned as he bit his lips.

Dillon caught Sheila's eye. "Mr. Franklin, you've never gone into the basement?"

"No. I'm a lawyer, not a handyman. Why would I need to go into the basement?" Roger asked.

"It seems there is a bedroom down there," Dillon said.

302   Victoria M. Patton

"I—I was unaware of any such thing. How do you know this?" Roger asked.

Damien tilted his head to the side. "We saw it. The door was open, and we could see the room."

Roger Franklin waved a dismissing hand. "Your warrant didn't allow for the search of that room. It was locked."

Dillon stepped up to Roger. "How would you know the door was locked if you have never been to the basement?"

"What?" Roger asked, giving sidelong glances towards the officers flanking him.

"You said you hadn't been in the basement. How did you know the door was locked?" Damien asked.

"I'm sure Shamus must have mentioned keeping the door locked. But I thought he was talking about a storage facility. Not a bedroom." Roger walked towards the front door. "According to your warrant, you had the right to search the office and the common spaces. Have you done that?"

Dillon nodded. "For now. We will be back with a crime scene unit to do a more thorough sweep of the premises. And the basement is a common area. You might want to brush up on your law, Mr. Franklin."

"You'd better have a new warrant." Roger opened the door to the home. "I have the authority of the Secretary of the Department of Human Services, and right now our concern is keeping the children safe. I think it's time you leave."

They all headed out the door.

Damien stopped and faced him. "Mr. Franklin, did you search Shamus' computer?"

"No. I don't know much about computers except turning them on. I do know you will need a warrant covering the computer." Roger said sneering at the Lieutenant.

"You must not have read the warrant, Mr. Franklin. It covered the computer in the office. As well as everything else in the office." Dillon smirked at his reaction.

"Well, you can't remove it from the home without a new warrant. You won't be let back in until you have that." Roger shut the door on them.

Detective Thomas stared at them. "This is going to be a mess. I will do what I need to on this end. Roger may have a lot of pull, but no one in this department will cover up what has been going on in this home. Damien, since this is technically your case, I don't have much authority. But I will let my captain know what's going on."

"You don't have to worry, Detective. Captain Mackey will be letting your boss know what's going on. I will make sure nothing comes back on you. Ask your friend to keep an eye on Franklin. For the day. I want to follow his movements." Damien tapped a message to his captain.

"I got it covered. My guy is around the corner. He's going to stay on him. We'll at least see if he goes anywhere these next twenty-four hours." Detective Thomas stood at his car door while Jimmy stood at the passenger side. "Listen, if you need Jimmy for anything, you send me a text. I know you have your own computer geeks, but he's handy, and he can be here in a hot minute."

"Thanks. We're dead in the water until we have another warrant. I'll keep you posted. Thanks for your help today. We appreciate it," Damien said.

"No problem, Lieutenant." Detective Thomas and his brother-in-law headed out of the drive.

Damien's phone rang. "Did you see my message?"

"I did." Captain Mackey's voice boomed through the Bluetooth. I put a hold on the crew heading down there. Caught them in time. We need to wait until we get that a new warrant. I've been on the phone with AD Reynolds and the chief. It looks like Roger Franklin has some pull. He has Tristan Rhinehart, the Secretary of DHS telling us we have no authority, and until we get some, we aren't going to be let back into the home."

"I have to wonder why this guy is putting up such a fight. We caught him in a lie." Damien motioned to Dillon in the backseat.

"Hey Captain, Dillon here."

"Hey, Agent McGrath."

"Listen, Shamus was abusing the girls at this home. But right now, all we have are a few records that don't match up, and some witness testimony that will be blown out of the water by a first-year law student."

"Damien, you guys get your butts back up here. Gather everything you have and let's get something to speed along getting a warrant. We still don't have a clue who killed these people." Captain Mackey covered the phone.

Damien heard a muffled conversation before the captain spoke again.

"Damien, the chief came in. The ADA will be here later this evening, around six. She wants whatever you guys have. Get your team together and gather all your information. We need to get into that home."

"Yes, Sir. We should be back at DC within the hour." Damien frowned at the disconnected call. "Okay. Looks like we're going to be busy." He glanced at the clock on the dash. Then double-checked his watch. "Crap, it isn't even ten yet."

Joe leaned his head against the seat. "Before we get to DC, run through somewhere to get breakfast."

"I could go for coffee now." Dillon yawned.

Damien took a turn leading them back into the heart of town.

CHAPTER SIXTY-FOUR

Chicago 11:30 a.m.

By the time Damien rolled into the parking garage at DC, Joe and Dillon had a cat nap, and the long morning was already wearing on him. He sat at his desk, going over the results from the lists he had put together at the house the night before. It was staggering how many were now missing or had committed suicide. "This is fucking unbelievable," he sighed.

Dillon walked through his office door. "Hey, I spoke with AD Reynolds. Even though we can tie Shamus to the abuse of girls, we have no evidence. Besides, Nancy," she snapped her fingers.

"Milligan."

"Yes, Milligan, we need other witnesses. All the workers can attest to is maybe Roger went into the basement, but mostly it was Shamus. He's dead. Have you heard from the ME down there?" She took a handful of jelly beans hoping the sugar would give her a boost.

"Preliminary results show a high dose of Fentanyl. Given orally. The doc found a small injection site on Shamus' neck. It looks like Ketamine. He's running a few more tests. The Ketamine dose was super low. He thinks it was enough to get control of Shamus. The killer wanted him to feel the slow death caused by the Fentanyl."

"Even with Franklin's connections to the Mancusso family, it's not enough. Right now, AD Reynolds says we have nothing tying Franklin to Shamus' actions." Dillon sat back in the chair with her eyes closed.

"Are you feeling okay?" Damien worried about the stress of this case.

"I feel fine." She laughed. "I've gotten used to waking up at this time. Or napping."

"I was going over the three lists again, you know the ones we put in my computer at the house?"

"We can't use the list from your brother, but the other two, they still show a huge discrepancy." She straightened, stretching her back.

"I'm hoping we can use it to connect Roger Franklin to Shamus' activities. There is no way Franklin isn't involved in some way."

"I'm sure he is, but at the most, we have the list he sent to Martin Escobar."

"How is he going to explain that?"

Dillon rubbed her temples. "He may say the lists originated with Shamus. So, any missing names are on him."

Damien gathered all his files. "Let's get everyone into the conference room. Maybe if we brainstorm, we can come up with something to push the warrant for the home. I'm also going to call Mr. Escobar, see if he has any pull with the family. If they give us permission to search, we don't need a warrant. They still hold ownership of the home."

Dillon perked up. "Backdoor...I like it." She stood. "I need to get a snack. I'll meet you there." She walked out first heading towards the Canteen.

"Hey, Dillon?" Damien said from his office doorway.

She turned around. "Yeah?"

"Grab a whole bunch of drinks. Get a variety. And place an order for several pizzas. I bet we spend the afternoon in the room." Damien winked at her. "Tell them to put it on my tab."

"You got it, Mr. Money Bags." She winked as she headed towards the elevator.

"Davidson," Damien said, walking past his desk. "Gather everyone working on this case. Get Detective Travis as well and meet Joe and me in the conference room." Damien nodded at Joe. "Get your butt in here." He pointed towards the main conference room.

Joe stood. Keeping his head down, he scooted his feet. "Yessir, yessir Master Kaine. Whatever you say, Master Kaine." He continued to shuffle into the room.

"I want to smack you sometimes." Damien laid his files out on the table. "How's Taylor doing?"

"She's good. Has a nasty cold, and didn't want to go into work today, but she went anyway." Joe peeked around the doorway. "She's dealing with the death of her parents. Even though she wasn't close to them anymore, it still hurts. That's her mom and dad."

"I can't imagine what's going on with her brother is making this any easier."

Joe nodded. "She's scared of her brother. I think that's what is keeping her from dealing with their deaths. You and I need to come up with a plan."

"As soon as we get this case over with, we will. I can get a phone like the one I make Dillon carry. We can track her and all her texts."

"Man, if she thinks I'm spying on her, she will be pissed." Joe sat on the corner of the table. "I won't look at her texts, but knowing where she is...I like that."

Everyone filed into the room. Dillon walked back in pushing a cart with a tub of ice and soda, along with some snacks. "The pizza's will be up soon."

"Did you say pizza?" Detective Jenkins wiggled his eyebrows at Dillon. "Are you tired of him yet?" he asked, nodding towards Damien.

"Yes. You got a better offer?" She giggled at his accent.

"You need a New Yorker." He ducked as Damien threw a wadded piece of paper at him. "Man, you throw like a girl."

Everyone laughed.

"You know you have to fight Detective Hall for her," Damien said, laughing at Dillon's expression. "He called dibs on you months ago."

Dillon looked at Officer Baker. "How do you put up with these guys?"

"You ignore them." Officer Baker sat at the conference table. When Detective Travis walked in, she looked down at her lap.

Dillon squinted, raising her eyebrow as Baker glanced at her. She watched as the young officer's cheeks blushed. Dillon sat next to her and leaned in. "When did that happen?"

Officer Baker smiled as she gave Detective Travis a side glance. "I don't know. I can't even explain it."

"Does he even know?" Dillon asked, taking a sip of her soda.

Baker's eyes widened. "No!" she whispered sternly. "And I want to keep it that way."

"Why? If you like him, tell him."

Officer Baker glared at Dillon. "You better not tell a soul. Not even that hunk of sex you sleep with. Or I will take you down."

Dillon roared back in laughter. Everyone turned towards her. "Sorry, Baker told me a joke." She sniggered as she leaned into Baker. "If you ever say he is a hunk of sex to him, I'll kill you. His head is already big enough." She touched Baker's hand. "Your secret is safe with me. But I may play matchmaker some time."

Officer Baker winced in pain. "I should've kept my mouth shut."

As everyone was settling down, a messenger brought in a package into the room. "Lieutenant Kaine?"

Damien looked up from his notes. "What's up Peppers?"

"This got delivered to another office by accident." He handed Damien the sealed envelope.

"Thanks." Damien set it under his pile of papers.

Dillon craned her neck. "What's that?"

Damien shrugged. "I don't know. I'll look later. I want to get going on this." He pulled his list of names he received from Mr. Escobar. "Okay. Let's settle down. Davidson, what have you come up with?"

"Every missing girl was last seen at the home or school. The school wasn't going to give me any records without a warrant. But I managed to get the office lady to at least tell me about some of the girls from the home. She said they seemed withdrawn. And several quit coming to school." Davidson took a drink of his soda and a bite of the muffin he took from the cart.

"Did she give you anything? Any kind of list, anything we can use?" Damien asked.

"She wouldn't go on record. She did give me five names of girls she remembers who vanished." He handed the list to Damien. "She won't say anything unless we get a warrant. She doesn't want to lose her job. But when she heard about Patrick Weinsted being murdered, she wasn't surprised."

Damien leaned into the table. "Why?"

"Three of those girls were picked up before school let out by Patrick. She remembers how scared they looked to leave with him. She didn't think much of it at the time. But now, she doesn't wonder if something else was going on." Davidson flipped through his notes.

"How long ago was this?" Damien asked.

Davidson looked up. "Those three girls went missing a few years ago."

"What about Dr. Theodore Osgood, you got anything on him?" Damien asked.

"It doesn't look like Theodore is involved at all. He fills in around the state. I would hazard a guess that Shamus took advantage of him being on call, but didn't set it up." Davidson took a bite of his muffin.

Damien scribbled some notes. "Officer Baker, did you read the diary?" Damien asked, dragging a hand down his face. He quickly looked at the names Davidson gave him and searched the list of names he had in front of him.

"Yes. Ivansky is in a meeting but, he and I spoke on the way home. From what the Morenos said, there is no way Clara committed suicide. She was blossoming. She loved the Morenos, and they loved her. She wouldn't have ended it like that." Officer Baker opened the diary. "The last entry was written right before her meeting with the therapist. This is what she wrote: 'I've come to terms with what happened to me. But only because of the love of my new family. They don't have to adopt me for me to know I am their child. I finally feel ready to tell my story and not hide in shame any longer. It wasn't my fault. And I shouldn't carry the burden any longer.'"

"Damn," Damien whispered. "Detective Travis were you able to get the crime scene photos of Clara's death?"

Detective Travis shook his head. "No. Since her death was ruled a suicide, the photos are in evidence lockup. I would've needed to put in a formal request, and I wasn't sure you wanted me to do that. However, I spoke with one of the officers who was called to the scene. Just told him we needed some answers that might help us in a case here.

"Her car was found in the parking lot of the therapist office towards the back of the property. The medical record stated she had ingested antidepressants, Ecstasy, and alcohol. That combination mixed with the heat in the car was a lethal combination. That officer first on the scene said it looked like a suicide to him."

Damien growled. "So, we have nothing on Clara, yet we all know she didn't commit suicide?"

"Well, not exactly. You asked me to look into the adoption and who might have known. When I searched the records, an email was sent to both Shamus and Roger Franklin. The State wanted Shamus' opinion on Clara's state of 1. They were looking for some more in-depth information about why Clara went into the hospital." Detective Travis handed Damien the email.

"As you can see from the response, all Shamus said was at this time he thought she needed more time in the care of the State's doctors." Detective Travis waited for a moment before continuing. "Here's the thing. Clara died a short time later. Within two months. I took the liberty of checking Patrick's life during that time."

Detective Travis produced another piece of paper. "These are the financials for Patrick. He traveled to Chicago several times during the two-month period. And he was here when Clara died."

Damien avoided looking at Dillon. He let his mouth drop open. "Get the fuck out!"

Dillon took the paper from him and read through the hotel charges and travel arrangements.

"Puts him in this area. That's a good thing," Joe said.

Dillon was about to speak when the pizzas showed up. She watched in horror as the detectives of VCU pounced on the pies as if they hadn't had any food for weeks. "Jesus, you'd think you guys never saw a damn pizza."

Davidson filled his plate. "Are you kidding? Wait until you have kids. The food hits the table, and if you blink, it's gone."

"Never gonna happen. Coach and Gunner are enough kids for me." Dillon took two pieces of pepperoni and grabbed another soda from the bin. Sitting back down in her chair, she focused on Patrick. "Okay, yes we can put Patrick in Chicago, but that doesn't mean he killed Clara. Without any concrete proof, it's nothing more than a dot on the map."

"At the very least, we might be able to connect enough of those dots to make the coroner change his ruling and make it an undetermined cause." Joe swallowed his bite of food. "It might help the Morenos get some answers."

Damien sat back in his seat. He watched as the men and women who worked under him laughed and joked while they took a minute to eat. Dillon caught his eye. She winked at him and smiled. He enjoyed watching her with his detectives and was grateful Phillip let her work this case with them. Giving everyone a chance to eat, he opened the envelope delivered earlier.

He didn't recognize the name or address on the return label and couldn't imagine who had to overnight something to him. He chuckled as he pulled the contents out, listening to Davidson talk about his kids. Damien's pulse sped up as he read the letter. "I need a pair of latex gloves. Somebody fast!"

Baker was closest to the door. She ran out to her desk and grabbed a box she kept in her drawer. Racing back into the room, she handed them to Damien. "What is that?"

"I'm not sure yet." He put the gloves on. He looked in the envelope, searching for an item. Dumping the rest of the contents out on the table. "Hey, Travis, put whatever is on this USB drive on the big screen. Just touch the outer edges, we need to dust it and everything in this envelope for prints."

"What is it?" Detective Travis asked.

"I don't know for sure. Don't start it until I tell you." Damien handed the letter to Dillon. "Read this."

She took the letter by the corners, reading quickly. "Holy shit."

"I know." Damien looked at Joe and the others at the table. "This package was sent by our killer."

Joe's hand holding his soda stopped mid-air. "No fucking way."

"Yes, fucking way." Damien sorted through the papers. "This guy sent us financial records of Roger Franklin, Shamus MacDougal, and Patrick Weinsted." He opened a little booklet filled with names of children and dollar amounts next to them along with who bought them and where they were sent. "He sent us trafficking information."

Davidson reached for the book.

"Get gloves on. I doubt we will find our killer's prints on anything, but maybe Shamus or Roger touched these items. Look at these names, I know you have been pouring over the girls, see how many you recognize."

He grabbed a pair of gloves from the box on the table. He took the book and began reading. "This is unbelievable. But, can we connect this to Shamus or Robert?"

Everyone grabbed a pair of gloves, wanting to ogle the new evidence.

There was an old picture attached to a receipt. "Holy shit, Madre de Christo." Damien stared at Dillon. "I think we have enough for a new warrant." He handed her the photo and waited for her to speak.

She sucked in a deep breath. "She was so tiny." Dillon stared at a photo of what appeared to be a little girl. Blond hair stuck out from the end of a tarp. Little pink tennis shoes stuck out the other end. She was lying in a hole dug outside the mechanic's shop. A second photo showed a very young Patrick standing next to the newly poured concrete. The picture had a date of 2007.

Dillon's gaze scanned the silent table. "This is damming...against Shamus and Patrick. Is there anything in there tying Roger Franklin to any of this?"

Damien sifted through the pages. "I see correspondence between Roger and Shamus."

"I have it ready, Lieutenant." Detective Travis stood next to the big screen TV taking up most of the back wall.

All eyes turned towards him.

"Roll it," Damien said.

Detective Travis used a pointer mouse and opened the only file on the drive. It zipped open and the screen filled with file after file. Pictures of girls with a corresponding number and amount. Correspondence between Shamus and Roger Franklin, along with certain emails between Patrick Weinsted, Shamus, and Roger.

"Wow," Joe said. "Where the hell did all this come from?"

Detective Travis sat at his laptop. He scanned a few of the files. "It looks like these came from Shamus's computer."

Damien glanced at Joe and Dillon. "When?"

Detective Travis opened a program and extracted the file information from the zipped file. "These were downloaded from Shamus' computer, the day after Chase was found murdered."

"Could someone have hacked into the home's computer and downloaded this stuff?" Dillon asked.

"Absolutely. Very easy to do." Detective Travis opened one of the folders. As the screen filled with the video, the room was silenced.

A video of the room in the basement played before them. A young girl was in the room, she appeared to be unconscious. Voices could be heard from out of the range of the cameras but the conversation was muffled.

"I recognize Shamus' accent. But I can't make out what they are saying." Joe leaned into the TV. "Do you?" he asked, looking at Damien.

"No. Can you do anything about the angle of the video or the conversation?" he asked Travis.

"No. Maybe if I run it through a filter." Detective Travis nodded at Damien. "I bet it was set to record onto the computer. There are tons of files in this folder of nothing but videos."

"Wait," Dillon pointed to the screen. As they watched the shadows of the two men could be seen moving. Within a few seconds, Dillon gasped. Roger Franklin walked into the makeshift bedroom. He appeared to inspect the young girl.

This time when he turned toward the camera, his words were perfectly clear.

"I think she should go to Costa Rica. The Commodore will like this one. I think she will bring a huge sum too. Clean her up though. Have her ready by tonight. I will send a car to take her."

Dillon pulled her phone from her back pocket as she stood and left the conference room.

"Davidson and Baker get everything together. All the files we have put together." Damien handed a few papers to him. "These papers are names from Roger Franklin that never made it to Escobar. Put them with the original lists that you have."

Davidson took the papers. "You got it." Davidson turned to his partner Jenkins. "You heard the man, put this shit in order."

Detective Jenkins glared at his Lieutenant. "Do you see the monster you've created?"

Damien laughed. "You'll live; I'm sure." He turned towards Detective Travis. "Make sure you can tell the ADA and AD Reynolds where everything came from. Organize this into a clear and concise package. Make a copy for Dillon and put it on a jump drive."

"I'll have it wrapped up with a bow." Detective Travis began cataloging all the files.

Damien stepped into the hallway and called his Captain.

Within minutes Dillon strolled up to him. "I need a copy of everything you got with the letter. We can put the original in evidence."

Damien poked his head into the conference room. "Send the zipped file to Dillon, Detective Travis. Do you have her secure email?"

"I do. I will send it now."

"Copy AD Reynolds as well for me, please," Dillon said.

"How long before you get the warrant?" Damien asked.

"You're not getting one?" Dillon asked him.

"Captain Mackey said if we need it, we will. He figured he would let you guys do the work. This case crosses so

many federal lines." Damien had to resist the urge to reach out a brush her hair out of her face.

"It does. I can't wait to see the look on Roger Franklin's face." She looked at her watch, two forty-five. "If the AD gets our warrant in the next few minutes. I'm going to call Tristan Rhinehart and tell him we need to speak to him and Roger today. I think we should take him down in the office. In front of everyone."

"I like that idea. Man, I was dragging, now I have a boost of energy." Damien turned as Joe walked towards him. "You got something?"

"I was looking at the stuff in the letter you got. There are some personal things from Patrick. I think our killer got some of this stuff from his house when he killed him." Joe held out a piece of paper. "This says 'my insurance policy'. It's a correspondence between Patrick and Shamus. He asks him for more money for taking care of some of the girls who didn't make the cut."

Damien read through the email. He looked at Dillon. "Do you think this was what the killer set out to do?"

She crossed her arms. "I can't say for sure. But I still believe the girl buried under the slab is the key. When we go through the records, maybe we will find her. I think the killer set out to kill those who hurt her. My guess is he stumbled on all this other information and changed his outcome. I would've have thought that killing Shamus would be his end game. Now, he wants to stop Roger."

Joe leaned against the wall. "And what better way than to show him as the mastermind and leave him left to face the music. Plus, if you guys play your cards right, you might be able to track down some of the buyers."

"And we are still no closer to knowing who the killer is." Damien sighed as he stepped back into the conference room. He began to clean up the empty boxes of pizza and empty soda cans.

Dillon helped fill the garbage can. "You may never find this killer. He has been one step ahead of us all along."

Damien looked at her. "That's not what bothers me."

"What bothers you then, Damien?" Joe asked.

Damien shifted his gaze between the two. "I don't know if I want to find him. He did us a favor. He stopped this child trafficking ring which has been going on under our noses for years. So what if he killed four people." He sat in a chair. "That's what bothers me. I don't want to find this guy. I know what he did was wrong," He leaned forward, placing his elbows on his knees. "What does that make me?"

Dillon glanced at Joe, then placed her hand on his shoulder. "It makes you human. It makes us all human."

CHAPTER SIXTY-FIVE

Dunes 3:00 p.m.

Roger Franklin walked into his office at the One Township. His was located down the hall from Secretary Tristan Rhinehart. "This place has no idea who really runs DHS," Roger grumbled as he sat at his computer. He pulled the USB jump drive from his briefcase and plugged into an open USB port.

He peered around the screen, making sure he had shut his door. Quickly typing out a series of commands he began erasing any correspondence on the drive. Roger had saved any and all documents he would need for work, but this way, he could wipe everything tying him to Shamus. As the program made each file poof away, he looked over the day's agenda.

His desktop phone buzzed. "Yes, Heather?"

"Mr. Rhinehart needs you in his office."

"Thank you." Disconnecting the call, he walked out of his office, locking the door behind him. Roger hummed as he walked towards his boss' office. He knocked before entering. "Hey, Tristan."

"Hey, Roger. What are we doing in regards to Shamus?"

Roger's brow wrinkled as the corners of his mouth turned down. "What do you mean?"

"We need to get all the facts about his murder. And we need to release a statement to the press. I want to look proactive. I don't want to be caught with my pants down. Are there any surprises I need to know about?"

Roger pursed his lips. "Have you heard anything about Shamus?"

Tristan sat in his desk chair. "No. Other than his murder is in connection with a few other people who are associated with the home. That's one reason I want to get ahead of this. I need you to find out everything Shamus may have been involved in."

Roger crossed his legs. "I was trying to wrap my head around some information which recently came to light after Shamus died. I needed to check out a few things. What I have been able to find is Shamus abused a few of the girls who came through the home."

Tristan's eyes almost popped out of his head. "What? Why are you now telling me this? Why the hell haven't I heard about this?"

"Listen it seems to have happened before you took over as Secretary. Years ago. As far as I know, there hasn't been any girls harmed recently. I'm sure the authorities can explain more." Roger was about to continue when Tristan's phone rang.

"Yes, Francine?"

"Mr. Rhinehart, an FBI Agent, is on the phone and wishes to speak with you."

"Thank you." Tristan clicked on the blinking button. "This is Secretary Rhinehart."

"Mr. Rhinehart, this is FBI Agent Dillon McGrath. I need to come and speak with both you and Roger Franklin about the recent murders of Shamus MacDougal and Patrick Weinsted."

"Perfect timing Agent, I was speaking with Roger about this."

"Great, Mr. Rhinehart, my team and I will be there in about forty-five minutes. Please have Mr. Franklin there with you."

"I will have Roger here." Tristan Rhinehart hung up the phone and interlaced his fingers, resting his hands on his desk. "Looks like I will get my answers. The FBI is coming here to gather some information. I want to give them everything they need. Any assistance. Am I clear?"

Roger grinned at his boss. "Absolutely. As long as what they want doesn't compromise this office, or they have a sufficient warrant for the information, I will cooperate fully." He stood. "I will be in my office. Let me know as soon as they arrive."

Tristan stood. "They won't need a warrant, Roger. For anything that pertains to the home. I want the information given freely. Do you understand? I know you like to grandstand sometimes, but this is not one of those times."

"I agree with you. I will do whatever needs to be done to make this office look good." He headed towards the door. "You know, I could always take over as the head of the home. I know how it is supposed to run. We can hire a psychologist to give the children the help they need."

Tristan nodded. "I think that will work. You do know the ins and outs of the home. I will tell Francine to draw up the necessary paperwork. I still expect you to do the legal duties required of this office."

"I can be here a few times a week and be at the home as well. I can put a house mother in charge to run the day to day aspects, and with the help of Martin Escobar, I bet we can keep this home running smoothly."

"I like it." Tristan waved him out as he began to speak to Francine.

Roger strolled to his office. He didn't have the proclivity for abusing the little girls, he was merely a broker. And now, with Shamus out of the way, he could move the girls around much faster and easier.

Once back in his office, he checked the progress on his computer. The files had been cleaned. He removed the jump drive and placed it back into his briefcase. He removed his phone from his pocket and accessed his secure text.

"Maxwell, I have the perfect girl for you. I need a few days to get her to you. We have had a few issues come up. I will email you with the travel details soon."

"The price is negotiable. I have had to wait longer than normal. My client is not a patient man."

"The price of this is negotiable. I want to make sure your client is happy and a repeat customer. I will contact you soon."

Roger smiled. As a good-faith gesture, he had no problems letting this girl go for a discount.

CHAPTER SIXTY-SIX

Chicago 3:15 p.m.

.

Dillon smiled at Damien and Joe. "They will be there."

"What does the warrant cover?" Damien asked as he grabbed his jacket.

"Everything. All the grounds, every room, every stone. AD is sending over a team of agents. He wants us to bring two CSU teams." Dillon paced Damien's office.

Joe walked up to the door. "Are we almost ready to go?"

Damien shook his head. "I need to make some calls." He first dialed Detective Travis. "Travis, I need you and a team to be ready to go in the next fifteen minutes. You guys will take Roger's computer from his office, hang on." He looked up at Dillon. "The warrant covers Roger's office as well, right?"

"Yes, it does. Anything he works on at the Department of DHS. It doesn't include the Secretary's office, he is not implicated in this at all," she said.

Damien went back to his call with Detective Travis. "Detective, you will take everything from Roger's office and any computers from the home Shamus had access to. Can you get two teams ready?"

"No problem."

"I want your team with us and the second team at the home. Bring any program you have to recover files. I'm sure he has wiped his computer. We know he wiped Shamus'. I want everything recovered, if possible," Damien said.

"You got it." Detective Travis disconnected the call.

Damien dialed another number. "Mr. Escobar, this is Lieutenant Kaine."

"Yes, Lieutenant Kaine. What can I do for you?"

"I wanted to let you know we may need your assistance later at the home. Will you be available later this evening?"

"Yes. Text me on my mobile, 312-555-2956. I can then meet you at the home. I hope you are closer to finding out what is going on with the prior residents and their murders."

"We are. I can't give you any specifics now, but I will fill you in later," Damien said.

"I look forward to hearing from you later, Lieutenant."

Damien looked up to see Dillon and Joe staring at him. "What?"

"Why did you call him?" Dillon asked as she walked out into the pen, followed by Joe and Damien.

"He is going to have to come in and take over that home tonight. The kids living there are going to need help. I wonder if there are any girls currently there who were being abused by Shamus." He turned to Dillon, who was on her phone. "Is your team here?"

"They just pulled in. I told them to wait in the garage for us to come down."

Joe grabbed his jacket. "Let's go arrest this *ball-bag.*"

CHAPTER SIXTY-SEVEN

The Dunes 2:55 p.m.

Damien gave a copy of the warrant to the CSU team who would go to Sunshine Valley and had instructed them to wait for the Federal team who would be assisting them. He had also told them to bring a ground-penetrating radar. He wanted to make sure there was a body before they went tearing up the concrete pad in front of the mechanic shop. As he pulled his SUV in front of the DHS building, several vehicles pulled up behind him. Federal officers gathered on the sidewalk, waiting for Dillon's instructions.

"They have no idea we're sweeping in with warrants to seize anything associated with Roger Franklin," Dillon paused. "Follow us, as soon as we identify Roger's office, I want you guys to go in and gather everything." She looked at Detective Travis. "You can do whatever you need to his computer. The warrant also covers his personal cell phone. Did you cue up the video I asked for?"

Detective Travis smiled. He handed her a tablet. "I did. I also included a few files showing his direct involvement."

"Very nice." Dillon turned toward her lead Agent. "I want you to arrest him. You guys take him back to holding in Chicago, and AD Reynolds will have instructions for you at that time." She glanced around. "Let's go."

Joe leaned into Damien. "She comes back and takes over. How do you like that?"

"I heard you," Dillon said as she opened the door.

"I don't mind. She can do the TV interviews, as well." Damien winked at her as she shot him a dirty look.

"Not on your life." Dillon stepped up to the receptionist's desk holding out her FBI badge. She handed Damien the tablet. "Where is Roger Franklin's office?"

The receptionist's eyes widened as she glanced at all the police and Federal officers standing before her. "Umm, I...I don't know if I should let you in. I should call Mr. Rhinehart." She picked up the phone.

Dillon reached over and took the phone from her hand. "Where is his office?"

The receptionist pointed to the glass doors behind her. "Go in through those, and his office is three doors down."

Dillon smiled at her. "Now you can call Mr. Rhinehart and tell him to meet us at Franklin's office."

Damien smirked at Joe. He leaned into Dillon as they walked through the door. "Admit it, you're feeling better."

She giggled softly. "Yeah, actually, I am."

As they headed towards Roger Franklin's office, everyone stopped their task at hand and watched. All eyes glued to the Federal Agents with boxes and the police officer following them.

Dillon saw who she assumed was Mr. Rhinehart beating a line towards her.

"Agent, what is the meaning of this? You said you had information and needed to speak with Roger and me. I wasn't expecting this." He stood defiant in their path. "I want to see a warrant giving you the authority to come in here."

Dillon stepped around him and opened the door to Roger Franklin's office.

"What's going on?" Roger Franklin stood walking around his desk. "I thought we were meeting to discuss the murder of Shamus MacDougal?"

Dillon walked into the office along with all the other officers. "Mr. Franklin, you are under arrest for kidnapping and child trafficking. "

Roger Franklin balked. "What are you talking about? Shamus was the one who was abusing little girls. I only just found out about his activities. I haven't done anything wrong." He leaned casually against the edge of his desk. A smirk pulled his mouth back.

He watched as a tech sat in his chair. "You will need my password, Jones1492!**." He smiled at the young officer.

Detective Travis nodded at him. "Thank you." He lifted an eyebrow at Damien.

Tristan Rhinehart looked at the warrant the Agent handed him. "I don't understand why you are arresting Roger." He glanced up towards the State's long-time attorney. "Roger, do you have any answers?"

"Normally at this time I would tell someone to ask for a lawyer, but I have nothing to hide, Tristan. I can only think because of what Shamus was doing behind all of our backs, they need someone to pin something on." Roger looked over at the young Detective at his computer. "You won't find anything but work-related stuff."

Detective Travis pulled a jump drive from his pocket. "You know, Mr. Franklin, the programs most people use to wipe their computer will only wipe one or two surface levels on the disk. It doesn't erase everything."

Roger shrugged and looked back at the Agent. "Have you searched Shamus' computer?"

Dillon smiled at him. "We did. And according to eyewitnesses, you had been in the office shortly before we arrived. But we have another tech over there now." She nodded at the tablet Damien held.

"Mr. Franklin, in your duties as the lawyer for Sunshine Valley home, can you account for why there is a discrepancy in the list of names you sent Martin Escobar and the lists which had been provided to him over the years?" Damien asked.

Roger sat up straighter. "I'm not sure what you mean."

Damien noticed a small bead of sweat line the man's forehead. "Over the years, Mr. Escobar received monthly lists from Shamus with the names of all the children who entered the home each month. On the list you sent him, there were many more names he hadn't seen before. Hundreds to be exact."

Roger waved him off. "My secretary probably mixed up the files. The one she sent him more than likely had names from other homes mixed in."

Damien tapped on the tablet. "Mr. Franklin, have you ever gone to the basement in the home?"

He shook his head glancing at this nail. "No. I'm a lawyer. I think I already answered this question for you. I have never been in the basement."

Damien held out the tablet. "Would you take a look at this video." He turned up the volume before he hit play.

Roger stepped closer to tablet. Tristan Rhinehart also stepped up to view the video.

Damien watched as the smug look on Rogers face melted away.

"This isn't real. You have doctored this video." Roger Franklin stepped back, waving his hands in protest.

"No. We didn't. This was taken right off Shamus's computer," Joe said as he stepped towards Roger.

Tristan Rhinehart's hand covered his mouth. He turned towards a man he thought he knew. "You're disgusting. You've been selling girls?" He glared at Agent McGrath. "If there is anything you need, ask. You don't need a warrant for anything. I'm calling our counsel to let them know what is going on. Unless you need me here?"

"No, Sir. One of the Agents will let you know if we need anything." Dillon watched as Mr. Rhinehart walked out of the office. She turned back to Roger Franklin. "We need your personal cell phone. Please empty your pockets as well." She motioned for an agent to cuff him.

Roger's face hung like a hound dog. "I'm not speaking until I have my lawyer present."

"Read him his rights Agent," Damien said as he handed the cell phone to Detective Travis. "Make sure that is a priority."

"I will, Lieutenant. I've been able to retrieve some of the files he erased. After this runs and I get it back to the ECD lab I will be able to retrieve more," Detective Travis said.

Dillon and the other's watched as the FBI Agents loaded boxes with contents of Roger Franklin's office. "Let's get over to the home."

Joe walked out first. At the SUV, he pulled out his phone. "Hey, I got a text from Newberry. He said his CSU team ran the radar over the slab. There is definitely a body under there. They have started breaking up the slab now."

"I was hoping we wouldn't find her there." Dillon looked out the window. "Unless we find some record of her or we can recover DNA and find a match in the system, we may never know who she is."

Damien started the SUV and texted Martin Escobar asking him to meet them at Sunshine Valley. He secretly hoped he wouldn't have to come back to this home ever again.

CHAPTER SIXTY-EIGHT

Tristan Rhinehart looked disgusted and appalled as he spoke of the horrors Roger Franklin and Shamus MacDougal had committed. He vowed to clean up the childcare system in Illinois so this never happened again. He watched as the Governor gave statements as well as every other Illinois politician. Kerry turned off the news conference.

He was impressed with Agent Dillon McGrath and Lieutenant Damien Kaine. He knew he had sent the information to the right people. The FBI had stated from the information they had uncovered they would be able to bring down one of the most prolific child trafficking rings. Several indictments were waiting to be handed down.

Kerry opened his desk drawer and removed a worn and faded envelope. One of two letters he ever received from his mother. Her stay in the penal system was what put him in the Sunshine Valley Home, and he hated her for that. His mother died within a few weeks of him receiving her last letter. Killed by another inmate.

That was six months ago, and what set him out on the quest for his sister. His mother had written to him in the hopes he could find her. She had explained she had given birth to a baby girl during a small stint of freedom. She had given the baby to one of her neighbors. Kerry dragged a hand down his face. Wiping the wetness from his cheeks. "What kind of fucking woman were you?" he said to an empty room. "To hand a baby over to a fucking neighbor." His face flushed with heat.

His mother's letter spelled out who the neighbor was. Had Kerry not had the computer skills he did, he never would've been able to track the little girl. The neighbor ended up dying of an overdose when Sierra was eight. The state searched for other family, but they couldn't even find a birth certificate for her. Finally, the state put her in Sunshine Valley, thinking she would be safe. That was in 2007.

Kerry crumpled the letter. Had he found this out earlier, years earlier, he could have helped her. He barely remembered the little girl when she came into the house. He'd left shortly after Sierra's arrival. He smoothed out the crumpled piece of paper. Flattening it on his desk. A process he had done several times over the last few months.

What he set out to do, he had accomplished. Kerry wasn't sure what he thought his actions would do for him, but he thought it would make him feel better. Help relieve the guilt gnawing at him since he had found out about his little sister. It was still there. He had no idea if things in the DHS system would change. That didn't matter now. He had punished those who had hurt Sierra, and all the other little girls who went through Sunshine Valley. He could live with that.

He had one more piece of unfinished business. He picked up the untraceable phone he'd purchased during the week and dialed.

CHAPTER SIXTY-NINE

Thursday 9 p.m.

Damien sat with his feet on his desk. He and Dillon had dropped off Joe and grabbed some Mexican food to take home. Mrs. C. had taken Gunner and Coach to her house for a few hours earlier that day. He stared at the dog who snored on the floor. "Does he look fat to you?" He pointed at the slumbering bag of fur.

Dillon opened one eye and peeked at the chocolate-colored blob. "He spent the day with Mrs. C., of course, he's fatter. How did the Morenos take the news?"

Damien sighed. "They were relieved to know that the ME would be changing the manner of death to unknown. That will allow the evidence we found regarding Patrick and Shamus to be examined. I think once the investigators look at everything, Clara's death will be ruled a homicide. Doesn't make her death any less hard to deal with. But at least they will know they made a huge difference in that young girl's life."

"Sometimes that's all you can ask for."

"I'm so frigging tired," Damien said. "Let's go take a bath. We don't have to be at DC until eleven a.m."

"Captain Mackey was feeling generous, huh?" She stood slowly. Her body ached, and her head throbbed. This had been the first full day of work she had done in weeks. "It may take me a few minutes to get up the stairs."

Damien laughed. "I can't carry you. We can crawl up them together." He turned off his desk light and grabbed his cell phone off the desk as it rang. Too tired he didn't notice who the call was from. "Kaine here."

"Thank you."

Damien stood rigid and snapped his fingers at Dillon. He put the phone on speaker, but motioned for her to stay quiet. "Who is this?"

"I think you know who this is. I didn't mean to kill so many people, but they deserved it."

"Why? Why did they deserve it? You had to know the information you sent us would've gotten them all arrested."

"Listen, I've deleted all my records from the DHS system. At the system. Not just on Shamus' computer. I also deleted my sister's information."

Damien's shoulders sagged. "The little girl under the slab."

"Yes. I'm not going to tell you her name. I only found out a few months ago I even had a sister. When I began my search for her, I found out all about Shamus and his nasty habit. The more I researched, the more I found out. I wasn't about to let them get away with going to jail."

Damien remained silent. His tired brain was jumbled with a thousand thoughts.

"I sent the information to you. I knew you wouldn't let Roger Franklin get away with anything. I also knew your girlfriend would make sure others were brought down. I'm sure she is there with you now. Hello Agent McGrath. I am truly sorry about your family."

Dillon scowled at the phone. "Thank you. I'm sorry about your little sister."

"Do you know how she died?"

Damien and Dillon stared at each other.

"Please. Please tell me."

"Preliminary reports say blunt force trauma."

Kerry's sharp intake of breath echoed in the office. "I know you don't condone what I did. I wanted you to know I don't plan on killing any more people. You won't find me, and I hate for you to waste your time searching for me."

"You're still a killer. A brutal serial killer," Damien said.

"I promise you, Lieutenant Kaine, I only wanted those who hurt my sister to pay for what they did. I won't do this again. It's not who I am. Let this one go, Lieutenant. Let my sister rest." Kerry paused for a moment. "I do have one favor to ask."

Damien stared at Dillon. "I don't know how I can help you with anything."

"I want my sister to have a proper burial. I will make arrangements, and you will be contacted by someone. When her remains are available for burial, will you honor my wish?"

Damien's head hung. He felt a hand on his shoulder. He glanced up to see Dillon's tear-streaked face staring at him. "Yes. I'll honor your wish and make sure she is buried. Make sure I'm the one who is contacted for this. I'll make sure it goes through."

"Thank you, Lieutenant."

Damien stared at the silent phone. Dillon wrapped her arms around him. "Let this one go. For us. For that little girl. For all the girls Shamus and Roger took advantage of. Let this one go."

THE END

Please leave a review wherever you purchased this book.

Other books by Victoria M. Patton

Damien Kaine Series
Innocence Taken
Confession of Sin
Fatal Dominion
Web of Malice
Blind Vengeance
Series bundle books 1-3

Derek Reed Thrillers
The Box

Short Stories
Deadfall

ABOUT THE AUTHOR

Victoria M. Patton is forced to share her home with a husband, two teenagers, three dogs, and a cat. If she isn't plotting her escape, she uses her Search and Rescue/Law Enforcement skills from the Coast Guard and her BS in Forensic Chemistry to figure out the best way to hide all the bodies and write amazing stories about the murders. If she has any free time, she drinks copious amounts of whiskey and binge watches Netflix. She is on most social media outlets, type in her name, you'll find her.

To learn more about her and sign up for her monthly email visit her websites:

www.whiskeyandwriting.com
www.victoriampatton.com

Made in the USA
Monee, IL
19 April 2021

66218559R00198